## A Connection

"You're not alone, Alex. Don't ever think you are."

She let herself smile at that. She had always been alone, in every fight she had ever waged. At this moment, she couldn't find it in herself to worry about it because she could see his lips parted and she knew he was going to kiss her.

She could describe his mouth on hers only as delicious. He tasted of mayonnaise and fresh bread and ham. And goodness, something she had never tasted on a man's lips. He didn't push, didn't press, just gently molded her mouth to his and easily played with her tongue. She felt his hands move to cradle her face and he lifted his lips from hers. "I'm in so much trouble," he said gruffly.

"I-I should go," she said, her voice nearly a squeak.

"Yeah. You'd better." He released her and slid one hand all the way down her arm to the tip of her little finger.

She walked over to the half wall and retrieved her sunglasses and purse. He followed her to the front door. Part of her didn't want to leave him, so she stopped before leaving. "What does this mean, what we just did?"

"You don't know?"

"I'm not very experienced at this. I don't mind telling you, you scare me."

Other books by Anna Jeffrey

*The Love of a Cowboy*

# The Love of a Stranger

## Anna Jeffrey

AN ONYX BOOK

ONYX
Published by New American Library, a division of
Penguin Group (USA) Inc., 375 Hudson Street,
New York, New York 10014, U.S.A.
Penguin Books Ltd, 80 Strand,
London WC2R 0RL, England
Penguin Books Australia Ltd, 250 Camberwell Road,
Camberwell, Victoria 3124, Australia
Penguin Books Canada Ltd, 10 Alcorn Avenue,
Toronto, Ontario, Canada M4V 3B2
Penguin Books (N.Z.) Ltd, Cnr Rosedale and Airborne Roads,
Albany, Auckland 1310, New Zealand

Penguin Books Ltd, Registered Offices:
80 Strand, London WC2R 0RL, England

First published by Onyx, an imprint of New American Library,
a division of Penguin Group (USA), Inc.

First Printing, April 2004
10 9 8 7 6 5 4 3 2 1

PUBLISHER'S NOTE
This is a work of fiction. Names, characters, places, and incidents either are the product of the author's imagination or are used fictitiously, and any resemblance to actual
persons, living or dead, business establishments, events, or locales is entirely coinci-
dental.

# ACKNOWLEDGMENTS

I appreciate my husband, George, a lifetime forester. His valuable comments keep me straight on what can and can't happen in the great outdoors. Besides that, he never stops supporting me and encouraging me in my writing endeavor.

I thank my sister, Pam. When I call her up and say, "Quick, listen to this and tell me what you think," she always listens no matter what she's doing, and she always has a valuable thought that improves my work.

I thank my daughter, Adrienne, for being my biggest fan and for spreading publicity about my books to anyone who will stand still and listen.

For the second time, I acknowledge my critique group, Fort Worth Writers' Group, and their ever-constructive comments. Guys, you know who you are.

# Chapter 1

Alex McGregor was in her favorite place in the universe—her hundred-year-old home on the side of Wolf Mountain in Callister Valley, Idaho. From behind a wall of windows two stories high, she looked over an exquisite panorama stretching before her—endless silver sky, majestic blue mountain, emerald valley pastures. Peace and beauty seeped into her soul.

The mid-July evening was quiet and hot. Through her open windows came the incessant chittering of uncountable birds and the soft roar of Swede Creek a few hundred feet to the north.

Her gaze swept down to the valley floor and landed on the Callister county road a mile away. There, a light-colored vehicle sped along, raising a plume of dust on the hard gravel surface. It slowed and made a right turn into her driveway.

Everything inside her stilled. No one casually dropped in. Only her best friend, Ted Benson, and her housekeeper, Lucille Arnold, ever came uninvited. And only a stranger would hazard her driveway without first calling for a report on its condition. "The Longest Mile," Ted had named it.

From so far away she couldn't recognize the make of

the intruder, but like a wary rabbit, it inched up the steep grade with jerky stops and starts. She knew why. Ragged potholes, oil-pan-busting stones and deep eroded ruts prevented faster progress.

When the rig reached her cattle guard and the second NO TRESPASSING sign, she could see it was a white pickup with a black canopy mounted on the bed. It disappeared into a shadowy tunnel of brush and thornbush at the driveway's midpoint. Plowing through the jutting limbs and scratchy branches could ruin a paint job. Damage might be avoided if a driver dropped two tires into the deep drainage ditch paralleling one side, but only those familiar with the road were aware of that option.

Alex knew the precise length of time it took to pass through the brush. She drew one side of her lower lip through her teeth and watched and waited for the pickup to emerge.

Minutes later, the bumper and grill came into view. The late-day golden sun gilded the license plate, making it unreadable, but one thing was clear. Its color was wrong to be an Idaho tag.

Tourists. Outsiders. Probably lost. Otherwise, how and why had they veered this far off the beaten path? More troubling was the fact that they had ignored her NO TRESPASSING signs, which even the local teenagers no longer disregarded.

She strode to the binoculars hanging beside one window, snatched them off their peg and homed in. The pickup was a late-model Chevy, the plates, California. She could distinguish the silhouettes of a male and female inside.

She lowered the binoculars and watched.

The pickup slowed to a creep where the driveway forked a few hundred feet from her front deck. There, the driver had two choices. The Y's left leg would bring them straight to her door, where she would tell them they had made a wrong turn and send them back to the county road. The right leg would put them on an old two-track known as Old Ridge Road. It traveled along the crest of a long, rocky hogback to the north side and behind her house.

To her amazement, the white Silverado turned onto the right fork, picked up speed and rolled along Old Ridge Road. As she watched it sink out of sight into dense green forest, she felt a little quake in her serenity. Trespassers could have only one destination—Granite Pond, a mile from her back door.

Two summers ago, she had ceased to tolerate *anyone* traveling beyond her house or visiting Granite Pond without her permission. Nothing had changed that so who did today's trespassers think they were? She charged through the kitchen, then the utility room and down the back stairs. In the basement garage, she mounted her Jeep Wrangler, backed out and followed the track of the Chevy up Old Ridge Road.

In a matter of minutes, she reached the intersection where a hundred-year-old wagon trace teed with the road. Erosion had turned the old wagon tracks into two knee-deep gouges, now grown over with grass bleached to beige by the merciless summer sun.

She braked and considered her options. She could follow behind strangers with an out-of-state license plate and confront them, taking a chance they weren't axe murderers. On the other hand, the old wagon trace, only a slightly better choice than driving cross-country, would lead to an obscure horse trail where she could look down on Granite Pond and the surrounding glade without being seen. She knew the horse trail well, had hiked it many times.

Choosing caution over confrontation, she yanked the Jeep into low gear, turned onto the wagon trace straddling the deep ruts, and ground her way higher up the hill.

Passable road soon played out and she parked, grabbed

the binoculars and set out on foot. She began to sweat. The air felt hot, as if heated by a furnace, and heavy as a tapestry. All around her, the eerie ambience of volatility showed itself in the dull, crinkled leaves of the underbrush. Dry grass and twigs crunched underfoot. Even the normally lush kinnikinnick had yellowed and become sparse from lack of moisture. In the ten years she had been spending summers in her Idaho retreat, she had never seen conditions riper for wildfire. A match, a spark, a lightning strike and the whole mountainside could combust.

At the top of a steep wooded slope, she knelt and looked down on Swede Creek. Fed by a glacier atop Wolf Mountain, it rushed from a gorge to the west, then tumbled along the flat meadow. Eventually it became a waterfall that plunged to Granite Pond, a crystal-clear pool so deep and cold no one she knew had ever been to its bottom.

The pond dominated center stage of a natural amphitheater, with limestone monoliths and tree-covered slopes rising on the sides. Even in today's dry conditions, thick green grass and a profusion of ferns grew around its banks. On the hottest day, standing at the edge of the glacier water, she could feel a chill in the air.

Magnificent natural wonders abounded in the Northwest and Alex knew that. But Granite Pond had a single unique feature—it was located on private property, bought and paid for by her.

And there beside it, the white pickup sat.

Some two hundred feet from the pond's bank, a low-roofed log cabin crouched almost hidden among tall evergreens, its one visible door framed on either side by small square windows. A Forest Service archaeologist had identified it as a Chinese miner's cabin, circa 1849, a rare and tangible insight into history.

She loved it, had paid workmen to cover the dirt floor

with wood and install glass panes in the windows. Then she had added an antique iron bed where she slept on warm August nights, a reclining chair where she spent hours reading or working intricate needlepoint designs that cleared her mind of all else. The idea of a thoughtless stranger dropping a cigarette or building a campfire anywhere near this precious place jarred her. Her resentment of the trespassers doubled.

Though she didn't recognize the pickup, the woman who climbed from the passenger side looked familiar. Alex watched her walk around to the driver's door. Even above the sounds of the waterfall, giggly feminine laughter echoed up. The man climbed out and pulled her to him.

Through the binoculars, Alex could see only the man's back, but he appeared to be tall with wide shoulders and short dark hair. She zoomed in on the woman.

"My God. Cindy."

Alex couldn't think of a female alive for whom she held more contempt than her ex-husband's trashy girlfriend, Cindy Evans. She would fight tooth and toenail to keep that woman away from Granite Pond and the old cabin.

She marched back to the Wrangler and rummaged for a weapon, found the handle to a heavy-duty jack in the back. Other than protection, she didn't know her intentions, but the hard, heavy feel of cold steel against her palm gave her courage. A search among scattered broken limbs yielded a straight, thick branch adequate for a staff. Using it to keep from slipping, she sidestepped down the hill.

At the bottom, the waterfall's roar absorbed the sounds of her footfalls. She crept from behind a wide-trunked pine tree to the front of the pickup for a clearer view. A few feet from the cabin's front door, Cindy teetered on one foot peeling off panty hose while the stranger's hands did something beneath her skirt. Without a doubt, they believed no one else was within miles.

"*Hey!*"

Alex swung the jack handle with all her strength. It thudded against the pickup's left front fender. The impact vibrated up her arms.

The stranger's head jerked toward her. Cindy shrieked, doubled over and grappled with her panty hose. "I didn't know you were home," she cried, as she twisted into her clothing.

"What difference does *that* make?" Alex stamped forward. "You can't come here *any* time." She planted herself in front of the stranger. "You get off my property."

The stranger struggled with his zipper, sputtering curses and glowering at the dented fender.

"I've called the sheriff."

A snort came from Cindy, accompanied by a glare of superiority. "Don't worry, Doug. She hasn't really." She sauntered around the Silverado toward the passenger door, straightening her hair. "Even if she did, he ain't gonna do nothin'."

The stranger's eyes cut to Cindy.

"C'mon. Let's get outta here," the tramp said. "She's crazy and she's got guns. She may pull one out."

"And don't you forget it," Alex said, anger making her voice shake.

"Oh, yeah?" The stranger's voice rumbled out in a raspy baritone. "If anybody's got a right to be pissed off here, lady, it's me." He stepped toward her. His finger jabbed at the Silverado. "Take a look at that fender. That's a new rig."

Fight-or-flight streaked down Alex's spine. He was a head taller than she, much bigger than he had looked in the lens of the binoculars. She had taken an urban self-defense class, could remember a knee to the groin, but no way would he get that close. She tightened her grip on the jack handle and backed up, putting space between them. She raised the jack handle. "Stay away from me."

"Doug," Cindy yelled from the pickup. "C'mon. Let's go."

The next thing Alex knew, the stranger had wrenched her weapon from her hand and was standing in front of her nose to nose. "I oughtta wrap this around your neck." He threw the jack handle to the side. "You owe me, lady. It'll cost a thousand dollars to get that dent fixed."

Alex backed up again, her eyes burning with tears. She hated crying, hated feeling afraid.

His expression softened. "Christ, don't cry." He raised a palm. "Look, let's calm down here. I didn't know"—he pointed behind himself in Cindy's direction—"the lady with me didn't know we weren't supposed to be here."

"That's a lie. She knew."

He stooped, picked up the jack handle and offered it to her. "Here. This looks like something you might need."

Alex could see in his eyes that he wouldn't harm her, though he might be mad she had struck his pickup. The sense of danger past, she forced her spine stiff again and snatched the jack handle from him. "I meant what I said. You get out of here."

"We're going. But don't think I'm forgetting that fender." He marched to the pickup, got in and slammed the door. She waited until the rig had crawled back onto Old Ridge Road before climbing up the hill to her Jeep.

By the time she reached her house and the living room windows, she could see the pickup making its way down the driveway, the taillights bobbing as it crossed bumps and potholes. Her thoughts churned. Long before Alex had divorced Charlie McGregor, he had taken Cindy to the cabin for clandestine trysts. Alex had even caught them there. That was bad enough, but what kind of arrogance made the woman believe she had the right to drag a stranger to it?

And who *was* the stranger? Though Cindy called his name, Alex had been so steeped in anger, a triviality like a name hadn't registered. His face seemed familiar in a distant, nagging way. With thick brows framing silvery eyes, a strong square jaw and defined lips, it wasn't a forgettable face. Good Lord. When had she noticed all *that*? She hadn't paid attention to such details about a man's appearance in more years than she could remember.

# Chapter 2

Doug Hawkins cursed to himself and switched on his headlights. What in the hell had he stumbled into? Oh, sure, he had seen the NO TRESPASSING signs, but his companion told him they didn't apply to her. The last thing he wanted in his newly adopted hometown was a fight with one of the local citizens over something as dumb as trespassing.

A dark tunnel of bushes, made darker by sundown, loomed just ahead. Their branches had already scarred the shit out of the right side of his truck on the way up.

"If you drive over to the right, your rig won't get scratched up," Cindy said.

If she knew that, why hadn't she already told him? He swore again and followed her direction. A front tire dropped into a deep hole and brought them to a jolting halt. "Goddammit! Shit." He shifted to a lower gear and labored forward.

After a good five minutes, they left the bushes to face an unbelievable rock-strewn path. It had been rugged enough driving up in daylight. Now, in the twilight, it defied description.

*Ka-thunk!* A tire collided with a boulder. Their bodies lurched. He swore louder and hoped for nothing more than to reach civilization without further damage to his truck. He only half listened as his companion seethed and fumed beside him.

"That's my special place. She won't let me go near it."

*Her* special place? Judging from what had just happened, there wasn't any question who *owned* it. He didn't reply. Navigating the downhill rock field took all of his attention.

A few minutes later, to his relief, he reached the county road with neither flat tire nor broken axle. Turning onto the smoother surface, he could now drive and talk at the same time. "Who the hell is she, anyway?" His passenger and the belligerent blonde obviously knew each other.

"Alex McGregor. She lives in Los Angeles, but she comes up here in the summer. She owns that ugly-looking old house we passed. Mean bitch. I wish she'd stay in California. Nobody wants people like her around here."

Doug thought about the log, stone and glass structure sprawled over a substantial part of the mountainside and decided Cindy's description of the house was about 98 percent wrong. "She's from L.A.? What is this, a second home or something?"

"I guess so." Cindy stared ahead, her mouth set in a pout.

"She doesn't work? Is she rich?"

"Humph. Richer than me. She acts like some prissy big shot, but she's nothing but a real estate salesman."

"You said that cabin belonged to a friend of yours. I wouldn't have gone up there if—"

"She's jealous. Just because—" His companion paused and sighed, obviously changing her mind about telling something. "Nobody in town can stand her. She thinks she's better than everybody." Cindy hugged her midriff and stared out the window. "She's crazy. Half the time she's either talking to herself or talking to cats."

Doug studied the woman he had picked up—or to be more accurate, who had picked *him* up—in the Eights & Aces Saloon in town. Long dark brown hair, pale skin, a few freckles. Late twenties. Not jailbait, but could be ten years his junior.

In rating easy lays, she had to be close to the top. That conclusion didn't require deep analysis. He had seen her for the first time ever today, when he went into the bar and asked if anybody knew the whereabouts of his old friend Ted Benson. Tavern romances weren't his style, but when she came from behind the bar to his stool and all but unzipped his pants and put her hand inside his fly, good sense and sound reasons to reject what she offered abandoned him.

What took more thought than classifying the barmaid was sorting out his own actions. Better than anybody, he knew the risks that accompanied a hookup in a bar. Yet he had let himself be not only hooked up but thrown into a fight in an isolated setting with a hard-assed loony. Dumb, thinking with the wrong organ. All of which proved that three years without sex was too damn long.

The lights of town came into sight, as welcome as an oasis. He could hardly wait to get back there.

At the Eights & Aces, he parked near the front door. "Let's go inside and have a beer." He had no desire to reenter the bar or to have a beer, but considering what he would have done with Cindy if they hadn't been interrupted, dropping her off out front seemed too rude, even for somebody who thought as little of most women as he did.

"You ain't mad, are you?" She turned her head and faced him, a plea in her eyes.

Oh, he was mad all right, but his anger was directed more at himself than her. He pulled on his door latch. "Let's go inside."

She didn't move. He scooted out, ducked his head back in and looked at her across the console. "Let's go in."

She stared out her side window, but didn't open the door. "It ain't me, Doug. It's her. Nobody can get along with her."

"I can see that." Boy, could he ever see that. The woman he had just tangled with had all the charm of a cornered badger. He rounded the rear of the pickup and opened the passenger door. Cindy climbed out with a scowl on her face. He grasped her elbow and steered her toward the bar's black front door.

As they passed the dented fender, he stopped and looked at it. From a few feet away, a mercury vapor light on a utility pole cast the white Silverado in a gray color and exaggerated the long wound on the fender. Over a foot long. Shit. The 4x4 was his pride and joy, the only vehicle he had ever bought new off the showroom floor. He closed his eyes, drew his hand down his face and shook his head. He guessed he should be grateful the headlight wasn't broken. He had insurance, sure, but . . .

Cindy looked up at him with contrite eyes. Doug blew out a breath, resigned. He caught her elbow again and urged her forward. "C'mon."

"My kids ain't home. We could go to—"

"I've got an appointment early tomorrow." That wasn't a lie. Tomorrow morning, he intended to take Ted Benson, his best friend from high school, whom he hadn't seen in fifteen years, to breakfast. "I need sleep. Let's have a beer and call it a night."

She jerked her arm from his grip. "You ain't gonna buy me a beer and just brush me off like I'm nothin'."

"Look, one hysterical female a day is all I can handle. I really do need to go home. That's where I was headed when I stopped in here. C'mon."

Inside the Eights & Aces, Doug sat at the bar and drank a beer with the barmaid, sharing empty, inane conversation and reaffirming his vow to give up women. At nine-thirty, he checked the time and deemed he had wasted enough of it at the Eights & Aces Saloon. Over Cindy's protests, he said good night.

During the twelve-mile trip from town to his new home,

his thoughts drifted to the pissed-off blonde. Other than a few drunks and dopers back when he had been a street cop, no woman had ever stood toe-to-toe with him like she did. For a few seconds he thought she might swing at him with that tool.

He had it out of her hands in an instant and could have flattened her if he had wanted to. She must have been able to see her disadvantage, but it didn't stop her.

He had been hot under the collar himself, but she was *incensed*—angrier than the circumstances warranted. Maybe the barmaid had nailed it—the blonde was crazy. Hell, maybe both women were crazy.

Crazy or not, from the looks of that house, she probably *was* rich, like the barmaid said, especially if she was in the real estate business in L.A. She damn sure could afford to pay for repair of his fender.

Just as mysterious as the woman was his own reaction. He didn't have altercations like the one he'd had with her. To do it went against his very nature and all his training. In his police career, back when he'd had one, his peers envied his self-control and calm approach to the most gut-wrenching of situations.

As he reached his driveway, what had been aggravating him all along dawned on him—the barmaid's comment about the blonde having guns. Volatile women wielding guns made him uneasy. He didn't doubt for a minute the blonde had them. Or that she knew how to use them.

*Leave it alone,* he told himself. *Whatever is going on between those two women is none of your business.*

He drove behind his house into the battered old barn, his temporary, makeshift garage. He climbed out and trudged through the fresh night air to his back door. Was this town big enough to have a body shop? He detested making a claim against his insurance for a fender repair and having his premium raised, but he also hated paying the bill out of his pocket. His every penny had a place to go. Maybe the pissed-off blonde would feel remorse and ante up.

And maybe pigs could fly.

Morning. Alex awoke to the thrum of Robert Redford's purr near her head and Maizie's body stretched across her legs. Through the open window came the early-morning cool. Without opening her eyes, she stretched inside the cocoon of covers, one foot, one leg at a time and finally arching her back and shoulders. She enjoyed the caressing feel of the warm bedclothes against her naked body. A human being hadn't provided that much comfort in years, maybe never.

As good as her bed felt, she couldn't lie in it and bask. She had things to do, among them an appointment in town at ten with the local real estate broker. He would be bringing a potential buyer from Boise to look over Carlton's Lounge & Supper Club, a millstone to which she had been chained for five years, nine months and thirteen days.

She threw back the covers and padded toward the bathroom. The cats hit the floor at the same time and trotted alongside her.

As she turned on the water and stepped into the shower, her thoughts centered on the stranger at Granite Pond. That nervous feeling she had noticed last night came back. She could define it only as a flash of awareness of him as a man. Odd, because she wasn't seeking a man and wouldn't know what to do with one if she had him.

She left the shower and wrapped in a thick terry-cloth robe, then sat down at the vanity and began to dry and style her long bob. The cats weaved between the vanity stool legs and her ankles, making little anxious chirrups. *Doug.* Where had she heard that name recently? She couldn't think of a real estate deal to which she could tie it. The stranger looked like a Doug, though. Tall and muscled, not like a bodybuilder, but extremely male and well proportioned. Funny how you associated a certain appearance with a name.

Hair and makeup finished, she returned to the bedroom to dress. For her meeting with the Realtor and his customer, she wanted to look professional but casual. She dressed in a pair of loose khaki slacks, a silk long-sleeved big shirt and brown alligator loafers, then set about tidying the bedroom.

Books and folders were scattered over the foot of her bed—engineering studies from the Utah Department of Transportation, Salt Lake City zoning regulations and building codes. There was a 36 x 30-inch site plan of Gateways, the huge retirement center proposed for construction in the upscale Avenues District in the foothills of the Wasatch Mountains.

Last night after she had calmed down, she had studied the documents into the wee hours. In the coming Friday's meeting in Salt Lake, she had too much at stake to risk the rise of some obscure question she couldn't answer.

She gathered the books and papers into a pile, refolded the site plan and carted all of it to her office in the front corner of the house. She didn't like Friday meetings, she thought as she slid file folders and documents into her big leather briefcase.

Maizie strolled across the desktop making little annoyed squeaks and Alex scooped her up and set her on the floor.

If something went haywire in an end-of-the-week conference, no time was left for the defect to be cured. Problems in real estate deals had a way of festering like untreated wounds. Minds could change over a weekend and by Monday morning a once viable project could be a dead duck. But with the Utah highway department's tight schedule, Friday had been the only choice.

Robert Redford leaped up to the desktop and arranged himself on a large rolled map lying to one side. The U.S. Geological Survey map showed Granite Pond and the sixteen hundred acres surrounding her house. A frown tugged between her eyes as the map reminded her of yet another problem, the genesis of which went back years, before she had divorced Charlie.

Kenny Miller, a local logger and Charlie's partying friend, now owned the five sections commonly known as Soldier Meadows that abutted the south of her property. Until a few years ago it had been part of her and Charlie's land. They had sold it to the logger.

The map was a sobering reminder. Kenny had called a few days earlier and told her he would start logging Soldier Meadows this year. He planned on building an access road across the right-of-way for which he had paid Charlie. The area was a strip of real estate twenty feet wide that traversed the rear of her property and would cross Swede Creek a short distance above Granite Pond.

She moved the cat aside and plumped the squashed map back into a roll.

She had received the deed to the house and acreage on Wolf Mountain in the divorce settlement, but there had been no document giving Miller Logging Company a right-of-way across her back fenceline. Kenny claimed to have made a handshake agreement with Charlie and paid him cash, but Alex didn't believe him. The crude lout was too shrewd to pay cash to someone as irresponsible as Charlie without obtaining some kind of documentation to prove the sale.

Many marketable trees grew in Soldier Meadows. She couldn't begin to calculate the board feet of timber. A logging operation might go on for several years. Daily heavy truck traffic no more than the length of a football field from her front door would devalue her home and property and make it unsalable. Her driveway would be changed—made wider, smoothed out. The grade would be lessened. Inaccessibility to her home would cease to provide security.

With Soldier Meadows being landlocked by her ownership on one side and national forest land on three sides, the law swung in Kenny's favor if he forced the issue. How could she stop him? Nothing had worked so far—not flattery, reason or compromise. She cursed her ex-husband for the umpteenth time. Since they were five years old, she had been cleaning up after him.

She rested her chin on her palms, thinking. Snafus and fubars were routine in her business. If Plan A failed, out of habit she went to Plan B. On a sigh, she picked up the phone and keyed in the number of her friend and lawyer in Boise. His assistant came on the line with a bubbly excuse for his absence.

"I'm going out of town myself," Alex said, "so I want to leave a message. Just tell Bob I think it's a waste of time trying to negotiate with a hardhead like Kenny Miller and I want to go ahead with the injunction. He'll know what I mean."

"I'll tell him, Mrs. McGregor. By the way, he told me to give you this referral. It's friends of his. Ed and Martha Anderson. They own an apple orchard out by Marsing, where Bob grew up. They need to sell real bad. Mrs. Anderson has cancer."

"I don't usually deal in residential property, but—"

"Oh, Bob knows that, but this is over a hundred acres. He says it looks like a good place for a subdivision and Hayes Winfield has made them an offer."

She sat forward with piqued interest. "The subdivision developer?"

"Yes. Do you know him?"

*Dirty old man, but rich.* "Only by reputation."

"Bob said to tell you he doesn't want these folks to get— well, to be taken advantage of. They need the help of someone who's smart and mean enough to deal with Hayes. Either that or find someone else to buy the property out from under him."

The assistant's last remark stung, revealing an opinion that had come from the mouth of someone she considered to be a friend. Alex moved past her hurt feelings, as she always did, with sarcasm. "Tell Bob, 'Gee, thanks.' What did Hayes offer them?"

"Bob meant it as a compliment, Mrs. McGregor. Honest. I don't know the amount of the offer, but he says, knowing Hayes, the orchard could be worth a lot more. I have the legal description for you and the directions to get out there."

Alex reached for a pencil. "Okay, shoot." She dashed off the information. "I appreciate the referral. I'm going to Salt Lake, but I'll be back by Monday. I should be able to get down to Marsing on Tuesday. Be sure the Andersons don't sign anything. Do we know how to get in touch with Hayes?"

"He's in Alaska. Should be back in August. Oh! I almost forgot. Bob and Mrs. Culpepper are hosting a party the end of August. They haven't decided on an exact day yet, but they want you to come. It's a fund-raiser for Ralph Cumley's reelection. Hayes is invited."

"That's a long way off, but yes, I need to meet Senator Cumley. I'm putting it on my calendar." Alex scribbled a note in her desk planner. Schmoozing with a politician was important. One never knew when such an acquaintance might come in handy. In this instance, it probably meant a campaign contribution, but that, too, was business. "Tell Bob to call me about the injunction."

"I will. You have a good day, Mrs. McGregor."

She hung up. "Right, I'll do that," she muttered.

Her living room clock chimed. No more time to dally. She picked up the USGS map. Her acreage backed up to national forest. She would stop by Ted's office first and ask him to help her pinpoint some obscure landmarks that would reaffirm in her mind the side and back boundaries of her property. To do combat with Kenny, she needed all the ammunition she could gather. When it came to plain old toughness in a backroom battle over money, many of the high rollers in plush offices in L.A. and San Francisco stood short in the shadow of Kenny Miller.

Blatant meows from both cats startled her out of her contemplation. "Stop worrying," she mumbled. "It'll work out fine." She left the office and started for the kitchen. The cats raced ahead of her. Food at last.

Doug finished the last phase of his workout with a hand weight, sitting on a chair at his dining table. For over a year he had ended either a run of several miles or a vigorous skiing workout on his NordicTrack the same way—repeatedly lifting ten pounds with his damaged left arm to a position parallel to the floor, then returning the weight to hang loosely by his side. The workout used to bring groans of pain, but most times now it brought only grimaces.

His Mickey Mouse wall clock—it had been a gift from a fatherless teenage boy he had once mentored in Los Angeles—told him he had to hurry to be on time to take his old pal Ted Benson to breakfast.

He reached for the towel draped across the back of his chair, wiped sweat from his face and chest, then rose and crossed the antiquated kitchen where his friend Bayer sat in a dull green cupboard weighted by eighty years of paint layers. He hesitated before taking the tablets on an empty stomach.

The concern was absurd under the circumstances. In the past two years, he had swallowed or been injected with every painkiller out there, from narcotics to over-the-counter analgesics. Now he used only nonprescription drugs that dulled rather than killed the pain but didn't cloud his thinking. He could live with pain. It had become as much a part of him as his leg or the left arm he had almost lost. What he couldn't live with was going through the remainder of his life muddleheaded. He had stood eye-to-eye with the grim reaper, and he no longer took tomorrow for granted.

"Fuck it," he mumbled, giving up the debate. He dropped a slice of bread into the toaster, then countered the aspirin with the toast and a long cold pull from the plastic milk jug. What he needed now was glorious hot water beating against his aching shoulder.

As he dressed in jeans and a T-shirt that heralded UCLA, he wondered if Ted would recognize him after all these years. He had some gray hair at his temples and a few facial lines, and at one-ninety he was a good twenty pounds lighter than when they had last seen each other. Even so, he was thirty pounds heavier than the day he left the hospital in L.A. two years ago. Of course, Ted had no way of knowing that and there was no reason to tell him.

# Chapter 3

"How you been while I've been gone, sweetie?" Ted came from behind his desk with a huge smile. Laugh lines fanned at the corners of his deep brown eyes. Alex relaxed, happy to see one of the few nonthreatening men in her life. She put her cheek against his and kissed air.

"You look pretty as a sunbeam. Sit down." He pulled a chair away from his desk and motioned to her. "Want some tea?"

"No, thanks. I'm in a hurry. I have an appointment with Frank Bagwell over at the café. He's bringing someone from Boise to look at Carlton's this morning. Maybe it's a real buyer this time. I've got to get over there and make sure the place is all cleaned up and shining."

"Hey, you've changed your hair." Ted smiled and touched the ends of her shoulder-length hair. She'd had it highlighted a few days ago in Boise. "It looks pretty. I like it."

Uncomfortable when men fawned over her, she averted her eyes and slid the rubber band off the USGS map. "Uh, thanks. Listen, I heard from Kenny a few days ago."

"Uh-oh, what did he want?"

"He wants to start logging Soldier Meadows. You know what *that* means. If you have time, maybe you would help me refresh my memory. Show me where my back line butts up to national forest and where my south line adjoins Soldier Meadows."

"Sure. Let's take a look." He cleared off a large space in the center of his desk.

She unrolled the map and spread it. "I have to be exact when I take up this access problem with Bob."

Ted's head tilted, his eyes questioned. "Culpepper? You're getting a lawyer involved in this?"

"I have to. It's already the middle of July and Kenny wants to start logging any day. I've told him he can't take his logging equipment across the back of my property, but he says he's going to anyway. I'm asking for a court order to stop him. I left a message with Bob this morning."

"Holy shit, Alex. Kenny won't take that lying down. What does Charlie think? He's in town, you know."

Alex felt the corner of her mouth twitch. Why her ex-husband continued to come to Callister she didn't know, but she couldn't avoid her suspicion that he was up to no good. "Really? Have you seen him?"

"No, but Pete and Mike saw him in the Eights and Aces."

"I don't care what he thinks. Resolving this access issue is mopping up another of his messes."

Ted's eyes leveled on hers for a few seconds, reminding her just how much knowledge he had of her ex-husband's shenanigans. Ted probably even knew the gory details of Charlie's philandering. Men always seemed to be aware of those things about each other. "And you know how many times I've done *that*," she added.

"Point taken. Let's change the subject and look at the map." He leaned over, the long, bony fingers of his right hand pointing out defining landmarks. His left hand rested on her shoulder and she felt the comfort of friendship in his touch.

* * *

"Hi, I'm Gretchen. Ted's in his office." The greeting came from a chubby girl with a toothpaste-commercial smile and a deep dimple in one cheek. "I gave him your note. He's talked about you so much, I feel like I know you."

"Uh-oh," Doug said, surprised at being *known* by the Forest Service receptionist. He gave her a wink. "Sounds like maybe I should be worried."

The receptionist's cheeks flushed. She pointed a finger to the right. "There's his office, second door. He's got somebody in there, but you can go in."

Ted Benson's name and title stood out in white letters painted on a rustic wooden plaque: ASSISTANT RANGER AND RESOURCE MANAGER. Ted had made it. His name was on a door.

Doug approached the office with a spring in his step. The heavy door stood ajar. A woman's low laughter floated from behind it. Doug tapped with his knuckle and peeked through the opening.

And there, before his eyes, perched storklike on one leg in front of a government-issue metal desk, stood last night's pissed-off blonde. The hand of the man he recognized as his old friend rested on her shoulder. Heated blue eyes and steel jack handles flashed in Doug's mind and his jaw tightened.

"Doug Hawkins! Get in here!"

Ted's jubilant voice shook Doug from his befuddlement. He willed his thoughts away from the blonde as he clasped Ted's outstretched hand. "Hey, Ted."

"Aw, hell," Ted said. "I gotta hug you." They hugged and backslapped until Doug stepped back. "Look at you. You haven't changed a bit."

"You either." Ted laughed. "Now we're both lying."

A hint of moisture showed in Ted's eyes and Doug remembered how softhearted he always was. His old pal's

formerly dark brown hair, though still thick, had turned a
salt-and-pepper gray.

"You really do look great, Doug. Are you?"

"I'm good, Ted. Not like new, but good."

Throughout the exchange Doug had watched the blonde
from the corner of his eye. Now she wrestled a huge map
spread over the desktop. She looked taller than she had appeared last night, dwarfed as they had been by tall trees and
canyon walls. Slacks covered her legs, but Doug somehow
just knew those long limbs would be tanned, shapely and
strong. From beneath a soft-looking shirt the color of
cream, the impression of lace showed and he pictured what
hid behind the little rounded edges. Something low in his
belly stirred.

"Gretchen found your note on the front door," Ted was
saying. "I hated not being here when you hit town, but I
had to go to school in Missoula. If I hadn't, they weren't
gonna let me fight fire this summer."

"No problem. I had plenty to do, getting settled in. Fire
fighting, huh? Is that part of your job?"

"Naw, it's volunteer. I do it every summer. If there's a
hot fire, they take all the free help they can get. Hard work,
but I like it. God, I'm glad to see you."

Meanwhile, the woman lost control of the map and
turned it into a heap of paper in the middle of Ted's desk.
"Here, sweetie, let me do it," Ted said.

She stepped back, her cheeks flushed, and gave the map-
folding project over to Ted, who deftly rolled it up, snapped
a rubber band around it and handed it to her.

"I don't know what's wrong with me today," she said,
hooking a sheaf of hair that looked to be twenty shades of
gold behind her ear. "I'm fumble-fingered for some reason."

Doug knew what was wrong with her, but like the gentleman he sometimes wished he was, he hid a smile.

She moved toward a chair in the far corner of the room.

In the looks department, she was something. The blind-filtered sunlight played on a classic face that could have come from a forties movie, but she had a body that came right out of Victoria's Secret and oversized clothing didn't hide it. The blue eyes that had confronted him last night watched him with such intensity, he had to suppress an urge to fidget.

"Small world, huh?" Ted said, drawing Doug's attention away from the woman. "Who woulda thought we'd get together again after all these years? It's gonna be like old times. Huntin' and fishin'. Just like when we were kids."

"I'm counting on it."

"You've come to the right place. This really *is* a sportsman's paradise, like I've been telling you on the phone." He turned to the blonde. "I want you to meet someone . . ."

She stiffened and stood straighter as Ted made the introduction. For the sake of decorum, Doug mustered a smile and extended his hand across the back of the chair she stood behind. He almost said they had met, but an anxious look in her eyes warned him not to.

Her chin dipped in an almost indiscernible nod and she offered only her crimson-tipped fingers in a handshake. He captured her hand in his and tried to hold her gaze.

She withdrew her hand and turned to Ted. "I don't mean to be rude, but I have to get going. Frank's waiting for me." She rounded the chair, touched Ted's cheek with hers and kissed air with heart-shaped lips. "Call me, okay?" She breezed through the doorway, leaving clean-smelling fragrance in her wake.

Doug stared after her until she disappeared, then remembered Ted's hand on her shoulder. "That the lady in your life?"

Ted looked up the hallway as if she were still there, worry obvious in his expression. "Naw. She's way out of *my* league. We're pretty good friends, though. She lives alone, so I help her out now and then."

*Friends, my ass,* Doug thought. Unless he had suddenly forgotten everything he knew about people, what he saw in his old friend was a hell of a lot closer to worship. Still, the statement had answered Doug's question, and he felt relief at hearing Ted wasn't connected to her in an intimate way. After last night's set-to, which still chafed, the feeling didn't make sense and he was annoyed at himself because of it.

Ted turned back, devilment in his expression. "Of course, I'm not the outlaw with women you always were. You've never met a woman who was out of your league."

Doug chuckled. If Ted only knew. "Shit. Don't think I haven't been raked over the coals by the weaker sex. And don't ever let anyone convince you they're weaker." Then, trying to sound more casual than his second encounter with the blonde had left him feeling, he said, "Damn, Ted, it's great to finally be here. This place is like a light at the end of a real long tunnel."

They laughed together again, followed by a stretch of silence. Ted became serious. "What's it been now, two years?"

Doug knew he meant the shooting. His heartbeat quickened as it always did when someone mentioned it. The catastrophic incident had taken the life of his partner and two ATF agents, had kept him in a hospital for months and caused him more physical and mental agony than he had imagined was possible. And it had cost his law enforcement career, which he would lament to his dying day. "Yeah."

"So what's the truth? I heard you were shot up so bad they thought you were dead."

The curiosity from a friend shouldn't be surprising, Doug supposed. The tragedy had been hashed over on national news for weeks and his trial had been on *Court TV.* Total strangers, if they recognized him, tried to open a discussion of it. "That's what they said. Must not have been my turn."

Ted shook his head, staring at the floor. "It's mean out there these days. I see it even in *my* job."

"Actually, I'm in pretty good shape now." Doug twisted and flexed his left arm to show it functioned, which was nothing short of a miracle. "I work out every day. Run a little. Don't put any pressure on myself. I feel great."

"Sit down, sit down." Ted moved to the chair behind his desk. "I want to hear everything you've been doing. After you got lost in that Los Angeles jungle."

Digging up old bones was the last thing Doug wanted. "Plenty of time for that. Right now I'm hungry. Let's go get that breakfast. I still don't have any food in my house."

# Chapter 4

"Dear God. Ted's old friend from California." Mumbling to herself and dodging dust-covered 4x4s, Alex strode toward Betty's Road Kill Café, two blocks up the street.

No wonder Doug Hawkins looked familiar last night. She had seen him in Ted's photo albums, holding strings of fish. Ted had told her about his old friend buying twenty acres of the old Stewart farm and moving here, that he had been a cop with LAPD and was nearly killed in some kind of police shoot-out. She had a vague recollection of seeing him on TV news two or three years ago, accused of murder or manslaughter or some kind of havoc. She should have realized who he was when she heard Cindy say his name, especially after seeing the pickup's California plate.

She had succeeded in swallowing a gasp when he stepped through the office doorway, but how could either he or Ted not have noticed her eyes almost leaping from their sockets or her knee-jerk reaction scrabbling with the map? How she hated being caught off guard.

He had recognized her, too, but, thank God, he hadn't humiliated her by mentioning the ridiculous scene at Granite Pond, an outburst she didn't plan to share with *anyone*.

Ted's snapshots didn't do the man justice. They showed a

rangy, athletic-looking boy, a description hardly fitting the flesh-and-blood man. He looked too clean-cut to be a criminal. Tall and lean, with tanned biceps bulging against the short sleeves of a white T-shirt, he looked like the jock Ted said he had once been. She could well imagine him in a football uniform, fading back to hurl a pass while a ton of human muscle rushed him.

The snapshots hadn't shown his gray eyes either, sentry eyes that had touched her everywhere. She didn't doubt the veracity of Ted's stories about this guy and women.

She conducted her professional life in a world of men, commingled with her share of Neanderthal types who suffered testosterone overload. She neither liked nor trusted them. Encountering one under normal circumstances, she kept a calculated distance, hid behind cutting retorts and refused to be intimidated.

This one made her warier than usual and she knew why. She had seen him in a state of arousal with his fly undone. The memory flew into her mind the instant she saw him in Ted's office and it was vivid, down to the color of his blue shorts. What was worse, that strange uneasiness had come back and escaping him was the only relief she could think of.

"What's wrong with you, idiot?" she mumbled to herself. "You live in Los Angeles. Tanned, sculpted males are thicker than fleas on a stray dog." True enough, but what she hadn't seen in a long, long time was a real live man with a hard-on. She felt as if she had been caught window-peeping.

Betty's Road Kill Café loomed a few steps ahead, its modern plate-glass door conflicting with a battered brick facade. The building was like the rest of Callister—old, used and dusty, with stories to tell of pioneer beginnings. It had been a brothel in the 1850s, with rooms upstairs. It still had rooms upstairs, but they were no longer let by the hour.

Betty rented them by the month to railroaders and seasonal
Forest Service employees.

No rivalry existed between Carlton's and Betty's Road
Kill as far as Alex and Betty were concerned. Alex fre-
quently ate at the café, and Betty and her husband were
customers at Carlton's.

Pushing through the entrance diverted Alex from her
mental hand-wringing. She was greeted by the rattle of a
cowbell Betty had tied to the glass door, the beat and twang
of Brooks & Dunn and air redolent with the aromas of
sausage and bacon and fresh, strong coffee.

Customers filled every table. Mostly Callister citizens
eating breakfast, but sprinkled among them were a few men
dressed in suits and ties, conspicuous out-of-towners. The
room hummed like a beehive.

She spotted Frank Bagwell, the only working real estate
broker in Callister. He was sitting in a high-backed wooden
booth by a window overlooking the street. He stood and
beckoned her over with a wave and she threaded her way
toward him through well-used tables and chairs.

Their meeting lasted only long enough to cover a few details and Frank soon left her alone with her cup of tea and a
paperback book ever-present in her purse.

Doug followed Ted out the front door of the Forest Service office building into the morning sun's eye-watering
brilliance. He could hear the shrill screech of steel against
steel in the distance. "What's that?"

"Sawmill's just up the road. Can't you smell the fresh-
sawn lumber?"

Doug took a deep sniff, filling his nostrils with the piney
fragrance and his lungs with fresh air—and doubting a
sawmill existed anywhere near Los Angeles County. "Cool.
I love it." He looked up at the clear azure sky. "And I love
that sky. Is there anything else in the world that blue?"

An unbidden image of Alex McGregor's eyes flew into

his mind. He pushed it aside and stuffed his fingers into his jeans pockets as he strolled up the street beside his old pal.

Inside Betty's Road Kill Café, Ted made a beeline toward the back of the room. Most of the diners nodded greetings as he passed. At a table near the kitchen, he swung one skinny leg over the chair seat and nodded for Doug to take the opposite chair.

Heavy ceramic mugs waited upside down at four places. A yellowed laminated menu stood between condiment jars and bottles in the center of the table. Doug reached for it and studied the choices.

A way-past-her-prime waitress wearing jeans came with a coffee carafe. "Morning, Ted." She turned over two mugs and poured them to the brim. "I saw on the news they got a fire over in Oregon. You going?"

"Hiya, Lorraine. Don't know. Might, if they don't get on top of it quick. Your boy still hauling logs over there?"

"Be doing it all summer. They're paying him a lot more than he can get around here, but his trips have been cut down. Tree-fallers quitting by eleven. It's so hot and dry, the birds are coughing. Supposed to get to a hundred today."

She pulled a pad out of the pocket of a ruffled apron and whipped a pencil from a helmet of frizzy blue hair. "You guys eating breakfast?"

Ted ordered a cinnamon roll, but Doug ordered his favorite morning meal—two eggs over easy, sugar-cured bacon and fresh biscuits with real country butter.

"You should have ordered an angioplasty with that," Ted said after Lorraine left with the order. "I can see you still like to eat. You still cook?"

Doug's mind took another turn down memory lane. Growing up, he had learned to cook from Ted's mother. Self-defense, she had called it, telling Doug often that the frozen pizza his brother and sister-in-law sold in their blue-collar bar was not a proper diet for a growing boy. "You

bet. Good food is one of the few vices I have left." He
picked up his mug and sipped.

Ted laughed. "Don't tell me you've given up hot
women."

Hot women. One hot woman had been the beginning of
the end of the police career of James Douglas Hawkins. If
he had never been called out to that domestic abuse scene,
if he had never met John Bascomb's wife . . . He stopped
his galloping regrets. Water over the dam. "Yep, that, too."

The waitress saved him from Ted's questioning by bringing breakfast. As he buttered a biscuit, he glanced past
Ted's shoulder and spotted the pissed-off blonde sitting
alone, absorbed in a book, in a corner booth across the
room. He tilted his head toward her. "There's your friend
again."

A bite of cinnamon roll filled Ted's jaw, but he looked
over at her.

"Interesting woman," Doug said and meant it. He had always been fascinated by a mix of balls and beauty in a
woman. "She strikes me as somebody who always does
something different from everybody else." He sneaked
peeks at her as he tucked into his breakfast.

Ted swallowed and laughed. "That's a pure fact."

"Look at her. The only one in this café who's not drinking coffee. She's having tea. With milk."

"Um, yeah. Wonder where Frank is. She was supposed to
meet him here this morning. Frank Bagwell. He's the real
estate agent down the street. She's trying to sell her bar."

"Bar? You mean, as in booze? Here?"

"Across the street, next to the grocery store."

"You said she lived in L.A."

"She does, but she owns Carlton's Lounge and Supper
Club. It's a long story." Ted dismissed the subject and
started a conversation about a high-country lake where
somebody he knew had caught some nice golden trout.

THE LOVE OF A STRANGER

Doug listened to the fish story, but continued to watch the blonde from the corner of his eye.

She didn't look their way once. She placed money on the table, then hurried out. The eyes of most of the men in the room followed her, Doug noticed, and he felt a tiny twinge of . . . what? He couldn't name the emotion, but it was strange and different.

"Not to sound like an old movie, Ted, but what's a woman like her doing in a place like this?"

"Kicking back, mostly. She's a high-octane real estate broker down in L.A. Shopping centers, apartments and such. A lot of stress, she says."

"And she's what, separated? Divorced?" Doug had to put effort into sounding indifferent.

"Divorced."

"From somebody around here?"

"Naw. L.A. Her and her ex own some restaurants down there. He runs 'em. He's a real asshole. Maybe you've seen 'em. Charlie Boy's Old South Barbecue."

Doug could think of several of the restaurant locations scattered around Los Angeles and Orange Counties. What came to mind was ice-cold beer, loud rhythm and blues and plenty of Southern atmosphere. He nodded. "Not bad food. He's an asshole? He beat her up?"

"Naw. She'd hit him back. Alex isn't one of those helpless females." Ted cut off another bite of his roll. "But when her and ol' Charlie were married, she put up with more from that guy than any wife I know of."

Doug had seen for himself that Alex wasn't helpless. After the confrontation in front of that cabin, he figured she wasn't afraid of a pack of wolves. "So why'd they get divorced?"

"Charlie's a drunk, but I suspect that's one of his more benign habits. I imagine he does a little dope. I wouldn't be surprised if he even sells a little. He used to come here to hunt in the fall, but I haven't seen him pick up a rifle in several years. Now all he does is party and chase women."

"In a town like this?" The last thing Callister looked like was a playground for the idle rich.

"Yep. It's crazy, but he's been back three or four times this summer. He's got a girlfriend here. Some of the gossips around town even think one of her kids is his. Cindy Evans. She's the bartender down at the Eights and Aces."

Doug's stomach rose and fell. He looked away, silently cursing and reminding himself of the deceitfulness of women.

"Alex was married to him for years," Ted went on, "and I think he tormented the devil out of her most of the time. Still does if he gets a chance. It's almost like he sits around and thinks up ways to harass her. She doesn't go around crying on people's shoulders, but I can see it in her when they've been in a row. Something must have happened last night. She looks like hell this morning."

Doug nearly choked on a bite of bacon and took a quick drink of coffee. He waited a beat for his stomach to settle. "She's not somebody you'd kick out of bed. Why'd she wait so long to dump him? They have one of those arrangements?"

"Alex didn't fool around, if that's what you mean."

"How do you know?"

"I just know. We've been friends since the first day I moved here. I would've known if she'd ever stepped out on ol' Charlie."

And if she did step out, Doug thought, the man across the table would have been the first in line to escort her. He shrugged. "She must have loved him."

"Hard to say." Ted shook his head. "Nobody, including me, understood it. My guess is it's the money that kept them together so long. Neither one of them could stand to split the pie. They're pretty rich. You ought to see her house."

*The ugly-looking old house.* Doug wished he had observed it more closely when he and Cindy had passed it.

"It's an old mansion. Built back around the turn of the century by the guy this town and county, even a mountain, are named after. She spent a fortune restoring and remodeling. It's full of neat stuff, looks like a museum. I keep an eye on things and take care of her cats when she's out of town. I'll show you the place one of these days."

Ted glanced at his watch. "Well, ol' buddy, I still owe the government a day's work. Pete Hand, a friend of mine, wants to go fishing over at Hell's Canyon this weekend. He's got a good boat. You up for it?"

"You bet. First thing I unpacked was my tackle. All I have to do is get a license."

"Fielder's Grocery sells 'em."

"Okay. Say, listen, I've got some time on my hands. I might be interested in that fire-fighting thing. Around here, that is. I wouldn't want to traipse off to Oregon, but if something happened locally—"

"Great. We can always use an extra hand."

"Anything special I need to know?"

"Naw. Every fire's different. For the local volunteers, it's pretty much on-the-job training. Being in good physical shape helps about as much as anything."

After he and Ted parted company, Doug bought a few groceries and a fishing license, then took the time to stroll up and down the main street of downtown Callister. What he saw was a drugstore, a doctor's office, a beauty shop. Two grocery stores, two gas stations and three bars. No fast-food restaurant, no discount store, no shopping center.

No street gangs. No teenage dope dealers wielding AK-47s.

Yep, you could leave your keys in your car and find it where you left it when you returned. He was reminded of his youth in a small town. He hadn't felt so much at ease in years. And having the company again of a good friend was a bonus.

When he reached the Silverado, the damaged fender glared back at him like a boxer with an injured eye. He had other things to do, so he put it out of his mind.

The wild blue-eyed woman who'd damaged it was more difficult to erase from his thoughts.

He started the pickup and crept along until he was beyond the city limits. No traffic met him, so nothing forced his thoughts away from the McGregor woman. She might live in L.A., but she was *from* somewhere in the South. She spoke with a hint of a drawl and dropped her *R*s and *G*s in that smoky low tone that summoned to mind erotic bedroom delights.

Before he could stop himself, he had conjured up a fantasy of her willowy body covered by ivory satin and lace or maybe just plain naked. He felt himself swelling against his zipper.

*Cool it,* he told his cock and reminded himself he had given up women.

# Chapter 5

The living room clock's soft *bong* brought Alex back to half consciousness. Her mind counted each strike until it registered nine. She jerked awake to see the night easing around her.

Good Lord. She had returned from town, eaten lunch, then begun her laundry. Sometime during the middle of it, fatigue had overcome her and she took to her chair for a nap, wasting time sleeping when she still had clothes to pack for her trip to Salt Lake. Shedding the grogginess of sleep, she forced herself to her feet, bent on removing lingerie from the dryer and folding it to be packed.

As she left the utility room, for no particular reason she looked through the window in the back door. Up Wolf Mountain, an orange glow showed against the dark sky.

An alarm clanged in her head. She yanked open the back door and stepped out onto the deck. The aromatic smell of wood smoke hung heavy in the warm night air.

Fear sent a spike to her heart. She dashed back into the house to the phone mounted on the kitchen wall, her loafer heels clapping across the hardwood floor. She stabbed in Ted Benson's number with shaky fingers.

When he picked up, she could tell she had awakened

him. "Ted. There's a fire on my mountain. It looks like Granite Pond."

"You sure?" His tone changed from sleepy to alert.

"Yes. It doesn't look big, but I can't tell from here. I'm going up there."

"No, Alex, wait. We'll be right—"

*Clack!* She hung up and was down the utility room stairs to her Jeep at a run, chanting a prayer as she went. "My house, my house. OhmyGod, please, not my house."

She had been around the Northwest during fire season enough to know forest fires almost always went uphill unless winds changed their paths. To her advantage, Swede Creek ran through the canyon behind and to the side of her house. If the winds didn't rise, the canyon updraft would take the flames in the opposite direction from the house.

She stopped the Jeep on Old Ridge Road, lunged out the door and looked down. Orange flames leaped out the windows of the old miner's cabin on one side. Like devil dancers, they skipped across the roof's wood shingles, climbed the log walls and threw themselves upward, crackling and shooting cinders fifty feet into the air. The glade and Granite Pond glowed red-orange. Smoke clogged her lungs. A sweet odor she couldn't identify filled her nostrils.

Suddenly, a woman appearing to be nude and colored a surrealistic orange burst from behind a nearby stand of trees, running across the clearing toward her, shrieking, stumbling, falling and stumbling again. "Help me! OhGod-helpme!"

Alex reacted automatically, half sliding, half falling down the steep hillside. As the figure closed the distance between them, Alex saw the woman had on panties.

Then Alex recognized her. *Cindy Evans.*

Cindy plowed into her and grabbed her. "Don't let him near me! He'll hurt me!"

The impact knocked Alex backward, but she kept her

balance, gripped Cindy's bare shoulders and caught her focus. "Who?" she shouted. "Who's trying to hurt you?"

"He's in there, Alex! He's in there!"

Alex shook her. "Cindy! Cindy! Stop screaming! Who is it?"

"Charlie!" She began to sob and shake. "Oh, God, Alex—it's—it's Charlie—He's in, in—the cabin."

Alex's head snapped toward the inferno the cabin had become. She shoved Cindy away and sprinted across the clearing, straight for the cabin's doorway. Overwhelming heat met her. She neared the door, but heat drove her back. Cindy appeared at her side and clutched her arm. Alex shouted, "Are you sure? How do you know?"

Cindy threw her head against Alex's shoulder, her voice hitching. "I know. I—just know. He's—in there." A paroxysm of loud sobbing overcame her and she clutched Alex's shirt with talonlike fingers.

Alex's eyes darted to the pond as her mind frantically searched for any kind of container lying around that would hold water. As she fought to rid herself of Cindy's clinging hands, she saw a train of headlights topping Old Ridge Road. Vehicles bounced down the washboard hillside. Local Forest Service firefighters. Alex wrapped her arms around Cindy, covering her nakedness.

Vehicle doors flew open with engines still running. People wearing hard hats and yellow shirts piled out and began strapping water pump cans on their backs. Axes and shovels in hand, they swept toward the flames like a wave of soldiers.

Ted Benson, trailed by Gretchen Peterson, came running. "Jesus Christ!" He turned and barked to Gretchen, "Get my windbreaker out of the truck. It's behind the seat."

Gretchen dashed away. Ted grasped Cindy's arms, attempting to pry her away, but the hysterical woman hung on to Alex's clothing with the strength of ten. Gretchen came back at a run, carrying the wrinkled nylon windbreaker and threw it around Cindy's body. With Ted's help, Cindy was coaxed and torn away from Alex. She latched on to Gretchen.

Freed, Alex dashed for the cabin door again.

"Alex! Where the hell you going? Stop!"

Balls of fire shot out the front door and through both windows as she neared. She danced from foot to foot as tongues of flame licked at her. Her flesh burned. Her hair singed. She threw her forearm across her face to protect it from the hellish heat.

Then, arms like straitjackets grabbed her from behind. She squirmed and screamed. "Charlieee! Let me go! I've got to get him out!"

"Alex! No—"

She broke free, moved closer to the front door, bobbing her head, seeking a path through the flames.

Someone grabbed her again, but she fought his hold. "He needs me! I've got to get him!"

Ted's shouts filled her ears as he pushed her to the ground. "Pete! Goddammit, help me! She's strong as an ox!" She kicked loose and clambered to her feet again, leaving him prone, but he grabbed her ankle, hobbling her.

Then a hulking form was in front of her, holding something dark and capelike, and everything went black. Her arms were pinned to her sides and she couldn't breathe. She shrieked and bucked and kicked with both feet. More hands held her. She was being dragged, then pressed to the ground by weight, and she felt less heat. The heavy cloth that stank of body odor disappeared from her head and she could breathe. Ted was straddling her.

A deafening *whoosh* jerked her attention to the cabin. The roof collapsed, a violent gush of flames soared and sparks rocketed. Imploding walls followed.

"Alex . . . Alex, you okay?" It was Ted and he was gasping for breath.

She couldn't answer, could only stare at the burning remains of the cabin. Ted lifted himself off her and she sat up slowly. Sourness rose in her throat. She turned and retched, emptying her stomach on the ground.

Ted reached for her. "Jesus, Alex—God, I'm sorry—"

"Hey, Ted!" The call came from up the hill. "Need that chain saw up here!"

"I hear you," Ted yelled and picked up a chain saw, shouldered it and backed away. "I gotta help, Alex. They're making a fire break. . . . Alex? . . . I gotta go. You okay now?"

She rolled to her hands and knees and looked around. The entire glade was on fire. Flames crept up Wolf Mountain in a red spiderweb pattern.

She felt a presence and looked up. Mike Blessing thrust an axe toward her. "Come on, girl. We need every hand."

He set her to work on a fire line behind two other firefighters. Backbreaking work, cutting brush and small trees, clearing a wide swath of the fuel that would feed the fire. She scarcely noticed, so perilous was the danger of a blowup and all of Wolf Mountain bursting into flames.

Grueling hours later, she staggered to a clearing the fire hadn't touched and dropped, limp from exhaustion. She propped her elbows on her knees and braced her forehead against the heels of her blackened, lacerated hands.

Fire no longer illuminated the small valley. Everything around her was darker than dark. Like neon, patches of red embers dotted the side of the black mountain in front of her.

She couldn't draw a breath without inhaling smoke. They had been fortunate. The winds hadn't risen, but without them the glade felt like a windowless room, the air reeking of the terrible stench of death and destruction.

As dawn turned the surroundings from black to purple and eventually deep blue, she could see herself. Her shirt and pants clung in scorched shreds. She was cut, bruised and burned. The flames had chased thousands of flying insects from their forest homes. Along with soot and dirt, bee and wasp stings covered her body where skin was exposed. Throbbing pain took attention to her hands and fingers. Her perfectly sculpted acrylic nails had been ripped off and several fingers bled through black filth.

Glancing to read the time, she discovered her Rolex gone. No telling when or where she lost it. It didn't matter.

In the dawn's pink light, she stared out on the smoking ruin. The people below her seemed to be moving in slow motion, their voices sounding muffled and far away. For a long while she had been functioning from an abstract place, seeing the disaster from somewhere above it all, as if this assault on her psyche were happening to someone else.

She closed her eyes and let her head fall back. *Oh, God. Charlie. I'm sorry. So sorry.*

Daylight. The temperature had cooled down to chilly and Doug shivered a bit. He hadn't been in Callister long enough to grow accustomed to the extreme differences in the daytime and nighttime temperatures. When he had volunteered to help fight fire, he hadn't expected to be called on so soon.

The landscape had taken on a drastically different appearance from what Doug had seen a little over twenty-four hours ago. Smoke, choking and thick enough to taste, swirled in the glade. His nose ran, his eyes watered. Voices weakened by exhaustion murmured here and there.

His left arm and shoulder felt as if they had been seared by the flames he had battled. The minute he climbed down from Ted's pickup and pulled on the yellow fire-retardant shirt and pants, somebody had shoved a chain saw into one of his hands and an axe into the other. He hadn't had such a physical test since leaving the UCLA hospital. He had always respected firefighters and rescue squads. This morning, he felt new and even deeper appreciation.

The grocery store and one of the churches had sent up water, coffee and cookies. Doug munched on a cookie and sipped coffee from a Styrofoam cup as he watched a doctor hovering over a charred body lying in the ashes. Somebody had said the doc was the coroner. Nothing unusual about that. A local physician acted as coroner in many rural communities.

Pretending to assist the doctor was a small man under a large hat that rested on his ears and eyebrows. He wore a badge and a tan uniform, so he had to be the county sheriff. He appeared to be trying to stay as far away as possible from the remains of the fire and the corpse. Typical small-town cop. Probably never witnessed a burned victim first-hand.

A bearded man carrying a cup of coffee approached and stuck out his right hand. "Pete Hand. We never got introduced. I'm a friend of Ted's." Doug shook hands. His new acquaintance turned his head and spit tobacco juice off to the side. "Looks like we're about wrapped up here. 'Preciate your helping out."

"No problem." Doug nodded toward the activity around the corpse. "Quite a shock for somebody."

"Maybe. Maybe not."

Doug paused for a moment, assessing the curious reply. "You know the vic's identity?"

"Yeah, I probably do." The bearded man's attention was on the sheriff, who was walking toward an aged white Blazer that had an encircled gold star on the door.

Doug, too, watched the sheriff as he slid behind the steering wheel, picked up a clipboard and began writing. "So what's the story? The sheriff got any ideas what happened?"

"Jim? I doubt it. He ain't the sharpest knife in the drawer. He says it was an accident. A lantern turned over. Gal named Cindy Evans and Charlie McGregor were up here partying. He talked to Cindy down at the hospital."

For a second, Doug's breath left him. *Shit.* "She was hurt?"

"Naw. Ol' Cindy's tougher'n a boiled owl. She's just shook up. Hell, who ain't?"

"McGregor's the victim?"

"Afraid so." Pete wiped his eyes on his shirtsleeve. "Bound to happen. He's been racing toward the edge of a high cliff ever since I've known him."

Doug leveled a long look at his new friend, surprised at the lack of sympathy in his tone. "Where was the ex-wife when the fire started?" He felt a little queasy as he waited for the answer, recalling the look in that pissed-off blonde's eyes as she charged him head-on with a jack handle.

Pete turned and looked toward the hillside behind them. "Her? Home, I guess. She's the one called the fire in."

Doug turned, too, and stared up at a woman sitting near the burned-out mountainside and looking small against its mass. "Isn't this her property? What was her ex-husband doing here?"

"That, my friend, is a long story."

Exactly what Ted had said yesterday. So more people than Ted seemed to know this woman had a long story.

Pete watched the activity around the cabin's ashes for a few beats, then spit again. "Well, I'm going to the house. Done all I can. See ya around. I expect this fucks up our fishing trip this weekend. Things get settled down, we'll do it."

"Uh, yeah, sure."

As Pete ambled away, Doug turned back to staring at the woman. He had never seen anyone who looked so alone. Even with the activity generated by the fire's aftermath and two dozen people milling around the glade floor, no one went near her.

He thought of approaching her, asking if she needed help, but before he could act on the impulse, Ted came from the trees left standing near the pond. He looked unsettled and pale through the layer of grime covering his face. "You okay?" Doug asked him.

"Yeah." Ted's voice came out weak and croaky. He turned away and spit on the ground, then Doug realized he had probably gone into the trees and thrown up.

Years of investigating homicides in a vast city had left Doug largely numb to violent death. He had grown the same sanity-preserving shell most cops did—not allowing themselves to be touched by the horror they dealt with routinely. Civilians, however, were profoundly affected. "Don't beat yourself up, Ted. A burned body's not a pretty sight."

Ted wiped his brow with the back of his wrist. "Man, oh, man. I thought I was tough. I've seen animals burned in fires, but it's not the same." He wobbled toward one of the trucks.

Doug glanced up the hill again at the McGregor woman, then headed for the tailgate of the pickup where Gretchen had laid out the water and cookies.

From her vigil on the charred hillside, Alex watched Ted's friend, filthy and bedraggled, trudge up the hill toward her, carrying two bottles of water. His gray eyes looked like mirrors against his grimy face. His whole body seemed to sag from fatigue.

He unscrewed the lid on a bottle of water and handed it to her. "You must be thirsty."

She nodded, only now noticing that her mouth felt as parched as the mountainside looked. From somewhere she dredged up a fragile thank-you as she reached for the water. Bracketing it with trembling hands, she sipped.

With a groan, the stranger eased himself down beside her, peeled off his hard hat and looked at her across his shoulder. "You all right?"

She nodded again, unable to find the spirit to speak.

The stranger looked down at the ground between his feet. "You know about the body?" His voice was low, guarded.

A lump sprang to her throat. She bowed her head and

swallowed, not wanting to risk looking him in the face. "It's my ex-husband."

"Did you know he was here?"

"No. Do—do I need to identify him?"

"You won't be able to. Just stay put. Let the doc and the sheriff finish."

She swallowed again. The lump wouldn't go away. "I have to see. I have to know—"

"They have ways of identifying him. There's nothing you can do. But the sheriff will probably want a statement from you."

Logic told her he had spoken the facts, and from what Ted had related of Doug Hawkins's history, he would know the procedure. In fact, he would be more qualified to ask her questions than the sheriff. Still, she glared at him, her mind resisting absorption of the horror that had befallen her former husband.

A flaming vision of Charlie's last agonizing moments filled her head. Had he called out to her, as he had always done when he needed help? A part of her wanted to break down and wail. She couldn't live with Charlie, but she had never wished fatal tragedy on him. "The sheriff is an idiot."

She watched in silence as the exhausted firefighters zipped the corpse into a body bag, then carried it uphill to the ambulance parked on Old Ridge Road. Her eyes stung, but she fought the tears and swallowed a sob.

When the ambulance drove away, the stranger stood up and offered her his hand. She took it and he pulled her to her feet. She steeled herself and walked with him down to the smoking ruins, hugging her elbows to hide her shaking.

The sheriff asked her questions; she answered. Dr. Thornton offered her tranquilizers; she rejected them. Ted offered to take her down to the hospital to have her injured hands treated; she declined.

Ted drove her back to the house in her Jeep. He urged her to let him take her to his apartment so she wouldn't be alone. Doug, who followed them in Ted's pickup, could take the pickup to town and leave it, he said. She told him no. Ted offered to stay with her in her house. She refused that, too. She had never relied on others for comfort or support. There had been no one on whom to rely.

No, she would find her way through this in her own way and in her own time.

# *Chapter 6*

Doug began his day on Saturday with a two-mile run, followed by a hearty breakfast. Though still sore from his fire-fighting experience, he set out cleaning the outbuilding he intended to fix up and turn into his workshop. To remodel his tumbledown house, he had to have a place to store his tools and supplies and do woodwork. The twenty by twenty building looked to have been a maintenance shop, probably for farm equipment. He planned to gut the old structure and rebuild it.

He had spent the three days since the fire laying out a plan for the work to be completed on the house before the onset of winter and making an estimate of the cost. He had also faxed résumés to Boise and Spokane law firms offering his services as an investigator and/or jury consultant.

His phone had remained quiet all week until yesterday, when a call came from the law firm of Henderson, Crowe & Culpepper, inviting him to Boise for an interview on Monday. He was eager to return to productive work in a familiar venue.

At noon he went into the house to grab some lunch and as he was making a sandwich, Ted called. "I'm on my way to Boise," he said. "If I hurry, I can catch a ride on a jump plane headed to Montana. They got a fire up north of Butte."

"Yeah? How long will you be gone?"

"I don't know. At least a week. Look, keep an eye on Alex, will you?"

"Why? Something else wrong?"

"We buried Charlie's ashes earlier today. Nobody showed up for his body, so they called Alex and asked her to take care of it. It's been hard. She says she's okay, but I don't like leaving her alone right now."

And Doug didn't like being assigned as her baby-sitter, but how could he say no to Ted? "What do you want me to do?"

"Just drive up and check on her. Make sure she's okay. She tries to be tough, but I know ol' Charlie frying in that cabin had to have torn her up inside."

Okay, he would baby-sit, and at the same time maybe satisfy his curiosity. Even as busy as his week had been, the aloof woman on Wolf Mountain had lurked in the back of his mind, along with a haunting hunch that the cabin fire was no accident. His hunches had always been accurate.

And there was his dented fender, which still rankled him. He hadn't taken the time to obtain repair estimates, but he didn't need one to know it would cost at least a thousand dollars. "I'll handle it. You just take care of yourself up there."

Wrapped in an oversized robe, Alex sat in front of her living room windows watching the shadows of the coming evening settle over the landscape. The cats sat on her lap and she murmured to them and stroked them. Her grip on her emotions was tenuous at best.

Like smoke, the week's events swirled through her mind. On Wednesday the owner of the Eights & Aces Saloon had knocked at the front door, told her Charlie's car was in the bar's parking lot and asked her what should be done with it.

For lack of another solution, she asked him to bring it to her house. He was happy to do what he could, he said, since Charlie had been such a good customer, and besides, the bar owner added, he had always wanted to drive a Cadillac.

Now the red El Dorado sat in the garage beside her Jeep. Since only Charlie's name was on the title, selling it would be a legal hassle if not an impossibility.

Being asked to take charge of Charlie's remains had been no surprise either. Who else would do it? Poor Charlie. He had no family she cared to hunt down. His associates—if there were any true friends, she didn't know them—had been mostly hangers-on who would have melted away if Charlie had ceased to pay the bar tab. For all their lives, she had been the one to pick up the broken pieces he left behind. Was it any wonder she'd had to take responsibility for him in death as she had so often done in life?

Callister had no funeral home, so after an autopsy, what was left of Charlie had ended up in a mortuary fifty miles away. With no one else to make decisions, she had consented to allow cremation and said she would handle the disposition of the ashes. It was the most and the least she could do.

She drove to the funeral home and picked up the eight-inch-square stainless-steel container. Then with Ted's help and a member of the county's road maintenance crew who also worked as the grave digger, the box had been buried in the Callister County Cemetery. She had even bought a family floral tribute.

While her mood remained gloomy, to say she was immobilized by grief would be a lie. She and Charlie had lived separately off and on for years before the divorce. Dealing with his binges and bimbos had long ago immunized her against paralyzing emotion where he was concerned. Their relationship had been an odd sort of bond, an inscrutable hodgepodge of insecurities and shared experiences and the comfort and shelter of lifetime acquaintance.

Memories crept in and it wasn't in her to spurn them. She pulled her robe tighter as a picture came back of herself and Charlie walking together down a dusty Arkansas road to their first day of school. The sun shone on his blond hair scrubbed clean in a galvanized number-two tub by a neighbor on the back porch of the McGregor shack. As they walked, he held her hand and made light of her faded, too big dress and secondhand shoes with worn soles and stitching loosening at the sides. Her school wardrobe had been a donation from a church. So had his. He was laughing, she was solemn. And hadn't that been the way they had lived their lives?

Maybe they hadn't cared about each other in a romantic way for a very long time, or never, really. But back then, over thirty years ago, on the first day of school, all they'd had was each other.

As she sat in front of the windows, sensing rather than seeing the incredible outdoor beauty, for the first time since the cabin conflagration, tears puddled and spilled to her cheeks, not for what had been but for all that hadn't. Indeed, the grave in Callister's prairie cemetery represented a decisive end to a long, unhappy chapter of her life.

Another grave winged its way through the halls of her memory, the one where she and Charlie had buried the daughter who had been their inspiration and motivation. He had never recovered from her death. Following her burial, he stayed drunk most of a year. Tortured by guilt, Alex believed, for the part he had played in the car accident that took the ten-year-old from them.

Alex checked him into a substance-abuse clinic, where he completed treatment and counseling. And soon after his release he had returned to the fog of addiction and irresponsibility where he felt no pressure and couldn't think a rational thought.

Amazing after all this time, how the pain could rip through the vagueness of memory as if the fortress within which she had enclosed it wasn't there. Amazing how it could still cut into her heart and inflict a fresh wound.

From out of nowhere, awareness of her own mortality nudged her, and she felt a gnawing urgency to get on with things, to make decisions. No more time to waste.

The trip to Salt Lake, put on hold by Judy, her assistant in her Manhattan Beach real estate office, had been replaced by the necessity to be in Los Angeles. Charlie's sudden death unleashed a hurricane of problems with the chain of ten restaurants the two of them had founded together and continued to co-own even after the divorce.

A California accountant confirmed what she feared. Charlie Boy's Old South Barbecue, of which her former husband had been the CEO, teetered on the edge of bankruptcy. Now she knew for certain why she hadn't received her monthly stipend from the restaurants all year.

The accountant insisted she return to California. Purveyors had to be paid. Three hundred employees, worried about their jobs, had to be reassured.

As always, when she thought of Charlie, thoughts of Carlton's Lounge & Supper Club weren't too far behind. On the one hand, she wanted to just get in the Jeep, drive to town and lock Carlton's doors forever. But her practical side, where worry over food and shelter remained as constant as summer drought, hesitated to close a profitable tiny business with an unprofitable large one floundering.

Oh, she knew she would be hearing the snickers of customers and seeing them talking behind their hands. Callister's citizens hadn't enjoyed such juicy gossip in months. This scathing new tale of Charlie McGregor's reckless antics and his cold, emotionless ex-wife already back to business as usual was the best one yet.

As long as they continued to lay down cash or credit

card for food and liquor, what difference did it make what they said?

In truth, she was more comfortable among Carlton's earthy customers than playing political games with the members of the multitude of professional organizations in L.A. to which she belonged. Having grown up among people to whom higher education came in low on a list of priorities, she understood those who made a living with their hands.

Of course, Carlton's would never pay off like a fat real estate deal, but running it was much less stressful. A disturbing thought sneaked into her musing. If forced to make a choice, she might pick Carlton's over her real estate brokerage.

But she didn't have to make a decision about that tonight. Tonight she had to change directions. Instead of preparing for a planned trip to Salt Lake, she had to prepare for a detour to Los Angeles. And she had only tomorrow to do it.

If she got under way Monday morning, she could make the nine-hundred-mile drive with only one stopover in Reno and pull into Manhattan Beach on Tuesday night. She left her chair, hauled her suitcase from the bedroom to the end of the living room sofa and resumed packing.

And packing was what she was doing when the churn of a diesel engine at low speed caught her attention. She went to the living room window and in the last glimmer of daylight saw headlights crawling up her driveway. As the vehicle drew closer, she recognized a Miller Logging Company dirty red truck.

The injunction crashed into her thoughts. She had talked to Bob Culpepper's assistant only a few days ago. Bob was out of town now. The injunction couldn't have been served. Or could it? Her heart lurched. *Damn.*

Since the fire, Kenny had been calling and leaving messages on her voice mail—two just today. She wished she had returned the calls. If she had, chances were he wouldn't be approaching her house now.

She rushed back to the bedroom and threw off her robe, grabbed from the floor the same silk noil jumpsuit she had been wearing at home for a week and slid her feet into tan leather mules. Her closets bulged with clothes, everything from casual rough-outs to designer labels, but since the fire her attention had been so fractured that even choosing clothing seemed too hard.

Outside, at the edge of the deck, she crossed her arms over her breasts and waited as Kenny killed his engine and dismounted. To her astonishment, he wore dark dress slacks and a white long-sleeved shirt. No cap. She had never seen him without a greasy Miller Logging Company gimme cap covering his close-cropped black hair. What could he be up to? Gooseflesh raised on her arms.

He began the ascent up her wooden deck steps. Even with ten feet between them, she saw his flushed face and suspected he had been drinking. Small black eyes in a square face, close-set under thick brows, glittered up at her. "I been calling you, Alex."

"I haven't returned any calls yet."

One hammy hand slid up the rail as huge black-booted feet hefted his dense body up the steps. His bulk filled the stairway. "That was too bad, what happened to Charlie."

When he reached the top step, she retreated a few feet. "Charlie made his own bed. What do you want?"

"My right-of-way across Old Ridge Road. I can't get to my timber in Soldier Meadows without it. I need your signature." He reached behind himself and pulled a folded paper from his hip pocket. "My lawyer drew up—"

"I'm not signing anything that has to do with logging and Swede Creek." She sidled to the front door, drawing a breath of relief that he hadn't come about the injunction.

"You still refusing to honor agreements you made?"

"Honor." The word was an abomination coming from Kenny's mouth. She placed her hand on the brass escutcheon that opened the door. "Just back up. We've already been through this. I didn't make any agreements—"

"It's already bought. I paid Charlie—"

"Perhaps you should have paid *me*. At least, *I* would have given you a receipt."

"I didn't come up here to pick no fight. Ain't you gonna invite me in so we can set down and talk like civilized people?"

"No." She didn't want him inside her house and the word "civilized" didn't apply to the brute standing in front of her.

"I got a deal for you. A good deal."

Hope sputtered to life. Last year she had attempted to buy Soldier Meadows back from him, but he had laughed in her face. Maybe he had decided to sell after all. Didn't she have too much at stake not to listen to his proposition? "Okay," she said on a great breath. "Come in."

When he passed through the doorway in front of her, a strong alcohol odor confirmed her suspicions and prompted her to question the wisdom of admitting him to her house. She led him into her office to the left of the entry and switched on a table lamp beside the sofa.

She didn't invite him to sit, but he seated himself on the sofa as if he were welcome. His weight sank into the buttery leather cushions. A shudder passed over her as she saw how grossly out of place he looked against the upholstery's rich oxblood color and the bronze nail heads outlining the fronts of the thick arms. He planted filthy work boots on her gray wool rug and she loathed the sight of them. Kenny was wealthy. It was his arrogance, not his bank book, that made him wear work boots with dress clothing.

Hunching forward, he rested his elbows on his spread knees, looked up at her and patted the cushion beside him. "Ain't you gonna set and talk?"

Alex thrust forth a defiant chin. "You aren't going to be here long enough for me to *set*. What's on your mind?"

Kenny looked down to his shirt pocket, plucked out a check and held it out between two fingers. "I want to buy you out. I got a check here—for five hundred thousand—"

"No. My home isn't for sale."

He didn't move a muscle or blink an eye. "Ain't nothing that ain't for sale, missy. You're a smart broad. You know what'll happen when I start logging next door to you in Soldier Meadows."

Alex was glad to be standing. It was good power psychology. She always conducted difficult conversations on her feet. And on a scale of one to ten, this one had to be a thirteen. "Oh? Have you found a new way to get over there?"

"I'm going across Swede Creek, blondie. Right across the back end of your property. Me and Charlie agreed. I'm taking my trees while they're prime. Them trees is the only reason I bought that damned ol' steep hillside. And you know me crossing Swede Creek was part of the deal."

Alex rolled her eyes to the ceiling. "Give me a break, will you? How many times can we have this conversation?"

She marched out of the office toward the front door. Almost there, she realized he wasn't following. She stopped, turned back and saw him still seated, his gaze intently focused on her.

Inside she sighed and swore. Butting heads with him

would only make her forehead bloody. Seeking another tack, she returned to the office. She moved behind her desk, clicked on the desk lamp, sat down and folded her forearms on the desk, eschewing power psychology and hoping for a rational conversation. "Kenny, look, I know you think I haven't considered this problem, but I've been thinking about it for months. You're right"—she patted the air with her palms for emphasis—"It isn't fair you paid Charlie for something you can't use. I know that. I'm still willing to buy Soldier Meadows back from you for more than you paid—"

"Nuh-unh. No point talking about it. You wouldn't pay what I'd want." He looked up at her from beneath a ridge of brow, his expression revealing she may as well have been speaking to Maizie or Robert Redford. "It's too hard to find timber that good anymore. I'm gonna take the profit from harvesting it."

"Listen, I understand how you feel. I'm the last person to fault you for wanting to make a profit. Driving trucks through the creek isn't necessary, though. You're an enterprising man. You know there's more than one way to skin a cat."

"Trucks is the only way to get them trees off the mountain."

"That isn't true. There's a couple of companies on the Oregon coast that do helicopter logging. If you hired one of them, you wouldn't have the expense of building a road. And you'd be doing a community service by preserving Granite Pond."

"Nuh-unh. Costs too much. The community don't get no benefit from that pond. You don't even let kids go up there anymore."

She drew a deep breath, dreading the very idea of the offer, the *expensive, desperate* offer, she was about to make him. "You know what it means to me to leave my acreage as well as the creek and pond undisturbed. If you get an estimate on the helicopter logging expense, I'd consider picking up part of it." She leaned to the left and opened her bottom drawer, lifted out a Portland phone book. "I'll even give you a name to call."

"Nope. It's too much money, but I meant what I said. I'll buy you out." His head tipped back. His eyes scanned the room and its dark, ornately carved floor-to-ceiling bookcases on two walls, the tall casement windows that made up the other two walls. Envy was so blatant in his eyes that she shuddered.

His gaze came back to hers. "I'm the only timber king around here now. I want to own this ol' Callister house."

*Owning* things was important to the ego of a man who had spent his youth not knowing where his next meal might come from. She hated being reminded they had that much in common. Her house had been built by a timber baron, a powerful motivation behind Kenny's desire to own it. If it belonged to him, she had no doubt he *wouldn't* log the five sections beside it. "And you think you can buy it for five hundred thousand?"

"Cash money."

"You offered me more than that last summer. This house has been restored and updated. I'm sure Charlie told you what I've spent. It and the timber are worth six or eight times that."

"I ain't paying you millions, missy." His gravelly voice—it had always reminded her of a rockslide—took on an ominous tone. "Forget that shit. You just better stop and think about what's going on around you and come to your senses."

Anger burned through her. Something at her core wouldn't allow her to be talked down to, even by someone common sense told her to fear. She sprang to her feet, her hand squeezed into a fist. "You're dreaming if you think threatening Swede Creek and the pond is going to drive me to sell this place for a fraction of its value. If

I have to lie down in the path of your equipment, I'll keep you from building a road across that creek."

The logger jumped up, too, and strode to the front of her desk. A vein throbbed in his temple. He stabbed the air in front of her face with his finger. "Charlie was right about you. You're a damn nut."

She couldn't let him see panic. She thought of King Kong and Fay Wray and stood her ground. "Charlie no longer has a say, does he?"

"Goddammit, you knew I was gonna log. You agreed."

"I didn't agree to anything about destroying Swede Creek or Granite Pond. Or using my driveway for a logging road. If I hadn't been preoccupied with something in Hawaii, this sorry deal never would have hatched."

"I paid Charlie cash, Alex. A *lot* of cash."

She had to maintain levelheadedness. Groping the recesses of her mind for another argument, she stepped back, away from his withering breath. "I sent you a copy of the environmental study I had done." She moved sideways to the bookcase, grabbed a copy of the thick engineering report off one of the shelves and slapped it onto the desktop. "Didn't you read it?"

He threw a hand in the air. "Them college pussies don't know shit. I seen Mother Nature do more damage overnight than my trucks'll do in a season." He stabbed the gray report cover with his finger. "That's nothing but a pile of paper."

Realizing that he was right pecked at her. She had paid thousands to scientists and engineers for an environmental impact study of logging the Swede Creek basin. Like children, they argued with each other. Their report was inconclusive, generating more questions than answers and weakening her position.

She clamped her jaw tight. "Okay. Here's a price for you. How does five million sound? Write me a check and the whole place is yours—house, trees, right-of-way, everything."

He stared at her, eyes hard and glinting. "Playing games with me, blondie, is wrongheaded. I already said I ain't paying you nowheres near that."

"Then we're wasting time. Good-bye, Kenny." She headed for the front door again.

"Wait—"

She stopped in the office doorway and turned back.

"I'll tell you what I *will* do." His eyes leveled on her mouth.

A premonition made her catch her breath. Good sense dictated she shove him out the door before he said what she despised hearing.

"I'll still stand behind that other deal. The one I tried to make you last year."

His prurient gaze traveled from her mouth down her body. A shiver raced from her neck to her tailbone. Wishing she had thought of underwear when she scrambled into the silk jumpsuit, she crossed her arms over her breasts. "The only deal I remember is the ridiculous price you offered."

"You know I ain't talking about money."

"You're insane."

"You think about it. A lot of women around here'd like to be Mrs. Kenny Miller."

"Then, dammit, buy one of them! And leave me alone."

Kenny laughed, a piglike snort more than a laugh. Vintage Kenny Miller. He walked to where she stood, towering over her. Her heart stuttered inside her rib cage.

"You got a mouth, I tell you. That's what I like about you. You ain't scared. Ain't nothin' gets past you. You ran circles around Charlie. He never knew if he was coming or going with you. I thought it was funny."

Alex didn't know the words to express her disgust, but

she did know she had to get him out of her house. She had seen with her own eyes he became a ruthless animal when people defied him and he had little regard for society's rules. She stamped to the front door again and jerked it open. Standing no more than two feet away was Ted's controversial friend, Doug Hawkins.

# *Chapter 7*

After climbing fourteen steps to reach her deck, Doug had just caught his breath when the massive front door popped open and Alex stared at him with a blank expression. He had figured she would be surprised at seeing him, but he hadn't expected her to be bowled over. Hadn't she seen his headlights or heard him drive up? "Hi. Ted asked me—"

Before he could finish his sentence, she leaned out the doorway, did a 180-degree visual sweep of the outdoors, then stared at his pickup, which he had parked in the upper driveway beside a red RAM dually. *Then* she threw him for a loop by grabbing his arm and pulling him into the house. "You're late," she said. "I was expecting you earlier."

*Hunh?* He thought he detected a tremor in her voice.

"I appreciate your doing this work. Did you bring the contracts? And the maps?"

*Contracts? Maps?* He hesitated a few seconds in the entry, looking past her shoulder to his left into a lighted office. He saw bookcases filled with books and a desk and credenza with a computer setup. A man—a *big* màn whose appearance said "blue collar"—stood in the middle of the room, his hands jammed against his hips.

Doug shot her a sidelong look as she grasped his arm and

urged him toward the office. Wondering what his unexpected arrival had interrupted, he sought a signal in her eyes. He saw nothing, but as tight as she appeared to be strung, he played along with the charade she had drawn him into. "Uh, well, they're in my truck. Want me to get them?"

"No," she blurted too quickly. "No, just come in."

One step into the office and he could feel the tension in the air, thick as syrup. Oh, yeah, she was afraid of something. Doug eyed the big dude, calculating if he could be the source of her fear. A little on the far side of forty, well over six feet and closer to three hundred pounds than two, the guy was big enough to terrorize a riot squad. He could break a 130-pound woman over his knee. He smelled of cologne and his face had the shine of a fresh shave, so it was clear the guy had dressed up for this visit.

She made no attempt to introduce them, but the man introduced himself as Kenny Miller and offered a right hand the size of a baseball mitt. "I hear you're a cop from California."

Remembering small-town life from his boyhood, Doug didn't wonder how a perfect stranger knew that. He shook hands.

Before he could say so much as his name, Alex spoke to Miller. "Our conversation's over." She released Doug's arm and sailed out of the office to the front door and held it open.

The big dude got the message, but took his time walking to the door. Eyes that looked like lumps of coal moved over her body in a way meant to insult her and Doug felt an urge to throw a coat around her. A derisive snort came from the guy's wide, lipless mouth. He stopped in the doorway and pushed his big square face close to hers. "You're wrong, blondie. This ain't over by a long shot."

A threat. And from the anxiety Doug could see in Alex, it could be a serious one.

She didn't say good night, just stared after Miller as he made his exit. Heavy footsteps clomped across the wooden deck, then down the stairs. A diesel engine, the red dually's, no doubt, fired with a clatter and she slammed the door so hard Doug feared its cut-glass panes might fall to the floor.

She stamped back into the office straight to one of the tall windows and looked out, watching the taillights descend the driveway. From where he stood, Doug could see their red glow, too. He kept one eye on them and one on her, reminding himself he had already judged her unpredictable.

He didn't think he had broken up a lovers' quarrel. The sleek-looking Miz McGregor didn't seem the type to take up with the man who had just left. Still, appearances sometimes deceived and hers tonight certainly did. Obviously braless in what looked like thin pajamas almost the color of her skin, she was dressed for intimate company. He tried not to wonder about the other article of underwear that was probably missing. He would bet all the cash in his wallet that one quick slide of the zipper in front of that clingy thing and she would be bare from neck to crotch. A charge of testosterone coursed through him and he felt himself swelling inside his jeans. *Jesus Christ.* His dick didn't seem to care that he didn't particularly like her.

The truck's taillights disappeared into the monster tunnel of brush halfway down the driveway. She turned from the window and confronted him, laser-blue eyes boring into his. "What are you doing here?"

Her tone would have frozen a lake and his immediate urge was to blow her off and leave, but he *had* gone to the trouble of braving that obstacle course called a driveway to get here. And he did feel that same mysterious pull he had felt in Ted's office the day he met her. He summoned a smile he hoped would melt the icicles. "Ted's request. He asked me to stop up and make sure you're okay."

"Why wouldn't I be okay?"

"I don't know. Why wouldn't you?" Dammit, she had put him on the defensive.

"Ted's worse than an old maid," she snapped as she moved to the desk and clicked off a small lamp.

Wow. And she and Ted were supposed to be friends. Doug was taken aback that she continued to be a bitch even when someone went out of his way for her. "Hey, babe, don't knock it. He's concerned about you."

"Nobody calls me babe, Mr. Hawkins, and that's a fact."

"Nobody calls me Mr. Hawkins, either. That is, nobody who's my friend." His voice came out sharper than he intended. How had she managed to bring out his worst for the second time? He was *never* rude to women. He didn't trust any one of them as far as he could throw the average grizzly, but he wasn't rude to them, especially well-built blondes.

"I'm a grown woman. I don't need someone to check on me."

She said it as if she hadn't just lost their little verbal contest. Maybe she didn't need someone to check on her, but she sure had been glad to see him a few minutes ago. "You sure about that?"

"Positive." Cutting in front of him, she went to the larger lamp by the sofa and switched it off, then strode from the office, leaving him standing in the dark.

He stood a few seconds looking after her. Difficult people had always intrigued him. Independent, self-sufficient assholes who cared not an iota what other people wanted or thought about their lack of manners. He wished he had the chutzpah to be one of them. His life would be—and would have been—so much simpler.

He hooked his thumbs in his jeans pockets and followed her. A stairway rose up across the entry from the office, but two wide oak steps took them down into a sunken living room that spanned half the front of the house. "What's with the maps and contracts stuff? What kind of game was that?"

She didn't answer. He couldn't tell if she hadn't heard him or if he was being ignored. Instead of pressing, he looked up and around. The ceiling had to be twenty feet high if it was a foot, crisscrossed by massive rough-hewn beams. Extra-tall windows made up the whole front of the house, giving the sensation of being suspended in a giant void. "Nice house," he said.

"Yes. It is."

So much for conversation. Through soft amber light cast from several well-placed lamps in the living room, they crossed more hardwood floors and layers of Navajo rugs. His gaze shifted from the surroundings to her ass, the firmness of which was all too evident. Yep, she was definitely a grown woman. He put her age at early thirties, but as well kept as she appeared to be, she might be older.

*Probably spends a fortune on face grease and spa treatments.*

Los Angeles was full of such places and he knew what beauty cost. He had shared life and an apartment for a few years with a wanna-be actress who thought nothing of blowing a hundred dollars on moisturizer instead of buying groceries.

They made a right into a long kitchen. She stopped abruptly and swung around to face him. Hands planted on her hips only emphasized the curve of her breasts and the raised impressions of nipples against whatever that thin thing was she had on. As delectable as that view was, it didn't distract him from seeing the scabs and abrasions on her hands and fingers. He still had some leftover cuts and bruises, too, but seeing hers reminded him a week hadn't passed since the cabin fire took her ex-husband's life.

She made an arc around the kitchen with one arm, a peeved expression on her face. "Would you like something?"

Now there was a loaded question. Though he could have shaved with the edge in her voice, that curvy body covered by a whisper of fabric, those bedroom eyes and generous lips were more than any man should have to restrain himself from latching on to.

"I meant refreshment," she added before a wisecrack could pop out of his mouth. She must have read his wicked thoughts.

A white, yuppie-style coffeemaker beckoned him from the counter. "Uh, got any coffee?"

"I don't know. If you can find it, you're welcome to it." She exited the room through a doorway on the opposite end of the kitchen.

Doug blanked out for a few seconds. She didn't know what she had in her kitchen? Did she expect somebody who had never been in her house to rummage around and look for coffee? Guess she wasn't into hospitality any more than she was into friendly chitchat.

"Okay," he said to the empty room and instead of analyzing the situation, turned his attention to locating coffee. The upper cabinets had glass-fronted doors through which he could see only matching dishes neatly arranged on shelves. No food. He resorted to searching the lower cupboards, where he found a partial small bag of Starbucks Breakfast Blend and except for a few cans of soup, not much else. He set the coffee to drip. Soon the aroma filled the room.

While he waited for the coffee to make and her to return, he took a look around him. The kitchen was great, right out of one of those TV cooking shows he sometimes watched. He didn't know the names of decorating styles, but skillful modernization didn't hide the galley-type kitchen's old flavor.

A long white granite cooking island with black speckles took up the center of the room. Above it hung a wrought-iron frame, with hooks holding well-used pots and pans. Was she a cook? Nah. Women like her didn't cook. Those utensils must have belonged to her ex-husband. Hadn't Ted said the guy was in the restaurant business? And hadn't Alex herself just shown a decided disinterest in the contents of her pantry?

From behind the breakfast bar of varnished oak that matched the floor, he could look across a dining room and one end of the living room. The décor was eclectic, but heavy toward Western. Nothing frilly. It seemed appropriate for her. She was the least frilly 100 percent female he had ever met.

Antiques. A few Indian artifacts and pottery and baskets thrown in. Some cowboy sculptures here and there and paintings that looked like originals hanging on the walls. Cowboys and Indians. She liked American history. He did, too. Ted had said her house looked like a museum and he was right.

From a perch on the back of a tan L-shaped sofa that could seat six or seven people, two fluffy orange cats watched him. Well, he had nothing against cats if they were friendly. The sofa appeared to be made of leather. Of course it was made of leather. This woman wouldn't own anything less. A packed suitcase lay open on one end of the sofa. "Humph."

The coffee finished with a gurgle. He pulled a thick mug from the upper cabinet and poured, then carried it to the windows and looked into the twilight. From a great distance, a long, low howl floated on the quiet air and startled him. Both cats leaped off the sofa, raced across the room and up the stairs. He heard a second howl and wondered if it could be a wolf. Callister Valley wasn't so far from where wolves had been reintroduced a few years ago.

As he watched the landscape fade to darkness, the utter isolation swallowing him struck him. He couldn't think of a woman he had ever known who would want to live in this place. Oh, sure, *anyone* would enjoy the house, but most females wouldn't like being so far away from the services

and protections society offered, like police and fire depart-
ments or, for that matter, neighbors. In fact, many *men*
wouldn't like it, either. The cantankerous Miz McGregor
was, to say the least, a little eccentric.

He looked across the valley to see if he could spot the
lights of his own house. Sure enough, he could. Some ten
crow-flying miles away, he estimated.

On a table beside a big puffy chair lay a paperback book
and he picked it up. A bare-chested, buffed-up guy and a
stacked redhead were locked in an embrace on the front. A
romance novel. Well, well, well. What did Miz McGregor's
choice of reading material say about her? He had read a
few romance novels, liked the sexy ones. Were those her
preference, too?

When he started to return to the kitchen, a piece of paper
on the floor near the steps from the entry caught his attention. He detoured, stooped and picked it up. A check for
$500,000, payable to Alex McGregor, and it was signed by
a Kenny L. Miller. Doug made a low whistle. What the hell
did this mean?

Miller didn't look like a rich man, but if he threw around
half-million-dollar checks, he must be. Doug's cop mind
and Alex's earlier behavior when she opened the front door
took him to thoughts of blackmail and payoffs. He carried
the check to the kitchen and laid it on the cooking island,
interested to see her reaction to it when she returned.

In the bathroom, Alex took a deep breath and slipped out
of the jumpsuit. She was furious. In the space of an hour,
two men she only casually knew had seen her wearing a
thin silk garment sans underwear. The hazards of having
people drop in unexpectedly. She should install a locked
gate across her cattle guard.

She felt both relieved and aggravated that Doug Hawkins
had appeared on her doorstep. She didn't know where the
meeting with Kenny would have ended if the stranger hadn't
showed up when he did. But at the same time she saw him

as a savior, she remembered he had ogled her in an even more lascivious way than Kenny did. Kenny's lurid stares annoyed her and she ignored them, but for some reason that could only be classified as ridiculous, under the scrutiny of Doug Hawkins, a total stranger, a giddiness had come over her and all she could think of was sex.

Despite all that, she did want him to stay a while, at least until she felt certain Kenny wouldn't return. For another undecipherable reason that had nothing to do with this stranger's friendship with Ted, she felt safe in his company. But what was she going to do with him?

The smell of coffee floated from the kitchen. So he found some. The last time she bought or made coffee must have been for Ted. He had been her only visitor all summer.

She armored herself in a pair of faded Levi's and an oversized blue T-shirt that hung to her knees, the least alluring clothing she could think of, then studied her face in the mirror. She hadn't put on makeup all week or even styled her hair. For Charlie's burial, she had simply shampooed it, combed it back and clasped it with a gold barrette at her nape. Now she brushed it vigorously, added a couple of flicks of mascara to her lashes, then a swipe of rose lipstick to her lips, all the while wondering why she was going to the trouble.

From the hallway leading to the kitchen, she saw her latest uninvited visitor standing beside her favorite chair, looking out the living room window. A light blue T-shirt stretched across his back. She had to admire the long triangle formed by wide shoulders and a trim waist. His knee-length khaki shorts fit well, too, over a tight bottom and long tanned and hairy legs. He would be the same age as Ted, which put him at thirty-seven or thirty-eight. She couldn't think of many men in that age range who didn't have spare tires around their middles and most, for sure, didn't have biceps that bunched when their arms moved.

She stopped herself. She *never* gawked at men's bodies. And if she ever felt a need to, she would buy a magazine.

He turned toward her and a smile quirked one side of his mouth. "I made the coffee. Want some?"

His voice was raspy, like he had just awakened. She had noticed it the day she met him in Ted's office. It sounded— she hated thinking it—sexy and seductive. "I don't drink coffee."

*Jeans.* Doug wouldn't have guessed her to wear jeans, ever. He returned to the kitchen and took a seat on a cast-iron stool at the breakfast bar. "So who's the gorilla and why're you afraid of him?"

"Did I say I was afraid?"

"Didn't have to. It was pretty plain."

She went to the cupboard. "It was not. He's nobody. A friend of my—" She blinked at the cupboard door, as if her thoughts had zoomed to another place. He waited for her to break down, as some ex-wives might when a long-term spouse had died tragically less than a week earlier. The cave-in didn't happen. "—of Charlie's," she finished.

*Hm.* What had distracted her? "Came to offer his condolences, huh?"

She returned to earth, opened the cupboard door and lifted out a heavy-looking teapot, then began searching the lower cupboards. She brought out a kettle, filled it with water at the sink, then set it on a burner.

Oh, yeah, hot tea. He had seen her drinking it in the café downtown. "Tea, huh? Never learned to like it myself. Cops thrive on coffee, the more like kerosene the better." He blenched at the choice of words, remembering the cabin fire had been started by a lantern. He tipped his head toward her suitcase. "Where you going?"

"I was planning to leave town before Charlie—" She stopped and drew herself up. "Not that it concerns you, but I'm going to California on—"

She stopped speaking when she spotted the check he had

placed on the cooking island. She went to it and picked it up. "Did you put this here?"

He shrugged. "Hey, babe, I found it on the floor."

Her jaw clenched, she tore it into one-inch pieces and flushed the pieces down the garbage disposal.

"Wow," Doug said, stunned. His blackmail theory washed down the drain with the check pieces. "I gotta say, that's the first time I ever saw somebody shit-can a half-million dollars."

She looked at him as if he had just disembarked from a space ship. Tears shimmered in her eyes, which only compounded his confusion. The kettle's whistle went off and they both startled. He rose from the stool, rounded the end of the breakfast bar and lifted the kettle off the burner. "Let me do this. You seem a little out of it."

"Be my guest." She left his side and took the seat he had vacated at the breakfast bar. Arms crossed over her chest, she watched him. Sure as hell, she was assessing him, trying to determine what he was about. Though he didn't want it to, the idea pleased him.

He had never made tea, but how hard could it be? He had seen tea bags while searching for coffee. He found them again—jasmine something—and dropped a couple into the teapot. Then he covered them with the boiling water. "How long before this is ready?"

Her body language didn't change. "A few minutes."

He braced his hands on the counter, waiting on the tea. "Look, if that dude's giving you a hard time, take it up with the sheriff. File a complaint against him."

"He and the sheriff are friends."

"So what? The sheriff's sworn to uphold the law. If a citizen files a complaint—"

"Where do you think you are, Mr. Hawkins? This is the Wild West. In Callister it's every man for himself."

He chuckled at that, though after seeing the sheriff at the

fire scene, a part of him didn't doubt what she said. "What, the sheriff would shine on an abuse complaint?"

A frown creased her brow. "Did I mention abuse? I can take care of my own problems. And I don't want to discuss it."

Yessir, she just might be the most exasperating woman he had ever met—and that was saying a lot. *He* wanted to discuss it in a big way. Now that he had spotted some kind of conflict and she had used him to escape it, he wanted to know what he had stepped in and how deep.

He found another mug like the one into which he had poured coffee and poured tea. "Let's see, you put milk in this, right?"

He crossed to the refrigerator and opened the door. Inside, he found close to nothing—a hunk of cheese so dried and cracked a rat would turn up his nose, a tub of butter and a quart of milk. On the lowest shelf sat three cans of Diet RC Cola and a gold box of Godiva chocolates. The combination made him grin. *Women.*

He reached for the milk, sniffed and deemed it fresh, then returned to the breakfast bar and added a blip to her tea. He pushed the mug toward her with a smile. "Who was it said tea without milk is uncivilized?"

She gave him a flat look. "I have no idea." She lifted the mug and sipped.

"So whaddaya think? I'm a pretty good tea maker, huh?"

Her mouth twisted into a sardonic smirk. "Passing."

He grinned, feeling he had crossed some kind of hurdle, and refilled his own mug with coffee. He moved around the end of the counter, sat down on the stool beside her. "Why don't you have any food in this palace?"

She swallowed another sip of tea, but didn't look at him. "I'm fine now. I have things to do. I don't think Kenny will be back. You can go."

"Go? Where am I going? How about you tell me what's going on with him? Maybe I can help you figure out how to deal with it. If he scared *you*, babe, he's bound to be a hard case. Hard cases used to be my specialty."

He would swear she almost smiled, but caught herself and sipped again. "I'm not sure that's an adequate description for Kenny. Thank you for the offer, Mr. Hawkins, but I don't need your help any longer. I really want you to go."

Doug groused aloud as he descended the driveway. Besides having a half hard-on for the past two hours, he was approaching the tunnel of bushes that had already scratched his new pickup. "Driveway, shit . . . insult to a man's intelligence." He veered to the right as Cindy had directed him last Monday night.

*You can go . . . Mr. Hawkins . . . I don't need your help any longer. I really want you to go.*

Damn her. What royalty did she think she belonged to? He had been two-timed, lied to and led down the garden path by any number of women, but never had he been sent home like some pesky little boy. His right front tire dropped into a hole and he had to shift down to pull out.

Forty-five minutes later he reached home. Hurt pride had switched to anger. He channel surfed, stopped on a documentary about salmon fishing in Alaska, but he couldn't force the loony witch on Wolf Mountain out of his head.

Who was the rough-looking dude who literally threw around half-million-dollar checks? Was she driving to California? Or driving to the airport in Boise? And when was she leaving? And why did he care? The sooner she left, the better. Once she was gone, he wouldn't have to worry about her. He never should have told Ted he would look after her.

The documentary ended and if someone had asked him where in Alaska it took place, he couldn't have said. Shit.

# Chapter 8

A blue steel hard-on stirred Doug to half-sleep. He lay there, savoring a filmy fantasy of disrobing a leggy blonde from thin beige pajamas. In the gauzy twilight of half-sleep, he cupped her ass with both hands, lifted her and sat her on the edge of a white granite counter. Her long legs came up and wrapped around his waist and . . .

He popped his eyes open, killing the erotic image. *Sweet Jesus.* He knew better than to even think of peeling the clothes off the honed body of a woman like Alex McGregor and stretching out next to her. Free-climbing a vertical rock face would be less dangerous.

His bedroom was semidark, so it was early. The departure from the Wolf Mountain witch came back to him and an edgy anger stuck in his craw. He couldn't think of the last time he had failed so completely at connecting with a woman.

Then he remembered the workshop. No rain in the weather forecast. This was the perfect weekend to tear the old shingles off the roof out there. A task that dirty and difficult ought to derail his libido. Then Monday, after his meeting at the law firm, he could stop off at Home Depot for a few tools and supplies and new roof shingles.

He closed his mind against Alex McGregor. From the

looks of the packed suitcase he saw on the end of her sofa last night, she would probably leave town today. With any luck, by the time she returned, Ted would be back from Montana and could worry about her himself.

By Sunday night the roof of his workshop and its old plywood interior walls lay in a burn pile on the ground and his pickup bed was ready to be filled with supplies from Home Depot.

Monday morning he dressed in slacks and sport jacket for the first time in months, even put on a tie, and headed for Boise for a nine-thirty appointment with Henderson, Crowe & Culpepper.

She had never liked Charlie's car, Alex thought, as she arranged luggage and boxes in its roomy trunk. He had seen a red Cadillac with all the whistles and bells as a success symbol. Her brokerage partner in L.A. knew someone who would buy it. Probably a pimp. All she had to do was deliver it. Ridding herself of the car and the hassle of selling it were worth the extra effort to drive it to Southern California.

The most dismal mood into which she had sunk in years had settled on her. First, she overslept. Packing and organizing had taken until late Saturday night. Even dressing had a bad outcome. For comfort on the long drive ahead, she put on white jeans and a yellow knit shirt. Then, in a hurry and still distracted by the meeting with Kenny the Menace Friday night, she spilled the chicken and rice soup she had heated for breakfast down her front and on her lap.

She had changed into khaki Dockers and a royal blue polo. Having to re-dress made her late and only compounded her negative frame of mind. Upon reaching Manhattan Beach, she would have a massage and a facial, then let her favorite hairdresser work on her color. Such personal pampering was bound to improve her attitude. Her fingers would need a few more days of healing before she could have a manicure, but she would do that, too.

Besides improving her outlook, all of the above were accoutrements of a successful Realtor and businesswoman. When she walked into a gathering of the managers of the ten Charlie Boy's Old South Barbecue restaurants, she planned to look like what she was—*The Owner.*

All the way to Boise, the Friday night meeting with Kenny and his parting warning replayed through her mind. *You're wrong, blondie. This ain't over by a long shot.*

Kenny was a monster and unaccustomed to people standing up to him. Who knew what he might do to coerce her home or a right-of-way from her? All future communication with him would be through a lawyer and she planned to take up the injunction against his road construction with Bob Culpepper in person today—just in case leaving a message with his assistant hadn't been adequate. She dared not leave town without her lawyer having a clear understanding of what had to be done.

She arrived at the law firm at eleven-thirty, half an hour late for her appointment. She was rarely late for a meeting. Embarrassed and irritated at herself, she apologized to the receptionist.

"That's okay," the smiling young woman said, picking up the phone receiver. "His nine-thirty ran a little late."

*Cheery.* Everyone in Bob's office was cheery. He stepped out with a big smile and invited her inside. Even *he* was cheery.

"I know I'm late," she told him. "I'll be brief."

"No apology necessary." He directed her to an armchair in front of his desk.

His first words were condolences. She skirted the subject of Charlie's death—what could be said, after all?—and launched a discussion of Kenny and his ardent desire to drive logging equipment across the back of her property. Bob told her he hadn't been back from vacation long enough to get her injunction against the road construction in front of a judge.

Employing the "squeaky wheel" theory, she insisted he give the injunction priority and press the environmental issues. A discussion of options followed and once a plan had been devised she was satisfied to bring the meeting to a conclusion. She picked up her purse. "Well, I have to be on my way. I'm headed to L.A.—"

"L.A.? But what about Ed and Martha Anderson?" The lawyer paged through a calendar on his desk. "I thought you were meeting with them tomorrow. I thought they were why you came to Boise."

"What? Oh—" Her memory zoomed back to the phone call before the fire. *Hell.* She had completely forgotten the Andersons, who were desperate to sell their apple orchard. She really didn't *want* to remember them now, but she had promised Bob. She pulled her small calendar from her purse and there the date was, written in blue ink—tomorrow morning at ten o'clock.

Alex had been a career salesman since before the word "salesman" became politically incorrect. Her income depended solely on commissions. Referrals were the lifeblood of her business. She *never* slighted one, a habit so ingrained it was automatic. Setting aside a meeting with a prospective client for the sake of illness, ennui or a death in the family was difficult if not impossible. Like a stage performance, the show had to go on. "With all that's happened, it slipped my mind, but yes. Yes, I'll be there."

She left the law firm and entered the multistory building's elevator in no better spirits, but she was glad she had stopped in to visit Bob in person. He might be a good lawyer and most of the time she liked him, but he hadn't seen her home or Granite Pond and she had never been convinced he understood her passion. Beyond that, it didn't hurt to remind someone who charged as much as he did that you were anxious.

To be at the Andersons' place in Marsing tomorrow morning, she would have to kill an idle afternoon in Boise, rent a hotel room and stay over. She could do nothing less. With her itinerary turned upside down and her thoughts in a jumble, it took great effort to call up the traits that separated her from her peers. But as the elevator began its descent, she called up the mental exercises that would put her in a state of mind to face a client with optimism and confidence.

Number one, she couldn't afford to ignore opportunities for commissions. The money might be needed in the coming days. She didn't know what financial minefield awaited her in Charlie Boy's Old South Barbecue.

Number two, meeting with a client would help her return to a routine, put her back on track toward some kind of goal.

And number three, which, if she admitted the truth, might be number one to her competitive personality, the potential buyer for the Anderson's orchard, Hayes Winfield, was a player in Boise real estate. A contact important to her future in the Idaho commercial arena, someone she needed to know.

When the elevator landed, she put on her sunglasses and hooking the purse strap on her shoulder, strode toward the front exit already planning her pitch to the Andersons.

She passed through the building entrance and a familiar raspy voice said, "Hey."

She turned and there leaning a shoulder against the marble wall stood the stranger, Doug Hawkins. Her heartbeat picked up and her brain went dead. Finally her tongue engaged. "Are you following me?"

His mouth tipped up at one corner, into that smirky grin that seemed to be a part of him. "Nope. But I saw you go inside a little earlier. I figured you had to come out sooner or later, so"—his right shoulder lifted—"I waited."

He had on dress clothes. Aviator sunglasses covered his

eyes and gave him a mysterious continental look. The sun highlighted strands of both gray and gold in his brown hair, which looked soft as a breeze ruffled it. What was he doing here in downtown Boise in front of the building where her lawyer officed? She looked up at him through narrowed eyelids. "Okay. I'm out. Is this part of making sure I'm okay? Don't tell me you're going to tail me everywhere I go."

"It's lunchtime and I'm new around here. Want to show me a good place to eat?"

She glanced at her wrist, then remembered she no longer had a watch. "Not really." Oh, hell, she had to eat, didn't she? "Well, I guess I could eat. All I've had is a little soup."

His head tilted back and he laughed, a rich male laugh that made an odd nervousness spill through her. "That's what I like. Taking a gal to lunch who's slathering for my company."

"I'm not a *gal* and you aren't taking me to lunch. . . . But I don't mind if we eat in the same place." There, that should shut him down. She knew his type. Movie star looks, cocky attitude, God's gift to women—Southern California was crawling with them. She started in the direction of the capital building's whitish dome looming on the horizon against a clear blue sky. "There's a mom-and-pop-type café up this street."

He shifted manila file folders and a neatly folded newspaper to his left hand and took her elbow with his right. She lifted her arm away. She might be ready for lunch, but she was far from ready for contact with a man who caused a change in her pulse rate. "How do you happen to be hanging out on this street?"

"Came to see some lawyers. Gonna do some work for 'em."

A slithery dread crawled up her spine. She stopped, snatched off her sunglasses and stared at him. "Who?"

"Malcolm Henderson and Bob Culpepper. Heard of 'em?"

The slithery dread reached her brain and made it ache. This couldn't be real. "I've heard of them."

His warm hand landed on the small of her back and he practically pushed her up the street. "I imagine everybody has. They look like heavy hitters."

"What kind of work?"

They reached the hole-in-the-wall café's front door before he could answer. A cute young woman labeled BRANDI, who looked like she could be a college student, made eyes at him, then led them to a booth with red vinyl seats. As they slid in, Brandi handed them menus and showered him with a dimpled smile.

"That's who you should be having lunch with," Alex told him.

"Unh-unh. I like older women." He grinned.

Alex rolled her eyes. She wouldn't let herself be taken in by phony charm. Or won over.

The café was crowded and noisy with loud voices and clattering dishes and the temperature was too warm, but it served good food. Many of Boise's businesspeople and the state employees and legislators ate here. He removed his jacket, folded it neatly across the back of the booth, then rolled up his cuffs.

Damn him for being attractive in a maroon tie and denim shirt, though she almost thought she liked him better in a T-shirt and jeans. Well, scratch that outlandish opinion. She had no business liking him in any attire at all. "What kind of work?" she repeated when the hostess disappeared.

"Little of this, little of that. They've got an armed robber on their hands—"

"They do not. They don't do criminals." She couldn't imagine a civil attorney of Bob Culpepper's stature taking on a criminal case.

"They do if they're court appointed. And neither one of them knows a damn thing about career criminals."

"I can believe that much. Bob Culpepper is the most righteous law-and-order man I—" *Oh, hell!*

His head cocked and he gave her a steely look with those silvery eyes. He did have the most interesting eyes—that pale gray color with an almost black ring around the iris. And lashes longer than some women's. "I already figured out you've more than heard of them," he said.

"Well . . . sort of."

The smirky grin formed again and he kept looking at her.

The waitress came and stood by expectantly, but Alex hadn't made a choice. She had been too rattled in his company to think about the menu. "Take his order first," she said, studying the offerings. "And bring separate checks, please."

"Make that one check," Doug said to the waitress, "and bring it to me."

He ordered the house special, a half-pound Grizzly Burger with all the trimmings, including a large order of fries and a milk shake. How could a man who ate like that stay so lean and trim? She ordered a tomato stuffed with tuna salad accompanied by a glass of water with lime.

"Looking in your cupboards," he said, "I wasn't sure you ate."

Not intending to be obligated to him in any way, Alex fished her wallet out of her purse and laid it on the table. "I don't want you buying my lunch."

"Hey, cool it. If I take a woman to lunch, I don't expect, or want, her to pay."

"You haven't taken me to lunch," she reminded him.

"Didn't anybody ever teach you to be polite?" He chuckled, winked at her, then tapped his temple with his finger. "In my mind, I'm taking you to lunch, so just relax and humor me."

"You didn't answer my question. Exactly what does

someone like you do for someone like Henderson and Culpepper and their bank robber?"

"Not a bank. It was a convenience store. They think there are errors in the police report, but I'll be surprised if they're right. I'm looking into it. But mostly I'm studying jurors. Jury consulting, they call it."

"And what qualifies you to do that?" Alex wasn't sure she wanted to hear the answer, knowing Bob Culpepper as she did. The meticulous attorney wouldn't hire someone who wasn't well qualified.

"A master's in psychology and fifteen years chasing misfits and outlaws."

Like an automated security system, all of Alex's defenses flew into place and locked. Her high school diploma had come via GED. She earned it attending night classes after she had worked a twelve-hour day in a restaurant and was too exhausted to function. And at the same time, she had taken care of a baby. She had educated herself further by reading everything she could lay her hands on, including complicated tomes on economics and finance, the understanding of which required her to keep a dictionary by her side as she read.

She often dealt with customers and clients better educated than she, but that was different. They would never see her in any setting other than professional and vice versa. Today, a two-foot table wasn't a wide enough barrier between herself and the too charming, overeducated man across from her. She added another rampart by sitting back and crossing her arms under her breasts.

Years of feeling not quite good enough, not quite smart enough sent a sneer sneaking to her lips. "Well, aren't you special?"

His teasing eyes turned serious. She suspected a caustic comeback hung on the tip of his tongue and she waited for it, wished for it so she could grab her purse, slide out of this booth and indignantly breeze out the door. What came instead was, "When you're a young guy with no money and no friends and a lot of time on your hands, one option's going to school."

She hadn't expected to sense that he was honest and down-to-earth, though she should have. Ever since she had known Ted, she had heard about Doug Hawkins and how he grew up an orphan, with nothing but brains, talent and guts going for him. The man was one of Ted's heroes. Ted even called him Superman. Now she felt guilty and bitchy, even thought for a second or two of apologizing for making such a catty remark. "Yes, I guess it would be."

He smiled and the room seemed brighter. For a man who had grown up poor, he certainly did have straight white teeth.

The food came. He analyzed the contents of his burger, then rebuilt it. "I doubt it's really made of grizzly," she said without a hint of a grin.

*He* grinned though and sliced the thick burger in half with his knife. "From what Ted says, you oughtta know. He told me you and your husband owned some restaurants."

She shrugged. One thing she wouldn't do was reveal her shortcomings by discussing herself. "Ted told me something about you, too. He said you like to cook. That you know a lot about food." She knew a few cooks. This stranger didn't resemble any of them.

"I like to eat, so I had to learn to cook. And yeah, I know a little." He went into detail about the difference between a good and bad burger and how you used nothing but the freshest tomatoes and crisp lettuce on burgers because the heat from the meat wilted them immediately and turned them to slop. And how you *always* salted fries right out of the hot oil.

She already knew everything he said. She had recipes on file for every kind of burger possible, had tried many of them, constantly upgrading the food served at Charlie Boy's Old South Barbecue.

He continued to talk—about food, about eateries around Los Angeles, about Charlie Boy's. He told her he had eaten in the restaurants, that he liked the food, even made some clever suggestions for improving it. She said little, didn't tell him that in all likelihood Charlie Boy's Old South Barbecue would soon be closing its doors forever.

By the time they finished eating, she found her mood had lifted. The waitress came with the check and Alex returned her wallet to her purse. While Doug paid, she took out her sunglasses. "I guess you're in luck," she said as they headed for the door. "At least I ate something cheap."

# Chapter 9

Doug felt like a fullback on the losing team. All through lunch he had carried the ball and been beat to shit by the opposition. The cranky Miz McGregor hadn't been rude. She had been . . . well, cranky. A sexy-looking curmudgeon.

After she kicked him out of her house Friday night, he should have known better than to expect anything different.

He guided her out of the café, into the brilliant sunshine. The temperature was warm, so as they strolled up the sidewalk, he hooked his jacket over his shoulder by his fingers.

Her perfume drifted to him. Pure. Clean. The same fragrance he had smelled that day in Ted's office. It reminded him of a soapy shower and conjured up an image in clear conflict with the prim shirt and pants she had on today. For some reason, he liked being close enough to smell her perfume. "How many poor innocent guys have you sliced to ribbons with that tongue?"

"I don't know any poor innocent guys."

"How about me? What have *I* done?"

"Humph. My guess is you're the least innocent of all."

He made a mental sigh. She was a tough nut. Buying lunch didn't seem to have bought much goodwill, not that he had expected to curry favor by doing it. He slapped a palm against his heart. "You hurt me."

Her head angled up, but her eyes were hidden by sunglasses. "Oh, please."

Okay, flirting wasn't effective either.

He had bought a Hershey's bar at the café's cash register, ever determined to put back on a few more of the pounds he had lost. Looking down at her with a mixture of frustration and amusement, he hung his jacket over his arm and unwrapped the candy. He remembered seeing chocolates in her fridge, so he broke the bar in the middle and handed her a piece. "Here. This was cheap, too. Maybe it'll make you sweeter."

Her lip twitched. Had she nearly smiled? She reached for the candy. They finished the block munching chocolate without talking. At the corner, he took the candy wrapper from her, wadded it up with his own and tossed it into a trash can. They had a block to go before reaching Culpepper's office building, scarcely enough time for him to figure out how to reach the most complicated person he had met in a while. "Where you parked?"

"In the underground near Bob's office."

He knew what was expected of gentlemen, so he caught her arm as they crossed the street. On the other side a manicured park butted up to the sidewalk. "Sounds like you know Culpepper pretty well."

"I call him when I need a lawyer."

"Which, in your business, is pretty often, right? You could have said you knew him right up front."

She shrugged a shoulder.

He searched for more personal dialogue. "Lemme guess. You're one of those control freaks. You enjoyed having the upper hand by not telling me."

"You're wasting time practicing your psychology on me."

He refused to give up. Or maybe he was just too dumb

to shut up. "So you sell commercial real estate in Los Angeles?"

She nodded.

"Los Angeles real estate. The golden fleece, I call it."

"Not as expensive as San Francisco."

"I'll bet you know a shit-load of high rollers like Culpepper."

"I wouldn't classify Bob a high roller. He's very conservative."

It was Doug's turn to shrug. He had no argument since he had come to the same conclusion. "I was surprised to run into you today. I saw your suitcase at your house. I thought you were leaving for California."

"I *have* left, but I'm sidetracked by a real estate deal."

Holy cow, persistence had paid off. She had answered a question. "Oh, yeah? Big bucks?"

She huffed. "Big enough to make me spend the night in Boise."

Amazed she had actually told him something of substance, even if it was very little, he pushed on. "Millions?"

She snorted a laugh and adjusted her sunglasses. "It's in Marsing. And that *ain't* Los Angeles."

Inside joke. He didn't get it entirely because he didn't know a lot about the esoteric world of commercial real estate. Knowing Idaho, Marsing, wherever it was, was probably small and rural. What he did know was she hadn't achieved success in sales by being a total asshole all the time. Did sharing a joke with him mean she was softening? Maybe so. Things were looking up. "Yeah. Thank God for that."

He nudged her arm and directed her into the park. She didn't seem to mind being diverted. They ambled along a shaded, meandering sidewalk beside a river. "That river have a name?"

"Boise."

"Boise River. Hunh. Big surprise."

She shifted her bag to the opposite shoulder. He gave her a sidelong look and saw again her injured hands and fingers and remembered the vulnerable woman he had sat down beside on a smoky hillside just six days earlier. "So how you doing?"

"Better," she said, looking straight ahead. She knew exactly what was in his mind and what he was asking, he thought with satisfaction. He had sensed all along they connected, even through the smoke screens she kept throwing up.

"Got a report from the sheriff yet?"

She shook her head.

Why not? Doug wanted to ask. And he wanted to ask about the autopsy, but reminded himself he was a civilian and it was none of his business. For all his curiosity about the fire, he had even more questions about her. That was the only explanation he had for hanging out nearly an hour waiting for her. "Hard thing, losing somebody you lived with a long time, even if you did split up. Like losing a card out of your deck."

"Sort of, I guess. I knew him since I was born."

*She tries to be tough, but I know ol' Charlie frying in that cabin tore her up inside.*

"Grew up together, huh?"

"We even escaped Arkansas together. Unfortunately, he was a disaster waiting to happen, but neither of us knew it then."

Half a dozen ducks waddled up beside them and she stopped and watched them as they crossed the sidewalk in front of them. "They're so busy. They seem to know where they're going." He detected a wistful note in her voice. She looked up at him and Doug wished he could see her eyes. "When Charlie was eighteen, he worked as a day laborer in the daytime, then as a busboy at night to keep a roof—"

From a few feet away, laughter came from a young couple lazing on a blanket under a tree and interrupted. Doug regretted losing the moment. They moved on. "Where'd he go wrong?"

"He was chased by demons even as a little boy. They caught up with him. In the bar and restaurant business, there are many tests of judgment and morality. He failed most of them."

The need to talk about her ex-husband must have been strong and who better to talk to than him? He had seen a countless number of such failures in his brother's bar business. As a cop, he had investigated their crimes. "What was it, booze, drugs?"

"Charlie was born doomed. Both his parents were alcoholics. I didn't know that's what you called it when we were kids. I just thought they drank a lot. I came to realize it later, after I studied alcoholism."

"Hard battle to fight. A person probably can't do it alone."

Her mouth turned down into a grim smile. "Hard. No one can imagine how hard life was for Charlie when we were growing up. Besides being a drunk, his dad had a violent temper. I used to bathe and bandage Charlie's cuts and bruises after . . . I remember once—I can't remember the year, but I must have been nine or ten—Charlie's dad beat him up so bad. I stood on his parents' porch and screamed through the screen door. 'You leave him alone,' I said, as if it would mean something."

A rush of admiration coursed through Doug. She had been a fighter, even as a little kid. "And did he? Leave him alone?"

She slipped a little finger beneath her sunglasses lens, wiping a tear, Doug was certain. She wasn't so tough after all.

"Actually, that particular time, he turned on me. When he did, Charlie got free and the two of us ran away, down to the river. We hid out the rest of the day, until we were sure his dad had passed out."

"Is that what you always did? Ran away?"

"Good Lord." She stopped and dug into her purse, removed a tissue and dabbed her eyes. "I apologize. I don't know where all that came from."

He didn't want her to apologize. He wanted her to keep talking. He looped an arm around her shoulder, wanted to pull her close, but didn't dare. "Don't apologize. I like hearing people's stories."

"Well, you wouldn't like mine." She shrugged his arm away. Oops. The curmudgeon was back.

"What were *you* doing while he ran from demons?"

"Surviving. I was the lucky one. They weren't after me."

He didn't have to hear the words to know her childhood had been no storybook scene, but he could believe demons hadn't chased her. She hadn't allowed it. She would have turned and faced them and whipped them to the ground. Demons had never chased Doug either, for the same reason. Some arcane force he had never understood had separated him from the booze sold in his brother's bar and the drugs that weren't sold but were available anyway. The woman beside him possessed the same gut-level strength. Amazing how much he had in common with her. He wanted the chance to tell her. "So how long you gonna be in California?"

"I don't know. A week. Maybe two."

"How're you passing the time between now and tomorrow?"

"Slowly. In truth, I need to be on the road."

"Want to see a movie?" He had to ask, had to do something to hold on to her company a while longer. Compared to most of the women he encountered socially, she was a breath of fresh air, even with her sarcasm and grouchiness. His brain didn't work fast enough to process all the questions he wanted to ask her. She hid behind a mask, which made her a mystery. And solving mysteries was what he had done for years. Not only was he good at it, he enjoyed it.

He gestured her toward a bench at the edge of the sidewalk and unfolded his newspaper, looking for the entertainment page.

"I haven't been in a movie theatre in years," she said.

When he found the page, he handed it to her. "How 'bout you pick one?"

She didn't take the page. "How about I say thank you for lunch and we go our separate ways?"

"What, afraid to go to the movies with me?" What was he doing, challenging her? He didn't have time to go to the movies himself. If he had an ounce of sense, he would part from her right now and stick to his original plan—stop off at Home Depot, pick up the items on his list and head back to Callister. But he had never been known for doing the sensible thing when it came to women. The idea of spending an afternoon with the cranky Miz McGregor held a masochistic appeal. He had always been willing to let the fairer sex torture him, to a point. "Here's a new one I've read is good. It's at a theatre in the mall. You want to drive or you want me to?"

"Really, I can't—"

"C'mon. What else do you have to do?"

"Nothing." She heaved a sigh. "My car's probably the closest."

She paid no attention to which movie he chose, other than to say she didn't enjoy blood and gore. They left the ninety-degree afternoon temperature and settled into the dark, air-conditioned comfort of the movie theatre. Their arms kept bumping as each of them tried to claim the seat arm and he solved the problem by tucking her arm beneath his. The next thing he knew, they were watching a sweaty, naked actor pumping between the spread legs of a glassy-eyed actress. Glistening muscles flexed with each thrust and the actress panted openmouthed. Doug glanced Alex's way. She was staring stone-faced at the screen.

"I want to go," she said all at once and stood up.

*Uh-oh.* Doug swung his knees to the side and let her

pass. In less than two minutes, they were outside. "Hey, I didn't know. It's supposed to be a good—"

"It doesn't matter."

Like a speed walker, she headed for that fire-engine-red Cadillac. He had been shocked when he first saw the car. Her classy, subdued look made him think Mercedes or Lexus. He would have never guessed she would own a red El Dorado with gold trim and wheels.

He followed her, lest he be left stranded in the mall's parking lot a long way from his truck. She fired the engine, he told her where he had parked and they must have broken a speed record crossing Boise. At his truck, he tried to apologize again.

"Just get out," she snapped.

"Okay. I'm out." He scooted out of the Cadillac and she was gone before he could dig his keys out of his pocket.

# Chapter 10

"What was I thinking, going to a sex movie with Doug Hawkins?" Alex mumbled to herself as she drove, headed for Kinko's. What ideas would he take from *that*?

At Kinko's, as she prepared a listing contract to present to the Andersons the next morning, a part of her mind stayed on Doug Hawkins and sitting there in the dark theatre, her arm tucked under his, her bare skin warmed by his. They hadn't been holding hands. What they had done felt more intimate somehow and she couldn't stop thinking how a real couple might leave the movie and go home, climb into bed and have sex, especially after being aroused by the love scenes in that particular movie.

She tried to picture Doug in bed, asleep on his stomach, his brawny arms bent around his pillow, his narrow bottom tight even while relaxed. She was sure he slept naked, as she did, and the image sent an odd uneasiness through her she had never felt.

"Good Lord, Alex," she muttered, "what is wrong with you?" The man was a criminal of some kind. Besides being involved in a nasty political free-for-all, he had been charged and tried for a crime. She wished she could remember the details. Maybe she would look them up in California.

After she finished at Kinko's, she checked into the Evergreen Inn, not decadently luxurious but plush enough for the rooms to cost two hundred dollars a night. She never paid for a hotel room without recalling the time she hadn't had the money to pay *any* price for a room, much less two hundred dollars. And she remembered just how arduous the journey from Level I to Level II had been.

Her large room reeked of artificial floral fragrance and the air conditioner roared like a wind tunnel. Two hundred dollars didn't muffle sound. Watching TV news, she dined on bottled water and cheese crackers bought from a vending machine in the lobby, but the afternoon wouldn't leave her mind.

Well, maybe it wasn't a sex movie. In reality, maybe it was a love story and a tender one at that, of a man and woman who shared a deep bond.

As some politician blathered at a talk show host on TV, a sense of isolation spread through her. *Deep bond.* It had been ten years since she had felt even a *shallow* bond to another human being. Longing welled up inside her for . . . .what? Love, companionship? Sex?

Sex. She couldn't remember the last time she'd had sex, couldn't remember how it felt to have a man around her, inside her or the emotions that accompanied it. She didn't even know if all her parts still worked. Well, she had to stop thinking about it.

A commercial came on and a smiling couple strolled past, arms crossed behind each other's backs, and she tried to imagine herself doing something similar.

*Silly,* she scolded herself. With whom would she stroll? Ted? He was her best friend besides her assistant, Judy, but she couldn't imagine him as a lover.

She thought of the handsome Lake Oswego shopping center developer who sent her presents. Could she become romantic with him? Once, after a nasty episode with Charlie, she had actually gone to an expensive resort with him, then chickened out at the last minute. He might still be willing, but the idea held no spark for her.

There was nobody. Her mind called up statistics and she did a calculation. She had forty-five more years to live. Forty-five more years without a link to another human being.

Then the image that invaded her reverie was that of Doug Hawkins. Her stomach flip-flopped. Exasperated by the thought, she left her chair and went into the bathroom, washed her face and brushed her teeth.

As she turned back the covers and plumped the pillows, she could see Doug Hawkins's smirky grin and how the cute hostess at the café had worked to get his attention. Well, that settled it, and good riddance. A jock with a Don Juan reputation would have no interest in a thirty-six-year-old woman. It would take someone younger, a *lot* younger, to feed his ego.

*Unh-unh. I like older women.*

"And the moon's made of Swiss cheese," she muttered.

Home Depot was closing its doors by the time Doug loaded his pickup bed with roof sheeting and shingles and insulation. He hoped he hadn't forgotten anything because through the entire shopping experience his mind had been on Alex. Her personality had him so flummoxed, he hadn't even thought to mention his dented fender, for which he still hadn't sought estimates.

The nighttime drive back to Callister gave him another two and a half hours to stew. They had communicated. She had opened up a little there in the park, actually seemed friendly.

*I want to go. . . . Just get out.*

What had gone wrong? Most women would have appreciated lunch and a good flick. And it *was* a good movie, probably award-winning. He had enjoyed it, or what he saw of it. He liked a good psychological drama with its share of plot twists, and the steamy sex scenes added an extra punch.

Was it the sex in the movie? Did she have something

against sex? Had her ex-husband failed in that department, too? For a woman with Alex's killer body not to like sex would be a monumental tragedy.

Sex with the aloof Miz McGregor. Unlikely enough for the thought to be a true fantasy. And a challenge.

"Ed Anderson? . . . Bob Culpepper told me to come see you."

A wizened man levered himself on his cane and creaked up from a rocking chair on the front porch of a two-story farmhouse. The porch floor's painted wooden surface gleamed. His thin gray hair was combed slick and he was wearing a white dress shirt and a tatty necktie, both of which Alex suspected he had donned for this meeting.

Behind the house acres of fruit trees climbed up a foothill in tidy, straight rows, their limbs loaded with ripening apples. The Norman Rockwell sight was made more so by the bright summer sun and the limitless expanse of blue, blue sky.

"He said you needed help selling your place."

The old man hung his cane on his forearm. A shaky purplish hand reached out as she stepped onto the porch. "Bobby told me you were coming."

They shook hands and exchanged farm talk. She knew about growing things. In her youth, her gardens had filled her empty stomach and her grandmother's and Charlie's as well.

Bob Culpepper had supplied her with a large survey map of Ed Anderson's acreage. She withdrew it from her leather attaché case. "I have the dimensions of your property, but I'm interested in the topography. The site preparation that has to be done will affect the price you can get."

"We can walk over some of it if you like. I take a little walk around it every day."

While Ed waited on the porch, she returned to her car for different shoes. For the sake of a listing contract on a prime property worth several million dollars, she didn't mind walking a mile or two. She had brokered thousands of acres to land developers. Many commercial brokers never bothered to walk the raw land they sold, but her on-the-ground knowledge had often given her a leg up on the competition.

She followed along as Ed pointed out obscure features of the property on which he had lived his entire life. At the same time, he told her anecdotes of the ups and downs of a farmer and father of three sons and two daughters. Alex listened, all the while making mental notes of the path of runoff water, the slope of the ground, the quality of the soil.

Ed told her the orchard had been in his family for three generations, how his children didn't want him to sell out, but the savings he and his wife had spent a lifetime accumulating had been depleted by medical bills.

Alex had heard variations of his story. She often dealt with elderly owners of valuable real estate. Many times she had seen them relinquish their hold on the earth to pay for medical treatment, which always saddened her.

Their walking tour in the morning sun raised a sweat, and Ed invited her into the house for a cold drink. While he shuffled about, breaking out ice cubes and taking a pitcher of lemonade from the refrigerator, Alex looked over the developer's offer. He didn't know much about negotiating with big shots, Ed told her, which was why he had to rely on her. "This is under market," Alex said. "Lucky you didn't agree to it."

"But he's the only one who's showed any interest. I don't want to make him mad. We need the money and we need it now."

Though she hadn't met Hayes Winfield, she felt confident she could convince him to pay market value for Anderson's property. And if for some insane reason he refused, she knew other developers to contact. "I understand your fears, but trust me. I won't let you get hurt and I won't make Mr. Winfield mad. We just need to get him to pay you a fair price."

"Bobby Culpepper told me you were the best, Mrs. McGregor. He told me to do whatever you said. If he feels that way about you, I know you're the right person for this job. Did he tell you he and my oldest boy used to play together? Culpeppers lived right up there." Ed raised a thin finger and pointed toward the window.

Alex's gaze followed his finger and she tried to visualize her suave and sophisticated lawyer growing up as a farm boy. She removed the listing contract she had prepared from her briefcase and laid it on the Formica table. Ed brought two glasses of lemonade and joined her.

"I'll need Mrs. Anderson's signature. I know how ill she is. I hate to disturb her, but—"

"She's upstairs. She had a hard time getting around this morning, so she took a nap. She's probably awake now. I can take it up to her."

Alex pulled her chair over to sit beside Ed. Paragraph by paragraph, they read through the agreement that would allow her to act as his agent in the sale of his property. She made sure he understood every part of it.

The reading finished, the document lay before him, the signature lines marked with a yellow neon highlighter. Alex removed a pen from her purse and placed it beside the contract, making a *tink* on the table.

The old farmer's demeanor changed as if the sight of the pen rammed home a deferred reality. His eyes became shiny with tears. She could have wept herself, caught up in his grief. Fortunately, Bob Culpepper had greased this one for her. Her emotions were still unsteady. She wasn't up to giving a lengthy pitch to persuade Ed Anderson what he should do.

Ed leaned forward on his cane, removed his handkerchief from his hip pocket and wiped his eyes. "This is a good home. It was built by my father. I was born here. It's been a happy place." He turned and looked at her with red-rimmed eyes. "I suppose Mr. Winfield will want to tear it down if he puts a lot of new houses here, won't he?"

Alex's heart ached. She couldn't alter the circumstances

time and cancer had wrought, but she could get Ed and Martha Anderson top dollar for their property, something they couldn't do for themselves. She forced an upbeat answer. "I won't mislead you. I honestly don't know what will be done with the house. Perhaps it will be moved to another site."

"If they move it somewhere, another family might learn to love it as much as Martha and I have. You ask them to move it, Mrs. McGregor. It's a good house."

"I can do that much," she said. "I promise."

He reached for the pen and began to sign the documents before him. Alex rose and crossed the kitchen to the sink, leaving Ed at her back. A black-and-yellow bird perched on an apple tree branch outside the kitchen window, bobbing its head and chirping. She concentrated on its activities, forcing away thoughts of her own uncertain circumstances. She didn't turn back to Ed until she again heard the *tink* of the pen on the tabletop.

She put her hand on his shoulder. "If I go upstairs with you to get Martha's signature, you'll be able to stay up there with her. I can find my own way out."

The old man nodded, levered himself up on his cane and shuffled toward the stairs. She followed, carrying her pen and the document that, after old age and illness, would change the remaining lives of Ed and Martha Anderson and their children.

From the doorway opening to the first bedroom, Alex saw the diminutive form of Martha Anderson. Medical paraphernalia crowded the room. A painted metal TV tray of neatly arranged medications stood beside the bed. Though the house was clean, the stench of serious illness and urine-soaked bed linen permeated the air. Alex felt a twitch in her jaw and a sting in her eyes. She had played this scene before, too, at her grandmother's bedside.

Ed approached his wife and put his hand on her shoulder.

"Mother, this here's Mrs. McGregor. She's the one Bobby said would help us. She needs you to sign something."

When the signature had been obtained, Martha's sunken eyes peered back at Alex. "I won't be here by the time you get this taken care of, Mrs. McGregor, so you look out for my Ed. We've never done this before."

She cleared her throat of the emotion swelling inside, bent forward and took Martha's hand. "I'll take care of him, Martha."

And she would.

Leaving with the signed contract in hand, Alex stopped in the doorway, produced a business card from her pocket and handed it to Ed. "I'm on my way to Los Angeles, but I have my cell on all the time. Hayes Winfield is in Alaska and won't be back for a month. I'll see him when he returns. Don't worry. If it doesn't work out with Hayes, I know someone else. I'll be in touch."

Outside, she stopped and cast a lingering look at the upstairs window of the Andersons' house. *Hayes Winfield. Snake.* Any developer would buy the property for two, maybe three times what Hayes had offered them. No wonder Bob Culpepper had wanted her to get involved. Ed would never have known the difference if she hadn't entered the picture. How dare Hayes try to cheat old people? She would show him. By the time she met him face to face, she would know all his weaknesses.

She had never been able to be unaffected by the real-life dramas in which she participated. Remaining detached and clinical was getting harder all the time. She only hoped the Salt Lake deal jelled so she could quit.

Seated and belted in, she pulled down the visor mirror. Her mascara had run. She removed a tissue from her purse, wiped away the black streaks on her cheeks and pointed Charlie's car south.

# *Chapter 11*

Though Alex had walked out of the movie, then kicked him out of her car ten days ago, she hadn't left Doug's mind. He didn't understand why the abrupt end to the afternoon mattered. What was more confounding, he couldn't keep himself from looking across the valley at night for her lights against Wolf Mountain. No woman had ever consumed so much of his mental energy.

Monday's mail had delivered a check for $1,000. No note, just a check. He would take it, but it wasn't enough to cover the fender repair. Damn her arrogance.

To make things worse, Ted and Pete had brought out burgers and beer a few nights earlier and most of the conversation had been about Alex. Pete laughed about her going hunting with Ted a couple of times and outshooting him. They talked about her long-lived feud with Miller and Cindy Evans, with whom Alex's husband had openly cheated for years.

And last, Pete told about her standing up to Miller in Carlton's when the logger beat hell out of a skinny kid he accused of stealing chain saws from a logging site. According to Pete, Miller would have taken a cue stick to the kid if Alex hadn't placed herself between them. Nobody else made an attempt to stop him. She appeared to be the only hero in Callister.

After hearing that talk, Doug found himself thinking dumb stuff, like wondering how it would be to take her hunting or fishing or if she would like the plan he had sketched for his kitchen. His thoughts bordered on being downright possessive.

Even with her filling some part of his every waking minute—and a few of his sleeping ones—he stayed busy with planned tasks. He finished the workshop—new roof sheathing and shingles, new electrical wiring, new insulation. A little paint on the interior walls and he would have a shop any half-assed carpenter would be proud to own.

Last week he had bought a firewood cutting permit from the Forest Service. He heard a checker at the grocery store say, "We'll be building fires by the middle of September." Hard to believe with afternoon temperatures climbing into the hundreds, but he took her at her word. He intended to cut, split and stack firewood—a first for him—and toward that end he devoted a day to shoring up the old woodshed a few steps from the back porch. He didn't know how thirty below felt, but a fire in the washed stone fireplace would be welcome on a frigid night.

And all of that had brought him to today's chore—tearing out the wall that separated the dining and living rooms. His vision for his home including making the living, eating and cooking areas open and airy. He liked watching TV or talking to someone sitting in the living room while he cooked. Before the shooting had altered his life, much of his social activity had revolved around cooking and dining and he longed to reach that place again.

The wall demolition turned into a nastier job than he anticipated and he'd had enough of it by late afternoon. To finish the task he needed a few items from the building supply store. He showered and shampooed away the paste of grime and sweat that had covered him all day. Nothing felt as good as clean hair and a clean body after a day of grungy work.

Afterward, weighing himself, he saw he had put on a couple of pounds, despite working hard every day. His body felt as close to normal as it had in over two years. He was returning to his old self. Good thing, too, because hunting season loomed and if he went for both a deer and an elk, he wanted to be in top shape.

He dressed in a T-shirt that said NEBRASKA and Levi's so worn they felt like chamois, then slipped his sockless size elevens into boat shoes and headed for town. Relaxed, he hummed along with a blues tune playing from a Boise radio station.

Callister Hardware & Building Supply, a block off the main street, would fit into one tenth of the average Home Depot, but Doug had found the owner—his name was Jack—to be friendly and accommodating. Supporting a small hometown business was good.

He chatted a few minutes with Jack, who told him no one had ever lived at the Stewart place except the man who built it and his children. Doug liked that, even envied it. He couldn't claim such constancy and deep roots. After his mother's death, he had lived in his brother and sister-in-law's house, but it had never been home. He moved out his first semester at Nebraska and returned only for an occasional visit. To a man who had hung his hat in apartments, first in Lincoln until graduation, then in Los Angeles until he finally bought a condo in Santa Monica, the idea of living in the same house for two generations was awesome.

He left the store owner at the cash register and ambled back where he found a display of blades for his Skil saw.

"Afternoon, Kenny," Jack's voice said. "What can I do for you?"

"Red paint. Hope you got it."

The name and the gravelly voice caught Doug's attention. He moved to the end of an aisle where he could see the cash register. The voice came from the big dude he had met in Alex's office at her house. He was dressed in a blue T-shirt and suspendered black pants that barely touched the tops of work boots. Work clothes. No longer than Doug had been in town, he had already learned the dress was that of a logger and the shortened pants were for safety and convenience. He stayed in place and watched and listened.

"Get any damage from that fire up at McGregor's place?" Jack asked, hefting a foot-square cardboard box onto the counter.

"Nah." Miller's reply was a growl.

"That was sure something, Charlie McGregor dying like that. With him not around to run interference with Mrs. McGregor, you gonna be able to get that right-of-way you need?"

With a knob-knuckled hand, Miller hoisted the box to his shoulder. "Damn straight. That bitch is a fuckin' nut. I'll be falling trees on Wolf Mountain before the month's out."

"Sure hope so. Hope it works out. Too bad, a man having to fight with an outsider when he's trying to make a living."

Growling an order to put the paint on his bill, Miller left the store and climbed into a late-model diesel truck, the same one Doug had seen parked in front of Alex's house.

Doug chose a saw blade and a short crowbar, then sacked up some nails. He took all of the items to the cash register where Jack waited with the 2x4s he had ordered. Since the store owner was a talkative guy, Doug quizzed him. "Was that the big-time logger in town?"

"Sure was. Don't know what we'd do without him. Keeps a lot of folks employed." Jack watched as the truck backed in an arc and churned out of the parking lot. His expression sobered. "Hardworking guy, ol' Kenny. He's in a scrap with one of our summer residents up on Wolf Mountain over a right-of-way."

"The California dame, right? A right-of-way to what?"

"Timber. Only thing around here that's worth anything."

"And she's holding him up? What's she doing?"

"He's got to build a road across her property to get his trees. She says no." Jack laughed a phony heh-heh-heh. "But if I know him, it's only temporary. If he says he's gonna be cutting timber by the end of the month, you can take it to the bank that's what he'll be doing. Not too many get the best of ol' Kenny."

Doug added up the few facts he now knew about "ol' Kenny" and determined the store owner had summed things up. And he now knew the crux of the feud between Alex and "ol' Kenny."

Leaving the building supply, still considering the man he had just seen, Doug nosed the Silverado toward Ted's office, his aim to catch his pal and buy him a beer. When he reached the Forest Service facility, Ted was just locking up and two men, one in cowboy garb and the other in a Forest Service uniform like Ted's, were standing on the sidewalk. Doug recognized the cowboy as Pete Hand, but not the other man. He beeped his horn.

Ted saw him and yelled across the street, "We're going to Carlton's. Come have a cold one." Ted lagged behind and waited for him, but the other two men sauntered up the block.

Doug wheeled into a space in the grocery store parking lot, his interest piqued by going to Carlton's. He had been curious about the bar ever since he learned Alex owned it. He jogged across the street to where Ted waited.

"Haven't seen you in days. You come to town to party on Friday night?"

"Partying might kill me. I've been to the building supply."

"Buying a lock for the gate?"

"Do I need one?"

Ted's teeth bared in a wicked grin. "Any day now these man-hungry women in Callister will find out you're single. They'll be out to your place in a stampede."

Doug laughed, though he didn't find the scenario funny.

"Actually, I was picking up some paint for the workshop walls and some studs. I'm anxious to get started on the house. I plan to work inside through the winter."

"No shit? When did you take a liking to construction work? You used to complain about having to help your brother with his building projects."

True. Doug's older brother, Steve, and his wife made a living from a blue-collar bar, but on the side they bought old houses, remodeled and resold them. Thus, Doug had learned carpentry and remodeling hands on as a teenager. Helping Steve had often conflicted with football practice and even games, a source of disagreement between him and his brother. "It's therapeutic. Thinking about fixing up that old place was what kept my head straight during . . . all that court crap."

*Oops, slip of the tongue.* He had nearly said too much about his troubles in L.A., where, after a trial that had gone on for months, a jury acquitted him of manslaughter. Thankfully Ted didn't ask a follow-up question.

"So how do you like it after a month in the hinterland? Twelve miles out in the country in the middle of twenty acres must be a big change after living in the big city."

"I'm loving it. It's quiet." The difference between life here and the treadmill that had been his existence in Southern California was laughable.

"Too bad you didn't buy *all* that old Stewart place."

"What would I do with three hundred acres?"

"Stewart's grass used to be some of the best in the county. It's too late in the year now, but come spring, you could get the irrigation ditches up in shape and maybe fertilize. Get a horse or two, some calves to fatten."

"What would I do with animals? . . ."

Carlton's Lounge & Supper Club fronted the main street. As Doug followed Ted into the smoky gloom, dust motes danced in the sunlight slicing through the open door.

Doug looked over the cavelike space. Nothing could seem more unlikely than Alex owning what stretched before him.

The room was maybe thirty feet wide. A massive antique bar ran the length of it and took half the width. His gaze roved over columns of dark curlicues and he admired a carved festoon of oak leaves and acorns crowning the top. Mahogany, Doug guessed. "Wow. Look at that old thing."

Stealing glances at their own reflections in a gigantic backbar's black-veined mirror, a few men sat on tall stools nursing drinks. Doug noted the stools were bolted to the wooden floor. "I think I saw that thing in an old western movie on TV the other night. A few gnarly gunslingers should be standing there swilling whiskey."

"Wait a while," Ted said with a laugh. "It's still early." He hitched his chin toward the back of the room. "There's Pete and Mike. C'mon. You haven't met Mike Blessing. He's an engineer with the road crew."

A row of tables marched in a line along the wall across from the bar, creating a narrow aisle. Pete and the man Doug had seen in front of the Forest Service offices sat at the farthest table back. Ted headed for the table.

As Doug approached the square table, the man Doug hadn't met rose with a big grin and introduced himself. Doug took a seat and had a déjà vu moment. The table's laminated top, scarred by cigarette burns, its edges ragged and chipped, looked hauntingly similar to his brother's joint back in Wilson.

Surveying the room, he tried to visualize a scene in such a small space where the big dude he had just seen in the building supply store beat a kid senseless. He could picture it, and just as clearly, he could see the woman who had whacked his pickup fender taking up for the kid. What he couldn't spot anywhere was a holder for cue sticks or a pool table. Ted waved at an overweight bartender, who returned the gesture with a hamlike arm. "That's Estelle Watkins. She's the manager when Alex is out of town."

Doug sized up the bartender's linebacker body. It was covered by a bright blue tent dress splattered with enormous pink and white flowers.

"I'll go get us a beer," Ted said. "No sense making Estelle walk any farther than she has to. I imagine she's been baling hay all day."

"He's not kidding," Mike said. "She really does bale hay."

Doug grinned. "Well, you don't see that every day. Say, where's the pool table?"

"Don't have one right now. You a pool player?"

"I've been known to shoot a game or two." Years trickled back. Doug had paid for his school supplies and clothing with money he won on pool games in his brother's bar. He had worked for Steve almost every night from the time he was old enough to push a broom until he left for college. As an underaged kid, he couldn't sell liquor, but Steve didn't stop him from hustling at pool.

"We only have pool when we ain't got a cook," Pete said, tilting his head toward a doorway leading to another room.

Trying to reason through Pete's remark, Doug glanced through a wide doorway to a room bathed in amber light and surrounded by the same dark paneling that covered the walls in the barroom. Two couples sat at tables with red-checkered tablecloths.

Ted returned with two frosted glasses of beer and slid one toward him. Lifting his glass, Doug tilted his head toward the back room. "That's a restaurant?"

Pete gathered himself from his relaxed posture and rested his forearms on the table, looking back over his shoulder to where Doug's gaze had stopped. "Yep."

"Food any good?"

"Doug's into food," Ted said. "He's a cook."

Pete raised his arm and waved and one of the dining couples waved back. "Right now, it ain't too bad if you like steak."

"The cook we've got now's an ex-con," Mike said. "Before he came along, nobody could get along with Alex for more than two weeks. She practically wore out the pool table hauling it in and out between cooks. Customers never knew if they were gonna get to eat or have to shoot pool."

His three companions laughed and Doug chuckled along with them. He could see Alex, cracking the whip while someone carried a heavy pool table in and out of the small space.

"But this one doing the cooking now's been here a few months," Pete said. "When she says jump, he asks how high."

Doug grinned. Alex's bar might look like something from the 1800s, but her selection of employees made it current and colorful. She appeared to be rigid and disciplined, but nothing about Carlton's fit her personality. "Customers don't get upset if they come to eat and all that's available is pool?"

"People around here don't get upset about much," Pete said, "especially what goes on in some café. Now the bar's another story. They didn't like it one bit when this place used to run short of whiskey. But that don't happen anymore. Since Alex has been running the show, the bills get paid. And she don't *never* run out of booze."

"That Alex is something else," Mike said. "Donald Trump in Sharon Stone's body. Awesome. Man, if I wasn't married—"

"She wouldn't spit on you, Mike. Why, look at Ted. He kisses her ass six ways from Sunday and she walks over him like he's a horse turd in the road."

"Cut it out, Pete." Ted turned to Doug. "Alex runs a tight ship and it's a good thing. I don't know what this town would do without Carlton's. There's always a wedding reception or a banquet of some kind. This is the only decent place in town for a group of folks to get together where they can eat and have drinks."

Doug had yet to see Ted cease defending and explaining Alex McGregor. Doug found himself wondering if she knew the depth of Ted's feelings.

"Unfortunately," Mike said, "the local culture, and I use the term loosely, doesn't know the difference between a decent place and any other. If the natives get bored and restless at the Eights and Aces across the street, they fight their way here to crash whatever's going on. Then all hell breaks loose."

Pete gave the engineer a pointed look. "Well, hell, Mike, so what? Nobody minds. Everybody has a good time. After all, we're all kin to each other."

"This is true," Mike said to Doug. "Either by birth or by marriage. And even if they aren't, most of them have grown up together. If it wasn't for the infusion of some fresh blood from Forest Service personnel or new schoolteachers, the whole county would be inbred."

"Just shut up, Mike. Callister is just as good a town as any other. We got a mayor and a city council. And we got commissioners. They keep things running just fine."

Doug kept his thoughts to himself and sipped at his beer. He suspected the town was really run by an oversized power broker named Kenny L. Miller.

# Chapter 12

Alex topped the last long hill just outside the Callister city limits in such an upbeat mood, she looked forward to seeing Carlton's Lounge & Supper Club again. She was a new woman driving a new vehicle, a sleek silver Acura MDX. The 4x4 SUV would be more usable all around than her Jeep Wrangler. And that was important because she had made a firm decision to move to Callister permanently. She had already set the wheels in motion.

In the past ten days in Los Angeles, her life had changed in ways she couldn't have imagined a month ago. Her brokerage partner met her in L.A. with not only a buyer for Charlie's car but a buyer for Charlie Boy's Old South Barbecue as well.

The entire chain was under contract for more than a fair price and she had negotiated retention of ownership of the valuable real estate on which the ten restaurants sat. The monthly lease revenue from the land and buildings would allow her to live comfortably for a very long time even if she had no other income. When she got her hands on the money from the sale of the restaurant fixtures and equipment, it would be invested in Boise income property.

Selling Charlie Boy's was a victory as well as a windfall. The buyer had surfaced from out of nowhere, but if he had not, she would have had to either stay in California and fight to pull the restaurant chain back from ruin or see its assets and years of hard work dissolve on a bankruptcy auction block. The first choice would have taken so much effort and time, even her real estate business would have had to take a backseat. The second choice would have broken her heart.

The Salt Lake retirement community deal would close soon and generate additional income. Scaling back her sales activity, if not quitting it altogether, seemed, at last, a real possibility. In terms of how and where she wanted to live, her future looked rosier than it had in years.

With so much good news under her belt, even battling with Kenny the Menace didn't seem so daunting.

Settling Charlie's affairs and negotiating on Charlie Boy's had kept her too busy to think of Doug Hawkins in the daylight hours, but the minute she relaxed for the evening and went to bed, he came back. Him and that damn movie they had watched in Boise. And sex. Whenever he came to mind, sex was her next thought.

While in California, she had told her assistant, Judy, she thought Doug might be interested in her. A long heart-to-heart ensued and Judy, as excited as a teenager, urged her to go for it. But Alex dared not step out on that limb. What if she slept with him, which might lead to caring about him? And if she let herself care about him, what if all he wanted was a warm body and in reality one much younger than hers?

She hadn't taken the time to research the scandal that ended his career with LAPD and no sane woman would get involved with an outlaw. She made a decision to give him a wide berth. She didn't need *any* man meddling in her new life.

When Doug looked up and saw Alex, his heart nearly leaped from his chest. Silhouetted in the doorway by the

afternoon sun's rays, she looked six feet tall. Like a mysterious stranger who "just rode in," she stood there, as if assessing the room for danger.

She moved through the space like royalty greeting her
subjects, smiling and chatting with imbibing customers
seated at the bar and at the beat-up tables, unbuttoning the
jacket of a severely tailored suit as she went. Her hair was
sleeked back and pinned up. Mike's earlier remark flashed
back. She did look a little like Sharon Stone.

She glanced toward their table, but her gaze slid right
past him. Had she not seen him? Was she snubbing him, refusing to acknowledge he had witnessed her vulnerable and
needy? Bullshit. The familiarity they had shared, though
brief, couldn't be erased for her any more than for him.

The scent of the clean-smelling perfume that intrigued
him every time she came near accompanied her. It hadn't
been expunged by her week-and-a-half absence.

He saw a mannish watch encircling her left wrist and a
delicate diamond tennis bracelet looping around the right.
The dichotomy could be a metaphor for her personality.

That was the thought process going on in his head, but
what was going on in his jeans was more raw. The thing
that had plunged him into a pit of lust was her blouse.
Light-colored and soft, it draped around the shape of her
breasts. Too well he could imagine his hands on them, his
thumbs brushing the nipples that showed as little raised
bumps through her blouse.

"Hi, guys." Her Lauren Bacall voice sounded low and
smoky.

He, Ted and Mike stood as she neared, but Pete stayed
where he was, resting his chin on his palm and looking
bored.

"You don't have to get up." Her mouth curved into a
slow smile. Light from the Budweiser sign above their table
glinted off the pencil eraser-sized rocks pinned to her earlobes.

Ted was grinning like he had won the lottery. "You look gorgeous, as usual." He reached for her hand and they brushed cheeks.

Doug stood there like a nervous teenager waiting to be acknowledged. When she dropped him no crumbs, he, along with Mike, sank to his seat, along with Mike, embarrassed at his foolishness.

Ted sat down, too, but didn't release her hand. "Just get back?"

"Yesterday. I spent the night in Boise. I'm brokering an orchard in Marsing. For a subdivision."

Marsing. Since hearing her mention it in the park, Doug had made it a point to learn it was a small farming community a short drive from Boise.

She withdrew her hand from Ted's, placed it on his shoulder and lifted one foot, flexing a slim ankle and showing dusty shoes. "Today was the second time I've tramped through it."

"In your high heels?" Ted's expression had grown even sillier as he tried to be playful. Watching him fawn over her made Doug uncomfortable as hell.

As the question of her sleeping with Ted zinged anew through Doug's mind, he chastised himself. Even if she did, it was nobody's business. Then the thought of her sleeping with Ted, or any man, fell on him like a rock and he realized just how badly he wanted to make his own erotic fantasies about her real. But how could he scratch that itch with a woman who ignored him?

Finally, her gaze moved his way and lingered long enough for him to tip the rim of his beer glass to her. She had a way of lowering her chin, but looking up with her eyes, which, with some women, a man might interpret as an invitation to something. With Alex, who knew what it meant? Or if it meant anything at all.

Her full lips turned up into another smile. He waited for her to say hello or at the very least, spear him with one of her sarcastic quips, but she did nothing that included him. Instead, she turned away and waved for Estelle's attention.

The bartender waddled to them, turning sideways to pass between the tables. She set down a glass of white wine and four fresh glasses of beer, then smothered Alex with a hug as they exchanged greetings.

When Estelle started back to the bar, Mike sprang to his feet and brought a chair from another table.

"Thank you, Mike." Alex gave him a smile and folded her jacket across the back of the chair.

Doug was irked. Not once had she smiled at *him* like that, not even after he had bailed her out of the jam she was in with Miller two weeks ago, whatever it was, or when they'd had lunch in Boise.

She took a dainty sip of wine, then turned back to Ted. "Why aren't you off fighting a fire?"

"Oh, guess they don't need me right now. I've got things to do here anyway. You're working on a big deal, huh?"

"Not so big. It's an old couple's property. They have to sell to pay medical bills. It's a sad situation. They make me want to cry."

"How come?" Ted reached for her hand again, lifted it and looked at the long crimson nails. She was wearing diamond rings tonight. Like her earrings, they glinted in the neon glow of the beer signs. Doug wondered if they were gifts from the deceased husband or some high roller boyfriend. "You got a manicure," Ted said. "Looks like your fingers are all healed up now."

She seemed distant and preoccupied, but hell, that was nothing new. Doug had seen her zone out and leave the planet in front of her cupboards that night in her kitchen.

She removed her hand from Ted's again. "This old couple. They're in their eighties. They've been married all their lives. Now, they're at the end. They're still in love and she's dying." She raised her eyes and looked past all of them, zoned out again. "I can't keep from thinking about how I'm getting older myself, and I'll never—" She stopped and beamed a wide, warm smile at Ted. "I think I've been driving too long."

*Never what?* Doug wanted her to finish. He wanted to hear anything that might give him a clue what made her tick. And he was envious of his old friend. *Jee-sus Christ.*

Ted's Adam's apple bobbed up and down. A noise came from Pete's direction and Doug turned to look. Pete's face was a picture of disgust.

"You guys have fun," Alex said, rising. "I appreciate your business. I'll buy you another round." She shot a glance at Pete. "You, too, Pete." She picked up her jacket and wineglass and sauntered in a loose gait toward the bar.

Ted appeared to be on the verge of leaping from his chair and following her. Doug silently swore he would tackle him if he so much as made the attempt.

Pete leaned toward Doug. "Now that's a sickening mess if I ever saw it."

Doug watched as she rounded the end of the bar. Tension coiled in his groin, drawing him up tight. What the hell was wrong with him? He navigated encounters with most women without an alert from down below, but every time he was around her, it happened.

She withdrew a rolled newspaper protruding from a purse so large it could only be called a satchel. Beside an avocado-green refrigerator stood a tall stool. She pulled it out, positioned a hip on the edge and hoisted herself up to sit, exposing a knee and a few inches of thigh. Then she toed off her shoes, raised her feet to rest on something he couldn't see and disappeared behind the newspaper.

He squinted to see what she was reading. The *Wall Street Journal.* That figured. She peered over the top edge and their eyes connected. She jerked the paper back to cover her face.

Shit. Doug turned away and involved himself with the BS going on at his table, watching her from his peripheral vision. Soon she closed her paper and folded it, slid down from her perch and put on her shoes as if readying to leave.

Goddammit, he didn't intend to be ignored. She had dragged him into her problems and then been remote and secretive. Her conflict with this logging dude stirred Doug's most primitive protective instincts. He carried his glass to the end of the bar where she had begun to stack magazines and newspapers on the bar top. "Hello again." He leaned forward and rested his forearms on the bar near the stack of papers. "Good trip?"

Alex stared at the stranger who was testing her determination to put plenty of distance between them. A part of her she hadn't acknowledged for years took in his muscled chest straining against his knit shirt that said NEBRASKA. She had to admit she enjoyed looking at him and he smelled like soap. "It was fine."

"You know, you've got just about the prettiest eyes I've ever seen."

What kind of remark was that? And what did he expect? Her pulse rate had kicked up but years of experience thinking on her feet enabled her to answer in a level tone. "They work well. What do you want?"

"I got your check. Thanks for sending it."

"Okay." She had no desire for conversation about an incident she wanted to forget. She reached below the bar, dragged out her purse and plopped it on top of the stack of papers she had gathered to throw away.

"Did you feel guilty?"

She may have felt a smattering of guilt when she first saw what she had done to his fender, but it had lasted no more than a millisecond. She gasped and fixed him with a look. "For what?"

"For beating the shit out of my fender." He grinned.

She couldn't keep from smiling. Men never teased her. "Maybe you should have kept your fender out of a place it had no business being."

"Touché." He lifted his glass to her. His head tipped back and he swallowed the last of his beer. She stared at the cords working in his neck. A little tuft of hair stuck out of the neck of his T-shirt. As had happened before, a weird uneasiness slithered through her. She had to get away from him. She switched her attention to rummaging inside her purse, searching for her keys. "As far as I'm concerned, the matter's closed."

He grinned again. "So, how'd it go in the City of Angels?"

"Fine." Dammit, where were her keys? She pawed deeper, sure she had dropped them into her purse.

He gestured toward her stack of newspapers. "That looks like serious reading."

Though he had been to school a hundred years, one thing she suspected he didn't read was the *Wall Street Journal.* Then again, maybe he did. Maybe he read everything. One more reason to separate herself from him. No way would she put herself in a position to be looked down on by an overeducated jock. "Reading's what I do. If you don't drink or pester the wildlife, there isn't much entertainment in Callister."

He winked. "Bet *I* could think of something."

Indeed. She rolled her eyes. "For your information, entertainment isn't why I come here." She removed her wallet and makeup pouch from her purse and laid them on the bar, followed by a packet of Kleenex, then plunged her hand inside the purse again.

"I'll bite. Why *do* you come here?"

He sounded as if he expected an answer. She could no more explain her reasons for her devotion to Callister to a stranger than to herself. And she wouldn't even attempt to explain them to *this* stranger. Something sharp pierced her finger. "Oh." She yanked her hand from inside her purse and examined her fingertip.

He reached for her hand, looked at her finger and rubbed

it. Then he leaned to the left and picked up her key ring loaded with keys off the end of the bar. "This what you're looking for?"

She snatched back her hand and the keys. "What do you want from me, Mr. Hawkins?"

"So we're back to that Mr. Hawkins crap." It wasn't a question.

"I promise you, that's preferable to the name I'm thinking." She began to throw items back into her purse.

He shook his head and raised his palms. "Okay, okay. Time out. Your tongue's sharper than mine." The teasing tone left his voice. "I'm trying to make friends here. Come back to the table and sit with us."

She leaned to the side and looked past his shoulder. Ted, Pete and Mike were behaving like chimpanzees and at least a dozen empty glasses sat on the table in front of them. They were tight as ticks. Typical for Saturday night. Eventually they would wind up across the street at the Eights & Aces, where a band always played on weekends. She slid a look back to her tormentor. "Why would I do that?"

He turned around and looked, too. "Okay, I see what you mean. Then have a drink with just me. We could go somewhere else."

Nope, not doing that, for sure. She'd already had lunch with him and gone to a sex movie. That was enough. She reached under the bar for a dry cloth, lifted his beer glass and wiped away the small puddle underneath. "There *is* nowhere else, and even if there were, I don't drink."

He picked up her empty wineglass. "You're drinking wine."

"Not that it's any of your business, but I never drink more than a glass. And I don't drink hard liquor at all."

"Why not?"

"I don't like alcohol." He was staring at her mouth and she fought an urge to lick her lips.

"Then why are you in here?"

Well, really. She could say she was afraid to let go of Carlton's as long as it provided her with a small income. She could say running a bar and restaurant was one of the few things she knew how to do with her eyes closed because she had done it for what seemed like forever. Or she could say she would lose her mind and fall into some kind of deep, dark hole if she weren't able to keep herself occupied with more tasks than one human could perform every day. But she wouldn't say any of those things, especially to a stranger, because they all called for an explanation she had no desire to give.

"You seem determined to pry into my life." She reached under the bar again and pulled out the bar's money bag, stuffed it into her purse. Estelle would be happy to be relieved of the responsibility for the bar's money. "This is none of your business either, but I'm unhappy to say that as much as I keep trying not to, I own this dump. The only consolation is, as revolting as it is, it isn't quite as bad as the boar's nest across the street."

"You mean the Eights and Aces. When Ted told me you owned a bar, I'll admit I expected something different."

How dare he? She squared her shoulders. "So?"

His head tilted back and he laughed. "Why do I think there's a story here that needs to be told?"

"I'm sure you'd find it dull."

"Hey, c'mon. Don't be so tense. Laugh with me."

"I'm not tense," she snapped. But she was more tense than if she were working a multimillion-dollar deal.

"See there? You're tense. Try me. My shoulder's just as dry today as it was in the park down in Boise."

What was he talking about? She hadn't cried on his shoulder, but unfortunately, in a moment of weakness, she had told him more than she had told anyone else in Callister. "This isn't a soap opera, Mr. Hawkins."

A spark flared in his flint-colored eyes. He clunked his empty beer glass on the counter. "No shit? Well, lady, I've known you what, two or three weeks? You've beat the shit out of my new rig, your ex-husband's burned to death under what some people might think are mysterious circumstances and you've dragged me into some kind of feud between you and a dude twice your size. Hell, he's twice *my* size. TV doesn't have a soap opera better than that."

Her eyes bugged. "Shut up. People can hear you."

He grinned. A teasing light came into his eyes. "Such a hypocrite. Sexy as hell, but still a hypocrite."

"Why are you harassing me? I haven't dragged you into anything. I don't expect anything from you."

"Look, Ted thinks a lot of you. I think a lot of Ted." His normally husky voice softened to something that sent a thread of warmth to unusual places. "If you're a friend of his, I'd like you to be my friend, too. Maybe I'd like you to be more than a friend."

A tiny little panic danced around in her stomach. What could she do about him? Well, one thing she could do was go home and leave him here. Maybe she couldn't keep him out of Carlton's. It *was* a public place and he was, after all, a customer, but she could keep him away from her house. "Hmm. Is that so?" She paused, crafting a reply that would shut him up for good. "I'm going home, Mr. Hawkins, but let me leave you with this. A friend of Ted Benson's might become a friend of mine, but there is *no* possibility a friend of Cindy Evans could ever enjoy that privilege. Frankly, I can't tell in which camp you fall."

He sat there blinking at her for a few beats, then slid his empty glass across the bar to where she stood. "Okay, goddamit, I give up. But let me leave *you* with something I just heard from the horse's mouth. Godzilla, who you were entertaining a couple of weeks ago? He just told Jack over at the building supply he'll be cutting trees in Soldier Meadows before the month's out. Now that didn't mean much to me, but I'm guessing it's *real* important to you."

The bottom fell out of her stomach. "What else did he say?"

"Other than saying you're crazy, that's it."

Alex's blood rushed. What had happened during her absence? She had to get home to her voice mail and E-mail. She ignored her nemesis, put her papers under her arm, hung her purse on her shoulder, then spoke to Estelle, who was busy at the other end of the bar. "Call if you need me."

His eyes were locked on her. "Can't take the heat, huh? Running off to hide in the palace? Want my opinion, sweet lips? This fight with Godzilla's ratcheting up. Just for the record, I'm putting my money on you. I believe you're meaner than he is."

She shot him the most venomous look she could summon, walked past him and left.

# Chapter 13

A week into August, days were still warm and sunny, but nights cooled down and Doug started sleeping under a blanket. Maybe he really would be building a fire in the fireplace by mid-September.

With a couple of coats of pale gray paint on the new plywood walls, he declared the workshop finished. He felt like breaking a champagne bottle across the double doors.

Inside the house, he had completed demolition of the wall between the living room and dining room and patched and installed new Sheetrock where necessary. The result was the light and open effect he had hoped for. The kitchen floor and cabinets came next.

Though pleased with his accomplishments, his spirits had been down all week after being handed his hat again by Alex in Carlton's. He tried to elevate his mood by reminding himself of what the painful past had taught him about surviving the battle of the sexes. Relationships with the fairer sex had to be viewed like streetcars. Soon as you rode one far enough, you boarded another. And sometimes, for one reason or another, you just never got on board.

Alex fell into the latter category. She had never even been friendly to him, in truth. She evidently had no interest in being so much as friends with him, much less anything else. The last thing he wanted was to be like Ted. For the sake of his pride and manhood, he could make only one decision about her. He would *never* set himself up for her rebuff again.

Still, he caught himself looking across the valley and pinpointing her house on the side of Wolf Mountain when washing his hands or preparing a meal or working out on the Track. Before he went to bed at night, he looked at the specks of light on the dark mountainside and wondered what she could be doing all alone in that mansion that must have at least twelve or fifteen rooms. Most nights, the lights were there and he felt more comfortable knowing she was home. With winter just around the corner, how much longer she would stay?

Finally, dawning came—the reason he couldn't seem to purge her from his thoughts. If Alex was anything, she was a warrior, with the instincts of an alley fighter. In a complex way, she fit his criteria. He had never liked helpless, simpering women. The feeling was a by-product of knowing hookers who had drifted in and out of his brother's bar, women who couldn't manage their lives and who were smothered with problems they, for various reasons, weren't capable of solving. He liked women who rose above life, took it by the neck and dealt with it. Like he did.

Annoyed at her, himself and the whole situation, he had avoided town all week and the discipline had improved his attitude. He used the early morning hours for working on his house, but he quit when the temperature rose and devoted afternoons to the work he had agreed to do for Bob Culpepper.

Thursday morning found him splitting pine rounds he had cut and hauled in a few days ago. He worked straight through lunch and by late afternoon had finished filling the wood shed. Readying to call it a day, he spotted Ted's truck wending up the driveway. He waved and walked over as Ted came to a stop behind the Silverado.

Ted climbed out, "Whatcha doing?"

"Firewood. Hard work, but I'd hate for cold weather to catch me without it." He set down his splitting maul and began picking up scraps of wood.

When he straightened, he realized Ted was staring at his body. Everyone stared when they saw his bare torso. "Did you work today?" Doug asked, hoping to distract him.

"Bad scars," Ted said.

"Yeah." Doug grabbed his T-shirt off a log and pulled it over his head. "Want a beer?" He started for the back door.

Ted followed. "Naw. A friend of mine wants to feed me supper. Mary Jane Masters. She wants to meet you, so you're invited."

"Date, huh? Cool. But I'm not gonna barge in."

"It's not a date. It's just supper. I told her I was coming out to get you, so get cleaned up and let's go." Ted made himself comfortable on the sofa and clicked on TV.

A meal cooked by someone besides himself sounded great and breakfast had been a long time ago. Doug showered and shampooed and put on clean jeans and a knit shirt. As they departed, he grabbed a chilled bottle of Chablis from the refrigerator and walked to Ted's truck. "So who's Mary Jane?"

"Just a woman I know."

"Yeah? You never said you had a girlfriend."

"She's a widow. Her husband got killed a few years back. Rolled a log skidder down a mountain on a logging job over in Oregon. She's from an old-time family around here. She's a schoolteacher. Could probably find you a date if you're interested. There's some single teachers and she knows all of them."

*Oh, Jesus.* If there was anything Doug didn't want, it was a matchmaking female trying to fix him up. "No, thanks. I don't have time for it."

"Just a thought. Winter nights get awful long and cold around here."

Doug softened his refusal of the offer with a laugh. "I've got good blankets."

They reached the city limits. "Mary Jane lives in town," Ted said. "I hate it. Every time I go to her house, everybody in Callister knows about it. Makes it damn hard to spend the night."

"It's about time I got to meet you, Doug Hawkins." A slender dynamo with a turned-up nose, a brilliant smile and short, brown hair pumped Doug's right hand. Energy and cheerfulness projected from her. "I've heard so many stories about you, I feel like I know you as well as I know Ted." She wiped her hands on her apron and took the bottle of wine Doug offered. "Ooohh, Chablis. That's so nice of you. How'd you know we're having chicken?"

She stood on her tiptoes and smacked Ted on the lips, then looked into his eyes with warmth and affection. That she was head over heels in love with him stuck out all over. "Missed you today. Wish you'd been with us."

Ted returned her kiss. "Me, too. How was shopping?"

Two tow-headed boys, maybe seven and eight, bounded into the room and embraced Ted's legs. He reached down and picked up the smallest one and Doug was struck by how natural and easy Ted looked with an arm around Mary Jane's waist and one of her kids perched on his arm. The boy Ted was holding hugged him.

"Boys, go watch TV 'til we're ready to eat," their mother told them. The older kid bounced out of the room toward a TV set in the living room and the one on Ted's arm squirmed to the floor and followed.

"Boy, they're wound up tonight," Ted said on a laugh. "They give you any trouble today?"

"No more than usual." She smiled up at him. "You've really spoiled them. All day long, they kept saying, 'Ted lets us do this or do that.' Then I had Mother talking nonstop, too. I just concentrated on keeping my sanity 'til she got out of the car."

Doug couldn't keep from watching the communication that passed between Ted and her. He could see they had more than an ordinary bond and felt a flicker of envy.

Ted released her with a chuckle. "I'll go give them a lecture." He went into living room and sat down on the sofa. "Hey, guys. What's up?" The younger boy rose from the floor and snuggled up beside him. "You guys gave your mother a bad time today, huh?"

"We didn't mean to," the kid said.

The older boy plopped down on Ted's opposite side. "Remember what we talked about?" Ted said to him. "Instead of making things hard for your mom, you should help her out, take care of her."

"I know," the boy said, morose. "It was Grandma's fault."

Ted put his arms around both kids and the three of them began laughing at the TV program.

Doug caught the wistful look in Mary Jane's eyes. "He's so good with my kids," she murmured, then with a sigh she turned away and started for the kitchen.

Doug walked behind her. "Can I help you do something?" A simmering pot filled the kitchen with a delicious aroma and an ambience of well-being.

"Sure." She smiled and handed him a bowl. "You can dish up the chicken. Promise not to judge my recipe. Ted told me you were an outstanding cook."

The kitchen table was set with matching dishes, place mats and napkins and a centerpiece of fresh-cut flowers. "Table looks nice," Doug told her.

"When Ted said he'd bring you, I drug out the good dishes." She smiled again. "Well, I guess we're ready." She went to the living room door and called Ted and her sons.

"This was delicious," Doug said after dinner. The welcome and the homey feeling touched him. The various apartments he had rented over the years and even the condo he had owned felt temporary, like camping out. They hadn't included a pretty table set with the "good dishes." He intended to turn his old farmhouse on twenty acres into a home that felt as comfortable and welcoming as the one in which he was a guest tonight.

Urged on by Mary Jane, he had eaten more than his share. "I haven't had homemade chicken and dumplings in years. Why don't you marry this woman, Ted? She can cook."

Ted's face turned red, but Mary Jane was unabashed. "I keep asking him the same thing myself. But I can't get past the witch on Wolf Mountain. I'm the *winter* girlfriend."

"Knock it off, Mary Jane. That's not true."

*Uh-oh.* Alex McGregor had been discussed before.

"Doug, you need to get a tag for steelhead," Ted said. "The season starts the end of September. Pete will take us fishing on the Salmon in his boat. Nobody runs the river better than Pete. He's real safety-conscious, too."

Doug watched Mary Jane's face. All he saw was resignation. If Ted's scolding and the quick change of subject had embarrassed her, it didn't show. "Great," he said, "that'll be fun."

Mary Jane sent her boys off to do their homework and the three adults visited at the table for a while. Soon Ted said it was getting late, stood up and began to clear the table. Doug helped. When the dishes were loaded into the dishwasher, he walked outside leaving Ted and Mary Jane a private good-night.

"She's crazy about you," Doug said, as they backed out of her driveway. "So are her kids. What did she mean, winter girlfriend?"

"It's a joke, sort of, but at the same time, it isn't. She bitches about the time I spend with Alex in the summer months. She thinks we'd get married if it wasn't for Alex."

"So, would you?"

Seconds of silence passed before Ted answered. "I don't know. Maybe."

"How much time do you spend with Alex?"

"I usually drop in on her a couple of times a week if she's around. Or I see her in Carlton's or she comes by the office. Sometimes she cooks supper, but mostly we go out for dinner somewhere."

"And you're still trying to convince me you're not sleeping with her?"

"No! I'm not." Ted gave a nervous laugh. "Mary Jane's the only woman I see that way. I don't think Alex is interested in sex. Or men."

"Don't kid yourself. She works at looking good. She—" Doug stopped himself. He had almost revealed more than he wanted to. "I just think a woman who looks like she does is not *dis*interested in sex."

"I imagine being married to ol' Charlie left her with a lot of issues. Might take some time to work through them. That's not what I'm after anyway. She needs a friend. I'm the only one she's got. Here, anyway."

"Mary Jane resents her."

"Big time." Ted sighed. "I might marry Mary Jane. But until I'm ready to give up my friendship with Alex, I couldn't. It wouldn't be fair. And besides that, Mary Jane would never let it alone. I'm just gonna wait a while and see what happens."

They passed the city limits sign, headed for Doug's house, but Ted didn't pick up speed. With the windows rolled down, the cool night air filled the cab with scents of pine and sage. Totally relaxed, Doug rested his elbow on the open window ledge.

"Man, smell that pine," Ted said, drawing in a deep sniff. "God, I love it."

Doug chuckled. "The fresh air does smell good."

"And look at those stars. Can't count 'em all."

"Yep. You don't see stars in Los Angeles. . . . Tell me something, Ted. Why haven't you ever gotten married?"

Ted's shoulders lifted in a shrug. "Hell, I don't know. My job's made it hard to meet women. I've always worked in these little towns like Callister. Most of the women are married and the ones that aren't, well—Until I came here, the only time I've lived anywhere longer than two years was Nevada. The gals I met down there were all hookers."

"How long you think you'll be here?"

"'Til I finish my career. About five more years and I'll have in my twenty."

"Then what?"

"Not going back to Nebraska, that's for sure. Nothing to do there except watch Mom take off on another trip. Now that Dad's gone, all she does is travel."

Doug remembered Ted's parents. Ted's mother had been the closest thing to a mother Doug had. She had done her best to hone the rough edges of a boy who grew up in an environment where downright coarseness wasn't out of place. To his regret, he hadn't learned of Ted's father's death until a phone conversation with Ted a few weeks ago.

"I like this town," Ted went on. "The people here would give you the shirts off their backs. You don't have to worry if you forget to lock your front door. The kids are safe in school. Fishing and hunting are great. It's a good place."

Doug did a calculation in his head. "You'll be what, forty-three? That's young to retire. What'll you do?"

"There's a half dozen big time ranchers around here. They're always looking for somebody like me. Good ranch managers don't grow on trees and with all the experience I've got with the government? Hell, I know one of 'em will hire me if for no other reason, just to interpret the rules."

Doug grinned and looked at Ted as memories flooded into his mind. Even before they were teenagers, Ted had worn cowboy boots and had a horse at his grandfather's farm. "You always were a cowboy."

"How about you? What happens next to Doug Hawkins?"

"I'm taking it one day at a time. I've got some feelers out. My cop days are over."

"And why haven't *you* remarried? The way women chased after you, it's hard to believe you've never done it again. I'm just an ordinary old sock. I always had a hard time getting a date, but you had your pick. I'm surprised one of those sexy-looking actresses down there in La-la Land didn't latch on to you."

Doug's thoughts landed on the drama queen with whom he had lived for a few years and had caught sharing his bed in his apartment with some mid-level studio executive. "Pete's right about women. One you can trust is hard to find. I haven't considered it since Diane. Had a couple of live-ins, but things just didn't fit."

"Mary Jane and I get along great when we're not arguing over Alex. With her being a teacher, I guess it makes sense she'd want me around more in the summer. And I do like taking those boys of hers fishing. They look up to me like I'm special."

The look on Ted's face told Doug just how affected he was by his relationship with Mary Jane's sons. "Rick's wife was a teacher."

"Rick?"

"Ricky Chavez. My old partner. He was killed the same time I got shot." A stillness filled the cab, making Doug wish the fact about his old partner hadn't spilled out of his mouth.

"I wish you'd tell me about it," Ted said softly. "You know I want to know."

Doug hesitated, wondering if he could tell someone who was as close as Ted had once been and whom he knew would be nonjudgmental. "Nothing much to tell. It was Christmastime. Everybody working short-handed. Rick and I got co-opted by the ATF into a raid on an old warehouse.

Just a few homeboys pushing a little dope and a few guns. They knew we were coming. It was that simple."

Doug paused and looked out his window. He could tell the story only to this point without choking up. He couldn't recount aloud the actual shooting or the last minutes of Rick's life with his head pouring blood onto Doug's lap. "Rick was my partner for ten years."

He stopped and attempted to will away the trembling that rose in his chest when he thought about the incident. Before moving to Callister he had been sent to a cardiologist to be checked out for the trembling and tightness. Anxiety had been the diagnosis. More drugs had been the recommendation. Instead of having the prescription filled, he left L.A.

"That's not simple, Doug," Ted said finally. "On TV, they said you shot a kid. Is that true?"

"Thirteen years old." Doug's throat ached as if it had swelled shut. The boy he had mentored had been only a year younger. "Shit, Ted . . . forget it."

"Right. Didn't mean to tear you up, buddy."

"Change the subject."

They turned off the highway and headed up the long driveway to Doug's house. Ted picked up the conversation again. "Now that you're here and settled down, maybe you'll meet somebody, get married and have a family. You're not too old."

Once Doug had taken for granted he would marry a loving woman and have kids and a house with a yard and blah-blah-blah. At some point in the past few years, a family was something he had ceased to expect. "Neither are you."

"Mary Jane's only thirty-two. Guess we could still have some kids."

"Diane was pregnant once," Doug said.

Ted pulled in front of the house. Doug hadn't left a porch light on and a quarter-moon gave gauzy, bluish light.

"I never knew that. You said you didn't have any kids."

"I don't. If you think life doesn't play strange tricks on

you. She wouldn't let me touch her without a rubber, so I don't know how she got knocked up. We hadn't made any plans for a family, so when she told me, I figured there'd been an accident. I thought, okay, we're old enough to be parents."

In truth, the news had swamped him with emotions and he had been thrilled, had gone out and bought a little Nerf football the very day she told him. "The next thing I knew, she'd had a miscarriage. Past tense." He didn't try to stop the bitter huff that burst out. "Which was a lie."

Ted didn't speak, just looked across at him wide-eyed.

"A month or so after she told me she lost it, I was cleaning her car. I found a receipt from one of those family planning clinics. By then, the professor she later married had entered the picture. Hell, for all I know, it was his kid."

"I wonder why my mom never heard about her being pregnant."

"I doubt anybody heard about it. We were in Lincoln. I didn't even say anything to Steve. Her mother knew, but she kept quiet. To this day, Diane's dad probably thinks I'm an asshole."

"Probably not. He's been dead quite a few years now."

"I'm going in," Doug said, pulling on the door latch. "This is depressing. Be sure to tell Mary Jane thanks again."

"Right," Ted said. "Be seeing ya. . . . And Doug? Thanks for trusting me."

"Why wouldn't I trust you, Ted? We're friends."

As Doug entered his dark house, loneliness stole through him. He clicked on his only living room lamp, then went to the kitchen and glanced at the Mickey Mouse clock. It was early, too early for bed. He wouldn't sleep, would just toss and turn all night. He could never sleep when memories got the upper hand.

He stepped out onto his front deck and glanced across

the valley toward Alex's mountainside. Visible in the darkness was the black expanse of Wolf Mountain silhouetted against a less-black, star-sprinkled sky. He squinted and looked closer and he saw them—Alex's tiny lights against the mountain.

He turned on the radio he kept tuned to an oldies station, then dropped into his rocking chair, propped his feet up on the deck railing and locked his hands behind his head. Until he came here and Ted dredged up old memories, he hadn't thought about his cheating ex-wife for a long time, or the fact that she had aborted his child.

Life might be different now if she had given birth. Even if she hadn't wanted the kid, he would have taken it. And now he might have a fifteen-year-old son to play ball with or a daughter to fret over. He would probably never have a kid now. Maybe thirty-seven wasn't too old, but he couldn't imagine what kind of woman he would choose at this stage of his life to be the mother of his child.

Mothers and children. His thoughts drifted to Mary Jane Masters and her kids. And Ted. Mary Jane was obviously a good woman, mother and homemaker. Learning that Ted put off her affection while he held out hope that something might flourish between him and Alex had been a surprise. It was one thing to fantasize about somebody like Alex, but another to allow the fantasy to take over your life and drive you to do something dumb. Only Ted seemed to be blind to just how unrealistic his pursuit of Alex was.

*Ted, Ted, Ted.*

Doug sighed and pushed to his feet. Before going back into the house, he looked across the valley at Alex's lights again. He had met just about every kind of nut there was, so he had met reclusive people. But they usually weren't as appealing as Alex. What would drive a woman like her to come to a remote, small mountain town and live alone in an old house stuck on a mountainside virtually impossible to reach without a four-wheel-drive vehicle?

Did she do or say something to make Ted think he had a chance with her? Was she aware his attraction to her kept him from making a move that would be good for him? Did she know Ted had had supper with Mary Jane and would she care?

What would she be doing tonight? Watching TV, reading? Was she lonely?

The questions shuffled like playing cards in his mind, even after he went to bed.

# Chapter 14

Doug awoke with a headache. After supper at Mary Jane's they had polished off the wine and added a few beers. He hadn't made it to the grocery store yesterday, so, out of eggs and bacon, he ate dry cereal for breakfast.

After a pot of coffee, he tackled painting the workshop's interior walls, then late in the afternoon, showered and shaved and drove into town for groceries, vowing to not be distracted. Before going home, he detoured down the side street where Alex often parked.

He didn't see the Wrangler, but he had heard Ted speak of her routine often enough to know she picked up the daily receipts late in the afternoon and helped Estelle behind the bar. Pete's truck was parallel-parked on the main street in front of the bar. Doug pulled in behind it, telling himself he was doing nothing more than stopping off to have a beer with Pete.

Finding Carlton's empty except for Estelle, he ambled to the far end of the bar and said hello. Today her tent dress was bright yellow with huge pink flowers and she was wearing a corsage thing in her hair—it matched the flowers in her dress—and Nikes on her feet. "Where's the boss today?"

"She'll be here. I hope she comes pretty soon or she

won't get away before the night trade starts. She doesn't like staying around here at night."

"Why's that?"

"Doesn't like being around drunks."

Doug lowered his head to hide the grin her answer triggered and wondered if she had ever thought it strange that a woman who didn't like drunks owned a bar, and a rowdy bar at that. He glanced at his watch. Alex did seem to be late.

No sooner had he paid for a glass of cold tap than she glided through the front door. Wearing dark slacks and a tan knit shirt, she looked sporty, clean and sleek as an otter. Inside, he felt the little burst of excitement seeing her always sent through him.

She breezed around him to her customary spot behind the bar and stuffed her purse under the counter. She fussed with something out of sight and came up with the zippered bank bag.

"How's it going?" he asked, unable to think of anything more imaginative and more nervous than any man of his age and experience should be.

"Fine. Where's Ted?"

Mental sigh. She seemed even more irascible than last night. "Don't know. Fishing maybe."

Estelle joined them at the end of the bar. Alex asked her if Kenny Miller had called. Estelle said no, but a lawyer in Boise had called three times. A crease formed between Alex's brows. "Damn." She stared at the floor, rubbing her temple with two crimson-tipped fingers. She was worried. What had happened now with Godzilla?

Customers began to drift in. A din of conversation and jukebox music grew in the small room. "Looks like a good Saturday night," she said to Estelle. "We're going to be full. I'll stay a while and see what happens. If the crowd gets too big, we'll call in extra help."

Several Forest Service employees drifted in, Pete and

Mike among them, and took their usual table. Pete spotted him and waved him over, pulling out an adjacent chair. Doug gave up his attempt to talk to Alex, crossed the room and took the empty seat beside Pete. "Ted's not coming?" he asked the men.

"He had a date," Mike replied.

"A date?" Doug hadn't heard Ted mention any woman other than Alex.

"He took Mary Jane Masters to supper up to the ski lodge," Pete said. "We were afraid he might back out if he knew we were coming here, so we didn't invite him."

Doug was muddling through that information when the front door swung open and a hulk filled the sunlit doorway. Only his silhouette showed until he closed the door.

*Miller.*

The logger's black hair was slicked back and shiny even in the low light. His long-sleeved shirt hung loose and un-buttoned, showing a gray T-shirt. Pete's glass clunked on the table. "Oh, shit."

Mike twisted a hundred eighty degrees and looked at the front door, then swore under his breath.

Everything about the logger looked agitated. He crossed the barroom with a bowlegged stomp that dared anyone to get in his way. Doug's pulse rate kicked up.

A sheaf of papers was clutched in the guy's hammy fist. He stamped straight to where Alex stood absorbed in a ledger at the far end of the bar and stopped in front of her. She looked up.

"You big-city bitch!" Miller's voice trembled. He shook the fistful of papers in her face. "Here's what I think of you and your goddamn injunction!" He ripped the papers in half, ripped them again and threw them at Alex's face.

She ducked to the left, avoiding being struck by the pieces. A familiar fist gripped Doug's gut. Defending against brutality was deeply ingrained. His butt was already off the chair, but Pete's restraining hand fell on his arm.

"Wait, Doug. He ain't gonna do nothin' stupid in a public place. It ain't your fight anyway. She can handle him."

Doug sat back on the edge of his chair, reminding himself he was no longer a cop and remembering the fire in her eye at their first meeting. Hell, she probably *could* handle him.

Alex snapped the ledger shut. "This is no place for this discussion." Her voice carried across the narrow aisle that separated the bar and Doug's seat. Doug heard a tremor, like that night with Miller in her office. She was afraid or nervous, or both. He stood up, carrying his empty glass toward the bar as if to order a refill.

"I tried to be neighborly with you, Alex," Miller growled. "You want lawyers? You got it. I got something that'll fix your ass." He yanked a folded document from his shirt pocket and shook it at her. "See this? You ain't keeping me away from my trees."

Alex stared up at him, giving no ground, not even when he pushed his bulldog face within inches of hers.

"Nobody wants to keep you from your timber, Kenny, but you left me no choice. Bottom line, you aren't going to build a road across my property and you aren't going to take logging equipment through Swede Creek. You'll have to go around."

"That'd cost a fuckin' fortune and you know it. I got news for you. I don't have to go around. I'm going right up Old Ridge Road. Legal."

As if on cue, the relentless jukebox stopped and the sharp exchange between them became audible to the room. Conversation ceased and Miller's voice notched up louder and stronger, obviously for the benefit of the customers. "You come in here to our town, bring your highfalutin ways, do any fuckin' thing you want to 'cause you think we're all backward."

"Do what you're going to, Kenny. But leave me alone." She moved around to a spot behind the bar and faced him.

He waved the folded document in front of her eyes again. "Your old man and I had an agreement, but even that don't matter anymore. You're gonna eat crow, missy, and everybody's gonna know it."

"I don't like crow and I don't eat it. I'm not discussing this with you. Your lawyer can call mine. I'm sure he has the number."

Alex's stemmed glass, half filled with white wine, sat on the counter. Miller grabbed it in a giant paw and threw it like a major league pitch against the backbar's mirror. The black-veined antique cracked in spidery lines all the way across. Mirror shards rained down on top of the assortment of liquor bottles.

Doug's adrenaline surged and he started for the bar where Alex and Miller faced each other. A couple of people on stools stood up and backed away.

"Estelle, call the sheriff," Alex said.

The bartender's eyes looked like two olives floating in buttermilk. Following orders, she reached for the receiver, but before she had pressed a number, Miller pointed a finger at her. "Estelle." His deep voice boomed. "You expect that boy of yours to ever work in this valley again, you leave the goddamn phone alone. This don't concern you."

Estelle returned the receiver to its cradle. An image of the big bastard wielding a cue stick flashed in Doug's mind.

"You leave Estelle and her family out of this." Alex's tone cut like a scalpel. "Your beef is with me. I warn you, Kenny, the Sierra Club or Friends of the Earth would like nothing better than to adopt Granite Pond. If that happens, you won't log Soldier Meadows in this lifetime, even if somebody builds a freeway to it."

*Godalmighty.* Doug couldn't believe she had threatened him. Miller became a smoking volcano. His black eyes darted. He seemed to be searching for something else to throw. Doug lunged, but before he could reach him, Miller's hand shot out and jerked Alex forward by the neck.

She scuffled with him across the bar top, slapping at his wrist and face.

The thud of a blow resounded. Alex stumbled backward. The next sound was the unmistakable double-click of a revolver being cocked. By the time Doug saw the scene clearly, Alex was backed against the backbar, shaking.

And leveling a short-barreled .357 at the middle of Kenny Miller's chest.

*Fuck!*

Blood trailed from her left nostril. A mouse had already swollen beneath her eye, but her gaze was locked on the logger.

The talk about her being a dead shot detonated in Doug's mind. His heart pounded against his sternum. One screwup and Miller was toast. Doug's senses heightened and intensified. His mind and body gave in to years of training and experience. He stepped closer, feeling as if he were walking in waist-high water. "Alex . . . listen to me. . . . Let the hammer down."

She didn't respond, didn't take her eyes off Miller. A bright red trail ran from her nose, down across her lips to her quivering chin and dripped onto her shirt.

Doug watched Miller's ashen face from the corner of his eye. *Don't move, asshole. Forgodsake, don't move.* "Alex? . . . Listen . . . I'm on your side. . . . Let me help you. . . . You know I won't hurt you. . . ."

Except for her shaking hand, no reaction.

"This bastard's not worth screwing up your life, Alex. . . . You know I'm right. . . . Put it down. Please." Seconds turned to a minute. "Please, baby," he said softly. ". . . Think about your future."

Despite her unsteady hand, she eased the hammer down and lowered the pistol, but she continued to stare at Miller. And blood continued to drip from her chin onto her shirt. She made no move to wipe it.

Doug released a breath and said a silent prayer of thanks

she was able to safely deal with the cocked revolver. As ridiculous as it seemed, he was glad she knew something about firearms.

Though her eyes stared, she appeared to see nothing. The pistol hung from her hand beside her thigh. Doug grasped her wrist with his left hand and the gun with his right. "Let me have it, baby. Everything's okay now."

She relaxed her hand and he took the pistol. He flipped out the cylinder and spilled the rounds in a clatter on the bartop, then stuffed the gun into his waistband and dropped the cartridges into the pocket of his jeans.

A sound like a deflating balloon came from down the bar. He saw Estelle slumped against the backbar, shaking her head. A sob burst out and tears gushed. "Estelle," he said, "it's okay. Stay—"

"You goddamn cunt." Miller's booming voice split the air. His weasel eyes glittered and he shook his clenched fist. "I'm gonna—"

"Hey!" Doug was on him in an instant, reaching across the bar and filling his fist with the logger's shirt. The bastard swung, but Doug parried and grasped his throat with a trained grip, fighting the urge to choke the life from the asshole. He yanked him forward until they were nose to nose across the bar. "You're pressing your luck, friend. Get outta here."

Miller's hands flew to Doug's wrist. He wheezed. Doug glared into his eyes for long seconds, then let go.

The logger staggered back, coughing, his hand bracketing his throat. Pure hatred burned in his eyes. He twisted and adjusted his neck, shrugged his shirt back into place. Bending over, he gathered the loose papers that had scattered on the floor when he'd scuffled with Alex. He stomped toward the door, but stopped before opening it and shook his fist. "You California sonofabitch!" He yanked the heavy door open. It banged the wall as he made his exit.

Doug turned to Alex. She was still braced against the

back counter, her fingers curled around its edge. A blood-stain had spread on the front of her tan shirt. She pushed away and strode past him and the staring crowd, making for the ladies' room. Voices in the room built to a crescendo.

When she returned, her face was clean, but she held a wad of tissue paper to her nose. Her right eye had already become a slit. She reached behind the bar for her purse. Without a look left or right, she strode the length of the room and left through the front door.

"C'mon, Doug," Pete said, coming up behind him. "Let's get outta here."

Pete and Mike followed Alex's path outside with Doug close behind. On the sidewalk, he looked up and down the street, but saw neither Alex nor her Jeep. "Is he gonna be waiting somewhere for her?" Doug asked the two men, craning his neck to spot her.

"I don't think so, but we'll check it out," Pete answered.

"What's wrong with that sonofabitch?"

"He's bad news, Doug. You don't want to mess with him."

Doug swore. "Hell, he could've hurt her bad." *Or she could have killed him.* The thought of either result made his gut clench. He scanned both sides of the street again. "Where the hell could she go so fast?"

"Look on the side street," Pete answered. "She usually parks around the corner."

Half a block down the side street between Carlton's and the grocery store Doug saw her at the Jeep door. He jogged to her side and found her stabbing the key at the door lock, but her hands shook so badly she kept missing the slot. Her teeth chattered. He couldn't tell if she was cold or in shock. He looped his left arm around her shoulders and reached for her key with his right hand. "Here, Alex. Let me unlock it."

She let the key ring fall into his hand. Looking at her, he

was convinced she would have collapsed before she succeeded in unlocking the door.

"I'll drive you home, baby." He guided her around the
rear of the Jeep. Twice, her knees buckled, but he held her
against him and kept her from falling.

She made an attempt to lift her leg to slide onto the seat,
but her foot raised only inches and she stumbled. "I feel so
weak," she murmured. Holding her waist, he slid his right
arm beneath her knees and lifted her onto the seat.

He took away the wad of bloody tissue she held to her
nose. The bleeding appeared to be subsiding. He pulled a
clean handkerchief from his back pocket and tucked it into
her hand, then guided it to her nose.

The temperature was cool, but perspiration beaded on
her forehead. He reached for her wrist and felt her pulse. It
was racing faster than he could count, but probably was
slower than it had been a few minutes earlier.

"Miller again, huh?" He said it attempting to break into
her trance. He passed his hand up and down in front of her
eyes and to his relief, she blinked. "You're gonna be okay.
Don't move."

He closed the door and rounded the vehicle to the driver's side, looking around for any sign of the logger. As he
scooted behind the wheel, Alex's head rolled back against
the headrest. He reached over her, pulled the seat belt
across her body and locked it into place.

He started up the Jeep, eased onto the street and drove
toward the city limits, debating if he should take her to
the ER. As they neared the turn leading to the hospital,
she mumbled, "Don't take me there."

Knowing she must have her reasons for not wanting to
go to the hospital, he complied with her request. Half an
hour later, at her house, he found her garage door opener
clipped onto the sun visor and drove the Jeep into the
garage. He supported her as she climbed the stairs leading

to a door, which put them first inside a utility room, then a short hall.

To the right lay the kitchen, but across the hall was a doorway through which he could see a king-sized bed. She veered toward the bedroom. The two cats trotted out from somewhere and began to meow and pace. She spoke to them and they came along as Doug walked her through a huge, luxurious bedroom into what he thought would be a bathroom. It turned out to be an exercise room with several pieces of equipment, but it opened to a bathroom, which was also huge, with walls of mirrors.

She wilted onto a vanity chair and he opened cabinet doors looking for a washcloth. When he found one, he soaked it with warm water, knelt beside the vanity chair and she allowed him to bathe drying blood from her face. She winced as he accidentally brushed her injury and he apologized.

Taking her chin in his fingers, he gently examined her eye and her swollen, reddened cheek. The cheek had absorbed the brunt of the blow, but the skin hadn't broken. While the skin around her eye would turn dark, the eye itself didn't appear to be injured. He had seen worse. "That sonofabitch," he muttered.

It was then that he saw the long, aged scar that began at her forehead and followed her hairline down the side of her head until it disappeared above her ear. Her hair style kept it hidden. "Car wreck," she said. "A long time ago."

This was no time for *that* conversation. He placed his fingers under her chin and tipped her head backward. "Open your mouth."

She frowned, but allowed him to look. "You've got a cut inside your cheek and another small one on the side of your tongue. You should rinse it with some salt water."

She frowned again and whimpered like a child. He wanted to wrap his arms around her and hold her, but he stifled the urge. Instead, he cupped her nape in his palm and brushed her cheek with his thumb. "I don't think anything's broken, but you're gonna have a shiner. Ice is what you need."

He moved on to washing blood off her hands with the washcloth. "How about a clean shirt or a robe or something?"

The bloodstained shirt was a pullover. She looked down at it and a tear slipped down her cheek.

"Hey, now. Don't cry. It's all over." Swallowing around the tight knot in his throat, he kept his voice soft. "I'll help you take it off." A thick robe hung beside the shower door. He reached for it and handed it to her.

Her chin trembled and more tears leaked, but she didn't break down. He mentally called Miller a few more choice names and as if she were a child, worked her arms out of her shirtsleeves, then eased the garment over her head. Blood stained the slope of her breasts and a white lace bra. For a moment, he thought of washing it off, but decided to leave that to her. He willed his eyes away from her chest and placed the robe around her shoulders. "Feel better?"

"I—I need some privacy," she said.

"Sure." He got to his feet and started backing out of the bathroom. "I'll just go make you an ice pack for that eye. . . . Just yell if you need me."

In the kitchen, he removed the pistol from his waistband and laid it on the breakfast bar, followed by the cartridges from his pocket. Oh, yeah, they were gonna discuss the gun, but meanwhile he searched in her cupboards, found a bowl and filled it with ice cubes from the refrigerator door. Using a dish towel, he tied a bundle of the ice cubes.

Soon he heard her approaching from behind and turned to see her coming up the hallway holding a large wet towel to her eye. She had changed into gray sweats. She sat down at the breakfast bar, leaned on her elbows and covered her face with the towel.

He carried over the little bundle of ice cubes and took a

seat beside her. "This will do more good than a warm towel."

She leaned on her elbows again and covered her eye with the cold pack. "I'm okay now."

"What about a doctor? If you don't want to go to the ER here, I'll drive you somewhere."

She shook her head and moved to the living room sofa. Her shoulders hunched forward as she hung her head, holding her face against the ice pack. She looked even more vulnerable than she had that morning after the fire.

He hooked his arm around her shoulder, then gave in to his urges and hugged her to his chest.

"I'm sorry, sweetheart. What can I do?"

"I'm so thirsty. Can you get me a Coke with some ice cubes?"

"You bet." Doug set her away and returned to the kitchen. He found canned Diet Coke in the fridge. He also noticed there was food. He sat beside her again and handed her the glass, watched as she sipped and winced.

"I think I need to go to bed," she said.

He thought so, too, and he ached to lie down beside her and hold her. "I could stay."

She shook her head. "I just want to go to sleep."

He wouldn't add stress by arguing. "I'll call Pete and ask him to come up and get me."

"You can take the Jeep. I won't need it until tomorrow."

If he had to leave her, that was the most practical thing to do. "You sure?"

She nodded.

He went back to the kitchen again, reached for a notepad on the counter under the phone and wrote his phone number. "This is my number. You'll call me if you need something, won't you?" He glanced at the gun and debated what to do about it. Finally, he left it where it was and picked up her key ring he had placed beside it.

"Those papers Kenny had," she said. "Did you see them?"

Doug shrugged. "I didn't look." God, he hated to leave her. "Look, I can take you to Ted's apartment. Or I've got an extra bedroom at my house."

She stiffened. Her eyes cut to him narrowly.

"Hey, believe me. You'll be safe."

"Don't trouble yourself worrying about me."

Doug sighed. "Well . . . keep ice on that eye." He stood up and started to go.

"Doug?"

He stopped and turned back. Her eyes were just as blue, but one was almost swollen shut. Her expression was not as defiant and daring as usual. Instead, it was soft and feminine. His knees turned to gelatin. He didn't know if it was from the adrenaline still coursing through him or because it was the first time he had ever heard her say his name.

She reached for his hand. "Doug, I—I thank you. For helping me."

His heart melted. His throat constricted. "You call if you need me," he choked out.

# Chapter 15

As Doug drove away, the image of Alex battered and alone haunted him. He had known his share of physical abuse over the years, first from years of combat on the football field, then from his days as a street cop. While he had never been beaten up, he had taken blows and he remembered how they felt. She might be strong and tough, but she wasn't made of steel. Being hit hard enough to black her eye and bloody her nose would affect her deeply.

His thoughts shifted to Miller. Doug had learned long ago never to underestimate a bully with a point to prove and a propensity for violence. Miller was capable of *anything* when threatened. In the future, in the place where he planned to rebuild his life and lead a quiet existence, Doug would have to watch his back. He regretted that.

A part of him wished he had never met Alex. Every time he went near her, something over the top happened. He swore aloud as a tire dropped into a pothole and the whole vehicle wrenched and squeaked.

Forty-five minutes later, he drove her Jeep into his barn. As he closed the swinging doors, he looked across the valley and saw her lights against the black mountainside. He went indoors. When he had left her his phone number, at the same time he had memorized hers. While it was fresh in his mind, he went to the front bedroom he had turned into his office and wrote the seven digits in his address book.

He studied them a moment, then looked out the window. The office's one window had the same view of her lights as his living room and kitchen. She had to be afraid up there in that barn of a house. If Miller decided to settle the score, he could do it in her isolated house and no one would be the wiser until it was too late. Dithering halted, Doug punched in her number.

She answered in her whiskey-pitched voice on the first ring.

He closed his eyes and pictured her beside him in bed, that voice whispering in his ear. The intimacy they had shared when she allowed him to remove her shirt came back and in his mind's eye he could see her breasts covered by lace. God knew this was no time to think of sex, but that was how she affected him. "I'm home now. I can see your lights are still on. I just want to be sure you're okay."

"How did you get my number?"

"I won't lie. I stole it off your phone."

"You can see my lights? From your house?"

"I'm looking at them now, out my window. Are you sure you don't want to go to a doctor?"

"I'll be fine. I just won't be dropping in on any important meetings for a while. Don't you live across the valley?"

"It's almost a straight line from my house to yours."

"I didn't know that."

"I look every night," he said, heartened. "I thought you were going to bed. Aren't you done in?"

"I couldn't sleep. I'm doing some work on my computer. I'll turn in pretty soon."

"Alex, do . . . do you ever get lonely?"

Seconds passed before she answered. "Sometimes. Doesn't everybody?" Her reply was almost a whisper.

"I think so. I sure do. The next time you feel like some company, maybe you could give me a call. Just to talk."

Another long silence amplified the low hum on the phone line. The next sound was a muffled sob and a sniffle he could tell she was trying to hide. "I have to go now. Good night."

A click and the line went dead. He walked outside to the front deck and stared at her lights. She was up there weeping. He wished he had taken her in his arms and held her, comforted her, let her cry against his chest. He wished he had demanded she let him take her somewhere to a doctor. He wished he were up there with her now. He wanted to be her friend and ally, wanted to be in her life, wanted her in his.

*Shit.* A bad night was ahead of him. He knew the signs. He punched on the television. An hour later she was still on his mind. He looked out his living room window and saw her lights. What good was he doing down here awake when she was up there in pain and maybe fear?

He went to the bathroom and brushed his teeth, then to her Jeep and shaved a good seven minutes off the trip to her house.

He tried the doorbell, but didn't hear it ring inside. She had to know he was there. No one could drive up without being seen. He banged the heavy brass knocker mounted between the two cut-glass panes, but she didn't answer. He tried the knob, found it locked. A tinge of panic darted across his stomach. Then the heavy door creaked opened and there she stood, looking small and bedraggled in the wide doorway. Her eyes glistened with tears.

Emotion swelled in his chest. He mustered a grin, feeling as awkward as a twelve-year-old. "Hi. I figured since we've both got insomnia, we could suffer together."

She stepped back to allow his entry. They reached for each other simultaneously. Her arms slid around his ribs and up until she clung to his shoulders and her forehead pressed into his chest. He could feel her battered soul and he held her for what seemed like a long while.

She took his hand and led him inside, down the two steps into the living room, to the sofa. He sat. She knelt in front of him and pulled off his shoes. He leaned forward, caught her hand and stopped her. "You don't have to do that."

Cupping her shoulders, he pulled her up, brought her with him as he leaned back to rest his head on the sofa arm. She nestled between his legs, her head on his chest.

"Rest now," he murmured, running his hand over her hair. "I won't let anything happen to you. Everything's gonna be all right."

She must have believed him because she handed him a fancy pillow for his head and neck and pulled the afghan that was draped across the back of the sofa to cover their lower bodies. She snuggled against his chest like a child and let out a great sigh. He folded his arms around her. Together they drifted away.

Doug awoke to the same thing that woke him every day—a deep ache in his damaged shoulder. But this morning, he didn't know where he was and a weight lay on his chest. He had a feeling he was being watched. He opened his eyes to see an orange cat perched above him on the sofa back. Green eyes stared down at him and a feline chirp came from the animal's throat.

The memory of last night fought its way through a sleepy maze and his orientation returned. He attempted to stretch his left arm without disturbing the disheveled blond head on his chest.

Alex moved against him. As usual, he had a hard-on. Normally, if he awoke in this condition, belly-to-belly with a good-looking blonde, he knew what steps to take next. None of them were appropriate this morning. She must have felt his erection because she sat up abruptly and moved down the sofa.

"There's a bathroom down the hall behind the stair." She

touched her swollen face and winced, then eased to her feet. "Use the shower if you like. Towels are in the vanity." She hobbled toward the kitchen.

Doug's left leg felt numb and his shoulder throbbed worse than usual. He leaned forward and dangled and flexed his left hand between his knees. He got to his feet and found the bathroom. In it, he discovered a tiled stall shower much bigger than his metal shower at home and a massaging showerhead. The luxury of room to turn around without bumping into the walls was too good to resist and the warm-water massage would feel good to his aching shoulder.

A little butterfly-shaped soap bar lay in a dish by the sink and from the vanity cupboard he pulled the thickest, sweetest-smelling towel he had ever seen.

After the shower, he finger-combed his hair and left it to air dry. He hesitated before leaving the bathroom, remembering last night. For her to have welcomed him as she did, then snuggled against him all night, she had to have needed someone. *Don't be fooled into thinking it's you, old buddy,* he warned himself. It could just as easily have been Ted or anybody else.

He returned to the living room, but saw no sign of her. Three weeks ago, she hadn't minded if he helped himself in her kitchen, so he did that. He opened the cupboard where he had seen coffee before. A new, unopened package of Starbucks Breakfast Blend sat there all alone on the shelf. But she didn't drink coffee. He distinctly remembered her saying so.

Mulling over that fact, he put on coffee for himself, then set water to boil for tea for her. By the time he put the tea to steep, the coffee had made, so he took two mugs from a cupboard shelf and poured himself a cup, behaving like he lived here. Leaving the second mug by the teapot for her, he ambled to the living room windows to watch the sun bring color to the valley floor.

A paperback—a romance novel—lay open in the basket beside the chair. Before he could pick it up, he heard her call, "Good morning." He turned and saw her enter the kitchen from the hall that led from her bedroom. He doused the pictures that she, bedrooms and romance novels all in the same stream of thought put in his head.

She was wearing jeans and a T-shirt and huaraches. "Hi," he said, and joined her at the cooking island. She smelled like soap and flowers and mountain mornings. "I opened your new package of coffee. Hope you weren't saving it for something special."

"Uh, no," she said. "I just bought it for—well, whatever."

Was she blushing? Good Lord, had she bought it for *him*? He couldn't tell, but she was damn sure stammering. A silly thrill darted through him. *Nah, you're daft,* he told himself, but he couldn't let go of the question. "Guess I misunderstood. I thought you didn't drink coffee."

"I don't . . . But everyone else does."

"Right."

Her right eye peeked from behind a purple lid. Underneath it curved a lavender crescent-shaped bruise. A reddened lump distended from her cheek. All of it looked painful, but if she was suffering, she gave no hint.

"I made you some tea," he said and smiled.

Her mouth turned up in an almost-smile, but she didn't look at him. "Thanks."

He took a seat on a cast-iron stool at the breakfast bar. "Eye looks sore."

"A little." She touched her cheek gingerly as she poured a cup of tea.

A lot, he figured, but he schooled his tone to be matter-of-fact. "If you don't want to see a doc in this town, I wouldn't mind taking you somewhere else. It's not that far down to Boise."

She lifted a small pitcher from the cupboard, walked to

the fridge and filled it with milk. "What's a doctor going to do but make an X-ray or give me pain pills?"

"It wouldn't hurt to have it checked out."

"No doctors." She poured milk into her tea.

Okay, fine. No doctors. He looked at the .357 lying on the counter where he had placed it last night and the cartridges strewn beside it. He wouldn't be surprised to see the sheriff any minute, coming to call her to account for brandishing a gun in the bar. Meantime, he took a closer look at the revolver. More firearm than he would expect a woman to own. "Good piece," he said, rolling morning stiffness out of his shoulder. "You get this thing in California?"

"Does your shoulder hurt? Ted's told me about your injuries."

Okay, so she didn't want to discuss the gun. "Just a little stiff." He grinned and winked. "War wounds."

"I hope you tried the shower massage. It feels wonderful. Did my sleeping on it all night hurt?"

"Just takes a little while to work the kinks out. You're worse off than I am. You calmed down this morning?"

She nodded, then came to the breakfast bar with her tea and sat down beside him.

"So what happens now? This seems like a good time to call up your buddy Culpepper."

"No need. He's done what I asked him to. Would you like some breakfast?"

He lifted a palm. "You don't have to serve me breakfast. In fact, I'll get out of your hair so you can rest." He stretched across the counter and picked up the phone receiver. "Ted should be home. I'll call him to come up and get me."

Her head snapped up. "No! I'll take you to your rig after breakfast."

Doug re-cradled the receiver. Okay, so she didn't want

Ted to know he had spent the night here. That must mean she knew how Ted felt about her.

"Don't you eat breakfast?"

"All the time."

"Then let's have breakfast. It's the least I can do after what you did for me." Genuine sincerity showed in her eyes and rang in her voice. She stood and walked to the refrigerator, opened the door and studied the contents with one-eyed earnestness.

"Anyone would have done the same," he told her with some doubt. So far, with the exception of Ted, Doug hadn't spotted anybody in Callister willing to help her.

"Everyone had the opportunity, but only *you* did something. People around here aren't known for heroics in facing Kenny."

"So I've heard." He didn't want to be known for it either, but it was too late now. He went to her side. "I can help you with breakfast. What are we making?"

She stacked bacon and an egg carton on his outstretched hands, followed by an onion and red and green peppers. "Spanish omelet and bacon. Right now I don't know how I'll pay you back, but I always return favors."

"It wasn't a favor. It was what had to be done."

She opened a cupboard door beside the fridge and lifted out a new jar of jalapeño peppers. "Ted's told me what a great cook you are. Perhaps you'd be better at this than I am."

He didn't believe she had bought so much food for herself and she hadn't done it for Ted, either. He knew—*knew*—she had stocked up on a few groceries with him in mind. And the knowing did strange things to his insides. He couldn't think what to say, so he stood there like a dummy who had never experienced a decisive moment with a woman. "Alex, listen . . ."

She looked up at him in that way she had and smiled. "What, you want to debate who's the best cook?"

She dragged more food from the refrigerator—butter, salsa, a hunk of cheese. She pushed the door closed with her hip and they took their stacks of food to the cooking island. Side by side, they worked. While she put the bacon on to fry in an iron skillet, he grated cheese, liking the closeness of sharing a task with her.

The pistol lay within arm's reach. The cop in him couldn't be suppressed, so as she broke eggs into a bowl and he chopped peppers, he tilted his head toward the gun. "I'll feel a lot better if you tell me you don't keep that in Carlton's."

She stiffened as she sliced off a chunk of butter and scraped it into a second cast-iron skillet. "No, of course not."

He could spot a lie a mile away. "Then you carry it in your purse? Got a permit?"

She dumped the beaten eggs into the sizzling butter and cut through them with a fork. "No."

"Then how do you get it into the bar?" He cocked his head for eye contact, but she kept her eyes on the eggs.

"I keep it wherever it's convenient. I have to get it from Point A to Point B, don't I? Why are you questioning me?"

Keeping his tone unconfrontational, he pulled four slices of bread out of the bag and began to make toast. "Just saying you can't carry concealed without a permit and you can't take a gun into a bar. Stiff penalties for both. A gun in a bar's a felony. Do you have an office in Carlton's, where you're able to keep it outside the barroom?"

"No." Seemingly unfazed by the possibility she had committed a crime that could have serious consequences, she gathered the cut vegetables and cheese and arranged them on the omelet, then folded it in half like a pro. "Would it be more acceptable if I wore it on my hip?"

"I think that's at least legal in this state. Look, I'm not trying to be argumentative." He tore off a couple of sheets of paper towel, placed them on a plate and began to lift the fried bacon slices out of their grease. "I'm just telling you that what you're doing is illegal. And foolhardy. It gives the good sheriff a reason to come after you."

She stopped and looked at him, one fist planted on her hip. "Well, now. I think that would be classified as my business, wouldn't it? Jim Higgins doesn't scare me."

Doug flinched as an icicle pierced him. He had thought he was making progress, but obviously not. Still, he managed a laugh, hoping he sounded lighthearted. "You're a regular outlaw, aren't you?" Determined not to get into another contest with her, he raised his palms. "You're right. It's your problem. Just tell me one more thing. Is Miller the reason you're packing a gun?"

"No. I bought it to defend myself against Charlie, in case he went completely off the deep end. I never dreamed I might have to protect myself from Kenny." She flawlessly scooped up the omelet and slid it onto a platter. "I think we're ready to eat. How's that toast doing?"

They ate at the long, shining table on heavy stoneware plates. The omelet was cooked to perfection. They chatted about books and movies. Surface talk, nothing deep. Still, it was something he hadn't done with a woman in a long time. She was warm and friendly and he thought she might be trying to make up for cutting him off at the knees when he had tried to discuss the gun.

He began to understand why Ted enjoyed her friendship. She was clever-tongued. She had to feel like hell, but she laughed and made cynical jokes about current events. Her conversation proffered no sexual innuendo or leading remarks, no misunderstood motives, yet he thought she was the sexiest woman he had ever met.

When his plate was empty, he rose and went to the coffeepot for another cup.

"If you're ready to go, I'll take you downtown." She stood up and carried her dishes to the sink.

*Oops.* Evidently there would be no lingering and relaxing over an after-breakfast cup of coffee. "Okay. No problem." He, too, cleared away his dishes.

Before he could count to double digits, they were on their way out the door. Easing down the driveway, she avoided the deep pothole that had grabbed him both going and coming in the dark last night. The road condition didn't distract *her* at all.

"I don't suppose you're gonna tell me what's really going on with you and this logging dude. All I've heard is the gossip. I'd like to know why I made an enemy of him last night."

# Chapter 16

A lex sighed. Her eye hurt, her cheek hurt. Did she owe it to a stranger to tell him the whole hateful story of her personal battles? Possibly she did owe him something. She had scarcely been civil to him since they met, yet he had come to her rescue twice. He couldn't be all bad.

And with his scruffy day-old beard and messy hair he looked more appealing than he should. In fact, he looked like they should be hanging around the house enjoying a private weekend.

She stopped the Jeep, put on the hand brake and twisted to the right. "Look high on the mountain over your right shoulder at that stand of timber."

The morning sun showcased the wallowing mass of deep green against the brilliant azure of a cloudless sky. Her heart ached if she let herself think that it had once belonged to her. "That's called Soldier Meadows. It covers most of the lower mountainside visible from here. It's about five sections. Charlie and I used to own it."

Ten years ago they had come to Idaho to raft the Salmon River, a change of scenery, a heart-healing effort after burying their daughter a few months earlier. Alex always read real estate ads wherever she saw them and she had stumbled across one touting "the only private property on Wolf Mountain." Knowing the rarity of private property in a bastion of national forest lands, she insisted they rush to inspect it. She hadn't known then that the pin dot on the side of a giant mountain would become one of her greatest obsessions. Her assistant had even accused her of replacing her lost daughter with a house and mountain in Idaho.

Doug twisted in the bucket seat and looked. "Sections? How big is that?"

"Six hundred forty acres. A square mile. Soldier Meadows is thirty-two hundred acres, more or less."

"Looks more like a forest than a meadow."

"It is mostly forest, but the name comes from a meadow where a post–Civil War army camp existed. It came with the purchase of the house. There was roughly five thousand acres in the beginning. Charlie sold the part that's Soldier Meadows to Kenny."

"Hunh. How'd that happen? And why?"

She heaved a breath, seeing that answering his question could be like removing her finger from a dam. "Charlie was drunk. I'd like to believe he didn't know what he was doing, but I'd be deluding myself."

"This is a community property state. He had to have had your cooperation when he sold it."

She might have known that as smart as this stranger was he would zero in on the point she didn't want to be reminded of. "That may be what I hate the most." Self-castigation for her complicity in creating this problem with no solution assaulted her often. She released the brake and eased forward.

"We fought over it for weeks and I thought we'd settled it. I thought I'd won. Then I had to go to Honolulu. I was representing some investors in a hotel deal. Charlie hounded me by phone and fax, lied to me by telling me bugs threatened to destroy the old-growth timber and something had to be done about it."

A bitter laugh escaped before she could stop it. "A little greed can be a dangerous thing. I'd spent a year putting the hotel deal together. The commission was . . . well, enviable. Charlie knew I wouldn't jeopardize the deal by rushing back to argue with him. I'm sure he deliberately waited until I was tied up five thousand miles away before reopening the argument."

"Nice guy. So how did it turn into a crisis with Miller?"

"Soldier Meadows itself has no frontage on a public road. Kenny can't get to it without crossing my property. And therein lies the dilemma. He claims he paid Charlie extra money in cash for a right-of-way that traverses Old Ridge Road and the upper end of my acreage, but I think he's lying. He's never produced a deed or any kind of documentation showing the access."

"You're right. He probably *is* lying. If he could show a paper and settle the disagreement, why wouldn't he do it?"

"Exactly. Furthermore, I believe he's too shrewd to give cash to someone as irresponsible as Charlie was. But Charlie died before—"

She stopped and shifted down to crawl over a large stone, suddenly feeling overwhelmed and exhausted by rehashing the details of a battle she had single-handedly fought since before divorcing her ex-husband. The enormity of the impasse made her feel small and ineffectual. It was bigger than she was, Kenny was bigger than she was. She had never felt so alone. She wanted to cry, but couldn't. Salty tears would hurt her sore eye.

It was too difficult to try to explain to a stranger who knew nothing about land and logging. She shifted gears again. "It's a boring story for someone who has no knowledge of timber or logging. Or no interest in it."

Doug's hand covered hers. "Wait a minute. I'm not bored. I want to hear the rest. And I'm interested." She stopped again, holding back the Jeep with a foot on the brake. "Didn't you hear what I told him in the bar? I refuse to let him drive logging trucks on Old Ridge Road or to ford Swede Creek. More than a dozen truck trips a day driving across the creek would destroy it and Granite Pond both."

The stranger looked thoughtful. "The traffic would screw up the creek bottom and send dirt downstream, right?"

"Yes. And into Granite Pond."

"Wow. Didn't your ex-husband know that would happen? Why did he want to sell so bad in the first place?"

They reached the tunnel of brush. She steered to the right, dropping the right wheels into the drainage ditch and inched forward through the shade. "I've never known for sure. I suspected for a long time Charlie was in over his head with something. He was always out of money. He gambled—ball games, boxing matches, horses. If he was losing, that could explain his erratic finances. I knew the restaurants were in trouble. I just learned how much while I was in California. He had raided them of cash. As half owner, I should have stepped in and found out what was going on."

"So if you sold over three thousand acres, I'm guessing we're talking a nice chunk of change."

"Yes, and Charlie got all of it. It was a cash deal. My part was I would let Charlie have my half of the money. In return I got a deed with just my name on it on this house and the remaining sixteen hundred acres. I guess I'll never know what he did with all that cash."

"May not. Cash has a way of disappearing."

Say something she didn't know, Alex thought glumly. She lifted her foot off the brake and they moved forward. "This place is my future. I want to live here. It's my escape from the madness in Los Angeles and from the stress and tension of the business I'm in. I've spent a lot of money remodeling and furnishing this house. If something happens to devalue it, my investment as well as all my plans are down the drain. I wouldn't be able to live here in peace if the pond and creek are ruined."

They arrived at the smooth surface of the county road and soon stopped behind his pickup, parked on the main street. She had told him the story, answered his questions. Now all she wanted to do was go home and nurse her wounds. She wouldn't even put in an appearance at Carlton's this week. She would leave the place up to Estelle. She slid the transmission into neutral and tilted her head to look across the console at him. "I didn't mean to suck you into my problems."

He turned toward her and smiled, but didn't hurry out of the Jeep. "Hey, my shoulders are broad," he said softly.

"I don't usually discuss my business in Callister, especially with strangers. I hope you respect that. The people here gossip about me enough as it is."

"We're hardly strangers anymore, do you think?" His hand covered hers on top of the gearshift and the gesture made her feel awkward and speechless. "I must not have made myself clear," he said. "I'm a good listener and I don't gossip."

She managed a smile. "Okay."

He scooted out, but stood just inside the door looking back at her, his hands hanging on the roof. "Thanks for breakfast."

She smiled again, forcing herself not to grimace from pain. "That's okay. Thanks again for helping me and for holding my head all night. I'm much better today."

"Would you like to go out for dinner some evening? I hear they have good food up at Indian Mountain Lodge. Or maybe we could drive to another town and catch a movie. Your pick this time."

Good Lord, he was asking for a date, like they were sixteen. "I seldom go out."

His mouth tipped into a big smile, probably one he hoped was charming. To her chagrin, it succeeded. "Couldn't you make an exception for a new friend who thinks you're a damned attractive woman and sexy as hell?"

She had no intention of playing dangerous boy-girl games. Best to clear the air right now. "I'm not interested in sleeping with you, Mr. Hawkins."

He stepped back and stared at her, his eyes narrowed. "Who the hell asked you to?"

"I know how it works with men like you. You think you can do me a few favors, take me to dinner and end up in my bed."

"Is that so? What, you think you're too damn irresistible to live without?"

"It doesn't matter what I think. Shut the door!"

"You got it!" He slammed the door with a whack.

She yanked the Jeep into first gear and pulled out of the parking space, fumed all the way from town to the county road. Why was he always so insulting? Every time she thought she might be able to like him, he made some smart-aleck comment. She should never have confided in him, was sure she would live to regret it.

By the time she reached her driveway, her thoughts had switched to the ongoing conflict with Kenny. The papers he had bandied about in the bar worried her. She should have made an effort to see what they were. Could he have learned about the old military right-of-way she had stumbled across last summer? Surely not. She had discovered it herself only by accident.

Perhaps she should call Bob Culpepper. She touched her swollen face. Better yet, she would go see him at home, go shopping in Boise, then see a doctor on Monday.

She tidied the kitchen, went to the bedroom and threw some things in a bag, called and left a message with Gretchen asking Ted to feed her cats and left for Boise.

What was wrong with wanting to bed a good-looking woman? The question didn't warrant debate or an answer. Who was he kidding by thinking it? Sex hadn't been the reason he had gone to her house last night. He went in friendship, because he had been concerned. Because, dammit, she had become important to him.

Doug made a left turn off the highway into his driveway. As it always seemed to do, reality lit up again. For her, he had been nothing more than a convenience. *You're a damn fool, Hawkins,* he told himself. *If you don't watch out, she'll be using you just like she uses Ted.*

He strode to his back door, jerked it open, tramped in and let the screen door slam behind him. His house was quiet and bright and clean with a cool, musty smell of freshly taped Sheetrock. He mellowed.

In the bedroom, he pulled off his boots and jeans and replaced them with running shoes and shorts. Out the door and down the lane to the county road and back. A couple of miles, another shower. He felt better.

The Mickey Mouse clock showed noon. Maybe he could catch Ted for lunch. He reached for the portable phone and punched in Ted's number. They met at Betty's Road Kill.

"Pete and Mike told me what happened." Ted waited until Lorraine Jones had left their table with their order for hamburgers. "And I've heard three versions of the story from other people."

Doug added his own version. In a tacit conspiracy with Alex, he omitted the footnote that he had slept all night at her house. No sense making trouble where none existed.

"What do you know about this feud that you haven't told me?" Doug didn't believe for a minute Ted didn't know the fine details of Alex's relationship with Miller or any other Callister citizen. "Money has to be what this is all about," Doug said. Money was right up there with passion as a motive for assorted crimes. "Tell me how much."

Ted shrugged. "A few million. I don't know exactly. Kenny's profit from logging the timber on the property that butts up to Alex's."

"Christ."

Ted shrugged. "Welcome to the Pacific Northwest. Trees translate to dollars, especially if it's virgin timber. Premium stuff. Damn little of it left that anybody's allowed to cut. Since most of it's old growth, I'm surprised some environmental group hasn't weighed in and tried to stop it. They may yet."

"Alex made that threat, something about the Sierra Club and something else. That's when he slugged her."

"I'm not surprised it pissed him off. Truthfully, I don't think Alex would do that. She knows as well as anybody if those folks got in the middle of it, Kenny could be left sucking wind from now on. The whole place would end up tied up in court 'til we all die."

Lorraine returned with their baskets of hamburgers and fries and Ted buried his fries in ketchup. "Even if it wasn't virgin timber, a logger couldn't ask for a sweeter deal. Close to the sawmill, close to town. Kenny's transportation costs will be nothing compared to what they might be if he was a hundred hard miles from the sawmill. I'm sure he wanted that ground real bad even though he must have known it's landlocked.

"I don't know for sure," Ted went on around a mouthful of burger, "but my guess is, mixed up with the booze and drugs and Cindy Evans thrown into the pot, Kenny somehow conned ol' Charlie into selling."

Doug compared Ted's comments to the story Alex had told him. He had seen too many lives ruined by booze and drugs in all strata of society. "Landlocked. You mean nobody can get to it without crossing somebody else's property." Alex hadn't used the word, but she had conveyed the meaning. He was adding new words to his vocabulary every day in this little town.

"Right," Ted answered. "That mountainside's steeper than a cow's face. Unless you're a wild animal, the only value it has is in the timber. If Kenny can't get it out, not only can he not make any money, he's stuck with a worthless piece of real estate to pay taxes on from now on. Hell, he couldn't even give it away, much less sell it."

"Last night in the bar, she told him he'd have to go around. Why can't he do that?"

"He'd have to cross national forest and that ain't gonna happen. Only other option is helicopter logging, but I doubt if there's enough stumpage to warrant the expense."

"Stumpage." Another word Doug didn't recognize, but he had heard enough to know it related to trees and their value. "Lemme guess. He figured if he could get his hands on the land, he could push and shove his way across the McGregors' property when he got ready to cut down the trees?"

"That's about the size of it. You have to understand the kind of man he is, Doug. He probably dropped out of school in the eighth grade, but that doesn't keep him from being smart and hard. Got a personality like a pit bull. Got that instinct to go for the jugular."

"Yeah, I can see he's more bite than bark."

"In a way, I admire the guy. He started with nothing— less than nothing. Somehow he scraped together money to buy an old truck and some worn-out equipment. For years he worked in the woods all day and worked on that old junk at night to keep it going, took on jobs nobody else would do. Now he's one of the richest men in the state and his reputation as a logger is as good as anybody's."

"Sounds like *you* don't have any trouble with him."

"Hey, man." Ted held a ketchup-covered fry suspended. "I've got the U.S. Government behind me. Even Kenny's not gonna bully the Forest Service."

"What's the law? What'll a judge say if Alex gets in front of him with this?" Doug stuffed the last bite of his burger into his mouth and pushed the basket away.

Ted did the same, shaking his head. "She doesn't have a prayer of winning. A judge will make her compromise."

"She must know that, so what does she hope to accomplish?"

"Wait him out? Hope for a break in her favor?"

"She must know better than that, too. For a smart woman, she does some dumb stuff. Like keeping a pistol in the bar. Did you know she does that?"

Ted sat back and sighed.

"It's a snub-nosed .357. A cannon. Did you help her buy it?"

"Lord, Alex doesn't need *me* to help her. She knows a lot about guns."

"Pointing a gun at somebody, particularly in a bar, could get her ass locked up. If I still carried a badge, I'd haul her in."

Ted shook his head. "What can I say? You can't tell her. She won't listen."

"I suppose the sheriff'll be—"

"Nah, she doesn't have to worry about Jim Higgins. He won't do anything unless Kenny pushes him and I can't see that happening. Kenny's a big dumb turd, but I don't think he'd sic the sheriff on her. Hell, he's in love with her."

Confused, Doug squinted. "The sheriff?"

"Kenny."

Doug shut his mouth to keep his jaw from dropping. "I knew she fucked around with somebody."

"Alex? Lord, no. It's not like that. But Kenny didn't even try to hide that he wanted to. Him and Charlie used to get drunk and he'd tell Charlie right out he was gonna take Alex away from him. Charlie would just laugh. That's one time where Charlie was smarter than Kenny. Alex told Kenny to leave her alone, but he didn't pay any attention to her."

"She had his attention last night when she whipped out that revolver. He was white as a ghost, as well he should've been. If she'd pulled the trigger, they'd still be cleaning up the mess."

"Kenny's not a guy to back up, but it probably did scare him when he saw her with a gun."

"This is the loosest place I ever saw. Doesn't anybody care about enforcing the law?"

Ted laughed. "Only if it's not too much trouble."

Doug stood and picked up the check. "I can't believe all this. I came here to lead a quiet life. I'm going home and study my map, find a new place to live."

Ted followed him toward the cash register. "Callister's a good place. There's a few rotten apples everywhere. You just happened to run into ours."

They parted at the café's front door. Doug drove the twelve miles from town to his house, trying to make sense of the past twenty-four hours and the revelation that life in this simple small town wasn't so simple after all.

That evening, he saw no tiny specks of light on Wolf Mountain and wondered why. The following day, he debated about calling Alex and asking about her injury, but remembering how they had parted, he rejected the idea. Then he considered calling her and apologizing, but for what? All he had done was ask her out.

No lights appeared on the next two evenings, either.

Surely, she hadn't gone on a business trip with her face battered. Since Ted must be feeding the cats, he would know where she was. Frustrated because he wasn't in that loop himself, Doug considered calling Ted to see if he could finesse the information out of him. *Don't be juvenile,* he told himself and rejected that idea, too.

# Chapter 17

On Tuesday morning, just after Doug finished his work-out, UPS delivered a small but heavy brown box. As he signed for it, the return address preoccupied him—Bynard's Antique Books, Boise, Idaho. He opened the parcel on his kitchen table and found a stack of well-used small books inside. The shipment had to be an error. He had never heard of the Boise bookstore.

He lifted out the top book and turned it in his hands. The spine was suede, the cover appeared to be fabric of some kind. For sure, the books were antiques. Printed on the spine was "The Winning of the West, Vol. I by Theodore Roosevelt." He opened the cover to the title page, covered by aged, crisp onionskin. Turning the delicate paper with care, he saw the publication date: 1905.

Five more like volumes, II through VI, were in the box. He lifted them out and fanned the ivory pages of each one. A square envelope lay on the bottom of the box. He pulled a folded note from inside it and saw embossed initials in one corner—"AM."

*Thanks for your friendship. Sincerely, Alex McGregor.*

He did a one-eighty and looked out his kitchen window at the distant smudge against Wolf Mountain he now could identify as Alex's home. His thoughts were a jumble. He had received presents from women many times, things like ties or sweaters he often didn't like. He could think of few gifts, if any, that had required study or deep thought on the part of the giver. How could she have known how much he would treasure so fine a gift?

His desire to call her outweighed his determination not to and he punched in her number, which for some arcane reason he still remembered. He heard one burr before he made a different decision, hung up and went to the shower.

At her house, he parked on the upper level at the front. She came around the corner of the deck clad in mud-crusted jeans and a loose dirt-smudged T-shirt, carrying several tomatoes. Her hair was swept back and held by a barrette at her neck. "Hi," he said, letting his eyes scan her clothing. "You mining for those tomatoes or what?"

She gave him an unsmiling, indulgent look. "My garden."

Her being a gardener was as far-fetched as her being the owner of Carlton's, but as he became more aware every day, nothing about her fit a conventional pattern. "You grew 'em? Hey, cool."

"I like growing things."

"Where'd you learn how?"

"My grandmother. It was survival training."

Her sunglasses were absent, so when she came closer, he saw that the swelling in her cheek and eyelid had gone down. Now she had only a dark crescent beneath her lower lid to show for Friday night's set-to. He glanced down at her lace-up walking boots. "Going hiking?"

She hesitated a few beats. "What do you want?"

"UPS delivered the books today. I came to say thank you."

"You're welcome." She looked up at him from beneath a hand shading her eyes. It was impossible not to notice that her eyes and the sky were the same clean color. "That means you're thanking me for thanking you. I told you, I always pay back."

"A set of antique books is a pretty special payback for a small favor."

She shrugged and began to dust off the tomatoes on her pants leg. "I thought you might enjoy reading them. Ted told me you like old things with history."

"I will enjoy it, but even if I never get it done, I'll still like owning them." He gestured at her boots. "Where you hiking to?"

"Granite Pond." She walked over and laid the tomatoes on the back deck. He picked one up and examined it. "It's a short-season variety," she said, eyeing him cautiously. "Nothing else will grow here."

"You don't say. Listen, maybe I could walk with you. It would be good for me."

A chirp came from her pocket and she pulled out a beeper. "I need to return this call first. Come inside if you like." She turned and started up the deck steps and he followed, his gaze glued to the tight jeans hugging her ass with each step. Inside, she made a left turn into the office.

He stopped in the doorway as she made her way to the desk. As interested as he was in everything about her, he still didn't want to eavesdrop on her phone conversation.

"You can come in," she said. "This is some information I'm expecting from my assistant. It isn't private."

He shrugged and stepped into the room. A wood floor squeaked underfoot. He hadn't paid a lot of attention to the office the first time he was in it. He hadn't had the chance because that night all he had seen was Miller.

The clean scent of furniture polish met him. A speck of dust couldn't be seen anywhere, but plenty of books were shelved in two walls of fancy bookcases. Everything from reference books to textbooks, fiction varying from the classics to erotica. He envied the collection. "Who's the reader?"

"I am." She keyed a number into the phone on her desk and put the receiver against her ear. "I have no social life."

Doug grinned at the cynical remark, but kept his back turned. As far as he could tell, Ted was the only person in town who didn't dislike her.

While she talked, he studied the wall above a long credenza behind her desk, saw photographs and architects' renderings of hotels, apartment buildings, shopping centers. He recognized an Orange County mall. Interspersed among the pictures of buildings were a few photographs, old and new, of Alex with assorted dignitaries.

Most ego walls he had seen weren't hidden in a private place where the outside world would never view them. He picked up a five-by-seven picture in a silver frame of her shaking hands with a former mayor of Los Angeles.

She hung up and came around the end of the desk. "What was this about?" Doug asked her, pointing to the mayor.

"Nothing much. He made a speech at a conference. Ready?"

"Sure."

As they started out of the room, almost hidden behind the door Doug saw a mounted mountain goat's head. Besides being an enviable trophy, it was an incredible specimen. How had he missed it when he had been here before? Then he remembered her turning out the lights and leaving him standing in the dark.

Below the goat's head he spotted a glass-doored gun cabinet. He saw a .22 rifle, a couple of shotguns and a 30.06. Even some pistols. Shit, she had an arsenal. Then he recalled Pete joking about how she beat all the locals in the Sunday turkey shoots, then gave away the turkey. "Your husband must have been a pretty good hunter."

"He was once, when he didn't drink so much. Where we grew up, everybody hunted. We had to."

"Where'd he get this guy?"

"He didn't. I did. It came from up on the Lochsa."

"You're kidding, right?"

"About which part? That I shot it or where it came from?"

"The first part. I know where it came from."

She laughed. "Why would you say that? You think a woman can't shoot a goat?"

He envisioned the steep, rocky crags where mountain goats lived. "That's not what I meant. I'm talking about where you had to go to get it. I'm in pretty good shape and a hunt that rugged would be hard for me. I can't imagine a woman even *wanting* to do it."

"I had a guide. He did most of the work, at least for half the trip."

"Half?"

"He hurt himself. He broke his foot."

Doug blinked as he considered the hazards such an injury in a wild remote area would raise. "While you were hunting?"

"I already had the sheep." She flipped a hand in the air. "It's a long, boring story. I will say, though, the whole adventure turned out to be the most difficult thing I've ever done in my life and I'll never do it again."

She walked out, toward the living room. Doug threw one last glance at the bearded, snowy white trophy. "Don't you have to draw a permit to hunt those?"

"I won the drawing. The permit wasn't transferable. If I hadn't gone on the hunt, it would have been wasted. I don't believe in waste."

A hundred questions danced around in Doug's head. Why would she have even signed up for the drawing in the first place? "Lemme see if I got this. You're saying going on a grueling hunt most men would find challenging was purely a philosophical idea, based on not being wasteful?"

"I'm not saying anything at all. You asked about it." She laughed again. "You're wondering just what a smart-aleck woman was trying to prove, right? It was one of those sur-

vivalist things, like some people do when they're diagnosed
with a terrible disease. I didn't have a terrible disease, but I
had Charlie. Challenging myself helped me clear my head
at the time."

Well, a man would never find life with her dull, Doug
decided as they stepped out the back door onto the deck. He
had to know the story that went with the mountain goat's
head, but he would save it for later.

A long hill began a few feet away from the back deck.
She stared toward the top of it as if reluctant to start the
climb. "I haven't gone up there since Ch—since the fire."

Doug would have paid to know what was going on in her
busy brain at that moment. Abruptly, she headed up and he
had to scramble to keep up. They were both breathing hard
by the time they reached the top and a road.

"This is Old Ridge Road," she said, as they stood in the
middle of a rugged two-track. "I told you about it. It's one
of the issues Kenny and I disagree on."

There was no way trucks of any kind were going to
travel on the narrow, rough road in its present condition.
Making it usable for heavy logging trucks would be no
small project. Understanding began to swarm in Doug's
head. He looked back toward Alex's house and realized she
might be able to see the traffic from her back door and
would certainly hear it.

In front of him lay the small bowl that closed in the
lower end of the creek, the pond and the waterfall that
dumped into it. Even before they arrived, he had heard the
rush of the waterfall. He remembered the sound.

In the noonday sun, the oval-shaped pond glittered like a
diamond nestled in the tall green grass that surrounded it.
Off to the distant left and at the beginning of Wolf Mountain's foothills was the pile of ashes and debris that had
been the log cabin. Behind it rose a steep hill with burned
tree trunks jutting from the blackened earth, looking as if
giant black toothpicks had been poked into the ground. A

sadness came over Doug. The glade had been unique and he had taken it for granted on his first visit. It would be years, if ever, before it returned to the same look.

Miraculously, the fire's path had taken it away from the valley floor. The separation between the charred hillside and the green grass and foliage on the banks of the pond and stream was as distinct as if someone had drawn a line.

He looked down at Alex's profile as she stared at the destruction. The uphill hike had made her cheeks rosy. Sunlight sifted through wispy tendrils framing her face. She wore no jewelry except small golden hoops in her ears. Now, up close and in daylight, he realized she had on little or no mascara. The dark, thick lashes that framed her eyes were natural. Her lips shone with just a hint of color. She was one of the most striking women he had ever seen.

A powerful urge seized him. He wanted to pull her into his arms, consume the sweetness he believed he would find in her mouth.

Her gaze was fixed on the cabin ruins as if her mind was far away. She shook her head slowly. "It was so beautiful." She looked up at him. "Didn't you think so?"

"It still is if you can shut out the scene to the left." He glanced down at the steep slope ahead of them that met the valley floor. "Let me go first." He stepped in front of her, turned back and offered her his hand.

"I don't need help. I'm up and down this slope all the time."

"C'mon. It'll be easier if you let me help you. Give me a chance to be a gentleman." Slanting him a look of skepticism, she placed her hand in his. "Put your other hand on my shoulder," he told her. Then, digging in his heels, he picked the way down the rocky decline.

Arriving at the bottom, he saw her eyes come to rest on the cabin ruins again. "There isn't much left," she said.

He was curious to get a second look at the ruins in a setting less congested than on the day of the fire. He tilted his head toward them. "Care if I take a look over there?"

She shook her head, so, not wanting to appear overanxious, he ambled across the clearing to the foot of the hillside. He didn't expect her to accompany him, but she came a few steps behind. There had been no weather to change how the ruins had been left, though there was evidence of visits by predators and, of course, the rescuers and firefighters.

He walked around the perimeter of the cabin's ashes, picturing how the old structure had looked when he had been here with Cindy before the fire. It had been close to dark that night and scrutiny of the cabin hadn't been what was on his mind.

A few parts of logs from the walls were left. Scattered among the ashes were twisted bedsprings, metal pieces from a chair's frame, a cast-iron stove scorched to a rusty red and looking misplaced on a brick hearth. It stood at an angle across what would have been a corner. Alex was right. Not much to see. "Where was the bed located?"

"On the opposite wall from the woodstove."

Doug measured the distance in his mind. He picked up a stick, squatted and slipped it through the twisted remains of the lantern that had been named as the culprit. Lifting it a few inches and studying it, he recalled being told once by a fire marshal that most metal collapsed at 1,500 to 1,800 degrees. "Real hot fire," he said.

He looked closer, but saw nothing to indicate a body had lain in front of the hearth. "What'd they say was the cause of death?"

"Carbon monoxide poisoning. And massive thermal injuries."

He looked up at her, squinting against the sun. With a vengeance, she was plucking the tufts from a plant of some kind. "Did the autopsy say if they found soot in the upper airway, upper lungs?"

"I haven't read it. What difference does it make? No matter what it says, Charlie's just as dead."

She was the worst liar he had ever seen, so he assumed evading the truth was something she was uncomfortable doing. The answer to his question must be yes. Charles McGregor *did* burn to death.

Knowing McGregor had been alive for some period while the cabin burned only elevated Doug's curiosity. He remembered the cabin having windows and a door. As small as it was, a window couldn't have been more than a couple of feet from the hearth, the door no more than five or six feet from the bed. Was McGregor passed out drunk? Otherwise, why didn't he get out?

*You're not a cop,* he reminded himself again. *So stay out of it.* "Right." He dropped the stick and stood up, pulled out his handkerchief and wiped his hands. "Where was Cindy when you first saw her?"

She pointed toward a cluster of standing, blackened tree trunks across the meadow. "She ran out from the trees over there. She kept saying, 'He'll kill me.'" She turned her back on the ashes and headed toward the pond.

"Was she talking about your ex?"

"I don't know. If somebody asked me if Charlie was a violent man, I'd say no, but at the same time, he could be unpredictable when he was drunk. I think he'd gotten to the point where brain cells were drowning faster than they could rebuild. That's what happens with alcoholics, you know."

When they reached tall grass, she stopped and pulled a tufted blade. A soft breeze brushed their faces. The grass rustled around their legs as they passed through it. Doug, too, bent and pulled a stalk of grass. They walked side by side, detufting grass stalks. "Was he belligerent? Obnoxious?"

She shrugged again. "What drunk isn't obnoxious? The

last year or two, he—well, he was lost. Pathetic, really. I
felt sorry for him."

"That's a charitable attitude."

"He didn't have the nerve to blow his brains out. His
method of suicide was death by drink. It was hard to
watch." She stopped and cut him a sharp stare. "You were
curious to see how I would behave up here, weren't you?
You came to observe me, to see if I'm the unfeeling bitch
everybody says I am."

"Not true. I wanted your company."

"That's nervy of you. You must know by now I hate
men."

"I don't believe it."

"Well, believe it. I've met few men I trust. Most of them
lie and scheme and their egos have to be constantly
stroked."

"Some men would tell you the same thing about women.
Neither sex has an exclusive claim on selfishness."

Her eyes softened and she gave him a measured look. "I
guess not. I admit I'm crotchety."

They had reached the edge of the pond, giving him an
opportunity to ease out of this conversation that could only
end in another argument. Their images looked back at
them. The action of the waterfall on the far end of the small
pool created a shimmy in its crystalline surface. The temperature was noticeably cooler. "I'll bet a dip in this is eye-
opening," Doug said, and shivered.

"It's glacier water. I've never known anyone who tried to
swim in it." She peered into the clear depths. "Isn't it amazing? They say no one has ever been to the bottom of it. It
must be thousands, maybe millions, of years old."

Doug had never seen her so animated. Her eyes danced
with excitement and he wondered what he, as a mere man,
could ever do that might put the same look on her face.
Mother Nature was tough competition. On that challenging
thought, he looked at the pond, too. It *was* amazing—

maybe a thirty-by-fifty oval, water clear as glass. Humans couldn't have laid the granite lining as precisely as the huge slabs came together. Water entered via the waterfall and left at the opposite end by way of the creek, which explained the water's purity. It looked shallow enough for wading. "Nobody knows how deep this is, huh?"

"Oh, I'm sure the depth has been measured sometime, somehow, but not since I've known anything about it." She made an arc with her arm that took in the whole small valley. "Now do you see why I don't want Kenny ruining this?"

"You don't think the fire has ruined it already?"

"The grass and underbrush will grow back. The Forest Service brings in tree planters every spring. When they come next time, I'll hire them to plant saplings." She pointed toward the mountain crest. "Up there is where Kenny wants to build his logging road. This creek and pond are in the watershed. The soil has talc. If it's disturbed to the extent logging will disturb it, it'll wash into the stream and turn the water cloudy as milk. The talc hangs in the water. It won't settle out for years and the fish will suffocate."

"There's fish in here?"

She crouched on her hands and knees and leaned forward, paying no attention to the cloud of mosquitoes that rose from the thick grass. "Look. You can see them. Little trout."

He squatted beside her and leaned forward, too. If she could stand a million mosquitoes, so could he. Sure enough, the fish were there. Small ones, maybe six inches long.

One broke the surface, then darted away. She jumped back, startled, then she laughed. "They're after the mosquitoes. We must have interrupted their lunch. They're so wild. They never see people. I usually don't bother them."

He rested his forearms on his thighs, looking around and

brushing hungry vampires off his bare arms. "I've spent a lot of time in the outdoors, but I've never seen a place quite like this. It suits you. It's like you are. Dramatic and wild."

Her head snapped to face him, suspicion in her eyes. "I'm neither of those things."

"What I meant is you're out there on the edge with the way you think and live. You don't appear to be trapped in the conventions most of us are."

She smiled and gave him a teasing look. "Ah. Well, that's a new description. I suppose it's an improvement over mean and crazy." She stood then, and he did, too. They were side by side, her shoulder touching his arm. She seemed unconscious of it, but he wasn't. She turned her head to look up at him and say something, but what she would have said was forever silenced by his hand cupping her jaw and his mouth settling on hers. He couldn't help himself. He had to taste her. He could think of nothing else.

Her breath caught, but she didn't resist. Nor did she return the kiss. "Kiss me," he murmured against her mouth. Her lips parted and let his tongue slide into her mouth. He delved for more. It must have felt okay because she didn't stop him.

Alex didn't stop him because she was shocked and because she had fantasized about kissing him. His lips were as soft and warm and nimble as they looked. They caressed her mouth. He tasted sweet and clean and he smelled spicy and male. She lost track of how long they kissed, but heat began to rise inside her, and for a reason she knew not, she moved her tongue against his.

A soft noise came from deep in his throat. His arm went around her waist and he hauled her against him. His hand crawled beneath her shirt, covered her breast and his palm gently circled her nipple. She began to feel dizzy and fluttery inside.

Something reminded her that barely a month had passed since she saw him ready to screw Cindy Evans in almost this same spot. She had no business doing this. She *would-n't* do this. "Don't," she choked out, and leaned back, putting space between them.

Her breath came in shallow shudders, his, shaky. His lips were shiny from kissing, his eyes heavy-lidded. He whispered her name and bent toward her again, but she jerked her head sideways and reached behind her, pulled his arm away and stepped beyond his reach. "I wish you hadn't done that. I wish I hadn't let you. And I wish I hadn't kissed you back."

She made for the hill.

His hand shot out and caught her wrist, stopping her. "What's wrong? Why are you upset?"

"I don't know why I let you come here with me. This place means nothing to you." She yanked her hand back and kept climbing, striding to stay ahead of him.

He caught up on the ridge road. "Alex, stop. Tell me what's wrong."

She broke and ran down the hill. Even with slipping on the steep surface and sliding in loose shale, he was well behind her by the time she reached her back deck. When he arrived, she had just finished removing her boots. He stood between her and the door. She looked into his eyes. "Leave me alone. Please. Just leave me alone. Please let me go inside."

He stepped sideways, allowing her to open the door. She passed in front of him through the back doorway and slammed the door.

From her living room windows, Alex watched the white Silverado bounce down the driveway and enter the tunnel of brush. She felt quivery inside. Her mouth tasted his kiss. She covered her lips with her fingers. She had to stop this. In California she had decided to stay away from him, which had been the right decision. But she liked him. She liked his keen intelligence, liked his no-nonsense approach to things, and he had a mysterious allure she couldn't put a name to.

Why couldn't he be just her friend, as Ted was? Silly idea, she thought then. He was like a character in a romance novel. Sexuality oozed from his pores, sparked from his too knowing eyes. Instinctively she knew he was an all-or-nothing kind of man. He wouldn't settle for friendship.

Scarier still, even if he could be "just friends" with *her*, she didn't know if *she* could be "just friends." She had this strange awareness of sex every time she was near him.

*Sex.* "Face facts, Alex," she mumbled. She was thirty-six years old, had been married and given birth, but she was as dumb as a virgin when it came to men and sex. She had fumbled through Sex 101 with Charlie and the result had been she became pregnant at sixteen.

Sex with her husband must not have been spectacular because she could scarcely recall it. Bells hadn't rung, she hadn't seen the stars she read about in novels. She hadn't wanted to tear off his clothes, hadn't wanted him to tear off hers, hadn't felt overpowering emotion. Sex with Charlie had mostly been a lot of trouble and made her want to take a shower. She hadn't missed him in her bed.

Damn Doug Hawkins for stirring up feelings she had no business having, for arousing urges she had no business pursuing, for making her long to experiment just one time.

She abandoned woolgathering in front of the windows, went to the phone in her office and dialed her Manhattan Beach office number. If there was anyone she could discuss Doug Hawkins and sex with, that person was her middle-aged assistant and mother of six kids, Judy. There was nothing Judy Moore didn't know about sex.

To say Doug wasn't in a bad mood by the time he returned to his own house was like saying a hungry wolf wasn't dangerous. No adjective existed in the English language to describe his frustration. He had never met a more impossible woman. Not once had an encounter with her had a favorable outcome.

What had happened to him that he couldn't leave her alone and move on? There had never been a shortage of women in his life. He hadn't *ever* had to pursue sex. It had always just been there. He had taken it or not taken it, as it came. The possibility that he wouldn't be able to hook up with a willing woman once he settled in Idaho hadn't occurred to him once. That he might meet one who would affect him like he hadn't been affected in years, if ever, hadn't occurred to him either.

What he needed was to forget about Alex McGregor and meet someone with no problems, some normal woman with whom he could spend time and have a normal sexual relationship. Or at least as normal as a single man could have. Good plan. All it needed was execution.

He was banging and slamming in the kitchen, hunting for something to devour, when he heard a car engine out front.

Long strides took him to the front door. When he stepped out onto the deck, Ted had just killed his engine. "I managed to escape for the afternoon. Get your tackle. Let's go up to Sterling Creek."

At the moment, nothing could have made Doug happier. He gathered his waders and his fly rod and flies. They headed north out of town and within an hour were casting lines into an incredible clear stream hemmed in by wooded, high canyon walls.

Peace crept into every part of him and Alex and her quirkiness seemed a million miles away. The majesty of nature always helped him regain his perspective. In Southern California, he had fled the city at every opportunity and spent time camping out, backpacking and fishing in the High Sierras. The escape had saved his sanity.

They fished hard, wading the edges of the rugged bank, and Doug lost himself in the dramatic scenery and the soft roar of the white water. By late afternoon, they had hooked enough rainbows and brookies to make a meal.

"I'll ask Mary Jane to cook these up for us," Ted said. "If it wasn't so dry, we could build a campfire and do it here, but I don't want to risk it."

That night Mary Jane fried the trout along with potatoes and onions. She added a salad and homemade bread and Doug gorged himself. By the time they helped her clean up the kitchen, the hour was late.

Ted leisurely drove him home. Doug felt more at ease than he had in years. He felt so comfortable in his old friend's company, over beers on the back porch, he told Ted the sordid tale of how his affair with the wife of a powerful politician and the fateful shooting of their drug-dealing thirteen-year-old son had ended a stellar law enforcement career.

"Did you know the kid was theirs?"

"Not at first." Doug had been on the receiving end of a morphine drip the day he learned he had shot and killed the child of his mistress. He barely remembered hearing it. "I didn't wake up for three weeks. When I did, I was in ICU. You don't get much news in the ICU. After that, I was stoned on painkillers half the time, in and out of surgeries."

One thing he did remember vividly. After being moved from the ICU, standing between two nurses, he had taken the longest walk of his life—half a dozen steps from a chair to his hospital bed. "A good three months had gone by before I got a clear picture of all that happened. By then, events were headed downhill at warp speed. Unstoppable."

"Was she somebody you loved?"

Doug shrugged. Even now he didn't know. "She was good-looking and fun. And needy. Bascomb pushed her around. That's how I met her, a domestic complaint. She said she wanted to leave him, but he scared her into staying. She couldn't seem to help herself."

"What happened to her?"

"Far as I know, she's still Mrs. John Bascomb. Wife of

one of the most powerful politicians in Los Angeles. That's what she wants to be, but I couldn't see it then. She thinks the position is worth the price she pays. By now she's probably hooked up with some other dim-witted bastard on the side."

"Man, oh, man. Shit just happens, doesn't it?" Ted yawned and stretched. "Well, I gotta hit the road. I'm riding fences with Pete tomorrow."

Ted pushed off the porch and Doug walked with him to his truck. As he started his engine, he gave Doug a sober look through the open window. "You've spent a lot of capital on women, haven't you?"

# Chapter 18

The tranquility Doug had found in the solitude of a mountain stream didn't hold over. Alex's rebuff at Granite Pond nipped at his heart with an ache akin to grief. The alien emotion had him bewildered.

He could manage the daylight hours without thinking of her so much, but work didn't distract him in the evenings. Nor did reading or watching TV. He went to bed with her on his mind, relived a dozen times the few seconds it took for her to look up at him with a tender gaze and say his name in that soulful voice or the night she had slept in his arms with her head on his chest.

And he couldn't forget the kiss at Granite Pond. She was passionate and fearless in so many ways. Would she be any less so in bed? He bet not and the idea of her hot and soft and ready was turning him into a sex-crazed fool.

To combat the growing lust, he threw himself into working on his house, finished half-done tasks, which included cleaning the old place's every nook and cranny. He scrubbed his bathroom plumbing hardware with lye and a toothbrush and discovered he didn't have to buy new plumbing fixtures after all.

After a week, he was still irritable. Food had lost its taste, a blow to his quest to gain weight. Music on the radio annoyed him. He couldn't even get interested in preseason football on TV.

He finished up his work for Bob Culpepper and Malcolm Henderson, driven by the thought of receiving payment for his services. He decided to take the files to them in person instead of sending them by E-mail or Fed Ex. Leaving Callister for Boise felt like a release from prison.

He hadn't seen his employers since the initial meeting. Renewing the acquaintance, he was pleased they still seemed to to have no concern about the scandal he had left behind in Los Angeles. He couldn't keep from thinking he should be looking over his shoulder, in case it jumped up to bite him.

At the end of the meeting, Culpepper followed him into the hallway. "Let's get a cup of coffee."

Such an invitation coming after a meeting always aroused Doug's suspicions. He strolled with the attorney down the street to a Starbucks, enjoying the eighty-degree temperature and wondering what bomb was about to drop on him.

The lawyer bought two coffees and led the way to a shaded table outside, away from other patrons. He spoke in a low tone. "I've got a client in Callister I'm concerned about. I'm wondering if you'd be interested in doing some investigative work up there."

The hair on the back of Doug's neck raised slightly. Culpepper could be speaking only of Alex. He swallowed a gulp of coffee that burned all the way down his gullet. "I don't do that kind of thing anymore."

The lawyer sat down, rolled up his shirtsleeves and loosened his dark blue tie. Normally, Doug liked seeing a man roll up his sleeves and get down to business. Today it gave him a chill. "This would be an investigation just for me and on the QT. It may not amount to anything."

"Who's the client?"

"A summer resident. Her name's Alex McGregor. You

may know of her. She owns a tavern and restaurant in town. Her former husband burned to death about a month ago."

"I've met her."

"Oh, good. I'm glad you know her. I believe she's involved in something that could be dangerous. Have you seen her in the past week or so?"

"Uh, last Tuesday."

"Then you know she was struck by a man named Miller. We served an injunction to—"

"I know, I know. I was in the bar when it happened."

"Then you must know why something wasn't done. Why wasn't an arrest made?"

Did Culpepper not know about Alex and the gun? "Look, Bob, the sheriff up there's more like Barney Fife than Wyatt Earp. There's talk he's in Miller's pocket, so Alex—er, Mrs. McGregor—didn't push it."

The lawyer sighed and Doug figured if anybody knew Alex's whole battle-worn history with Miller Logging Company, Culpepper did. But he didn't appear to know his client had come close to shooting the logging company's owner.

"What I want to talk to you about," the lawyer said, "is I don't trust the investigation Higgins made of Charles McGregor's death. The death certificate indicates Charles burned to death, but I haven't been able to find out how it happened."

"The sheriff must have a report of some kind—"

"The report has been conveniently lost, can't be found. I'm worried. I fear for Alex's safety."

The hair on Doug's neck stood straight up. "You're gonna have to tie it together for me, Bob. How does her ex-husband's accidental death relate to her safety?"

"Because the same people she's in conflict with now, and has been for years, were associates of her ex-husband's and they have a link to each other."

"You mean Cindy Evans and Kenny Miller."

"Those two and Charles McGregor were an unholy alliance if there ever was one. Since the day Charles sold the neighboring sections to Miller Logging, there's been constant turmoil. His dying strikes me as too convenient. It's a feeling I have."

"Do you happen to have any facts to go with that feeling?"

"No, but I believe they're there. That's why I'm talking to you."

Doug blew out a breath, glad his eyes were hidden by sunglasses. He didn't want to be involved in this. His crime-fighting days were a thing of the past and Alex would resent the hell out of him snooping around. "So, what, you're thinking Cindy and Miller together were somehow responsible for the cabin fire? And McGregor's death?"

"I don't know. That's why I want someone to take a look at it. Did you by any chance ever see that cabin?"

"Yeah, I saw it. Both before and after. Actually, I helped out fighting the fire."

Pure glee almost leaped from the lawyer's eyes. "Oh, good. What did you think?"

"I'm not an expert on fires. I'm acquainted with one of the Forest Service firefighters who was there. He believes it was an accident. A turned-over lantern." Doug hesitated. Admitting his true thoughts to Culpepper would be as good as agreeing to do the investigation. "I'll admit, I had a couple of questions, but hey, I'm just naturally suspicious. Comes from being in the questioning business a long time."

"That's okay. Go ahead and tell me your analysis."

"Well . . . the cabin was small. Not much bigger than a large bedroom. It had windows and at least one door. I question why McGregor didn't get out. Or, if he was passed out, why the woman with him didn't get him out. Mind you, I have no factual basis for those questions. The explanation could be simple."

"It isn't the woman who worries me."

"Miller? That's painting with a broad brush, Bob. There's no evidence Miller's guilty of anything but being an overbearing asshole. Last I knew, that wasn't prosecutable."

"If the sheriff's report's lost, how do we know what evidence there might be?"

*Fuck*! One vicious conflict with the most powerful man in the county was enough for one lifetime. Now Culpepper wanted him to take on another in a different county. Doing it could derail his plans to spend the rest of his life in peace and quiet. "Look, you don't need me. If you launch a new formal investigation, subpoenaing Cindy Evans will end it in a matter of hours. I'll bet she's told Sheriff Higgins the whole story."

"Alex doesn't want me to do anything that will create more friction. She's accepted Charles's death as an inevitable occurrence."

*He's been racing toward the edge of a high cliff ever since I've known him.* Pete Hand's words at the fire scene echoed in Doug's head. "She's not the only one. I've heard somebody else say the same thing."

"But if I had facts, a good cause, she would go along."

Something pushed him to stay in the conversation. "Exactly what do you want from me?"

"Just find out if there's any reason to go further. Besides finding out how Alex's ex-husband wound up dead on her property after he had been ordered by the court to stay away, I want to approach the attorney general about the sheriff. But I need facts."

"I haven't been in Callister that long. I'm not well acquainted with all the players, but I think I know this much. If I agree to dig around and discover what I think will be easy to find, if you don't follow through and put people away, Mrs. McGregor will be in an even tougher spot than she's in now."

"You don't have to worry. Even if I weren't an officer of the court, I'd do this for her. She's a wonderful person, one of the most generous people I know. Except for a church or two, she's the only charity in Callister. I'm stunned all the time at what she's willing to do for that little town."

"Like what?"

"You haven't heard about her foundation?"

"Guess that's one of the tales I missed."

"She buys medicine and food, even clothing for needy families. Right now I'm arranging for an elderly woman's house to be reroofed and painted before winter sets in."

Of all he had learned of Alex, Doug had *never* heard what Culpepper had just told him. "Is that a fact?"

"Don't mention it to anyone. She does it anonymously."

"Hunh," Doug said, taking a few minutes to reconsider the lawyer's request. Finally, he decided a woman who comprised the only charity in town deserved to be supported. "Shit," he mumbled, stalling the commitment. "Christ. . . . Okay, I'll do it."

For the first time since they had sat down with the coffee, the lawyer smiled. "Great. And thanks. I'll pay you, of course. By the way, you aren't interested in being the sheriff up there, are you?"

Doug laughed. "Not a chance."

Alex, Cindy and Kenny Miller bounced around in Doug's brain all the way back to Callister. His charge sounded simple enough—persuade Cindy Evans to tell what happened at the cabin the night of the fire. How to do it and what can of worms the revelation might open were scary to contemplate.

*Alex.* An anonymous charity? Who would think the self-centered Alex McGregor gave away money? How many dimensions could one woman have? While he thought her beautiful and desirable and all he could think about was crawling between her legs, at the same time he agreed with

Ted that she was greedy and self-centered. So much for surface perceptions. If Culpepper hadn't mentioned her gen-
erosity, Doug doubted he would have taken on secretly
investigating something he wanted no part of.

When he saw the lights of town on the horizon, the clock
on his dash glowed nine-thirty. At the city limits, he slowed
and cruised up the main street, recognized Ted's truck in
the parking lot outside the Eights & Aces. With no particular reason to rush home, he decided to go inside and have a
beer.

The Eights & Aces Saloon did business in a building
over a hundred years old. It was a genuine country-western
honky-tonk that drew a huge crowd from miles around on
weekends when a popular band played. Doug hadn't been
in it since the day he had met Cindy Evans and gone with
her to Granite Pond. His eyes took a moment to adjust to
the haze inside the barnlike building.

Tonight, a few couples sat around tables in the semidarkness near the dance floor. Butch Wilson, a sawmill worker
he had met in Carlton's, sipped a beer at the horseshoe bar.
Cindy was washing glasses. Her face broke into a smile as
she came to where Doug stopped at the bar.

He nodded a greeting to Butch, then ordered a draft from
Cindy. "Ted's truck's outside. I thought he'd be in here."

"He is." She tipped her head to the right. "He's over in
the corner with Pete Hand and Mike Blessing, getting
drunk. And entertaining the Queen of Swede Creek."

"Who's the Queen of Swede Creek?"

"The bitch. You know. *The* Alex McGregor? You won't
have any trouble recognizing her. She's the one with the
black eye."

Butch sniggered, but Doug ignored him.

Peering through the dim light, sure enough, Doug saw
*the* Alex at a table in the corner with Ted, Pete and Mike.
The day had already been testimony that the world was full

of surprises, so he shouldn't have been startled at one more. "Hunh. I'd better check this out."

Cindy scowled and harrumphed. Doug left the barstool, beer glass in hand, and crossed the dance floor to where the foursome reveled.

Alex had on mud-covered faded Levi's and a cropped T-shirt with a large swipe of dirt down one side. He was reminded of their hike to Granite Pond a week back and the warmth of her bare breast beneath his palm. Another erotic fantasy evolved in his mind. Last week, he thought he had mastered the irrational fascination Alex aroused in him. Now it roared back. In spades.

"Doug," Ted said too loudly. "Pull up a chair."

Doug dragged over a straight-backed chair from another table and straddled it, resting his arms on the chair back. Tabletop litter—empty shot glasses, a salt shaker and lime rinds—told the tale. Jesus. This woman who didn't drink was doing shooters? Doug grinned. "Looks like you guys are having a good time. How long you been here?"

"I dunno," Mike slurred, "but if I don't leave pretty soon, my wife won't let me in the bedroom. I won't get any for six months."

"Where you been, Doug?" The question came from Ted.

"Boise." Doug let his terse reply stand. He wouldn't discuss his business, especially in a bar.

Alex hadn't said a word since he arrived, didn't acknowledge his presence. Maybe he would have been surprised if she had. One look and he saw she was a little tipsy. She sat sideways in the chair, her shoulders leaning against the wall. One hand rested on the rim of a beer glass, a loose-fitting gold bracelet draping into the glass.

With hair disheveled and little makeup, she looked as if she had just risen from bed—or more like she should be *taken* to bed. The bruise around one eye showed, even in the room's dim light.

Someone dropped some coins in the jukebox and country

rock music swelled with a pounding rhythm. "Let's dance, Alex." Ted reached across the table and took her hand.

She listed as she rose from her chair, but caught herself on the tabletop. Their joined hands passed over all heads at the table, causing the T-shirt to lift and expose her midriff and navel. Pulling her along, Ted teetered toward the hardwood square in front of the jukebox.

Doug turned to Pete. "What's *she* doing here?"

"Damned if I know. She came in with Ted. Something about somebody's birthday. Snooty bitch. She keeps ol' Ted turned inside out and she don't give a shit about him. She just uses him."

Doug stared at Pete and suppressed an urge to defend Alex.

When the song ended, Pete and Mike applauded and whistled. Alex and Ted tacked back to the table, sweating from the vigorous workout on the dance floor. Alex licked her full lips and wiped her forehead with the back of her hand. Doug hadn't thought she would know how to dance or that she would enjoy music, two things he liked himself. He had never imagined her in any kind of social situation.

"Now we need a slow one," Ted said.

Alex sank to her seat, but Ted went to the jukebox and dropped in more coins. "When a Man Loves a Woman" and Michael Bolton's voice filled the room.

Alex's eyes closed and her head swayed back and forth to the rhythm. Ted returned and led her to the dance floor again. He pulled her close and appeared to be lost in a reverie all his own.

Unable to force his eyes to leave her, Doug watched her languid movement to the sensual music. He didn't like seeing Ted's arms around her, didn't like seeing her so vulnerable. And he didn't want these guys leering at her.

The song ended, only to repeat. She parted from Ted, returned to the table and flopped onto her chair, leaving him to find his way back from the dance floor alone.

Cindy appeared, a bar towel thrown over her shoulder. "Okay, that's it. I ain't serving you any more drinks. You're all too drunk. You're gonna get me in trouble. Go home."

Doug walked around the table to where Alex sat. She looked up at him from under lazy eyelids and he felt as if somebody had hit him hard in the midsection. He took her hand and urged her from her chair. "This is good music. Let's don't waste Ted's money."

As if it were something she had done a thousand times, she allowed him to lead her to the dance floor. He placed his right arm around her waist in the traditional position. As her body came against his, he stifled a groan.

He moved her near to the speakers where the jukebox cast an ethereal glow from a kaleidoscope of lights and where no other sound could be heard above the beat of the music.

He felt her warmth, smelled her perfume, her essence. He had never been near her when she didn't have a distinctive scent. His dick stretched and swelled and felt like a rail spike pushing against his zipper and her belly. He expected her to pull away, but she didn't. "You always smell so good," he told her.

She slipped her right hand from his, slid her arm around his waist and melted against him. Her head nestled into his shoulder, her body fit against his with the precision of jigsaw puzzle pieces and he felt the heat of her breasts against his chest.

"This is fucking music," she mumbled and snuggled closer to him.

*What?* Had he heard her right? His mind reeled, but he managed to laugh a little. "You've had too much tequila. You need to go home."

"I know. Today's a bad day. Many black thoughts."

Black thoughts? He couldn't say the same for himself. In fact, the thoughts flitting through his mind were closer to purple. He couldn't resist encircling her waist with his other arm and drawing her closer. He rested his cheek against her hair. The room spun around them and they were alone in an eddy of heat and surreal lighting. He closed his eyes and let himself be sucked into the ambience.

Remembering where he was and keeping himself from grabbing her ass with both hands took all of his concentration.

The music ended, but he continued to hold her. She didn't move. They couldn't stand in the middle of the dance floor all night, so he raised his hands to her shoulders and turned her toward the table. He partially steered her, partially supported her, hoping his problem in the front of his pants wasn't noticeable.

"Where'd everybody go?" Alex frowned and slid down to the chair.

"They went home." Cindy piled glasses and debris onto a tray. "I'm closing up."

"I'll take you home, Alex," Doug said. "You can't drive."

"I drove here and I can drive back."

"No. You live ten miles from here." He left her propped against the wall and went across the room to where Butch Wilson was still sipping beer at the bar. "Butch, the lady needs a driver. I'm gonna take her home. Follow me and bring me back, okay?"

"Sure."

"Lady, my ass," Cindy sniped. She unloaded her tray with a clatter on the stainless-steel drainboard.

Doug returned to Alex, put his arm under her elbow and urged her to her feet. "C'mon. I'm taking you home."

She stared at him like she might tell him where to leap, then let him guide her outside.

"I'll follow you soon's I finish my beer," Butch Wilson called after them.

# Chapter 19

Doug closed the heavy front door behind them. "Take a deep breath. It'll help clear your head."

Alex crooked one arm around a roof-supporting post on the covered sidewalk and stood for a moment, head tilted back, inhaling the cool night air.

"Where you parked?"

She frowned and thought a few seconds, then pointed toward Fielder's parking lot in the next block. He held her close to his side and walked her to her Jeep.

"I think I've had too much to drink," she slurred. "Where did Ted go? Why did he leave?"

"Couldn't tell you. Where's your keys?"

She shoved her hand into the right pocket of her jeans, which slipped down her hips and exposed her navel and her flat, oh-so-kissable stomach. She dangled the keys on two garnet-tipped fingers.

Doug grasped the keys, then helped her into the Jeep's passenger seat. As he buckled her seat belt, he glanced back to see if Butch had left the bar yet. There was no sign of him, but Doug started the engine and headed toward Alex's house anyway. She leaned back against the seat and closed her eyes.

Fifteen minutes later, they left the county road and began

the climb up her driveway. At the jolt from the first pothole, she opened her eyes and straightened in the seat. "Ted said you're a cockhound."

Doug's neck did a sharp ninety-degree toward her. *Ka-thunk!* The Jeep's left tire collided with a boulder.

She giggled. "I'll bet you thought I didn't know a word like that."

For lack of a quick retort, Doug laughed.

"So, are you?"

Christ, had Ted really said that? Doug couldn't imagine him making such a statement to any woman. He shifted gears and eased forward. "You've had too much to drink. You don't know what you're talking about."

"But I still know what a cockhound is." She giggled again.

Now he was curious as well as amused. "What? What is it?"

"It means you like to fuck."

Oh, boy. Thank God they were at her house and he would be rid of her soon. He struggled to hold her as she half fell, half stumbled out the Jeep door. "The safest place for you, lady, is in bed. I'll help you upstairs."

"You want to go with me?" Her liquor-clouded eyes leveled on his face. "To bed, I mean."

"I am going with you. Into the house." He put an arm around her waist and supported her up the deck steps. He tried the front door and found it unlocked. "Jeez," he mumbled, thinking of the treasures inside her house.

Inside, she pulled away from him. "It's coffee you like, right?"

"No, I—"

But she had already sailed toward the kitchen, leaning only slightly to the left. He trailed behind her. She reached into the cupboard and brought out the package of Starbucks, dragged the coffeepot across the spotless counter and started the coffee-making process.

"You could use a cup or two yourself," he said, placing his hands on his hips and watching her.

"Not I. Never touch the stuff." In the midst of the flurry of activity, she set out two mugs, confusing him as usual.

She pressed the ON button with a flourish, turned around and bumped into him. His hands automatically caught her waist. He laughed. "Careful."

She didn't push him away. He could feel her heartbeat, the heat of her breasts against him, and knowing all he had to do was run his hands up a few inches to touch them only added to the pressure straining below his belt. She looked him dead in the eye and didn't move.

After what had happened on the dance floor and what she had said to him in the Jeep, he wasn't embarrassed that she could feel his erection. He figured she already knew the plumbing worked anyway, had felt it the morning after they had spent the night on her sofa. "Wow," he said softly, "does this mean we're friends?"

Before she could reply, a rumble erupted from the coffeepot. She started to turn toward it, but he stopped her. He didn't want her to move. "Wait." He ran his gaze over every part of her face, halted on her parted full lips. "God, you're a beautiful woman, Alex."

"You say that to all the girls."

"Only if it's true. Can't you tell how much I want you?"

He watched her draw a measured breath, then she turned away and poured coffee for both of them.

He was no more in the mood for coffee than for a discussion of quantum physics, but he accepted the mug she offered. "So how come you're out drinking with the guys tonight? You're breaking all kinds of rules—hard liquor, coffee."

She sipped from her cup and peered across the brim with that catch-me-if-you-can look. All at once she turned and tossed her coffee down the sink drain. "I don't know why I poured this. I really do not like coffee."

He set down his mug and caught her waist again. "What *do* you like, Alex?" Her face tipped up to his and he looked into her liquor-clouded eyes. "I've been wondering since the first time I saw you."

Her head cocked, her eyes studied him and for the briefest moment he could feel a hum in the air between them.

"That day in the parking lot," she said softly, "you did want to sleep with me, didn't you?"

Doug didn't know whether to laugh or cry. He couldn't think of anything he wanted as much as he wanted at this moment to haul her off to bed. "Did. . . . Do."

Her lips curled into a smile. "Sometimes I get tired of sleeping alone."

*Oh, Jesus.* Another one of those surprises was about to spring up in front of him. He eased her back against the counter, braced his hands on either side of her, dipped his head and brushed her lips with his. "It's a damn shame, a woman like you sleeping alone." He covered her lips with his and tasted the sweetness of her mouth.

A light flashed in the living room and an engine revved outside. Doug lifted his lips from hers. "Shit."

She stiffened and sidled out of his reach. "That was insane. You'd better go."

Before he could organize thought, she was on her way to the front door. She held the door open. "Go."

He stopped in front of her at the door. Butch Wilson's headlights spotlighted them in the doorway.

"Don't you dare kiss me again," she said.

"Coward."

"Go."

Weak in the knees, he left her house and climbed into Butch's truck. "Ain't never been up this road before," Butch said as they crept along. "If you can call it a road."

Doug was in pain, ached all the way up in his belly. "Yeah, I know what you mean."

"She's sure an odd duck."

"Odd." A short word to describe the most unpredictable, complicated woman Doug had ever met. He shifted his position. "Yeah."

"Every man in town's wished he could get in her pants, but she don't have nothin' to do with people around here much."

Doug grunted to hide both his discomfort and his annoyance at Butch's remark.

"Ol' Kenny Miller's plumb crazy about her. He told the woods boss over at the sawmill he'd sign one of them marriage agreement things and give her half his timber holdings if she'd marry him. Every gal in this county'd cream in their jeans to have Kenny come after 'em the way he used to chase after her. I can't believe he belted her. She must've really pissed him off."

Butch had Doug's immediate attention. "Were you in Carlton's that night?"

"Naw, but I heard about it."

"You know Miller pretty well?"

"Been falling trees for him ten years."

"Long time," Doug said. "Good guy to work for, I guess."

"He's okay. He works hard. Always has."

One thing Doug had learned about the citizens of Callister—almost any sin could be forgiven if a guy worked hard. His curiosity veered to the document Miller had pulled out of his back pocket in Carlton's. He remembered Alex asking about it. "I don't suppose you'd know what the beef between him and Alex McGregor is all about? Why would he go into her place of business and jump on her like that?"

"He's prob'ly trying to get even. I thought you was there. They said you kept her from shooting him."

"But I didn't know what the fight was about."

"She's trying to screw him out of a way to get to his

trees. Trees means everything to Kenny. Lord, he'd murder somebody over a stand of trees."

Doug withheld a reply to the unwitting prophetic comment. "He paid Charlie McGregor extra for the right-of-way to Soldier Meadows," Butch added, "but it was in cash. Since he can't prove it, the blonde told him to go fuck hisself."

"Did anybody see him pay?"

"Naw. It don't matter no more anyway. Kenny's found a way to fix it. That's one thing about Kenny. He always finds a way."

"What's he doing?"

"I don't know all of it. I heard him telling the gal that works in the sawmill office. Somebody made a mistake a long time ago in a survey." Wilson pointed his thumb back over his shoulder. "He's gonna own that old ridge road him and the blonde have been fighting over. He's trading the Forest Service a hundred and twenty acres for it. She ain't gonna be able to stop him from using it to haul his logs out."

Doug took a few seconds to digest the new and startling information. He wished he knew enough about logging and Forest Service policy to ask intelligent questions. "The Forest Service trades land? How does that work?"

"I dunno. It's going on now. 'Course it takes a long time to get stuff done with the Forest Service. They always have all these papers to fill out."

Doug might not know exactly what the trade meant, but intuition told him if a trade was good for Miller, it was bad for Alex. "Complicated situation," he mumbled.

"Yessir, it is that. A lot's happened between her and Kenny . . ." Wilson's voice trailed off as a boulder loomed in the headlights.

Doug was glad he stopped talking. Sharing deep thoughts about Alex with Butch was something he didn't relish.

The next morning, with great effort, Doug skied in his living room. Eight a.m. and he was exhausted. Last night was the first time in more years than he could count back that he had been driven to relieve himself in a towel.

In bed, he had mulled over the conversation with Butch Wilson for hours. Then when he finally dropped off, the familiar, bloody nightmare, absent for months, visited him. The dream was always the same: himself in a dark, crumbling warehouse, wounded, bleeding and slumped against a wooden crate in filthy water. Two downed ATF agents lay beside him, his friend Rick Chavez's head gushed blood onto his lap while hip-hop music boomed around them and faceless armed men closed in. When his automatic clicked empty, he always woke up with an outcry. He suspected the dream wasn't far from the reality, though he remembered only surreal snatches of events after he had been hit.

Unable to return to sleep, he found his mind drifting to Alex and sticking there like an old phonograph needle on a seventy-eight record. A truth as profound as life and death came to him. He loved her, plain and simple. It was the only sane explanation for the possessive feeling he had for her. He was fascinated by the contradictions in her quirky personality, entertained by her cynical sense of humor, challenged by her quick wit and unconventional approach to life. And he believed she had more heart than any woman he had ever known.

Last night convinced him she had an interest in him. All he had to do was scale a tall wall, swim a deep river and break down an unknown number of barricades.

And if he felt all of that, how could he not be concerned about her problems?

*I believe she's involved in something that could be dangerous.*

Bob Culpepper's words echoed in the back of his brain. Just how dangerous *was* Kenny Miller?

He had to get to Cindy Evans. She was the key that

would open the vault of information that could expose
Miller if he was guilty of something and possibly put the
good sheriff away. As dark as Doug's mood was when he
awoke, he resolved that today was as good as any to see
what he could wheedle from the barmaid.

But first he had to settle something with Ted. His old
friend's intentions with Alex were unclear. Doug believed
they were based on hope more than fact. Still, he couldn't
pursue Alex as long as Ted held some kind of ideal of winning her.

*Ted.* An intelligent, mature man, but he seemed to have
no pride where Alex was concerned. His mooning over her
like a lovesick calf had made him a laughingstock among
his friends. Even if he succeeded in capturing her, a relationship between them could be as destructive as it was
temporary. Christ, Alex would grind a softhearted soul like
Ted into little pieces and spit him out and never notice what
she had done. Besides what Doug felt for Alex himself, he
didn't want to stand by and watch a friend's humiliation.

Alex shifted in bed, but didn't open her eyes. What had
she done? The memory of Doug bringing her home, then
the two of them standing in the kitchen smooching like
teenagers was veiled and distant, but the fact that he had
wanted sex wasn't. She had been so tempted. If his ride
hadn't shown up outside, she might have invited him to
stay. Oh, Lord. She prayed to die. She deserved it. She
would never drink again.

She eased up to sit. Her head pounded, her tongue was
paralyzed, her mouth tasted like moldy socks. How could
she have spent the evening in a bar, and a competitor's es-
tablishment at that, drinking and carousing with three men?
Had she lost her mind?

Guilt battered her. Getting drunk to wipe out memories
was Charlie's tactic, not hers. Ten of her daughter's birthdays had come and gone since her passing and Alex had

managed to get through them sober. What had happened yesterday?

It had been the trip to the grocery store that unhinged her. Two girls, maybe nine or ten years old, had been arguing over a cake mix purchase and they had asked Alex to help them decide. A memory had rolled over her, the day Holly wanted to bake a birthday cake for Charlie. They had spent an entire afternoon laughing and baking and creating and true to form, where Holly was concerned, Charlie had gushed over the finished product as if it came from the finest bakery in Los Angeles. She could still hear the laughter and remember the fun they'd had.

Tears burned her eyes. Would she be haunted until her dying day? She had dropped her guard for only an instant and there the memories were, lurking and luring her into a black canyon of self-pity. And on the canyon floor she had fallen into a river of tequila.

"Stop this," she said, sniffing away the tears. "Just stop this. It was a hell of a long time ago." She would work outside today. All day. Many outdoor chores needed doing. She would work hard and not think.

She stood up, waited for her head to clear, then padded to the shower.

Doug came to a stop in front of the reception desk in the Forest Service lobby. "Hi, beautiful. Ted in his office?"

Gretchen grinned, showing her dimples. "He's back there, but we may have to get the EMTs any minute. Pete's already called in sick and I heard Mike Blessing's wife's looking for a divorce lawyer. It must have been quite a party."

"Don't blame me." Doug grinned and winked. "I wasn't even in town." He saw Ted through the partially open door of his office, his elbows resting on the desk, his fingers massaging his temples. Doug tapped on the door and stepped into the office. "Hey, buddy. How about a shot of tequila?"

"Shit." Ted didn't open his eyes.

"You're pale as a ghost. You look like hell."

"I feel worse than I look. My head weighs fifty pounds."

"Shooters? You should have known better. That's for young bucks with no brains." Doug flopped into a chair opposite Ted's metal desk and propped an ankle across one knee.

Ted's hand trembled as he stopped his massage long enough to sip from his coffee cup. "Don't remind me."

"How about a big greasy breakfast over at Betty's? I'll buy."

"Food. God, I might puke any minute." He reached for his handkerchief and wiped beads of sweat from his forehead. "I haven't had a hangover like this since college."

"Maybe you should go home and crawl back between the covers."

"That's where I'd be if I didn't have to go through this damn report." A file folder lay open between his elbows. "I don't know how I'm going to concentrate on it. Just looking at it makes my eyes cross." He closed his eyes and groaned. "This day will be forty-eight hours long."

"What was Alex doing there last night? I thought she didn't drink."

"Just one of those things. She was running some errands in town. It was, uh—oh, one of those hard birthdays. She didn't want to be alone." His eyes opened to a squint. "How'd she get home?"

"I took her."

A swift flush flagged across Ted's face. "I thought so. That's why I left."

"Somebody had to, Ted. She had no business driving. You guys left her."

Ted's expression darkened. Tension swirled in the air. "That made it damn convenient, didn't it?"

"Hey, what's the problem?"

"Just remembering old times."

Doug's inclination was to say go to hell, but this was Ted. "I didn't screw her, if that's what's bugging you. What, you think I'd hit the sheets with a woman too drunk to know her mind?"

To Doug's amazement, relief flickered in his friend's eyes. Doug sat forward in his chair, bracing a palm on his thigh. "Ted, I'm gonna tell you something as a friend. Alex is a mountain you're never gonna see the top of. She doesn't care about you in the same way you care about her and she never will. Give it up. Do yourself a favor. Marry Mary Jane and have kids. She loves you."

A muscle in Ted's jaw tightened. "Mind your own damn business."

Shaking his head, Doug stood up and turned to go.

"It's *you* she wants," Ted said behind him. "I can see it. In all the years I've known her, I've never seen her want any man. But she wants *you*. And I know how it goes with you, old buddy, how it's always gone. It's just a matter of time before you'll be fucking her and to you it won't mean shit."

Doug's spine stiffened. Turning back, he stabbed the air with his finger. "Ted, because we've been friends for so goddamn long, I'm gonna forget what I just heard, but if you ever say anything like that to me again, I'll knock your friggin' teeth out."

He stamped out the door.

# Chapter 20

After the exchange with Ted, Doug had difficulty keeping his mind on buying groceries, but he managed. Afterward, he stopped by the Exxon station and filled his gas tank before leaving town. Country living required more organization than he had anticipated in the beginning. For instance, a couple of times he had found himself at home with barely enough gasoline to get back to town.

On the drive home, he rehashed what had happened between him and Ted. He couldn't remember a quarrel with Ted Benson ever, about *anything*. And for sure not about a woman.

The county road that went past Alex's driveway made a sharp right turn off the main highway. As he approached the intersection, his thoughts turned to her. She would wake up this morning with a hangover. She would need food in her stomach, but did she have anything to eat in her house? Did she know about the Forest Service land trade with Miller? He had bags of groceries in the back of his pickup and as if the Silverado had a will of its own, before he knew it, he had made the turn onto the county road leading to her driveway.

Reaching it, he put the transmission in crawl and let his truck creep up the rugged roadway. By the time he parked on the upper level, she was waiting for him, hanging on to a shovel with one hand and a rubber hose spouting water with the other. From the looks of the puddles and dirt piles, she had been digging something from the end of a drain pipe. She had taken on a physically demanding project to punish herself for last night. He grinned to himself, pleased at just how well he knew her.

She was wearing huge canvas gloves and mud-covered rubber waders that reached clear past her knees.

He brought the pickup to a stop. As he opened the door and slid out, she looked at him with unsmiling eyes.

"Hi. Thought I'd better come up and check on you." She didn't reply, so he pushed on. "What you need is a bigger pair of boots."

She peeled off one glove, pushed those two-hundred-dollar sunglasses to her forehead and frowned. "Don't tell me what I need."

He guessed a friendly reception was too much to expect. After last night, today she probably felt cornered and embarrassed. He went to the back of the pickup, pulled a jug of cold milk from one sack and opened it. "Those sunglasses do a lot for the boots. Where'd you get 'em, Rodeo Drive?" He offered her the milk, letting a twinkle steal into his eyes. "A real fashion statement."

She stared at the milk for a few beats, then re-covered her eyes with the sunglasses. Nope, not in a joking mood. But she did drop the shovel and reach for the milk, almost greedily.

"For somebody who doesn't drink, you sure made up for lost time." He picked up the shovel. "Let me do this. You must feel awful." He tilted his head toward the water hose. He wouldn't put it past her to spray him when his back was turned. "Why don't you turn that water off?"

She handed the milk carton back to him, then clumped toward the faucet mounted on the side of the deck and shut off the water. He felt more at ease.

He placed the milk carton inside the pickup, then plowed the shovel into the pile of mud plugging the drain. "You drank those guys under the table." She crossed her arms and watched him dig. "Poor old Pete couldn't make it to work today."

She made a sarcastic snort and pushed back a golden sheaf of hair. Her hand trembled. She had to be glad he took the digging chore away from her, though she would never admit it.

The back deck rail was roughly head high. She propped an arm on the rail and leaned her forehead against it. "I guess I should thank you for bringing me home. I'd might have killed myself or someone else if I'd driven. Everybody just left me."

"You're welcome. In truth, it was my pleasure."

She glared at him. "Do you have a reason for being here?"

With the drainpipe freed of mud and rocks, he stuck the shovel into a mud mound and chuckled. "I know a few hangover remedies. I'll trade you one for picking up where we left off last night when Butch showed up."

"As usual, I don't know what you're talking about." She flung back her hair in a gesture of defiance.

He moved to her side and rinsed mud from his hands under the faucet. "You expect me to believe you don't remember telling me you're horny?"

Unflinching blue eyes fixed on his. "I did no such thing."

"Yes, you did. Not in words, but you said it. Now that you're as sober as I am, don't you have the guts to do what you really want to? I say let's go for it. I've got nothing but time and you look like you need to lie down anyway."

She scowled, blushed from the neck up and appeared to be studying a pattern of rocks on the ground. "People say and do things they don't mean when they drink too much."

"Maybe. But they also sometimes lose their inhibitions and say and do what they really want to."

"This is silly." She spun on her heel and headed for the deck steps.

Reflexively, he grabbed her forearm and brought her around to face him. "I'm trying to be friends with you, but you're the rudest person I've ever met."

She squared her shoulders and hoisted her chin. "How many times do I have to say it? I've got all the friends I need. But even if I didn't, this doesn't strike me as a friendly conversation."

"You know what your problem is? You're a snob. And you're a coward. You're scared to death you might come down to earth and do something normal and like it." She attempted to jerk her arm away, but he held on firmly.

Her eyes shot sparks. She kept her captured arm rigid, her hand in a tight fist. "Let. Me. Go."

"What if I don't? You gonna shoot me?"

She tugged her arm against his strength. He cupped her nape with his free hand and hauled her against him. She looked into his eyes, her lips trembled. He couldn't help himself, he crushed his lips to hers.

The warmth and sweetness of her mouth gentled him and maybe her, too, because her lips parted and let his tongue slip into her mouth and play. God, he wanted her. He moved his hand to clasp her ass and press her pelvis against the ridge in his pants. When he had to breathe, he tore his mouth away and heaved for air. She, too, was breathless. "You'd better be careful," he said. "Nobody kisses like that who wants it to end there."

A torrent of emotions showed in her eyes—anger, fear, passion. He was positive he saw passion. "About that hangover," he said. "I may not be able to cure it, but I guaran-damn-tee you I can make you forget it."

Her face flushed. She pushed hard against his chest, her gaze locked on his. "Damn you," she said in a throaty whisper. "Turn me loose, you . . . rapist. Just get the hell off my property. Right now."

He backed away. "You're a handful, Alex McGregor. You're a handful. It's gonna happen between us and you're gonna love it as much as I will."

"You're dreaming." She marched to the deck stairs, the rubber waders chuffing and her perfect ass twitching in the tight jeans. A few treads up the stairs, she turned back. "You're as arrogant as someone else I know. Maybe you'd like to black an eye on the other side."

"You know better than that."

"What I know is your reputation. Just because I said something I shouldn't have, don't think I'm going to be another one of your bedroom statistics. I mean it. Leave me alone." She whirled and continued clumping up the stairs.

"And what statistics are those?" he called to her back. "You think I'm making marks on the wall by my bed?" She kept climbing. "If fucking you was all I wanted, I could have done it last night. All I had to do was send Butch Wilson down the road. I came to tell you I heard something you might like to know, something that might be important to you."

A few more steps. "The only meaningful thing you could tell me is that you're leaving town."

"Yeah? Well, how about this? Roads. Old military roads. But screw it. You're so goddamn smart, you can figure it out for yourself. When it's too damn late." He turned and strode toward his pickup.

She stopped at the top step and looked down at him. "All right, Mr. Hawkins. You have my attention. What about roads?"

"Across your land. A screwed-up survey and a land trade by the Forest Service. Get your buddy Culpepper to check it out."

"Wh-what do you mean, land trade?"

"A hundred and twenty of Miller's acres in exchange for Old Ridge Road."

"How do you know that? Who told you?"

"A reliable source." He climbed behind the Silverado's steering wheel and fired up the engine, then stuck his head out the window. "Don't call me Mr. Hawkins. Last night, we talked about fucking, babe. That makes us first-name friends."

He turned around in her driveway and began the rocky descent, watching her in his rearview mirror. Christ, that hadn't gone at all the way he wanted. He was amazed anew at what a gutsy broad she was. She never gave up. He could see how even Godzilla might come out the loser in this battle.

The feel and scent of her in close contact hung in his mind. If last night's episode hadn't erased the idea of seeking the company of some more ordinary woman, today's encounter killed it forever. There could be no other woman.

He stiffened his legs and rearranged his pants. She was still standing on the stairs when he lost sight of her.

He reached the highway and the choice of a left turn that would take him back to town or a right turn that would take him home. He thought of his commitment to Bob Culpepper, which made him think of Cindy Evans, which made him think of Miller. He glanced at his watch. Most likely, Cindy would be at work at the Eights & Aces. A slow weekday afternoon could be the best time to talk to her, especially since he had no desire to get trapped with her in a private place.

Alex refused to move until his pickup left her sight. Only when the rear of the vehicle sank below a rise in the road did she collect herself. She clumped to her gardening shed at the back of the house and peeled off her rubber boots. Then she padded barefoot to the kitchen. With trembling hands and perspiring brow, she filled a glass with ice cubes. She reached into the refrigerator for a Diet Coke, then concentrated on not allowing the liquid to boil out of the glass as she poured it over the ice. Just a small exercise in mind control.

She felt funny between her legs. Tingly and swollen and wet. Muscles up inside her flexed and made her shudder. Never in her life had she been kissed like that. Good Lord. He had put his tongue into her mouth and she had let him. What was worse, she enjoyed it. Her heart beat faster just thinking of it.

He was right. A part of her hadn't wanted things to end there. What had she started? She carried her drink to the sofa and sat back against the soft leather, closed her eyes and pressed the cold glass to her temple. Her head throbbed with every heartbeat.

Old military roads. Had Kenny discovered the old wagon trail, the extension of Old Ridge Road that crossed the back of her property? Would he try to claim the right to use it? And what could he be trading?

She couldn't concentrate on Kenny and the old road because her mind kept drifting back to Doug and his kiss and what he had said. *Was* something going to happen between them? Of course not. Sex had ceased to be a part of her life years ago. Still, how would it feel, his naked body against hers? How would his—she couldn't make herself say the word—how would *he* feel hard and swollen inside her? The sensation eluded her. Too many years had passed since . . .

She sat up abruptly. *Damn.* Liquor had fried her brain. She had too much to do to waste a minute on such thoughts. She rose and carried her glass to the dishwasher. She had to call Bob Culpepper and ask him what kind of land swap Kenny could be engineering with the Forest Service.

The cool, dark atmosphere inside the Eights & Aces belied the balmy day outside. Country-western twanged from the jukebox sitting on the corner of the unlit stage across the room. Doug gazed toward the horseshoe bar. Cindy looked busy cleaning and glancing at the soap opera play-ing on a TV parked at an angle on the end of the horse-shoe's back leg.

As Doug approached the bar, she looked up and gave him a once-over. He would have sworn her eyes landed on his belt buckle. He took a seat on a tall stool, glad the high bar stretched between them. "Whatcha doing?"

She threw her towel over her shoulder and planted a hand on her hip. Her ample endowments thrust against tiny buttons straining to hold a tight knit shirt together. "Clean-ing. That tell you how bored I am?"

Doug glanced at the stainless-steel bar deck and its re-flections of soft overhead lighting. In his youth, he had been responsible for cleaning in his brother's tavern, so he knew keeping the stainless glowing called for some dedica-tion.

"Where ya' been?" She returned to wiping off water spots and fingerprints. "I ain't seen you in a long time."

"Yes, you have. I was in here last night." Doug dug out his money clip and peeled off two dollar bills. "Draw me a Bud." He looked around, saw only a couple and a group of several at tables in the semidarkness near the expansive wooden dance floor. He turned his attention back to Cindy.

The corners of her lips twisted into a smirky smile. "Oh, yeah, I forgot. You're the one that hauled the Queen of Swede Creek out of here."

She reached into the freezer and pulled out a frosted glass, filled it from an oak tap, then bent forward in an ex-aggerated gesture and placed the glass in front of him. Mammary flesh threatened to spill from her shirt's V neck all over the bar top. "That was some black eye Kenny gave her. Everybody in town's talking about it."

"I don't doubt it."

She checked her nails, applied a liberal helping of strawberry-smelling lotion, then moved to the beer cooler. Out came a can of Coors Light. She brought it back to the bar deck, popped the top and gave him a grin that could only be labeled a leer. "Gonna buy me a beer?"

*Cheap enough.* Doug could see she was relaxed, maybe already had a couple. "Sure." He produced his money clip again and added two more dollars to the bar top.

"Long as somebody pays for it, the owner don't care." She picked up the towel and wiped away the wet ring left by the beer can. The slope of her breasts plumped with her arm movements.

"So what's everybody in town saying?" he asked, bringing her focus back to Miller and Alex.

She shrugged. "Surprised something didn't happen before."

"You know these people pretty well, don't you? Miller, Alex? Charles McGregor?"

"Yeah, I know 'em. Me and Charlie—well, it wasn't any secret about me and Charlie." She took a long pull from her beer.

"The talk is Miller's a friend of your family's."

"He used to live at our house when we was kids."

"You mean with your parents? How come?"

"Hell, he had to live somewhere. He couldn't stay at home. His daddy beat him up all time. Him and my oldest brother was always friends, so my mom let him move in with us. She treats him like one of her own kids."

"Hunh," Doug said, wondering what that fact said about Cindy's mother and brother.

"You didn't come in here just to talk about them—"

"Hey, I'm new in town and there's a lot of gossip." Doug sipped. "Just trying to keep all the players straight."

"Kenny's a good guy. He ain't real polished. He never did finish school, but hell, who did?"

"So let me see if I've got this right. Miller and Charles McGregor were friends, you and Miller are friends and you had something going on with Charlie. You guys were the Three Musketeers, huh?"

She frowned. "What does *that* mean?"

"Nothing. Just that the three of you were good friends. I even heard Miller has a thing for Alex."

"Well, yeah. But not as bad as he used to. If he ever got her, though, he'd wish he hadn't." She picked up a package of Marlboro Lights and a plastic lighter from beside the sink. "Hey, over there," she yelled across the room to the customers. "Anybody need a beer?"

A decline came back.

She sauntered around the end of the bar to where he sat and squeezed sideways between him and the neighboring empty stool. Her pelvis slid along his hip and the beast in his pants gave a twitch. "I don't know why Kenny'd want somebody like her. He's rich. He could have any woman around here."

She rested her palm on his thigh as she reached in front of him to retrieve an ashtray, engulfing him in the smell of strawberry lotion and cigarettes. "You think she really would've shot him?"

Doug didn't know the answer to that one, but he did know that many killings were crimes of passion and the incident in Carlton's fit the criteria. "Anybody's guess," he said.

"Why're you asking all these questions?" Her warm, soft breasts pushed against his biceps. If she came any closer she would be on his lap.

"Just making conversation."

"You lonesome or something?" Her eyes traveled down to his fly and back.

"Are you?"

"A little. Since Charlie's gone."

She pulled a cigarette from her pack and hung it from her lips. Doug hated cigarette smoke, but to hear what she had to say, he would endure. He picked up her lighter and clicked it. The tiny flame in the dim room spotlighted her heavy mascara as she drew on the cigarette.

"Yo, Cindy! Bring us two Black Velvet and waters." The call came from one of the customers seated at the table for two.

"Oh, hell," she said and slid off the stool. "Okay," she yelled back. She laid her smoke on an ashtray, ambled behind the bar and filled three glasses with ice. She deftly spurted shots of golden liquor from the bar well into two of the glasses and Doug smiled inwardly, recalling the bar business. Black Velvet wasn't the most expensive whiskey on the market, but it cost more than the brand most profit-minded bar owners served from the well.

Cindy grinned, pulled a bottle of Black Velvet from a shelf off the backbar and poured a shot and a half into the third glass. "I'm gonna have one, too." She giggled. "We charge extra for BV, but they're half drunk. They won't know the difference. Want one?"

Doug ground his teeth, fearing the interruption had closed a a window of opportunity. "No, thanks. Don't drink the hard stuff."

She set the Black Velvet and water she had poured for herself on a napkin at her place at the bar, then sashayed across the room, carrying the customers' drinks on a tray, her hips swinging with the gait of walking in high heels. She unloaded her tray and picked up empty cans on her way back to where he waited. To his relief, when she returned, she hiked a hip onto the stool and put a few inches of distance between them.

He forged ahead, hoping to recapture the stream of conversation that had been cut off. "Must not have been easy, losing Charlie like you did. You were with him when he died, huh?"

She finished off her beer, then squeezed the can together in the middle with a loud crack. Buying time to think about her answer, Doug figured. "I wasn't *with* him, but yeah, I was there."

"You must be the only one who knows what really happened."

"Yeah, well . . . it ain't something I talk about. I told Jim, but that's all. I had to tell *him* or he was gonna blame *me*."

"Does somebody need to be blamed? I thought it was an accident."

"Hell, yes, it was an accident." She sipped at her drink. "Hm, that hits the spot. You don't like whiskey?"

Doug grunted.

"Charlie did. That Charlie. I'll never forget him. He was real nice to me most of the time, but . . ." She pulled another cigarette from her pack and propped it between two fingers.

Doug picked up her lighter again and held it for her. "But what?"

"Sometimes he made me nervous. He was kind of—well, weird—about sex and stuff." She blew out a long stream of smoke. "Charlie liked watching. Maybe as much as he liked doing it. Does that make you hot, watching?"

Doug turned that information over in his mind. Did Alex know this about her ex-husband? He took a long sip from his glass to hide his surprise. "You mean watching you? With somebody else?"

"A lot of times that's the only way he could, you know, get it up."

"This is a real small town. Must not have been easy to find somebody willing to—"

"Oh, I know people." She faced him, her elbow resting on the padded bar edge, a short skirt baring her spread thighs nearly to her crotch. A mound of breast flesh and the black lacy edge of a bra showed only inches away on one side of her shirt's V neck. "I bet you don't have that problem, do you?"

"What was wrong with him? He drink too much?"

"That was part of it. Mostly he just liked weird shit.

Sometimes he wanted somebody watching *us*. You ever done that? Let somebody watch you, you know, do it?"

"Uh, no."

"You think it's weird? I always thought it was. I didn't like it much."

"Who was the watcher? Miller?" Doug managed to keep the question casual though anticipation of the answer kicked up his pulse. Cindy turned back to the bar and downed her drink in one long gulp. Doug angled his head, seeking eye contact. "Hey, look at me. Miller was the third person?"

Her head swung around to face him, her eyes wider than a deer caught in a spotlight. "No."

"Hey, you already started—"

"Oh, hell. . . . Sometimes he was."

"And you went for that? You said you didn't like it."

"What the hell am I gonna do? I been screwing with Kenny since I was—well, I don't know how old. He's like my brother. Not that I ever fucked my brother, but Kenny and me ain't blood related. You know what I mean?" She pulled out another cigarette and lit up again. "If you ever tell, I'll say you're lying. Kenny would beat the crap out of me if he knew I told somebody he was like that. Even my brother don't know it."

Smoke curled between them as Doug studied her. Miller was in the cabin the night of the fire. Doug had zero doubt. But when did he leave, where did he go and how the hell had McGregor wound up dead? Doug took the cigarette from between Cindy's fingers and crushed it out in the ashtray.

"Hey, what're you doing?"

"I'm doing you a favor. Ever hear of a guy named Jack Dunlap?"

"I dunno. Seems like a name I've heard."

"He's the state attorney general. Some people in his office wonder why the sheriff didn't do a better job investigating Charles McGregor's death."

"It was an accident," she blurted. "Jim said so."

"But you know different, don't you?"

She slid off the barstool and returned to the bottle of Black Velvet, poured a shot into her glass on the bar, then picked it up.

"Look, I'm not a cop anymore. What you say to me can't hurt you. I want to help you out of the mess you're in."

She tossed back the whiskey, grimacing at the burn. "It was what Jim said. The lantern turned over."

"You the one who helped it turn over?"

"No!" she said fiercely. "Me and him—what're you trying to say?"

"I'm telling you there are those who believe there was more to the cabin fire than a turned-over lantern. If you were McGregor's girlfriend, you must have cared about him—"

"He was messed up, but—" Her chin quivered. A tear crawled from the corner of her eye. She slashed it away with the back of her hand. "He was gonna get me out of here. He was gonna take me to California."

"Then he must have cared about you, too. If you had that kind of relationship and you had nothing to do with his death, don't you want the truth to come out?"

Her eyes met him, shiny and wet, but she said nothing.

"By the time Jack Dunlap's office finishes, there won't be any secrets anywhere and charges will land on all of you. I can help you buy yourself some points if you tell the right people what happened to McGregor."

She poured another drink. "I already told. Me and Charlie was having a good time. We got drunk. And we might've smoked a little. That's all."

"Then how'd the lantern get turned over?"

"Charlie fell and bumped it."

Even if Doug hadn't known it would take a major bump

to turn over the lantern, the lie was so apparent in her eyes, anyone could have detected it. "Know what a subpoena is?"

"No."

"It's a summons. If the attorney general opens an investigation, you'll be called. You'll have to tell the truth or face perjury charges. Then it'll be too late for me, or anybody, to help you."

"What're you talking about? Jim already said—"

"Take my word for it. Higgins isn't the final authority."

He could see a glimmer of fear in her eyes. *Bingo*. All at once she laughed a nervous titter and rolled her eyes. "Shit. I told those guys—"

The door swung open and half a dozen men burst in. "Hey, Cindy. Bring us a pitcher." They made their way to a table. She turned back to him, in control again. "It's happy hour. I gotta go to work."

*Fuck!* A pen lay on the bar. Doug picked it up, pulled her napkin close and wrote his phone number. "Time's running out. Use your head. Think about what I said." He reached for his money clip again and dropped a twenty on the bar. "That should cover those shots of Black Velvet."

Driving home, Doug organized his thoughts. If Cindy had told the sheriff how McGregor died and the death was something other than an accident, Doug couldn't even list all the charges that could be leveled against the man the county had elected to enforce the law. Cindy, at the least, could be charged with conspiracy and obstructing justice. Then there was Miller himself. Doug's gut told him the logger was involved in what happened to McGregor. The only unanswered questions were how and why.

# Chapter 21

Alex awoke Thursday morning in what her grandmother would have called "a state." She felt like a snare drum was tattooing inside her body. She hadn't been able to reach Bob Culpepper the previous afternoon to discuss the land trade and today, his assistant had told her, he would be in court all day. She worked at her computer and made phone calls. Patience wasn't one of her strong traits, so at midmorning she called Ted and grilled him about the trade.

"It's news to me, Alex," he said. "Land trades are done down in Boise. We never know about them up here 'til they're finished."

"Look, do me a favor. You have contacts in the Boise office. Pick a few brains for me. Find out anything you can."

"Sure, Alex. I guess I can try."

"Ted, don't you understand? I have to know if this is true. And if it is, I have to stop it. The first thing Kenny will do is build a road across Swede Creek. He'll either divert the water that feeds Granite Pond or shut it off altogether. He can do that, can't he?"

"In theory, I suppose—"

"Ted, if something happens to Swede Creek's flow, even for a short time, the waterfall will cease to exist. Granite

Pond would turn stagnant and dry up. My God, the grass and the beautiful ferns would die. The wildlife will stop coming to drink. And that's just the beginning. Besides me, doesn't anybody care about that?"

"Sure, Alex, but—"

"Then after the bastard destroys something that's ancient and beautiful, he'll drive off with his trucks and his money like nothing ever happened."

"Alex, you're getting awfully upset."

"Upset! I'm not upset, I'm hysterical! I'll tell you this much, Ted. Even if I don't own that old road, Granite Pond is still mine and I'll fight him 'til I die."

She hung up in Ted's ear, shaking with frustration. She could think of no one who would know the details of the trade—that is, no one except the man who had told her about it.

*Damn.*

After yesterday, did she dare call him? Would she be able to talk to him without thinking about—

Would she be able to even look at him without picturing—

Her checks warmed as naughty images flitted through her head. *Stop this,* she told herself. In truth, despite her nastiness to him, and despite the fact that all he thought about was sex, he had showed her true friendship more than once.

She marched to the kitchen, picked up her purse and keys and headed for the Wrangler.

Doug was just finishing a shower when he heard a rap on the front door. He picked up his Levi's cutoffs from the bathroom floor and pulled them on, then grabbed the shirt he had left on the back of the living room sofa after he finished his run. Opening the door, he met Alex.

"Hello," he said, trying not to show astonishment. He didn't know why she had come to his house, but after yesterday, she had to have one helluva good reason.

Her eyes roved down and up his body "I-I'm sorry." She stepped back and started to turn. Shit. His lack of clothing had embarrassed her, but it was too late now. He grabbed her wrist. "Wait, Alex. Come in." He pulled her into his living room, then shrugged into his shirt.

He could see she was uptight and tense. She looked around, no doubt taking in the construction mess, the bare, newly taped Sheetrock walls and his NordicTrack, weights and weight bench that half filled his living room. Compared to her house, his place was a shanty. He made an open-palmed arc around the room. "You caught me at a bad time. Everything's under construction."

She faced him, but he couldn't see her eyes behind the dark lenses of her sunglasses. "Yesterday, you said something about Kenny trading for Old Ridge Road. I have to know about it."

Ah, her reason for coming. He shrugged a shoulder. "I don't know any more than what I said. Something about a mistake in a survey and a land trade between Miller and the Forest Service for that old road behind your house."

She was shaken. He knew that if he could see her eyes, they would be boring into him. "You want to sit down?" he asked her.

"No. Where did you hear about it?"

"Butch Wilson told me Tuesday night. He heard Miller tell somebody who works in the sawmill office."

She buckled and sank to the wide sofa arm, her purse still hooked over her shoulder. He gave her a squint-eyed look, unable to determine if a new crisis had developed or if the trade was a continuation of an old one. "Why do I get the idea you already know all about it?"

"Not *all* about it." Her shoulders sagged.

Recovered from the surprise at her visit, he walked over to her and gently removed her sunglasses, then slid her purse off her shoulder. She didn't even resist. "Tell me about it." He set her purse and sunglasses on the half wall that separated the kitchen from the living room. "It sounds like a big burden for one woman to carry."

He reached for her wrist again, led her around the sofa arm and urged her to sit down. "How about something to drink? I don't have any tea, but I've got some Pepsi, some Gatorade."

She sat on the edge of the sofa cushion, her elbows resting on her knees. "That's just what I need. A double shot of a power drink."

He couldn't keep from grinning. He would be worried if she didn't have a sharp comeback. "Want it on the rocks?"

"No. I don't want anything to drink." She stared into the blackened opening of his rock fireplace. "You know, I almost wish you hadn't stopped me from shooting Kenny."

"No, you don't." He sat down beside her. "You'd be in jail"—he ran his finger down her spine—"and I'd never get the chance to make love to you." He didn't know why he said that, unless he had already crossed over to the assumption that the day would come.

She shrugged away the gesture. "Just drop that. You aren't going to get the chance anyway."

He leaned forward, too, his bare knee touching her denim-covered one. "Yeah, I know. Now, tell me what's got you rattled."

"I feel so damn stupid." She pressed the tips of her fingers against her forehead. "It's my fault for ignoring it. I should have done something back when I could have."

She stood up and walked around his coffee table. He stayed seated, waiting for her to confess the mistake she thought she had made.

"You remember me showing you Old Ridge Road that day we went up to Granite Pond?"

He remembered more than that, like the sweetness of her mouth and the warmth of her body pressed to his. And that she had run away from him like he might hurt her in some way. "Yep."

She began to pace. "Well, it travels on up the mountain. It stops at my back fence, then runs along the back line of my property, a strip of land about twenty feet wide." She stopped and looked at him. "Remember me telling you about the army campsite in Soldier Meadows?"

"Yep. I remember that, too." He laced his fingers behind his neck, watching her.

"Back then, the strip of land was a road that went to the campsite. You can see the tracks even now. When Charlie and I got the divorce and I was given the Idaho property, I got a stack of old documents that were sort of the history of the property." She came back to the sofa and sat down on the edge of the cushion, as if she were poised to bolt. He had started to learn the edginess was a natural state for her. "Where Charlie got them in the first place," she went on, "I don't know, but some of them were copies of old field notes from the original survey. I was reading through them one day and found where the government surveyor had written the description of the army's road in 1870.

"I was blown away because Idaho wasn't even a state then. I researched and learned the government started surveying soon after the Civil War. By 1870 my property had already been claimed, so the government laid out the road on adjacent unclaimed property."

Doug loved true historical tales. He sat forward, his interest piqued. "Wow. Wonder what the army was doing camped in that spot?"

"I don't know. The Sioux were all around this valley then and mining was going on. Maybe the army was protecting miners. Anyway, the government resurveyed in 1947 and found errors. Their corrections put the road on what's now my property. The people who owned the property then had it under fence and contested the survey. They fought with the Forest Service for years. I couldn't find any record where the ownership was ever determined."

She got to her feet and started pacing again. "Then a few

years ago, the government made more corrections in township corners in this area and the road ended up on Forest Service land. I didn't even know it until I did the research. But it's still inside my fence, which hasn't been moved in well over fifty years."

The light went on in Doug's head. "So you're saying the Forest Service land that's inside your fence is what they're trading to Miller?"

"I'm not sure yet, but I think so. And I don't know how to stop it."

All that Doug had heard about Miller paying for the right to use the road came back to him. "Why would Miller pay your ex-husband to use a road you and he didn't even own?"

"I suspect Kenny thought it would be easier and cheaper to just buy it and be done with it rather than start a row that would call for lawyers and court."

"Can't Culpepper help you? Or Ted? How about Ted?"

"Ted doesn't know about it. I've never told him. I guess I hoped if I kept quiet nobody would ever make an issue of the fence or the road. It's not like a flood of people ever go up there. I haven't even been there myself in over two years. My hikes usually end at the glade and Granite Pond.

"I knew it was a problem when Kenny bought the property, but I was still married to Charlie then and my concentration was too fractured to think about it. I suspect nothing would have changed if Kenny hadn't decided to log. One thing loggers do is research property records before they start cutting trees. It's lawsuit city if they cut timber off the wrong piece of real estate or drive where they aren't allow to and so on."

"I don't get it. Isn't there some kind of rule that if something's been a certain way for a long time it stays that way?"

"Sometimes that applies to private property, but not to government-owned land. I've had experience confronting the Forest Service and the BLM over unclear boundaries. The government always wins."

"Always?" It was an empty question. He knew the answer.

"Always."

Doug shook his head, more confused than he wanted to reveal. "So where does all of this leave you?"

She released a heavy breath. "I'm waiting for Bob to tell me. He hasn't returned my call." She walked toward her purse. "I have to go. I was hoping you knew more details." She picked up her sunglasses and hung her purse on her shoulder. "I came here for another reason, too. I've been thinking about how you didn't have to get involved in this, but you did. Kenny's a terrible person. Now you'll be on his list. I'm sorry."

Doug felt like tugging on his ear to make sure he had heard right. All that Bob Culpepper, then Cindy, had told him rushed into his memory. He stood, too, walked to her and he smiled, hoping to reassure her. "Hey, he's not the first bad guy I ever met."

She smiled, too, and wiped the corner of one eye with her fingertip. *Tears?* "No, I'm sure he isn't," she said. "I should add, I'm sorry I've been mean to you."

For some reason he didn't like hearing her apologize. He clasped her elbow and urged her toward the kitchen. "I'll bet you didn't eat breakfast, so how about some lunch? I've got some fresh ham. Believe it or not, they stock Boar's Head at Fielder's."

"You're really into food, aren't you? Why don't you weigh three hundred pounds?"

He flashed her a grin. "I work hard." He steered her to a chair at his antique round oak table and took her purse and sunglasses away from her again. "Now, you sit right here while I make a couple of gourmet sandwiches."

Alex took a seat on an oak straight-backed chair and looked around. His house had an open, airy feeling she liked and it smelled of freshly taped Sheetrock. It was also very neat and spotlessly clean, even with construction debris stacked here and there.

He began to gather sandwich fixings from the refrigerator. Indeed, she hadn't eaten since lunch yesterday and she was hungry. He was obviously at home in a kitchen, even where the cabinets were wooden boxes with plywood laid across them for countertops. "This is temporary," he said of the cabinets, as if she didn't know. "I'm buying new cabinets from Home Depot."

He hadn't buttoned the shirt he put on, so a long strip of his chest and flat hairy stomach was exposed. He didn't seem to be embarrassed by his scant clothing and she had to admit she didn't mind looking at him. Besides being long and lean, he was tanned to golden and beautiful.

"This is a small house," he was saying when her mind came back to the conversation. "It's the only one I've ever owned. In L.A. I lived in apartments 'til I bought a condo, which wasn't much different from an apartment."

"Where did you live?"

"Santa Monica. Not too far from the ocean. Want your bread toasted?" He turned and gave her a frontal view of his body.

She took full advantage of the sight. His torso showed well-defined muscles and dark hair that trailed down his flat stomach in a whorl and into the waistband of his cutoffs. His maleness leaped out and clutched her and she found herself wondering if he had on underwear under those cutoffs. "Uh, it isn't necessary."

While he spread mayonnaise on slices of sourdough, he launched an explanation of the changes he had made in his house and those he had slated for the future. "I'm gonna add a couple of rooms soon, one for the exercise equipment"—he gestured toward the NordicTrack—"and a master bedroom and bath."

She sensed a shyness about him, like maybe he wanted

her approval, and it reminded her of a little boy. "It looks like it'll be wonderful when you're finished."

She hadn't been in the house when the Stewarts owned it, but she remembered the family. "The Stewarts used to farm. I thought there were several hundred acres here. I thought all of it was for sale."

"Three hundred twenty acres, but who needs all that land? I bought just twenty acres. The rest of it's still on the market." He brought two thick sandwiches to the table, then pulled ice trays from the freezer and broke out ice cubes.

"You should always buy land if you can."

He took two cans from the refrigerator and poured Pepsi over the ice. "Good financial advice, huh?"

She smiled, unable to recall all the land she had bought and sold over the course of her real estate career. The profits had indeed made her well off. As they sat across the table eating, she sensed Doug Hawkins was a steady man, comfortable with who he was, calm and assured he was usually right. Nothing like Charlie, who had spent his life hanging from the roof by his fingertips. She wondered how it would be to routinely share meals with a man like Doug. It wasn't a serious thought, really, just something to pass the time it took to chew.

Finished with her sandwich, she sat back. "That was great. Thank you. But I really do have to go."

She stood up and he did, too. He came around to her and took her hand. "I wish I knew more," he said, rubbing the top of her hand with his thumb.

She liked her hand in his and didn't pull it away. She looked up into his incredible serious silver eyes. "I'll get to the bottom of it. I probably already know most of it. I just have to figure out a strategy. This is what I get for trying to be sneaky. If I had tried to deal with all of this back when I first found out about the survey error, I wouldn't be faced with disaster now."

"You're not alone, Alex. Don't ever think you are."

She let herself smile at that. She had always been alone, in every fight she had ever waged. At this moment, she couldn't find it in herself to worry about it because she could see his lips parting and she knew he was going to kiss her.

She could describe his mouth on hers only as delicious. He tasted of mayonnaise and fresh bread and ham. And goodness—something she had never tasted on a man's lips. He didn't push, didn't press, just gently molded her mouth to his and easily played with her tongue. She felt his hands move to cradle her face and he lifted his lips from hers. "I'm in so much trouble," he said gruffly.

"I-I should go," she said, her voice nearly a squeak.

"Yeah. You'd better." He released her but held her gaze as he slid one hand all the way down her arm to the tip of her little finger.

She walked over to the half wall and retrieved her sunglasses and purse. He followed her to the front door. Part of her didn't want to leave him, so she stopped before leaving. "What does this mean, what we just did?"

"You don't know?"

"I'm not very experienced at this. I don't mind telling you, you scare me."

# Chapter 22

At her desk in her office, Alex keyed on the SPEAKER button to answer the phone's insistent warble and heard Bob Culpepper's voice.

They exchanged small talk before the lawyer broached the land trade. Alex had already given his assistant the few details she knew. "I've made a few phone calls," he said, "and done a little research. Here's the bad news."

A nervous titter escaped her throat. Sitting down at her desk, she picked up the receiver. "Okay, let me have it."

"The trade is near completion. A hundred twenty acres off Miller's north side in Soldier Meadows for the no-man's-land strip across your back boundary line."

Alex almost stopped breathing. It was one thing for a disaster to be under speculation, but another to hear about it officially. Her mind raced in all directions. "Then, we-we have to get to the Forest Service. I know they can't protect Granite Pond, but they won't want Swede Creek to be damaged."

"If Miller doesn't stop the creek's flow altogether, the government may be ambivalent about collateral damage from building a road across it. I'm waiting for a call from them. It's my understanding they like Miller's deal because it squares up their boundary abutting his property on the west side. When it's done, the disputed boundary will be firmly established."

"And he-he'll own the access to his timber." Alex hung on to the receiver white-knuckled, as if she could squeeze a positive answer from it. "There's legitimate environmental issues. Radical groups have stopped countless logging jobs. Some Eskimos in Alaska stopped road construction northeast of Sterling Mountain on the risk of pollution to the Big Salmon and they don't even live in Idaho. All they did was write a letter to the right people and a big logging job has been on hiatus ever since."

"That was on public lands, Alex, not private property. This isn't California. Here, the courts have a healthy respect for ownership rights. And you've told me many times, so do you. Besides, do you really want to start a firestorm in the community where you own a business and are making your permanent home? It might be different if you could be sure you'd win, but—"

"Okay, okay. I get the point."

"I've already presented a brief to Judge Cobb making the environmental argument. It'll be a week or two before we hear, but I don't expect him to rule in our favor. Look at Callister. Half the community is unemployed. The same is true of most of the neighboring towns. Logging's too important to the economy in that part of the state."

She fought back tears. "Dammit, Bob, why didn't this come up when Charlie and I bought this property ten years ago, or when we sold the five sections to Kenny? Why hasn't it ever shown up in a title report?"

"I don't know, but that's another matter. Did you have it resurveyed when Miller bought the five sections?"

"No. We used a metes-and-bounds description. I knew this meandering road problem was hanging out there, but when it wasn't mentioned anywhere, I assumed the Forest Service had resolved it in our favor." She heaped recrimination on herself. A woman who had been in the real estate business fifteen years should know better than to assume *anything*.

"Lesson learned," the lawyer replied. "It won't hurt my pride if you check everything out for yourself."

"I don't need to check it out. I trust what you say."

"You'll be down Tuesday, right?"

Dollar signs raced through Alex's mind at such a velocity she could hardly compute them, the value of her home and surrounding property flying out the window.

And Granite Pond. An ancient, irreplaceable wonder of exquisite beauty was on the brink of disappearing forever.

Bob's voice seemed far away.

"What? I didn't hear you. What did you say?"

"The twenty-seventh. Next Tuesday. The fund-raiser for Ralph Cumley, remember? You're supposed to make contact with Hayes Winfield. Ed and Martha Anderson, remember them?"

"Yes, of course I do. Yes, I'll be there." Alex paged through her desk planner, studying her schedule. "You know, Bob, I should leave here a day earlier so we can sit down and talk face-to-face. I can be in your office after lunch on Monday." She scratched a note into her planner and returned to the pending disaster. "What are the chances of getting some help from your friend Senator Cumley on this? As hot as everything environmental is, he should want to jump in with both feet."

"We can discuss it with him, but bear in mind Miller's got some influence, too. Sizeable campaign contributions, you know."

"Crap. Well, I'll see you Monday afternoon."

"Right. See you then."

As Alex hung up, her thoughts collided, trying to sort out the news she had just heard and its consequences. She flipped through her phone index, landing on *M*. Kenny's phone number glared up at her from the middle of the page. She wanted to punch in his number and rail at him, call him names and threaten him with doom, but she stopped herself. She had already made one colossal error. She would play her cards close to her vest until she could see everything on paper with her own eyes. Sometimes lawyers made mistakes.

Three days had passed since kissing Alex had left an imprint on Doug's psyche as distinct and permanent as the scars on his chest. Even a weekend of nonstop sports on TV hadn't distracted him. He couldn't stop thinking about her. He stayed busy during the daylight hours on various construction projects, but kept his nightly vigil checking her mountainside for lights.

Every part of him had wanted to follow her away from his house last Thursday. At the same time, he knew better than to do it. She needed time to come to terms with what was happening between them. He hoped she would come back or call him, but it hadn't happened yet.

He hadn't seen or heard from Ted since the exchange between them in the Forest Service office on Wednesday. He was heartsick. Ted was more like his family than his older brother was. At erratic intervals between texturing Sheetrock and watching sports on TV, Doug debated what to do about their suddenly uncertain friendship. He had turned the problem over in his mind so many times, he could no longer remember who owed whom an apology.

He was on his knees repairing his fence in the morning sunshine when a green Forest Service pickup drove into his driveway. Ted. Doug stood up, waiting for his old pal to alight and walk over to the fence. Ted's usual light-hearted mien was absent. He put out his right hand in stony silence. Their eyes connected and Doug gripped his hand firmly.

Patches of color appeared on Ted's cheeks. "Got a cup of coffee?"

Doug felt embarrassed himself, but what the hell? He and Ted had shared too much to let things they never should have said come between them now. "You bet."

Inside the kitchen, Ted looked around. "Boy, this place is looking great."

"I'm accomplishing a lot." Doug poured steaming coffee into a heavy mug and handed it to Ted. "Have a chair."

Ted took the cup and sank to a chair at the oak table in the kitchen. "Can't stay long."

"I'm glad to see you. I appreciate your coming out."

"Got any sugar?"

Doug turned to his makeshift cupboard, lifted out a sugar bowl and set it on the table.

Ted scooped out a spoonful and dumped it into his mug. "We've known each other a long time. So I figured I'd come out and tell you a story."

"Shoot." Doug poured coffee for himself.

"When I went to work for the Forest Service"—Ted paused and sipped from his mug—"my first assignment was over in Oregon in the high desert. One time I found a coyote pup. It was pitiful, all starved and beat-up. I don't know what happened to its mama, but it would've died if I'd left it. Turned out to be a little female. I wanted to make her a pet. I thought, hell, why not? They're just like dogs, right?"

"I guess so."

"I named her Misty. Built a pen and took care of her. Doctored her, fed her every day. Lord, I even had the vet give her shots. She gentled down, let me pet her, got to where she would play with me. I damn near forgot she was a wild animal."

"What are you getting at, Ted?"

"Let me finish." He took another sip from his mug.

"The longer I had her around, the more fascinated I got with her wildness. She was always on the defensive. I never knew when she was gonna bite a chunk out of me. No matter how well I took care of her, there was always that glassy fear in her eyes like she was waiting for me to hurt her. It's that thing nature gives 'em, that instinct to survive."

A shiver passed over Doug as he recognized the analogy in Ted's story. The parallel to Alex was right on the money.

"I knew I oughtta let her go," Ted said, "but it was a long time before I gave up and turned her loose."

Doug studied the bottom of his empty cup. "And your point?"

Ted's eyes raised to his. "Alex has got that coyotey look to her, Doug. I'm saying she's a damaged soul and she's a survivor. It's a bad combination. Awful hard on the people who live around her and try to care about her."

Doug snickered, though he wasn't amused. He closed his eyes and massaged them with his thumb and forefinger. "Who the hell needs a coyotey woman?"

Ted snorted and stood up, went to the coffeepot and refilled his cup. "Hell, Doug, none of us *needs* one, but when were *you* ever hot for any other kind? Even when we were kids, you always took up with the one who had parents that beat hell out of her or more problems than any teenage kid oughtta have. Those poor little girls you rejected, the ones who didn't have anything going for 'em except good looks, normal personalities and cute asses? I used to feel sorry for 'em. They didn't have a clue what it took to capture your interest."

It was true. Though the few women Doug had called friends over the years—mostly cops—were strong, tough people, the one he had married and the ones with whom he'd had affairs were just the opposite. He sighed and rubbed the back of his neck, then rose and went to the coffeepot. "I'm different now," he said, keeping his tone even and pouring another mug. "I'd like to be with some-body who's ordinary, plain ordinary."

"Well, Alex McGregor ain't it. Of all the labels I might hang on her, plain or ordinary ain't one of 'em."

Doug gave a self-deprecating chuckle. "I don't know if I've ever known a woman who's tougher than I am."

"That's what keeps your head screwed up. She is and she isn't. You look at her and you think any woman who's that soft and girl-like is bound to be so helpless she needs you to slay dragons for her. Then she'll come up with something that shows you helpless is the last thing she is and you'll never have any real influence on anything she does."

Doug sighed mentally. "*That's* the truth."

"Knowing it doesn't keep her from worming right into your guts. Those eyes, that centerfold body haunting you at night. She's pushing you away the whole time, but sometimes she'll do or say something that makes you think she'd be lost without you. So you can't leave her alone. She's like a damn narcotic."

"So? Are you warning me to keep my hands off Alex McGregor?"

"Just trying to pass on something I know that maybe you don't. Friend to friend." Ted stood up and strode to the sink, tossed the remainder of his coffee down the drain and set his empty mug in the sink. He started for the door, speaking as he went. "I gotta go to Boise tomor-row on Forest Service business. Want to ride down with me?"

"Maybe I will. I can deliver my bill to Bob Culpep-per."

Ted stopped. "Culpepper? Alex's lawyer? What're you doing for *him*?"

"Jury consulting."

"I'll be damned. Small world. Well . . . meet me at
seven at the office."

"Right."

As he watched Ted drive away, Doug felt a renewed
and profound respect for his old friend, who was wiser
than he had given him credit for.

# Chapter 23

Alex arrived in Bob Culpepper's office at one o'clock, an hour earlier than scheduled. She'd had all weekend to stew over the land trade. She paced in his assistant's office until being admitted to an oak-furnished conference room.

She met Bob in the middle of the room. They hugged and she kissed the air beside his cheek. Survey maps and field notes lay in a neat line down the long conference table. She studied them, going from map to map, document to document.

She took the end seat at the conference table as if it were her own and folded her arms on the tabletop. "Let's get right to it, Bob. What's our strategy?"

The lawyer took a chair to her right. "I see the damage to the creek and pond as our only strong point, though even that's a long shot. Like I told you on the phone, I doubt if Judge Cobb will be sympathetic."

She chewed on the inside of her lip. "When is the trade scheduled to be final?"

"Could be anytime. Needless to say, Miller's pushing to start logging ASAP. The paperwork is pretty far along. If everything fell into place, he could start in the next week or two. We might cause a delay by calling for an environmental study."

"I've had that done before. The result was a storm of confusion, but let's do it anyway. I feel better knowing we're doing something. You know me. I can't stand to sit on my thumbs." She rose and walked along the length of the table, examining the maps and documents again.

Bob removed his heavy-framed glasses and leaned back in his chair. "If you and Charles had known this might occur, you probably wouldn't have sold off the five sections and put yourself in this position."

She huffed a humorless laugh. "Guess again. Charlie knew Kenny intended to log. Deep down, so did I. What other reason could he have for buying the property? But at the time of the sale, it was too much trouble to fight with Charlie over it."

"There's something else you should know, Alex." The lawyer looked up at her with a grim expression. Ominous music began to play in her mind. "Miller's sued for the right to use your driveway to get to Old Ridge Road and ultimately to the old army road that will take him to his own property."

Alex felt her brow crunch into a painful frown. "What? That's *my* private property. He can't do that."

Bob left his chair and came to her side in front of a large map of Wolf Mountain. He replaced his glasses and traced a curved line with his finger beginning at the county road with which her driveway intersected and going uphill to Old Ridge Road. Just as she had feared all along, the route ran roughly three hundred feet from her front door, then along Old Ridge Road a mile behind her house. She wanted to scream, pound the tabletop with her fists.

"Your driveway's the only road that's ever been carved out of Wolf Mountain. Believe it or not, Miller's using the environmental impact argument as a reason he should be given the right to drive on it."

Alex's stomach began to shake as a picture of logging trucks driving past her front door, then circling behind her house rumbled through her head. "Bullshit. He couldn't care less about environmental issues." She battled tears. "With this survey error surfacing and his suit, I suppose the injunction we filed is worthless?"

"Not entirely. It addresses our environmental concerns."

"I guess I need to tell you something I did, in case it comes up before this is over. You know when Kenny hit me? I threatened him with a gun." Alex kept her eyes lowered and drew a circle on the tabletop with her fingernail. "I lost my head for a minute. One of Ted's friends, Doug Hawkins, probably kept me from pulling the trigger."

Bob opened his mouth to speak, but she raised her palm and shook her head, not letting him have the chance. "Don't give me the lecture about carrying the gun and all that. What am I supposed to do? If I hadn't had the pistol that night in the bar, he might have really hurt me."

Bob sat in silence for a few beats, then shook his head. She couldn't read his thoughts or his body language, but for some reason, he didn't make his usual speech about going to the attorney general. Puzzling.

"When Higgins is up for reelection," she added, "I believe he'll be defeated. I'm planning to donate quite a lot to helping his opposition."

"But Alex, the problem goes further than the sheriff. If Higgins is under Miller's thumb, do you think a new sheriff won't soon be, too? The population of Callister County is under three thousand people. Do you really believe there's a citizen up there who isn't influenced or affected in some way by Miller? Money and brutality make a heavy hammer. And what about Charlie? I still think we should—"

"No, Bob. Charlie was a tortured soul in a death spiral. I saw and accepted that fact long before catastrophe happened. The only thing surprising was the time and place. He's buried now and this is probably the first time ever he's been at peace. I want to let him stay that way. I'd rather concentrate on trying to save my home and the creek and pond."

The lawyer sighed and raised his palms, surrendering the debate. "And what if his death, the sheriff, the logging— what if all of it turns out to be one and same problem?"

She dredged up an insincere smile. "Offhand, I'd say that's one of those bridges we cross when we get there." She picked up her purse. "Guess we've covered it,"

The lawyer began gathering the documents and maps into stacks and rolls. "You mentioned Doug Hawkins. He's doing some work for us on a case we've got coming to trial."

"Oh?"

"He's a hell of a good man. It's too bad what happened to him in California."

"You mean his getting shot?"

"The whole thing. When you were down there, didn't you hear about it? It was on the news for months, all over the country."

"You mean John Bascomb's kid? I heard the talk, but who pays attention?" She huffed a humorless laugh. "I work for a living, remember?"

"There was more than the teenager's death. Three cops were killed—two ATF agents and another LAPD detective. Doug was fired, driven out of town, you might say. You didn't know that?"

"It was quite a while back, as I recall. I remember the boy because I have a passing acquaintance with that nut, John Bascomb. I've butted heads with him once at a city council meeting. I must have forgotten about the cops."

"We feel fortunate to have Doug working with us. It's not easy to find somebody with his qualifications. . . . So, Alex, after Miller hit you, you didn't have any pictures made, did you?"

"I don't keep a photo album, Bob." She was still mulling

over the plight of her home and property. "Dammit, I can't win this, can I?"

The lawyer looked down at the table. "I don't know."

"You mean no." She heaved a sigh. "Of course, I do have an ace in the hole. I could always marry the bastard. Then I could poison his food."

"Who? What do you mean?"

Alex mustered a smile and kissed her friend and lawyer's cheek. "See you tomorrow at cocktails, Bob. I'm ready for Hayes Winfield."

She left Bob Culpepper's office with weight in her chest and time on her hands. Her emotions hovered in a chasm of depression that threatened to drag her to the bottom if she didn't find something positive to think about.

As if on automatic, the positive thought her mind drifted to was Doug Hawkins. She couldn't forget the strength and comfort of his arms around her. If he were in front of her right now, she would fall into his embrace and let him soothe her as he had done before.

Then there was the fact that he wanted to sleep with her. And maybe, as far-fetched as the notion seemed, maybe she wanted to sleep with him. Nothing had erased the memory of his hungry mouth and the fire his kisses built inside her. A thought of him sneaked in every day from some remote place and caused her to lose her train of thought, sometimes in midsentence.

Bob's remarks about him had aroused her curiosity. Though she hadn't had time to research his past while in Southern California, she had time now. And the library was within walking distance. She set out in that direction.

"So that's where I am," Doug said to Bob Culpepper after updating him on the meeting with Cindy. He had just pocketed a hefty check from Henderson, Crowe & Culpepper for services rendered. "I'm hoping she'll feel pressured and call me. If I don't hear from her soon, I'll try something else."

The lawyer nodded. "I've already talked to Jack Dunlap about the situation. He wants to turn it over to the state police in Meridian."

"Meridian?"

"Callister falls in Region Three. Meridian is where the headquarters is located."

"State cops, huh?"

"Yes. They have detectives." Bob laughed. "Idaho isn't like Los Angeles. We have a small population and not much capital crime, comparatively speaking. The state cops handle most of it."

"Cool," Doug said, liking the idea of a dearth of murder and mayhem. "Give me another few days to see what happens with Cindy. By the way, I heard the Forest Service might be making some kind of swap involving an old military road on Alex's property. Is that possible?"

Bob Culpepper slumped against the tall back of a tan leather chair. "When it comes to real estate owned by the feds, anything they want to do is possible. They make all kinds of trades as long as they don't lose any real estate. It's an even hundred-twenty-acre swap. I'm under the impression it hasn't been made public. How did you find out?"

"One of Miller's employees. So what happens now?"

"Alex is screwed."

"Does she know it?"

The lawyer nodded. "It's a disappointment, but we're dealing with it. Say, I just learned we have another friend in common."

"We do?"

"Ralph Cumley. He tells me he knows you from years back."

"I'll be damned. I haven't seen Ralph in years. Since I

worked narcotics and he headed up an antidrug commit-
tee."

"My wife and I are having a little benefit on his behalf
later this afternoon. Reelection time. You might like to drop
in and say hello—"

"May I interrupt?" A female face poked through the
doorway. A slender blonde entered the office. "Edith told
me I'd find an attractive single man in here."

Culpepper drew her to his side. "Doug, this is my wife,
Angela. Something tells me you're about to be tagged for
cocktails with the senator."

"Jacket and tie," Angela said, looking him over.

Doug laughed, looking down at his khakis and knit polo
and slip-on shoes. "Afraid I'm out of luck."

She placed her hands on his shoulders and turned him
around. "Hmm, I think one of Bob's jackets would be too
small. I'll be right back."

Culpepper chuckled as she breezed out the door. "Once
my wife's mind is made up, it's hard to change it."

Mrs. Culpepper hustled back into the room waving a
business card, which she thrust into his hand. "Here's an
address. Bob's assistant is making arrangements for you to
pick up a jacket and tie. Oh, and a shirt if you need one."

"Hey, really, I appreciate it, but even if I get dressed up, I
still can't make it. As much as I'd like to see Ralph, I don't
have wheels. I rode down here with a friend from Callister
who's going back right away."

"Oh, that's no problem. We have another guest from Callister who's going back tomorrow. I'm sure you can get a
ride. I'll arrange it and introduce you at cocktails. We're
gathering in a banquet room at the Evergreen Inn. Just get a
room upstairs and sleep over." She placed a slender hand
on Bob's forearm. "Honey, let Doug borrow your car to go
pick up a jacket."

Culpepper dug into his pants pocket and pulled out keys.
Before Doug could protest, Angela hurried him out the

door, describing where he could find Culpepper's Mercedes.

He left the law firm suspecting—no, *knowing*—that Alex was the Callister resident who would be present at the political event and the person who would be driving him home. The opportunity of spending time with her in the close quarters of an automobile pleased him even more than renewing his acquaintance with Senator Cumley. Meeting Ted in front of the building, he told him he was going to hang out overnight for a fund-raiser for an old friend and that he had a ride home.

He found Culpepper's car parked in a covered garage below street level. Once he had picked up the clothing, he rented a room at the Evergreen Inn. He scarcely had time to shower, shave and dress before he was due to put in an appearance at the party upstairs.

Alex hated cocktail parties. She was bored half an hour after she arrived. She hated the dress she had on. She had bought it to wear to something in L.A. There, it was typical attire; in Boise, it was a costume. Even the music irritated her—bad pop plinking from a grand piano in the far corner of the meeting room, made worse by the hollow echo of poor acoustics.

The reason for her attendance at this shindig was nowhere to be seen. She hadn't met Hayes Winfield, but had seen his pictures many times. She scanned the crowd of a hundred or so for a mane of white hair and there, across the room, she saw . . . *Doug Hawkins.*

She felt a dull thud in her stomach and swore under her breath. Angela hadn't told her who needed a ride back to Callister, but now she knew. Doug was the passenger whom she had agreed to shuttle. They had parted on good terms a few days earlier. She didn't like having him learn what she was up to tonight.

The ruggedness synonymous with his jeans and knit

shirts was just as evident in dress clothing. His shoulders seemed even broader in a structured jacket and his loose-fitting khakis hid what tight-fitting jeans didn't. Scolding herself for her naughty thoughts, she found an inconspicuous corner and turned her back so he wouldn't see her.

Before long, Angela found her and dragged Doug over. "Alex, this is the gentleman without transportation I spoke of earlier. Doug Hawkins." Angela clung to Doug's arm and looked up at him with fluttering lashes. "This is Alex McGregor. She's being kind enough to let you ride back to Callister with her."

Alex forced a smile. "We've, er, met."

"Oh. Well, that's wonderful." Angela gushed and fluttered more. "You won't have to waste time getting acquainted."

Alex shot her a flat look, then swerved her attention to Doug. His eyes roved over her appreciatively, all the way to her toes, and she knew he was taking in every square inch of her dress—or lack of it. She felt as if her nipples had peaked and she resisted an urge to look down. "Uh, where are you staying, er . . . Mr. Hawkins?"

Doug's eyes came back to hers and drilled her. "I'm in this hotel."

"Good. That's good. I'll be leaving at eight—*promptly* at eight. I'll meet you in front of the elevators. I have an appointment and I do not want to be late."

He grinned, his even white teeth contrasting against his tanned face. "Ma'am, I'm at your mercy. All I ask is that you don't hurt me."

He was smirking. He was laughing at her, *laughing* at her discomfort while his eyes undressed her. A young woman wearing a tiny dress—maybe she was fourteen—appeared and placed a dainty hand with multiringed fingers on Doug's forearm. "There you are," she said. "I've been wondering where you disappeared to."

Doug's silvery gaze focused on Alex as he covered the

young woman's hand with his. *Well, on closer examination, she might be fifteen.* Alex gave him a wry smile. He winked, then traipsed off with the sixteen-year-old.

Angela gave a little gasp of delight. "What was that all about? Was he flirting with you?"

Alex rolled her eyes. "Where is Hayes, Angela?"

"I saw him come in a few minutes ago. He didn't bring his wife, which is a little upsetting. Without her here to ride herd on him, nothing in skirts is safe from the old lecher."

"I want to make an appointment with him for tomorrow morning. Let's go find him."

"You mean you don't have an appointment already? But you just told Doug—"

"Just because I don't have one now doesn't mean I won't by the time this soiree is over." Angela's expression contorted into one of worry. "Don't worry, Angela. Mr. Hawkins will get home."

"I envy you. I'd like to take him home myself."

"He's spoken for," Alex shocked herself by saying.

# Chapter 24

Doug watched Alex and Angela Culpepper approach a knot of laughing guests across the room. He had seen her dressed mostly in casual clothes and a business suit once, but never like she was tonight. Except for her arms and shoulders and a hemline extending no more than a few inches below immodesty, black slinky knit fabric smoothed over her body like Saran Wrap. Nothing, yet everything, was left to the imagination.

Even the throat-high neckline was a tease because when she turned her back, he could see she was bare to the waist. The substantial amount of visible skin was luminous, the color of honey. He saw no sign of a tan line anywhere, which sent an erotic thought slinking to his groin.

Her utter femaleness was like a living thing, elemental and dangerous. He tried to avert his eyes, but they defied his will and moved to her long legs, covered by sheer black stockings stretching down to black spiky heels.

In the group and giving her his undivided attention was a short but solidly built middle-aged man with a florid complexion, intensified by overstyled white hair. He held a drink and a large cigar in the same hand.

When Alex moved, the old guy's eyes shifted between her breasts and the hem of her dress. His right hand in a

way meant to be casual, moved to rest on her hip. She made
no attempt to move his hand, nor did she seem put off by
where it was. The hand remained until someone else joined
the group and required the man's handshake.

What was she doing here dressed like a hooker with a
diamond-covered old fart rubbing her ass and drooling over
her tits? She shouldn't be throwing herself at somebody
like she was doing. Doug wanted to grab her by the arm,
yank her out of the room and tell her to go home and put on
some clothes. He had seen nightgowns less revealing.

He watched as she left the white-haired man's group. She
wandered through the room as if she were lost. She stopped
at the windows that looked out over Boise. He picked up
two glasses of champagne from the bar and moved to
where she stood with her back to him. He touched her bare
back with his finger. "Do you dare?"

She turned to look at him, almost eye-to-eye in high
heels. She splayed her hand across her chest and caught her
breath as if she was startled. The diamond earrings he had
seen her wear before glinted from her earlobes. Her
makeup didn't quite hide the fading yellow bruise beneath
her eye, but most people wouldn't notice, much less wonder about it. But then, who would look at her eye when so
much of the rest of her could be seen?

He offered her one of the flutes of champagne. She lowered her eyes, hesitated a few seconds, then took it.

He looked up and down her willowy form. "Wow. Look
at you."

A wary look cut from the corner of her eye.

"Gives a whole new meaning to the, uh, *little* . . . black
dress." He didn't try to hide the edge in his voice. "No need
to ask if you're packing heat. I can see there's no place to
hide something as bulky as a .357."

"What are you doing here, anyway?"

He stuffed a hand into his pocket. "The senator and I go

way back. And I'm the token charming single guy, babe. No cocktail party is successful without at least one."

She laughed and flung back her hair. It fell past her shoulders like a shimmering golden waterfall. Her arm crossed her midriff, making a rest for her elbow as she held her champagne glass. A flirty gesture if he had ever seen one.

"Then why are you wasting your time on me? You should be charming someone who needs it."

He winked. "I am, dumplin'. I am."

"Dumpling?"

"And what are you doing here? Besides picking up horny old rich guys?"

A smile almost broke across her face, but she caught herself before it happened. "This is business."

"Now there's an interesting proposition. No pun intended. The last time I saw somebody doing *business* in a dress like yours, she was on a street corner in Hollywood."

"Humph. Don't make fun of me. Something important is at stake here."

"Other than the taxpayers' pocketbooks, what could possibly be at stake at a function like this?"

"A nice commission." Then she added a serious afterthought. "And a beautiful old apple orchard on a hillside. It'll soon be replaced with a subdivision full of second-rate houses marketed as dream homes."

"You're confusing me, which is nothing new. Are you fer it or agin it?"

"In principle, I'm against turning agricultural lands into subdivisions, but that's beside the point. Principle has never paid a single bill for me. I intend to sell it to Hayes Winfield and be paid well for doing it."

He couldn't keep from chuckling. "Miss Pragmatic. By all means, don't let lofty ideals get in the way of fast money."

"One thing I never do, Mr. Hawkins, is let reality get

cluttered by immaterial idealism. If my refusing to sell it
would change anything, I'd refuse, but if I don't sell it,
someone else will." She looked at him with her usual penetrating gaze. "I don't know how much you know about
being a real estate broker, but it probably has something in
common with being a cop."

There she was, with that Mr. Hawkins crap again, but intrigued by the riddle in her last remark, he withheld a caustic comeback. "In what way?"

She looked at him with her usual penetrating gaze. "I
don't know how much you know about being a real estate
broker, but it probably has something in common with
being a cop."

There she was, with that Mr. Hawkins crap again, but intrigued by the riddle in her last remark, he withheld a caustic comeback. "In what way?"

"After you do it for a while, there are no more lofty
ideals. And there's not much faith left in human nature either. The difference is I deal in greed instead of crime."

Doug chuckled. "Most of the time, it's not easy to separate the two."

She turned her attention back to the room and looked out
over the guests.

"At least your black eye's almost unnoticeable now. I
suspect you can get by without explaining it to these politicians' wives. I doubt if they'd understand a gunfight in a
saloon."

"I don't waste my time trying to explain anything to
politicians' wives."

With a hawk's eye, she watched a group across the room
and the same white-haired guest he'd seen her with earlier.
He could almost see a calculator working behind her eyes.
"The red-faced old bastard who had his hand on your ass, is
that Hayes Winfield?"

"Where he had his hand is none of your business."

"Does he know he's in your crosshairs? And why him?"

"He's a developer with cash. And lots of it."

The green-eyed monster's sizz elevated to a roar in Doug's ear. He riveted his eyes on hers. "In that dress you ought to be able to sell him the Brooklyn Bridge."

"Cute. What am I going to have to do to get this nonsense to stop?"

"I've told you what it's going to take for me to be a good boy. What was it you called it that day in your driveway— an 'indiscriminate roll in the hay'? I'm guessing one night in your bed would turn me into a regular lapdog."

Her mouth clenched tight. "If I thought it would make you leave me alone, I might just do it."

She took a step away, but he stepped forward and grasped her arm, bringing her up short and turning her back to face him. He pulled her close, close enough to feel her heat, drink in her scent, see the tiny twitch of her rigid jaw. He leaned forward and brushed her ear with his lips. "Don't tell me you haven't been thinking about it."

Her head jerked up. Daggers flew from her eyes. "I'll tell you this much. If this is your idea of a seduction, it has failed miserably."

He held her gaze, determined to be the stronger one, but he relaxed his hold on her arm and took a sip of champagne, chuckling softly. "I wonder if Winfield can tell what he's in for. You'd better be careful. You'll give that old man a heart attack."

"It's called salesmanship, Mr. Hawkins. Bear in mind, there's all kinds of marketing. And I'm a pro."

She turned and sashayed across the room with her loose-hipped gait. And all he could do was stand there and wonder just what was she wearing, or not wearing, under that dress.

Well before midnight the party began to wind down. Guests straggled away. Some, including Alex's only reason for being present, were a little drunk. A few, more than a little.

She found an out-of-the-way spot near the door, poised for the opportunity to say good night and escape. She had been anxious to leave from the moment she made contact and secured an appointment with Hayes.

Now, as she leaned against the wall and watched the shrinking crowd, she saw Doug Hawkins talking to the senator across the room. His hair appeared to be darker in the banquet room's dim light. It looked messy and sexy, as it always did. Why couldn't he be ugly?

She couldn't keep herself from watching the good-looking fool. Young women had hung around him all evening, swooning over his every word. Older women fell all over him, too. She had seen at least two business cards transfer from manicured female fingers to his jacket pocket.

Well, what did she care? She had been mistaken, letting down her guard last Thursday.

He turned away from the senator and headed her way. The man walked with a swagger, his hands shoved into his pants pockets, pushing back his jacket, comfortable with who he was. She could feel his eyes touching her every-where and she crossed her arms over her chest.

He joined her against the wall, placing his shoulder beside hers. "I don't suppose you'd be willing to kiss and make up."

*Ha!* She smiled. "No. I wouldn't."

"I suppose that means I'll have to catch another ride."

"It isn't necessary. I'm one of the good guys. I wouldn't leave a flea-bitten dog stranded. We don't have to talk to ride down the road together."

"Since there's no public transportation back to Callister, I appreciate that."

She kept silent.

"I suppose it wouldn't make any difference if I said I was out of line earlier."

"Yes, you were. Why would you be so obnoxious?"

He blew out a breath. "Aw, hell, Alex . . ." He turned and braced a hand against the wall. "I might as well say it. I think I'm in pretty deep here. I'm not handling it very well. Go somewhere with me, supper, a drink. Away from here. I'll be a gentleman. I do know how."

The latter she believed and she was tempted, but tomorrow's mission came before anything else.

"Please?" he added.

"I can't. I need to get to bed. Tomorrow I have to be alert and on my toes."

"What's so important about tomorrow?"

"I have to get a signature on a contract. I expect it to be difficult. Not getting the signature, but enduring the process."

"Whatever that means. Breakfast, then? We could meet in the lobby."

"I'm really letting you off the hook, but I guess we could do that. On one condition."

"Which is?"

"We call a truce and cut out the insults."

He chuckled. "We can do that. But damn, how will we communicate if we can't insult each other?"

"You're entirely too smart-aleck for your own good."

She moved toward the door and he followed. They strolled through the empty lobby without talking. When they reached the elevators, he asked her which floor. She told him, he punched the UP button and stood back. The car rose with a purr. Though they were the only passengers, they stood side by side against the back wall, arms touching as they watched the progress of the lighted numbers above the steel doors.

He loosened his tie and stripped it off, pushed it into his pocket and undid his collar button. Seeing him do something so personal sent a tremble through her stomach and she thought of the unplanned intimate moments they had

shared—her seeing him with his fly undone at Granite
Pond, his helping her out of her shirt in her bathroom, her
seeing him scantily clothed in his living room. Still, watching him remove his necktie almost seemed more intimate.
"You don't like ties?"

The corners of his mouth tipped up in a smile. "Haven't
worn one since I was last in court."

The car landed at her floor and the doors glided open.
When she stepped out into the hall, he followed. Her heart
made a little bump. "You don't have to escort me. I can find
my own way."

"But why should you?"

At her room, she turned to say good night. He leaned
down, his hands cupped her face and his mouth covered
hers. It was a gentle kiss, his agile mouth shaping her lips
to his. It left no doubt of his desire, but there was more. She
tasted the loneliness and need of a man who had spent the
whole of his life alone, as she had. Her lips parted and welcomed him. His tongue came in and her arms slid up
around his shoulders. A keening sound came from him as
his big body pushed hers against the doorjamb. He bent his
knees and fitted his rigid organ against the notch of her
thighs and a thrill of awareness crawled through her. She
had an insane urge to reach between them and wrap her
hand around his erection.

His mouth dragged to her ear, his breath heavy and warm
against it. "Invite me in," he whispered gruffly.

"No, I—"

"Sh-shh. Say yes." His gaze came back to her eyes, and
if she had wanted to look away she couldn't have. "I
promise, I'm not selfish in bed."

Her heartbeat had gone from slightly bumping to thun-
dering in her ear. She shifted, but found herself trapped
within the heat of his closeness. "I—I should tell you something."

"I'm listening." His warm lips brushed beside her nose,

the corner of her eye. His fingers played with the button at her nape, the only fastener holding her dress in place.

She felt dizzy and hot in places she usually didn't notice. "It's—it's about sex."

"Oh, yeah." His hand slid down and covered her breast and she shuddered with a sensation she didn't want to end. His tongue flicked at the corner of her mouth and she could swear her knees weakened. "I haven't had sex in . . . in about eight years is my guess."

He stopped kissing her and frowned into her eyes. "Say that again?"

"I knew that would cool your jets."

Seconds passed while their gazes held. "Didn't work," he said softly and kissed her again.

His warm palm covered her bottom and pulled her against him, but she squeezed her arms between them and pushed him away. "I'm going in. I have to be ready for my meeting tomorrow. I don't want to be distracted."

His hand braced against the door facing. He looked rumpled and sexy and altogether appealing. "Is that a no? Or a later?"

"I don't know." And she didn't.

He leaned forward and placed an openmouthed kiss beneath her ear. "I'm taking your word about the importance of tomorrow, but my jets aren't cooled." He turned the doorknob, pushed open her door. "Damn, I want you. I hate to leave you."

"Doug, I—"

He caught her arm, gently nudged her inside. "No more talk. I'll live." He placed another gentle kiss on her lips. "Lock your door. Sleep tight. And don't forget the old Chinese proverb. I've saved you. You belong to me."

He pulled the door shut and left her standing alone in her room.

"Oh my God," she mumbled and threw her purse into her suitcase.

# Chapter 25

Doug waited in the hotel lobby with the *Los Angeles Times* and a Styrofoam cup of coffee bitter and black enough to match his mood. Through the night he had stripped Alex out of that black dress a dozen times. He felt as if he had been hard all night.

Then, while busting his ass to be in the lobby by eight, he cut himself shaving with hotel soap and a throwaway razor he had bought in the gift shop. Now *she* was fifteen minutes late. He glanced up every time the elevator landed. As he rose to refill his cup, the doors glided open and there she stood.

His heart did a back flip. Her hair was pinned up in a knot at her crown. She wore a purple-looking suit and gray high heels. The skirt struck her at mid knee, a sharp contrast to last night's costume. And an improvement. The suit, no doubt, had a designer label. Her jewelry was understated but elegant. The Sama sunglasses covered her eyes. She looked every inch the woman in charge as she rolled her suitcase off the elevator and took command of the lobby.

He placed his empty cup on a lamp table beside his chair and stood, folding his newspaper and tucking it under his arm.

"I'm in a hurry," she said. "My appointment's at ten. Let's grab something in the coffee shop."

"Nice outfit. You look good in purple."

"Thanks. It's mauve."

"We're certainly short this morning. Bad dreams?"

"Don't you dare start pestering me."

She led the way to a counter in the coffee shop and ordered hot tea with milk and a bagel. For the sake of expediency, he abstained from his usual he-man breakfast and ordered toast and coffee. She ate without removing her sunglasses.

Before he could reach for his wallet, she paid the waitress for both their meals, stood up and headed for the door. He had no choice but to tag along behind her to what looked like a brand-new silver Acura SUV.

"Great wheels," he said, folding into the contoured passenger seat. "This must have cost you a commission or two."

She ignored him, drumming long ruby fingernails on the steering wheel while she waited for an opportunity to move into the busy morning traffic.

She maneuvered through the double lanes of cars for a distance, then pulled into a suburban strip center made up of one long line of nondescript offices. They crawled along as she read addresses. She turned abruptly into a parking space and stopped with a lurch and a squeak of tires. On a plate-glass door directly in front of them, painted in an arch of gold letters, was WINFIELD HOMES, INC.

She switched off the ignition and rested her elbows on the steering wheel, then rolled her shoulders several times, closed her eyes, hooded them with her hands and took deep rhythmic breaths. Was she doing some kind of meditation routine? Doug kept his silence.

When she raised her head, she gave him a heart-stopping smile. "Showtime," she said and reached for a portfolio lying on the backseat. Holding it close to her breast, she angled her head toward him. "Go in with me?"

"I'll just wait here and take a nap." He slid down into the comfortable bucket seat and closed his eyes.

"Please? I'd really appreciate it."

Sincerity rang in her voice and curiosity leaped into his head. Without opening his eyes, he arched his eyebrows. "Why?"

"Because if you're with me, he won't have his hands all over me and I'll get out of there faster."

After spending a miserable night, Doug had a low bullshit quotient, but he opened his door and stepped out. "I don't know why, but I'm gonna do this. Consider it payment for the ride home."

"Forget it. I don't need your help. I'm sorry I asked. You've ruined my concentration." She slammed the door, pivoted on her left foot and stepped onto the sidewalk in front of Winfield's office.

He took a long stride behind her and gripped her upper arm. The momentum of his propelling them through the front door brought them to an abrupt stop in front of a receptionist. Alex's arm jerked from his grip and she threw him a poisonous look. The young blond receptionist greeted them with a shiny crimson smile and ushered them into Winfield's office.

The old fart rounded the desk as they entered. Alex introduced Doug as her associate. Winfield shook his hand and spoke to him, after which Doug felt dismissed. Curiosity at what he had let himself in for overrode his frustration and he took a seat on an out-of-the-way sofa parked against the wall.

All of Winfield's attention gushed on Alex. "Darlin', I'm so glad you had the time to stop by. It's hard to do business when everybody's having a good time."

*Or when everybody's drunk,* Doug thought.

Winfield put a huge arm around Alex's shoulders. "I didn't

know until last night you were Ed Anderson's agent. Why, if I'd known, I would have contacted you before I talked to him."

Alex unbuttoned her suit jacket. A lacy, body-hugging top peeked from underneath. It was beige, almost the color of her skin. "His attention is on caring for his wife, Hayes. He didn't feel he could spare the time and energy to negotiate. Mrs. Anderson is dying of cancer, you know."

"Isn't it a sad thing?" Hayes placed his hand under Alex's elbow and guided her to a chair in front of his desk. She sat. "Folks who've spent their lives at hard work sacrificing their home to pay doctors and hospitals." Doug rolled his eyes and leaned back, cocked an ankle across his knee. Winfield returned to his desk chair. His leer darted between Alex's chest and her crossed knees. Doug wished he had waited in the car.

"I know how busy you are, Hayes." Alex unzipped her portfolio and lifted out a single page. "To save time I took the liberty of preparing a letter of intent." She slid the page across the desk.

Winfield fixed his half-glasses on his nose and read. His florid complexion changed from faint to vivid. "Why, darlin',"—he looked over the top of his glasses—"I think you misunderstood. This isn't the price Anderson and I discussed. Why, this is quite a lot more."

"Oohh, it is? He didn't tell me you and he had discussed a price." Her words sounded as saccharine as Winfield's. Doug could swear that what had been a subtle hint of the South in her voice became a full-fledged Southern drawl. "My market analysis determined the property can sell for even more than this letter of intent states."

Winfield sniffed and stared at the page. He looked more than a little pissed.

"Ed Anderson isn't a greedy guy, Hayes. He just wants a reasonable and . . . *fair* price."

"Well, darlin', I don't know if I'm a buyer at this price."

The old bastard shook his head and sighed. "There are so many expenses to development. You know that. And risk. We don't ever know what we're going to run into when we take equipment in and start work. And then there's all the regulation these days. By the time we satisfy the government agencies, I'll be paying interest for months before I can turn a spade. I feel sorry for the Andersons, but—"

"Oh, I know you do, Hayes, and I certainly don't blame you if you don't feel you can swing this one." She propped her elbow on the back of her chair. Her suit jacket slipped up and back at the same time, exposing one lace-covered breast.

She reached for the letter, pulled it back to her side of the desk and continued in a honeyed voice. "I hope you don't think I'm trying to pressure you to do something you don't want to, Hayes. If this project isn't for you, that's okay. I'm in contact with someone in Portland—"

"Portland?" Winfield's large hand smoothed down his jaw.

"Yes. Perry Morris. Morris Homes? Do you know him?"

"I don't believe we've met."

"Oh, you'll have to meet him. He's such a strong, imaginative developer. I've done a lot of business with him, so I've seen what he can do with a beautiful piece of land like the Andersons'. Perry will have great ideas for creating green areas and preserving the natural landscape. Maybe even a private park dedicated to the city later. Believe me, Boise will be impressed."

Winfield's gaze lingered on Alex's breasts. His face grew even redder and Doug's fuse grew shorter. "He's accustomed to the high cost of dirt in Portland," Alex added, "so he won't have any trouble with Anderson's price. I've already found a lender, so that speeds things along."

Winfield pulled the letter back and reread it, growling and clearing his throat repeatedly. Alex shifted her knees, her jacket hanging open. Doug expected to see sweat break out on Winfield's brow any minute.

She stood up in front of his desk, a pose that placed her lap wrinkles in Winfield's direct line of sight. The only thing that kept Doug seated was the fact that Winfield's stare finally left her wrinkles and traveled up to her face.

The developer glanced Doug's way and Doug did his best to keep his expression impassive. Then Winfield opened his center drawer and removed a pen, giving Alex a reptilian smile. "Well, now, we don't want Portland land men coming in here, do we?" He signed the document with a grand gesture, called the receptionist and instructed her to make copies.

Doug wanted to expel a breath of relief. For a minute, he had feared Winfield wouldn't sign. The old lecher came around the end of the desk and put his hand under Alex's arm, his knuckles nudging her breast. "You know, darlin', when I saw you last night at Bob's party, I wondered why you were there. Now I know, don't I? I wonder if I've been given a fast shuffle."

"Don't be silly, Hayes. Bob and Angela have been friends of mine for a long time. They always invite me when they have a party. It was just a wonderful coincidence running into you there."

The receptionist met them with copies as they walked out of Winfield's office. Alex turned and shook hands with him. "I'll follow up with a contract, Hayes. I can't wait to see your development. I know we'll all be proud of it."

Back in the car, she heaved a deep sigh. "Well, thank God that's done." Doug could see she was talking more to herself than to him. She backed out of the parking space and wheeled into the traffic. "I've been tied in knots over this one. If I hadn't gotten involved, that crook would have screwed Ed Anderson to the wall."

She stopped the car on the side of the road beyond sight of Winfield's office and let it idle on the shoulder while she dug a cell phone and planner from her satchel. She flipped through pages, keyed in a number and made an appointment to stop by somewhere in an hour.

Doug had been simmering since the exhibition—and exhibition was the only word for it—in Winfield's office. "Is that the way you handle all your business deals?" He knew he sounded like a self-righteous fool, but he didn't know any other way to express how he felt.

"Not always." She pulled back onto the pavement. "Never, actually."

"He had you naked thirty seconds after you set foot in his office and you planned it that way. You teased him. Today was a continuation of last night."

She slammed on the brake, bringing the SUV to a screeching halt on the side of the road and causing them both to lunge forward. "What is wrong with you? When did any of this become your business?"

"When you dragged me into it. I watched you, Alex. You were doing a number on that guy last night at the party. Why didn't you just screw him then?"

Her lower lip trembled. "Don't accuse me of that. I wouldn't do that."

He couldn't tear his eyes away from her lace-covered breasts showing from beneath her suit jacket. "And you gave me that celibacy act when I made an honest pass at you. Shit. I had a hard-on all night."

She shifted gears and killed the engine then propped her elbow on the steering wheel and turned to face him. "I don't know why I should explain anything to you, but I'm going to."

He gave her a wary look, waiting for the arm twist.

"I go out of my way to earn my pay. Just as you probably did when you were policing, I sometimes do things I hate because I judge them to be necessary."

He harrumphed. "I'd like to meet your client and tell him how far out of your way you went for him last night. And today."

"Don't say that. And if you really want to meet him, you can, in about twenty minutes. The people I'm representing are elderly. This is a desperate situation for them. They need all they can get from the sale of their property to pay their bills and to live. I promised Bob Culpepper I would help them.

"Since Ed Anderson had already started a dialogue with Hayes, it made the most sense to go after the bird in hand. Otherwise I would have had to start from scratch looking for another buyer. If I hadn't wrapped things up fast, I'd have been letting Bob down as well as the Andersons. I had to get Hayes's signature before he cooled off."

"One thing's for damn sure. He wasn't going to cool off looking at you."

"Where do you get off making cynical remarks about anything I do? I'm not the one with the reputation of a satyr. It was a business decision. I could have waltzed around in a conventional way with somebody like Hayes for weeks or months before accomplishing what I did in the past twenty-four hours. I've been studying him since I got the listing from the Andersons. I know how affected he is by attractive women. I can't help it if he's a dirty old man. I determined that the fastest way to get it done was to . . . well, to . . ."

"To make him think he was going to get a little of the great Alex McGregor?"

"No! It would never have gone that far. I didn't make him any promises. But if I would have, so what? Is he any different from you? You've been undressing me with your eyes since we met and you're trying to get me into bed with you. None of it concerns you. Why do you even care?"

"Because—" Because why? He knew what he felt, but he couldn't imagine it rolling off his tongue. An intangible current passed between their eyes. He returned to staring out the window, seeing nothing. "Cover up your tits. I'm not impressed. And I *don't* care. You're right. It doesn't concern me."

"Then why are we arguing?"

"You're slick, Alex, I'll say that for you. Pretty slick. Somehow you've turned this around so I feel like I've done something I need to apologize for."

"You don't have to apologize," she said softly. "Look, I'm a hard worker. I don't want you to think I achieve success because of—well, because I earned it any way except through honest effort."

He turned to her. "I could ask you the same question you just asked me. Why do you care what I think?"

Seconds of silence passed as she stared at him. "I *don't* care what you think," she snapped. "I'm just tired of arguing with you." She shifted back to a driving position and cranked the ignition. "Look, it's a three-hour drive. Can we please just cool it 'til we can part company?"

In silence, they sped along a country road into the foothills outside Boise, past rolling orchards and farmhouses. Soon she pulled into the driveway of a twenties-vintage home. An old man met her on the front porch. She handed him a copy of the letter she had brought from Winfield's office. The shriveled-up old guy broke into tears and wiped his eyes.

Doug sat in the car watching and listening to their conversation. Only a first-class ass with no feelings wouldn't have been touched by the tenderness with which she treated the elderly man.

Doug's anger began to sneak away. He knew only two things. His head was a mess and his heart was in serious trouble.

# Chapter 26

"This is the last decent place to eat lunch between Boise and Callister," Alex said, pulling up to a gas pump at a truck stop outside Boise.

They hadn't talked since arguing earlier. She needed gas and intended to eat lunch. If he didn't want to join her, he could sit in the SUV and wait. She should have left him in the SUV when she went into Hayes's office and avoided the quarrel altogether.

It went without saying that a man as stubborn as Doug Hawkins wouldn't appreciate her effort to get Hayes's signature. Still, a perverse part of her wanted to bask in his jealousy. Having a man feel possessive about her was a new experience.

She popped open her gasoline cap and slid out of the Acura. Doug appeared at her side and took the gas nozzle from her hand. "Women don't pump gas when I'm around."

She smiled inwardly at the attitude, but appreciated his doing it. Her DKNY suit wouldn't recover from grease or gasoline stains. "Thank you," she said and smiled. "Meet you inside?"

He smiled, too. "I'll be there."

And just like that, the argument went away. Inside, before he came in, she paid for the gas and eliminated the op-

portunity for another squabble. She waited for him before
ordering lunch. She had grilled chicken, but he asked for a
caveman-style lunch of chicken-fried steak, mashed potatoes with gravy and rolls. As they ate, she chatted about the
real estate business, in which he showed enough interest to
ask relevant questions. She queried him about jury consulting because she had never known anyone who did it.

When they finished lunch, he insisted on buying; so did
she. They settled on splitting the check. But they laughed.

As they left the restaurant, a blanket of fatigue fell
around her. Tension had kept her rigid since Friday and the
earlier episode dealing with Hayes had drained her. "I don't
suppose you'd be interested in driving," she said.

He grinned. "I'd prefer it."

Sure, he would. Superman wouldn't be content riding as a
passenger with a woman driving. She gave him a bland look
and handed him the keys. "Knock yourself out." She seated
herself on the passenger side. A gesture of peacemaking, she
told him, but in truth, being relieved of the two-and-a-half-
hour drive suited her fine. He shoved on his aviator sunglasses and assumed the role of pilot as if he weren't even
surprised to be asked.

As he drove, she settled into the warm welcome of the
gray leather passenger seat, watching the landscape whiz by
and letting stress drift away. She thought about the day coming soon when she would no longer participate in charades
like the one in which she had been involved for the past
twenty-four hours, when she would quit selling real estate
and survival would no longer be a daily clash of wits.

"Car drives nice," he said. "I like it."

"Hm. I think I do, too."

"You traded that red Cadillac in on it?"

"No. The Cadillac is . . . was Charlie's car. My partner
has a buyer for it, but I'm still hassling getting the title
cleared up. Red tape."

"Ah."

The message in his reply made her laugh. "You thought that car was mine?" She laughed again.

"Okay, okay. How would I have known any different? So, did you have fun at the party?"

"I enjoyed meeting Senator Cumley. Parties like that one aren't my thing, but I go to them when necessary. In my business, networking's important. And don't say anything about my dress. Did you have fun?"

"Visiting with Ralph was good, but I'd rather camp out in the mountains."

She laughed. "Me, too."

His head turned toward her. "Really?"

She couldn't see his eyes behind his sunglasses, but she heard the surprise in the question. "You seemed to have a good time. You made some new friends. You were surrounded by people all evening . . . well, women." She winced as she said it. Now he would think her jealous.

"I met a few new people . . . .Women. Nobody I'll be calling."

Damn. He *did* think she was jealous. "Perhaps you should. If you're going to live here, you should get to know people."

"I'm trying to get to know *you*. And you're hardly one to advise somebody to get to know people."

"Oh, no you don't. We aren't going to talk about me."

"What else is there?"

"There's you. You could tell me the truth of why you came to Callister."

Doug's heart made a little thump as all he had gained with Alex came into jeopardy. Truth. He wasn't sure of the truth himself. He remembered only that he had left Southern California like a captive raptor that had been freed to return to the wild. "Simple fact. To start over."

"That may be a fact, but I've found that facts and truth are often different."

She was too damn smart. He wanted her trust, so he

pumped up his courage and opened Pandora's box. "What do you want to know?"

"I spent a few hours in the Boise library, reading old newspapers and—"

"You did what?" He flicked a glance away from the highway, in her direction. *Shit.* He wanted to yank off his sunglasses and chew on them. That she might dig into his California past shouldn't surprise him. Still, he hadn't expected it.

"I'd appreciate it if you'd watch the road. I don't want me, you or my new SUV to land at the bottom of one of these canyons. You know, I remember when John Bascomb's son was killed. I know him and I know Los Angeles politics. I believe the DA was grandstanding when he brought a manslaughter charge against you. A waste of taxpayer money considering he never had a chance of a conviction."

Doug couldn't stop a bitter snort as those agonizing days came back to him. The Acura's leather bucket seat felt like quicksand, sucking him down to a place he desperately didn't want to go. "That's what my lawyer said, but when you've been indicted and your fate is in the hands of a bunch of lawyers and the court system . . . take my word for it, it's a scary place to be."

"According to the newspapers, you're used to scary places. I read one story where you talked home invaders out of murdering a whole family."

Oh, yeah. He remembered those lunatic losers. Three days and nights of terror for dozens of people. "What kind of a library were you in?"

"Wasn't that true? Didn't you do that?"

"But I had control of that one. It's different when you're in control."

"What I didn't learn from my reading is why John Bascomb hated you so much. You were doing your job and his son's criminal activities weren't new news. He went after you hard, so there must have been another reason."

The woman whose vehicle he drove would see through a lie as if it were cellophane. He didn't have to be a genius to know a misstep at this moment would annihilate any possibility of a future relationship with her. On a wing and a prayer, he stepped to the edge of a sheer drop, gripped the steering wheel tightly and gave her an answer. "I had an affair with Bascomb's wife."

Silence for long seconds while he could hear his heartbeat. She broke it first, with an insincere laugh. "Well, that explains some things."

The SUV seemed colder. "I knew better," he said. "Suffice to say, I kick myself daily."

"I hope you found it worth what it cost you."

"Not for a minute."

"I've always been amazed at what men will risk for sex."

"Hey, did you want me to lie? I made a mistake and I can't undo it. I've paid, big time. But I'm not gonna kill myself. The best I can do is live with it and try to avoid bad judgment in the future."

And none of that was a lie. No day went by that he didn't think of some part of the ordeal and regret most of his actions. When she had no comment, he added a footnote. "Obviously you've never done something that haunted your every minute."

Her head turned away and she stared out the passenger window. "In truth, I—" Her voice faltered. "Everyone makes mistakes. Let's move on."

Doug was grateful. He didn't know what either her words or her body language meant, but maybe she had a secret that went deep. In any event, moving on was fine with him.

A frank, honest answer wasn't what Alex had expected. As much as the gory details of his life and his affair with a married woman might interest her, to delve into it would be an obscene invasion of his privacy. Beyond that, was she prepared to be as honest about her own closeted skeletons as he had been about his? In a word, no.

Doug reached across the console and took her hand. "Alex, I'm not proud of what I left behind in L.A., but if there's an upside, it changed my life, changed who I am."

"I can see where it would have." She moved her hand and crossed her arms under her breasts. "According to the papers, people all over the country thought you were a hero. You had a fan club."

"That was part of the insanity. Unfortunately, the fan club didn't pay my lawyer. The legal fees bankrupted me."

"I'm sure."

"It's all settled now, but there was a time when I didn't know if it ever would be. To answer the question you're *really* getting at, the manslaughter charges were dropped and the lawsuits are settled except for mine against the City of Los Angeles. Possibly I'll get my pension back if I live long enough. The bankruptcy's been discharged. Now I'm just broke."

"But you bought Stewart's place."

"Framing houses. Thank God my right arm wasn't injured. When I was able, I went back to swinging a hammer. When I first moved to Southern California, that's how I made a living. And I sold my condo for a nice price. An ocean view is worth a lot."

"Sounds like you're clean as a whistle."

"I am. So now I'm helping out guys like Culpepper." He reached across the console and placed his hand on her knee. She didn't move it. "And trying to figure out the most intriguing woman I've ever met."

And how many women had heard *that* line? Still, she respected, even envied, the ease with which he admitted mistakes. She had never been able to be so open.

Soon they saw Callister on the horizon. Kenny Miller and his logging plans barged into her thoughts. "I think I've lost the battle for Wolf Mountain. In a few weeks logging equipment and trucks will be traveling past my front door."

"You're not gonna try to stop him?"

"Short of shooting him, I can't stop him." She sighed, giving up. "But Bob keeps trying."

"So what happens next?"

"If Kenny's trucks are driving past my house day after day, I can't live there. Logging that much timber will take years. He offered me five hundred thousand dollars for the house once. Maybe I'll just sell it to him and look for somewhere else to live."

"Sounds like you'd be losing a lot of money."

Alex had never tallied what her obsession with her house and Callister had cost her in dollars and cents, didn't want to know. "Yes, but there's nothing new about that in Callister."

"Come live with me. You like to fix up old houses. Help me fix up mine. I've still got years of work to do."

She looked his way and saw his smirky grin. Of course, he was kidding, but for a silly minute she thought the suggestion wasn't such an outrageous idea. Perhaps sharing quarters with Doug Hawkins wouldn't be half bad. He was a glib-tongued, entertaining companion, he had proved he would protect her and she couldn't keep from wondering how it would feel to share days with a man so—she hated using the word—macho.

Or to share nights with a capable lover. She had no doubt he was a capable lover. She laughed, abandoning outrageous musings. "I'm hardly an ideal roommate. I'm selfish. I want everything my way."

"We all want things our way. It's the way we are. So how long before Miller starts cutting down trees?"

"It could happen any time."

As they drove through town on the way to Doug's house she realized a comradeship had evolved between them. She didn't know if it had begun weeks ago when he took her home after Kenny hit her or last night when he told her she was his. It didn't feel like a bad thing.

The late-afternoon sun was casting long shadows by the time they rolled to a stop in his driveway. Doug reached across and cupped her nape, rubbed her taut neck muscles with his thumb. "Come in. I'll buy you a beer."

"You know I don't drink beer."

"Figure of speech. I'll scare up a Pepsi."

She shrugged and smiled. Were they engaged in a continuation of what they had started at her hotel room door last night?

"Okay," she said, just like that.

She sat in her seat as he unfolded his lanky frame from behind the wheel, wondering what she had submitted to by saying *okay*. His heated good-night kiss as well as his less-than-subtle attempt to invite himself into her room had made falling asleep difficult last night and had come back to her at least a dozen times throughout today.

As he opened her door, he offered her his hand. She stepped out and let herself be tugged along toward the neat deck where a rocking chair sat. Seeing it brought to mind his saying he watched for her lights at night and she felt a thrill at that. She glanced over her shoulder and could indeed spot her house against the mountain across the valley.

The bare wooden floor creaked as they stepped into the living room. He went to the refrigerator and returned with two cans of Pepsi. He popped the tops and handed her one. "Be right back." He disappeared and came back with a pair of wool-lined slippers "Here," he said. "You can lose those high heels."

"Okay. I guess." Alex stepped out of her shoes and into his. They swallowed her narrow feet. They both laughed. "These are what size?"

"Eleven. How about the jacket?"

She shrugged, ambivalent. "Okay." He helped her slip out of her suit jacket and hung it on one of the NordicTrack's ski poles. He placed a hand on her back and she felt herself being ushered into the living room to the only seating besides the chairs at the dining table, a thick-armed, distressed-leather sofa crouched across from a rock fireplace. A wrought-iron coffee table with a thick glass top huddled on a nubby rug that looked like cotton. All in all, a masculine domain.

"I'm debating if I should keep the wood floor or put in carpet," he said. "Whaddaya think?"

She glanced down at the oak floor. "Looks like good wood. It would be worth doing over."

"Have a seat." He went to a CD player tucked into bookshelves lining one wall.

She sank to the edge of the sofa, holding her Pepsi can with both hands and forcing herself to move past the awkwardness she felt. Even if she hadn't been thinking off-limits thoughts about him earlier, she still would have felt out of place. She didn't visit in people's homes except to discuss real estate they wanted to sell. As many years as she had known her assistant, Judy, she hadn't been inside her house more than once or twice.

While he selected a CD, she studied his shelves. Many of his books appeared to be textbooks, which reminded her how much better educated he was than she. Without question, she was overmatched and a familiar need to be on the defensive began to creep in.

Billie Holiday's voice rose softly from small speakers on either side of the CD player. "You like blues?" he asked.

"Well . . . a little, I guess."

"I'll bet you don't even listen to music."

"I do. When I'm working in my office and when I'm driving. But I don't pay much attention to it. I don't know the names of artists. Or songs, for that matter. Believe it or not, when I was a little kid, I could play the guitar."

He grinned and tucked back his chin. "The hell. Don't do it any more, huh?"

"I don't have time."

"You know this one, don't you? Billie Holiday?"

"I know the name. And I know her history. I just don't know her music."

"Stick with me, babe. An old guitar player should appreciate the finer points of rhythm and blues." He winked.

She smiled at his joke. Maybe the reason she liked him was because he joked, unlike most of the men she knew.

"You look uncomfortable. The bathroom's in the hall, just around the corner. If you want to get out of those panty hose, I won't tell anybody."

That sounded good. She felt tired. Topping off the stress of the last few days with a heavy lunch had left her logy. "Maybe I will." She set her Pepsi can on the coffee table and found her way to the tiny square bathroom that had obviously been added on years back. It was maybe a quarter the size of her bathroom on Wolf Mountain.

Back in the living room, she stuffed her panty hose into her shoes. He was lounging on the sofa, bare feet propped on the coffee table's glass top. "Feel better?"

Seeing his feet jolted her. She hadn't seen a man's bare feet in years. His were long and wide with a high arch and tanned, and she wondered if, when he lived in Santa Monica, he hung out on the beach. "Uh, sure."

"Sit," he said, patting the seat beside him. "Put your feet up."

She did as instructed and closed her eyes, trying to ignore the sight of her own narrow feet beside his wide ones and the fact that with ridding herself of panty hose, she was without underwear. The mellow sounds of "My Man's Gone Now" filled her head. "Your music. More old things with history." From out of nowhere, a shiver passed over her.

"Cold?"

"No. Just unwinding."

He stood up. "Remember the night in the Eights and Aces, when we danced?"

She gave him a grimace. "Don't remind me."

His hand reached for hers and he drew her to her feet and into a dance position. "I told you, I don't judge."

"Well, I do. That night was awful."

"You're being hard on yourself. You're not the first person to try to lose a bad day in a bottle of hooch."

"If there's anybody who knows problems don't disappear in liquor, it's me."

"Do you remember what you said that night?"

It should offend her for him to remind her of her off-putting behavior, but it didn't. The question in his soft, gruff voice was seductive, for though she might like to forget, she hadn't. An odd sensation traveled through her belly. "You mean about the music? Or . . ."

"Either. Or both." He held her against him as they swayed in place, his cheek brushing hers. He took her hand to his chest and covered it with his own. She could feel his strong, steady heartbeat, feel his warm breath against her temple, smell his scent. She had never felt so secure. She closed her eyes and leaned into him.

"That's it. Just relax." The next thing she knew, his hand had closed over her nape, he was tilting her head back and his lips settled softly on hers. His kiss was earnest. Noninvasive. An endearing hum came from his throat and he drew back. "Oh, lady. You are so sweet."

She felt herself being danced backward into the hall, knew she was being steered to his bedroom. "This is scary," she said, but didn't protest.

"No. Loneliness is scary. This is normal."

His left hand moved down and cupped her bottom and pressed her to him, to where he felt hard and huge. She didn't pull away, but when he increased the pressure and moved her against him, anxiety darted around in her rib cage. "This is dangerous. We shouldn't be—"

"Shhh," he whispered. "Don't be afraid."

But she *was* afraid. She didn't know how to behave, had

forgotten how to respond. Still, she made no effort to stop him. "I'm not," she lied.

He kept kissing her eyes, her nose, her ear. Her breasts began to feel heavy and achy and that funny feeling in her belly seemed to be moving lower. She raised her arms around his neck. Something brushed against her calves and she opened her eyes. They were standing beside a bed in a small, tight room dimly lit. "This is crazy," she whispered.

"No. Fighting each other the way we've been doing is crazy."

Then his hands were under her skirt, clasping her bottom, his palms burning hot against her bare skin and sending little prickles clear to her toes. She sensed his strength as he lifted her slightly, eased her back onto a puffy comforter and followed her down. Her skirt hiked up around her waist and she felt herself exposed. A jolt of panic shook her. "I'm— I'm out of practice at this."

"Riding a bicycle," he whispered, squeezing her bare hip. "You don't have to do anything. Leave it to me." His skilled hands pushed her top up past her breasts. His head bent down, his mouth closed hot and wet over her nipple and he sucked her through the lace of her bra. The odd tickle down below turned into a driving need and she couldn't stop the little noise that pushed from her throat.

Doug could feel her tension. He vowed this would be good for her if it killed him. And ready as he was, it just might. He kissed her again, swirling his tongue around hers and at the same time smoothing his hand down her belly and cupping her sex. He wove his fingers through her tangle of damp curls and parted her. She was so wet. Any misgivings he had that this might be one-sided vanished. His dick turned hard as a crowbar. He drew a deep breath, slowing himself down before he went off like an anxious teenager.

"Open your legs a little," he whispered.

Her knees fell open. He pushed a finger into the hot, soft sheath waiting for him. Her breath caught, her eyes flew open and locked on his. "It's okay." He drew out her moisture and played with her, slowly stroking the layers of her sex. "You feel so good . . . . Like silk."

She began to make frantic little grunts. He moved over her and knelt between her knees, watching her face. A crease showed between her eyebrows, her mouth twitched, but she didn't open her eyes. Her fingers gripped his biceps. Her hips lifted and she pushed herself against his hand. He found the core of her sex with his fingers and rubbed slow and easy.

"Oh . . ."

"Come . . ."

"Oh . . . I don't—I don't know—"

"Tell me when—" He leaned down and kissed her, sliding his tongue into her mouth and keeping rhythm with his fingers.

"Oh . . . I think—" She sobbed an outcry from deep inside as she went over. She finished with little whimpers that were pure pleasure to hear. When she reached for him, he let himself stay in her arms, holding her in his. "But you didn't," she said in a tiny voice.

"Oh, baby, I will. We're just getting started." He kissed her long and deep and she returned a kiss so hot and passionate he could have whimpered himself. "Oh, Alex . . ."

He should undress. He should undress her, but he didn't want to stop for even a few seconds. He moved down, trailing his open mouth down her body until he reached her smooth belly. "You're so soft . . . so sweet . . ."

"Oh . . . you're . . . whiskery—"

"Does it hurt? . . . I shaved early—"

"No . . . .No, it's . . . umm . . ."

"I don't want anything to hurt you."

"No, it's fine . . . . It's—Doug . . ."

"Lift your knees. Let me—oh, Jesus, you're beautiful."

"Doug . . . you shouldn't—"

"Don't stop me."

# Chapter 27

Doug struggled for the right words, knowing the wrong ones could be devastating and not ready to say all that he felt. Except for Alex's missing panty hose, they were both still dressed and he was sprawled on top of her. He wanted to stay right there for the rest of his life, but he pulled out and moved to her side and tried to bring her with him. She tugged down the hem of her skirt and covered herself, then turned her back on him, drawing her knees up into a fetal position.

He expected her to be embarrassed. Her participation had been anything but reticent if several powerful orgasms could be used as indication.

He gingerly placed a hand on her side. "Hey . . ."

Disheartened when she didn't respond, he gave her a little shake. "Hey, talk to me."

When she didn't speak, he turned her to face him. She didn't look him in the eye with that laser gaze he had come to know. In fact, she looked almost shy. Her hair was tossed in disarray. Even in the room's low light, he could see her mouth was swollen from rough kissing, the skin around it red from his late-day beard. She looked sated and seductive and he longed to hear her say something, even a sarcastic remark.

He buried his face against her neck, breathed in her clean smell. "It's okay," he said softly. "It went okay. You're so good . . . Jesus, sweetheart." He wrapped his arms around her and held her, could feel her body trembling, though she lay still as a statue.

All at once, she sat up and pulled away from him, straightening her clothes. Okay, no soft talk. She stood and raked her hair back from her face with her hands. Maybe she needed the bathroom. He braced himself on one elbow, looking up at her. "Clean towels and stuff are hanging in the bathroom."

Without a word, she left the bedroom. Shit. He got to his feet and hiked up his jeans. He turned back the bedcovers, glad his bed had clean sheets. The waning sun had brought a cooler temperature. When she came back, they would crawl under the covers and talk. He would tell her his feelings, drag hers out of her, make her understand the depth of what had just happened.

He sat down on the edge of the bed, marveling at fate's strange twists. When he saw her at Culpepper's party yesterday, never in his most far-out imaginings could he have predicted that twenty-four hours later they would have the most incredible sex. He had suspected her cool facade hid a passionate woman, but Christ Almighty, he hadn't expected a volcano. Yet another part of the ever evolving Alex McGregor. "Thank you, Jesus," he mumbled, rolling his eyes heavenward.

The sound of a car engine just outside startled him. Heart in his throat, he sprang to his feet and stamped up the hall to the bathroom, calling her name.

She wasn't in the bathroom. *Fuck.*

He reached the kitchen window just in time to see taillights as that fancy SUV got to the end of his driveway and turned onto the county road. *Fuck!*

His gaze shot to where she had left her shoes. No shoes. He stood for a moment staring at his dark living room. She had left her suit jacket behind. It still hung on one of the ski machine's poles. Billie Holiday crooned as if nothing had gone wrong. "Goddammit," he muttered.

His socks and shoes lay by the sofa. He pulled the socks on and shoved his feet into the shoes. Then he yanked a windbreaker from his small front closet and grabbed her suit jacket. As an afterthought, he stopped off in the bathroom for his toothbrush and set out for her house.

Mired in self-censure, Alex sat at her breakfast bar with a spoon, a box of saltines and a jar of peanut butter. The cats sat nearby, watching her. Had her brain entered a new body? It must have, because the old body had defied all reason and common sense directed by her cerebral organ.

She had been a fool. Even knowing his reputation, she had let a jock superstud lead her to his bed like a lamb to slaughter and he'd had her under him in no more than what, thirty minutes, an hour? He probably had spent longer seducing Cindy Evans. An image of Cindy in his arms at Granite Pond flashed in her mind. It made her brain ache. Her heart ached a little, too, if she admitted the truth.

Oh, he had been clever and so polished a caution light hadn't even come on in her head. The jerk had softened her resistance even more by bringing her his slippers, thus ridding her of her shoes and a few inhibitions. He had even talked her into removing her panty hose for comfort. For comfort? Hah. As much as he knew about women, he probably *knew* she wasn't wearing panties. She should have been. At least panties would have made it less easy for him to . . .

Her cheeks flamed at the thought of how she had done everything and anything he urged in his deep whisper, how he had touched her everywhere with his fingers, even his eyes. She had lain there spread open, letting him look his fill, then he had used his mouth and tongue to . . . On his order, she had even wrapped her legs around his waist and taken him deep inside her, had begged him, actually *begged* him, to . . .

She groaned and squeezed her eyes shut against the memory. "You stupid woman," she mumbled. "How could you be so juvenile?"

The crunch of tires on gravel halted her self-flagellation. Had he followed her? Surely not.

She heard heavy footfalls on her wooden deck steps. Peering around the corner from the kitchen to look through the front door's glass panes, she saw he had reached the top step. A tight knot pressed against her chest wall. Her first impulse was to turn off the lights and ignore him.

"Stop being dumb," she said. "Just tell him it was a mistake and stop him before he ever comes inside." She strode across the dark living room toward the front door and turned on the entry light. Its cut-crystal globe splashed shapes and shadows over the hardwood floor. A tear had sneaked from the corner of her eye. She wiped it away with her fingertips, then stepped outside to meet him.

The entry light cast a soft glow through the door panes. The night air raised goose bumps on her bare arms and she hugged herself for warmth.

With the grace of an athlete, he crossed the deck toward her, his eyes boring into her. Her heart thumped.

"Alex—"

"Don't say anything." Her determination to stop him weakened, but she met his eyes with steel in her spine. "You shouldn't have followed me."

He opened his palms in question. "Why did you run away?"

"This isn't right for me. Being involved with someone is not right for me." The temperature had dropped at least twenty degrees. She was so cold her teeth started to chatter.

"You're freezing." His hands reached out and uncrossed her arms, then drew them around his torso, enclosing her into his jacket and cocooning her in warmth. "Doesn't that feel better?"

It felt wonderful. "Not necessarily."

"Now, tell me why I'm not right for you."

"Because. You add complications to my life."

"Sweetheart, your life is a freeway pileup. If anything, I'm a stabilizing factor." His finger tipped her chin up, his head bent and his lips touched hers so gently it seemed they were hardly touching at all.

She couldn't make herself resist. His head angled left, then right as he softly sipped and flicked her lips with his tongue. Though she intended to be defiant, the same fire he had built in her belly earlier started smoldering again. She pushed against his chest halfheartedly with one hand, but he kissed her again, his tongue finding hers. The remnants of her resolve withered. Tears rushed to her eyes and she couldn't stop them. "You sneaked up on me. You didn't even ask me if I wanted—"

"It didn't seem to be the time for a debate."

"I hope you're pleased. You won. You've conquered—"

"Won? Conquered? You see this as a battle?" He held her, stroking her hair and soothing her. "Aw, Alex. You're such a fighter. . . . Jesus, sweetheart . . ."

The endearment in his deep and dusty voice fell on her ear like the most lyrical of poems. A feeling of belonging spread through her. In her entire life, no one had ever called her "sweetheart" or whispered loving words of any name. Her fists knotted around his jacket front as her tears wet the front of his shirt.

He rocked her and held her until she pulled herself together. She could feel his cheek against her hair, the warmth and strength of his big body. She didn't even want to stand against his determination. "I don't know how you manage to drive me crazy and make me feel good at the same time."

He set her back with a deep, soft chuckle and looked into her face. "That must mean we're making progress."

"I suppose you want me to invite you in. You probably think I'll let you spend the night."

His grin came lightning quick and little-boy charming. "I brought my toothbrush."

She couldn't hold back a laugh. He was the most audacious man she had ever met. Resisting him was exhausting. "It's a good thing. If there's anything I can't stand, it's a man with dirty teeth."

She led him inside. "We didn't eat. Are you hungry?"

"A little. You mean you've got food?"

The cats trotted along beside them to the kitchen.

"Peanut butter. And maybe some jelly."

"Grape?"

She smiled as she took a new jar of grape jelly from the cupboard. "Picked the grapes myself, squeezed the juice with my own feet, slaved over a hot stove."

"Just what I thought. Were you wearing those waders when you did it?"

She gave him a bland look and picked up the jar of peanut butter. "Get the spoon and the crackers." She headed for the bedroom, casting him a sly glance over her shoulder. "If you coax me, I'll let you lick peanut butter off my tummy."

He tilted back his head and laughed. "Lead on, lady. I'm a master at coaxing and I've got the fastest tongue in the West."

Damn it all, she couldn't keep from liking him.

Hours and spoons of peanut butter and jelly later, Alex lazed with her back against Doug's chest, arms draped over his knees, in her Jacuzzi's warm, frothing water. Through a faint mist, the light of two dozen candles flicked shadows onto the walls and reflected in the mirrors. The whirlpool's motor whirred softly, muffling sound. Her muscles felt so mushy, if she'd had to move suddenly, she wouldn't have been able to.

"You liked it when I ate you," he murmured.

She felt her cheeks warm and hesitated before answering. "Maybe."

He chuckled softly. She could feel the gentle rumble in his chest. His arms slid around her and his hands covered her breasts. "There was no maybe about it. You liked it. So did I." He placed his lips against her ear. "Was it better with or without the jelly?"

"Stop it. You're embarrassing me."

"You weren't embarrassed when I did it, were you?"

She hesitated again. "No."

"I knew we'd be good together." He picked up a sea sponge and squeezed a trail of water down her arm. "You knew it, too, didn't you?"

She didn't answer. "A penny for your thoughts. . . . And if they're dirty, I'll make it a nickel."

Her eyelids felt too heavy to open, but she smiled at recalling what they had done with the peanut butter and jelly. No man's mouth had ever touched her most intimate places, no man's sweeping tongue had ever been inside her or reduced her to a mindless desperate being. "I thought we'd never get all that peanut butter and jelly washed off."

"You're the one who offered your tummy. I would've been content with a cracker."

She giggled. Oh, his teasing was good for her. "Here's a thought for a penny. In all the years I've owned this house, besides me, no one's been in this tub."

"Does that mean I'm special?"

"Or maybe I should qualify that. No one I *know* about."

He clasped her shoulders and urged her to sit up and when she did, he began to soap her back in slow circles. She closed her eyes and rolled her neck to one side, felt his teeth bite into a tender place on her shoulder. "No one you know about?"

"Charlie could have brought someone—"

"He'd do that?"

"He'd do that. And then some."

"Is that why you didn't have sex for eight years? Because of his chasing around? Was it really eight years?"

She hadn't anticipated that question popping up, especially at a moment like this. "Charlie and I were like cousins. I don't think he wanted me for sex and I didn't want him that way either."

"Sweetheart, I'll tell you this without even knowing the guy. If you two were married, he wanted you for that. So how come you kicked him out of bed?"

She opened her eyes and turned to face her inquisitor. "Now you're prying."

He clasped her arms, pulled her between his open knees. "I know. I'm nosy." He trailed his wet fingers down her jaw. "I want to know all your secrets."

She plucked the sponge from the water, squeezed it over his shoulders. "Should we trade secrets? I'm sure yours are juicier."

"But yours are buried deeper. C'mon," he said softly. "You like fucking. Tell me why you quit it."

She gasped and frowned. "What makes you think I like . . . that?"

His hands slid up her sides, cupped her breasts and lifted them, circled her nipples with this thumbs. "There's nothing wrong with liking it. You're evading the question."

She loved his hands on her body, but he was getting too close, digging too deep. She should give him the answer, then see how fast he could dry himself, get dressed and get the hell out of her bathroom, her house, her life. She should have thought of telling him earlier. She scooted to the opposite end of the tub.

"Okay, here's one for you. This one's probably worth a quarter. I had VD. A particularly virulent strain of gonorrhea." She hoisted her chin and waited for his jaw to drop, waited for him to say, "See ya around." Neither happened.

"Gonorrhea." He looked at her intently as a drop of water dripped off his chin.

She hung her elbows on the tub's edge and plowed ahead, giving him an out. "Don't you want to know where I got it? Don't you want to know if I was engaged in prostitution or something?"

He picked up the sponge and squeezed out water, but his eyes never left her face. "Yeah, I want to know."

"Charlie. That's how I learned he had other women. He caught it from one of the waitresses at Charlie Boy's, Number Six, I believe it was."

"He's a bastard."

"Want to know something else? Those condoms you've been so worried about? With me, you don't need them. My chances of getting pregnant are somewhere around one in fifteen thousand. And now that I'm over thirty-five, I think it's even harder."

He continued to stare at her, his eyes unreadable. "Heavy odds," he said finally.

Tears began to burn behind her eyes. Dammit, she didn't want to cry. She couldn't remember the last time, if ever, she had told anyone the hateful story and saying it aloud affected her in an unexpected way. She scooped up water and bathed her face. "It's not that I'm sterile. It's scar tissue. Somebody's little soldiers would have to be very determined troopers."

His hand wrapped around her ankle and he pulled her forward until she was between his open legs again. His hands cupped her bottom and he lifted her to straddle him. "So why didn't you divorce his ass?"

"I did file. Wrangling over a settlement went on forever and—" The tears leaked out again.

"That's enough." He lifted her off his lap, then stood up and stepped out of the tub.

So. Telling him about her past *had* affected his feeling for her. "What is it?" she asked, wanting to hear his rejection in words and at the same time fighting tears of disappointment waiting to gush.

He gripped her wrists and pulled her to her feet, then out of the tub. He reached for a towel and began to dry both of them with rough, sure swipes of a thick towel. All she could think was she had lost him. Lost him before she ever had him. She had known from the outset getting a involved was a mistake. What man wouldn't drop her like a hot potato once he knew her sorry history? "I tried to tell you from the beginning we shouldn't—"

He scooped her into his arms and carried her back to the bedroom. They sank to the bed together, a tangle of arms and legs. Face to face, a foot apart, his hands cupped her face and he kissed her fiercely. "Listen to me," he said gruffly, his eyes glued to hers. "None of it matters. Not your past, not mine. All that's important is us right now and how good our lives are gonna be because we're together."

Her chest ached with emotion. She wanted to say it was too late, too much had happened for them to ever overcome.

But her throat had closed and she couldn't speak. The tears she had been holding back leaked out.

He pushed her to her back and moved over her. In a quick maneuver, his hard, smooth penis glided into her and her deepest muscles responded on their own. They flexed around his thickness, holding him where they wanted him most. A soft groan came from deep in his chest as his head dipped and his mouth devoured hers.

They kissed savagely with tongue and teeth, as if they hadn't just spent hours making love. She arched to him, wrapped her legs around his hips. Then, heat. Friction. And his bare flesh sliding against hers in a steady rhythm and she wanted it to never stop. Sensation began to gather in her deepest places. She wrapped her arms around his head and shoulders and hung on for the ride.

"Let go," he whispered, his body taut and straining.

Orgasm thundered through her in waves and little mewling sounds hitched from her throat. She cried out, plunging over the edge.

"Oh, Jesus," he said, wrapping both of his thick arms around her and chuckling against her neck.

"What's so funny?" she managed to ask.

"Nothing. I'm just so damned happy. You make me feel like a kid."

"Did you—" She couldn't say the word.

He moved wet strands of hair off her face and kissed her. "Did I what? Come?" He chuckled again. "Oh, yeah. Couldn't you tell?"

"Well, maybe." They kissed more. She loved his mouth, loved the taste of him.

"You're so innocent," he said softly, his arms bracketing her head, his silver eyes looking into hers. "I've never known anyone like you."

"But I'm not. I've done things."

"We've all done things. It's human nature. All I know is I'm happy. And I want to make you happy."

# *Chapter 28*

From the end of Alex's long driveway, Ted saw a pickup parked in front of her house. He threw what was left of his doughnut out the window and sat forward, peering over the steering wheel. He didn't expect Alex to return until this evening. *Nobody* should be parked in front of her house. He jolted and banged up the road faster than was prudent.

When he drew close enough to recognize Doug's Chevy, Ted's heart fell to his shoes. Was Alex home? She had to be. It was six o'clock in the morning. Too early for Doug or anybody else to drop in for coffee. "Fuck," he muttered, his thoughts in turmoil. Not confident what to do, he cranked down his window and slowed his truck to a crawl, looking for signs of life. Except for the whistling wind accompanying the cool front that had moved in overnight, the surroundings were quiet.

He parked beside the Silverado and made no attempt to soften his footsteps as he mounted the deck stairs and crossed to the front door. He knew the doorbell didn't work, so he banged the knocker, then let his arms hang loose, snapping his fingers while he waited for a response. None came.

He jogged down the steps to the basement level. Peeking

through the windows in the garage doors, he saw Alex's mud-spattered Jeep and her new Acura. He refused to jump to conclusions. There was a rational explanation for everything. Taking the steps by twos back up to the deck, he returned to the front door and tried the knob. The heavy door opened. He stuck his head inside and called Alex's name before letting himself in. He called again and the cats trotted to meet him.

As his eyes roamed the room, Alex appeared in the kitchen doorway. Ted jumped when he saw her. "Alex! Lord, you scared me! I couldn't tell if you were home."

She was barefoot. Her hair looked like she had been caught in a wind tunnel. Her hands tightened the belt of a silky beige robe. "I just got in last night," she said.

Ted's heart began to pound, but he struggled to keep his tone light. "What's Doug's rig doing here?"

Maizie and Robert Redford purred and brushed Alex's ankles. She sidestepped them and ran a hand through her disheveled hair. "He spent the night."

Ted couldn't find words. He stared at her.

Maizie and Robert Redford meowed in chorus, weaving between her feet. "Dammit, cats . . ." She bent down and picked them up, one on each arm. "Ted—"

"Hey, Ted." Doug came into the kitchen, sleepy-faced and hair askew. He, too, was barefooted and the button at the waistband of his jeans was undone.

Ted didn't need a drawn picture. The image of Doug and Alex together was all too vivid. His memory flew back twenty years when his steady's best friend had told him Doug could make a girl do anything he wanted her to. The pedestal on which Ted had placed Alex began to crumble.

"Hey, yourself, buddy." Ted couldn't keep his words from sounding clipped. At this moment, he hated Doug Hawkins. He turned his eyes back to Alex. "Guess you don't need me to feed the cats. Wish I'd known. I wouldn't have made the trip up here."

His eyes began to burn. Jesus Christ, he thought he might cry. He strode toward the front door, hurrying to escape before he embarrassed himself. "Ted," she said, but he didn't stop. He yanked the door open and slammed it behind him. The windows rattled, but he didn't care if they all shattered.

"Ted, dammit, stop . . ."

Alex dropped the cats, then tightened the belt of her robe and stepped outside into the chill. Ted had already reached the bottom of the deck stairs. By the time she hopscotched across the cold, wet planks, his truck had turned down the driveway.

She began to shiver in the damp morning air and went back into the house. She shut the door firmly and rested her forehead against it for a moment, the pain and disappointment in Ted's dark eyes hanging in her memory. Returning to the kitchen, she found Doug spooning cat food onto two plates. The cats paced and meowed and brushed his pant legs with determination. "I forgot to call him and tell him I was home," she said. "Why didn't you say something? Or do something?"

Doug held a spoonful of cat food suspended. "Like what?"

She crossed her arms. "I don't know. We should have done something."

Doug put down the spoon and rounded the end of the breakfast bar to where she stood. "C'mere." He pulled her into his arms. "Did you think we could keep this hidden from Ted?"

"No, but I didn't intend to drop it on him like a concrete block. He's a friend."

"He's my friend, too. More than that. He's like a brother. I know him. He has to sort this out and he will. He just needs a little time."

Tears leaked from the corners of her eyes and she shook her head. "I don't like hurting a friend. I don't have that many in the first place."

Doug kissed her brow, then tucked her head against his shoulder, petting her hair and rubbing her neck with his thumb. Being petted was such an alien experience, she didn't know how to reject it. And maybe she didn't want to. "So you've always known how he felt about you?"

"I didn't encourage him. I never made him think there was anything but friendship between us."

Maizie and Robert Redford yowled in harmony and she glanced to where they were sitting at the back door. "They want to go out and I have to wipe my nose."

Doug produced his handkerchief, dried her eyes and wiped her nose. He framed her face with his hands and looked into her eyes. "And a pretty nose it is." He kissed the tip. "When I first met you, I wouldn't have guessed you'd care about Ted's feelings."

"Well, I do have to live up to my reputation."

He smiled and kissed her. "He isn't mad. He's coming to terms with something hard. I'll talk to him."

He had taken her. His oldest and best friend had taken the woman he loved. There was nothing left to be said.

Ted drove through town, nosed his pickup north toward the mountains, lost in his thoughts. His stomach felt like somebody had slugged him, like back in high school football. He still remembered how a belly blow felt.

Funny. Being hit in the stomach hadn't bothered Doug all that much. Doug just plowed on, never cried uncle, never said he'd had enough. He had that thing in his gut, like that damn coyote over in the Oregon desert. That was the fundamental characteristic he shared with Alex, the thing that made them alike. Hell, they deserved each other.

What had made him, ordinary Ted Benson, think he might have a future with a woman like Alex? What did they have in common? On his best days he was no match for her. His buddies were right in their criticism of how she treated him, how she made him look the fool. Not that she meant to. He had let it happen by not summoning the will to demand her respect.

And she had so damn many problems all the time. Her whole life was just one constant fight with somebody. He thought of how Mary Jane kept her own troubles hidden to keep him from worrying. He thought of how she opened her heart and home to him, and her body, with nary a question about his stupid obsession with a shooting star.

Doug had nailed it, him and all that damned psychology he had studied. Alex McGregor was indeed a mountain Ted Benson wasn't destined to scale. Why, forgodsake, had he thought he wanted to, especially with a woman as sweet and loyal as Mary Jane waiting for him?

He climbed ten slow miles on a winding road before he reached his destination, almost halfway up Callister Mountain itself. The snow line was probably less than half a mile away.

Parking near the edge of a steep decline, he slid out and moved around to the front of his truck, then squatted on the balls of his feet and looked over the grand panorama coming to life before him, trying to remember if he had ever been here so early in the morning.

He usually came to this spot when troubles assailed him. The limitless horizon helped him realize anew that he was less than a grain of sand in the scheme of things. The maw before him always gave him the urge to call out and listen for his echo, but he had never done it. Disturbing the solitude in that way would be like cutting into his flesh with a sharp knife.

He drove into the alpine fir trees he loved. There was snow, but it was light and the road wasn't frozen. A light skiff lay on the dark green branches, making the whole place look like a Christmas card.

At the Double Deuce Ranch's cattle guard he turned around and headed back to town and to the Forest Service offices. His watch showed seven-thirty, but he didn't see

Gretchen. A few employees talked and laughed in the break room, readying for the day. He didn't join them. He went to his own office and hung his uniform jacket on the coat tree standing like a sentinel in the corner of the room.

He closed his door, then took a seat behind his desk. The first thing he always saw when he sat down was a picture hanging on the opposite wall—an enlarged snapshot of himself and Doug when they were young guys, holding a string of fish between them. Naturally the biggest fish hung on Doug's end of the stringer.

He leaned on his elbows and rubbed his eyes, trying to corral his thoughts. The fingers of his right hand found a pencil lying loose. He spun it again and again on the desk blotter, concentrating on the revolutions.

In a few months he would be thirty-eight. Other than his job and a little money in the bank, what did he have to show for his nearly forty years? Since the day he left his parents' home, apartments with spartan furnishings had been where he hung his hat. He had never owned a house, didn't even own a good horse.

He opened his left top drawer, pulling it all the way out, and felt blindly in the back under boxes of paper clips, staples and rubber bands. His hand emerged with a navy blue ring box. It had been hidden in the back of the drawer for four years. He opened it and stared inside. A diamond solitaire set on a gold band nested in the slot, a matching wedding band beside it.

When he had bought it, it seemed like a large stone, but now it looked small and trifling. He could afford something bigger. But Mary Jane wouldn't care. She would be happy with just the gold band. She cared about *him*.

He took the rings from the box and slipped them on his little finger, holding his hand out flat in front of him, studying the stone. He pulled his handkerchief from his rear pocket and polished both rings.

Gretchen's voice came from the lobby; she was running

late. He was in no mood to trade sarcasm with her this morning. He slipped the rings back into their velvet slots and snapped the lid shut. He shrugged into his jacket, dropped the ring box into his pocket, then dialed Mary Jane's number.

Her rushed hello came on the line.

"Headed out?"

"Hi," she said softly. He closed his eyes and pictured her sweet smile.

"Teacher's meeting this morning. Can I call you later? I was just on my way out the—"

"Don't leave yet. I'm coming over."

Alex left for Los Angeles on Monday, headed for one last meeting with the developer of the Salt Lake retirement home project and his architect. She had planned to drive, but Doug persuaded her to fly. He didn't want to think of her driving alone with a fall storm from the west moving across.

Returning from taking her to the Boise airport, he found his thoughts dominated by the previous four days. The real Alex was nothing like the cold image she projected to the community around her. The real Alex was warm and funny and affectionate. He couldn't imagine the will and discipline it had taken for her to live for eight years with virtually no human touch, couldn't relate to all of her reasons for doing so. It didn't matter now. There would never be a lack of contact between him and her.

He had been at her house day and night since Wednesday. They survived on canned soup and what they could throw together to make a meal from her meager kitchen stores. They spent more time in bed than out. He had come so many times, he felt sore. He should have known that once undertaken, her approach to sex would be no less ardent than how she tackled everything else.

Then yesterday, he witnessed a metamorphosis. Right before his eyes, she changed from his passionate lover to a terse, calculating businesswoman as elusive as a shadow. She spent a good part of the day on the phone, another part packing her suitcase and gathering documents. The ease with which she switched roles worried a dark place inside him and Ted's story about the coyote in the Oregon desert kept rolling over in his mind. He worked at putting aside his doubts. He couldn't expect her to abandon the life she had carried on before knowing him, could he?

She had begged him to go to Los Angeles with her, but he declined. Nothing, not even she, could make him return to the City of Angels. He had left nothing there but bad memories, a washed-up career and a reputation as a rogue cop.

Since keeper-of-the-cats was now his title, he would stay nights in Alex's house, but he would spend his days at his own place. Her home might be a mansion, but to him its maze of fifteen rooms and dark hallways and corners held all the warmth of an empty skyscraper. In her absence, he planned to replace his old shower in the one bathroom in his house. He had been putting it off, not wanting to live for a week without showering.

He thought of Cindy Evans. More than ten days had passed since he had approached her in the bar offering her an opportunity any sane woman would have taken. Plenty of time had passed for her to wrestle her conscience and get in touch with him. He was slipping. In the past he wouldn't have let a potential witness languish so long. He would make another attempt to talk to her this week.

Reaching Callister, he drove straight to his little farmhouse. The red message notification light on his voice mail box blinked at him as he entered the kitchen, an unusual occurrence since few called him at all, much less left messages. He pressed the PLAY button and the machine voice denoted the date of the message as Thursday. The next voice he heard belonged to none other than Cindy Evans.

"You know what you said, about helping me and all? I've been thinking about it. You prob'ly don't know it, but I got four kids I gotta think about. If you still want to talk, then okay."

*Thursday. Four days ago. Shit!* He glanced at his watch, saw the time to be well past noon. He abandoned his plan to work on his bathroom and headed for town.

The young guy working the bar at the Eights & Aces told him Cindy had gone to eastern Idaho. One of her cousins had a baby and she went to help out, wouldn't be back for a week or two. He handed over a sealed envelope with Doug's name scrawled across the front.

Doug waited until he was seated in the pickup before he opened the envelope. Inside was an out-of-town phone number. As soon as he reached home, he tried it.

"You gotta come over here," Cindy told him when she came on the line. "I ain't going back to Callister for a while."

She said the name of the town where she was, but he would have to call her when he arrived and meet her somewhere away from her cousin's house. Her cousin wouldn't understand. "Promise you won't tell anybody," she said. "I mean people like Ted or Pete Hand."

"Not a soul in Callister will know we've talked," he assured her. After they hung up, he dragged out his map and studied the route to Challis, Idaho. To his aggravation, there was no short and easy way to get there from Callister.

Minutes later, Ted called. "Hi, buddy." He spoke as if nothing were different. Doug was relieved to hear from his old friend. He hadn't had much time to think about how to resolve the issue that shouldn't be an issue between them.

"Ted. How's it going?"

"You home alone?"

"Alex went to California."

"Put the coffee on. I'm coming to see you. I need a favor."

A fresh pot of coffee waited when Ted arrived within the

hour. They shook hands. "Come in, come in," Doug said, taking Ted's jacket and hanging it on the handlebars of the ski machine. "Come into the kitchen."

Doug poured coffee and gestured for Ted to sit down at the table. "You said you need a favor. Just name it."

Ted stirred sugar into his mug. "Mary Jane and I are finally gonna do it, after all these years. I want you to stand up with me."

"God, Ted, that's just great." Doug reached across the table and shook Ted's hand again. "She'll make you a good home. And you'll be a good dad to her kids."

"She will. And I will. I guess I knew all along someday I'd marry her if she wanted to. She said yes, so . . ." Ted shrugged.

"When?"

"Four weeks. At that old Christian church downtown. It's no big deal. Not formal or anything. I'm just going to wear a regular suit, so you don't have to buy new clothes."

"You do me honor, friend. I didn't know if I'd ever hear from you again."

"I wasn't mad, Doug." He looked at the floor. "Hell, I couldn't be mad at two of the people I think the most of in the whole world."

The warmth of long friendship and the feeling his family was restored affected Doug in a powerful way. "Thanks. I don't know if you care, but I'm happier than I've ever been. Alex is—well, we're—Christ, I'm just happy."

"Where'd you say she went? California?" Ted snorted a laugh. "Ah, well, that's a pattern. Don't I know it. It'll probably always be that way with her. Running up and down the road to somewhere."

"I'm going to work on it. Part of what drives her is insecurity. Maybe I can convince her if she'll settle down, I can take care of her. I'm not as rich as she is, but I can still take care of her."

Ted nodded. "Maybe you can even get her to work on her driveway. I've put hundreds of hard miles on my truck feeding those damn cats. Guess that's your job now." He looked around the room. "Whatcha working on?"

"The bathroom. When it's done, I'm finished with carpenter work 'til spring. In a couple of weeks I start doing some jury consulting for a law firm in Pocatello."

"That's good, right?"

"It's a referral from Bob Culpepper. He's turned out to be a friend as well as a good contact. Some more things are coming up in Boise in the next couple of weeks. When I got out of the hospital, I wondered if I would ever again be able to fill a whole day. Now I've got all I can handle. And no pressure."

"Like my mom always says, door closes, another opens. So you're gonna be content here, then. In little ol' Callister?"

"Yep. I'm here for life. Alex, too."

"Me, too. If I even hinted I wanted to take Mary Jane and the kids off somewhere, I'd have to fight her whole family. . . . Well, I gotta get going. I'll let you know the plans when they're all made."

"That'll be great. Just tell me if I can do anything."

Alex called the following evening. She had heard from Bob Culpepper. The judge ruled in Miller's favor. The logger was free to start work immediately. She was devastated.

Though three months ago the news wouldn't have affected him, an unexpected jolt shot through Doug when she told him and he longed to be with her, to comfort her. "Come on back," he said. "Just get on a plane and come home. I miss you."

When she said she couldn't return until Friday, he realized he had only a few days to see Cindy. He didn't want to have to tell Alex what he and Bob Culpepper were up to until everything came together. And he didn't want her thinking he had something going on with Cindy. He did something he hadn't anticipated he would ever do. He told her a lie.

# *Chapter 29*

A distant buzz ripped Doug from a sound sleep and he took a few minutes to orient himself. His eyelids flew open. Chain saws? Shit. Had Miller started? He left Alex's bed, went to the kitchen and made coffee. While it dripped, he stepped outside and looked around, saw nothing different, but like a swarm of angry bees, the sound continued without letup.

On his mind this morning was Cindy Evans and the crime he was convinced had occurred at Granite Pond. Before embarking on a three-hundred-mile trip, he wanted to take one more look at the cabin ruins without Alex hovering at his shoulder. He called Ted and asked him to go along. An experienced firefighter's take on the fire at the scene would be valuable information. Ted met him in Alex's front driveway midmorning. The minute Ted's feet touched the ground, he cocked his ear. "That's chain saws."

"She lost the battle with Miller."

Ted looked at the ground. "I hadn't heard. Judge moved fast, I guess."

"How does it work, when somebody sets out to log three thousand acres of trees?"

Ted laid out the scenario—tree-fallers first with chain saws. One of Miller's cat skinners would walk a CAT up and start work on Alex's driveway, which would be widened, smoothed up, the grade reduced. Old Ridge Road, too. Both would be made passable for logging trucks. "It'll break Alex's heart to see that," Ted said in conclusion. "Not if I can help it," Doug replied. "Let's go."

They trekked up to Old Ridge Road and down to the glade surrounding Granite Pond. To Doug's surprise and dismay, the cabin site had been scoured clean of rubble. "Do you know what happened to the debris?"

"Alex hired somebody to clean up and haul it off."

"Fuck," Doug grumbled. "I didn't know that." He headed for the cabin site with Ted walking beside him. "Did you find out how McGregor got here that night?"

"Cindy's rig." Ted pointed toward the waterfall end of Granite Pond, a good hundred feet from where they stood. "It was parked over there."

"Four-wheel drive?"

"Yep. She drives an old Blazer."

Doug walked to where he had parked his pickup the evening he came here with Cindy, slightly to the right of where the cabin's front door had been. It seemed like a more logical place to park. "Wonder why she parked it way over there?"

Ted shrugged. "She told Jim they went fishing before they got down to serious partying."

Plausible, but not likely. Doug chuckled. "Wonder if they caught anything."

In response to Doug's questions, Ted filled in a few facts Alex had not. He was convinced the accelerant had been lantern fuel, a container of which could be found in every garage or storage shed in Callister County. The lantern's scorched skeleton was no longer present, but Doug's memory scrolled back to where he had first seen it beside the brick hearth.

Could Cindy have offed her lover, then set the place on fire? If so, what had been Miller's role?

Moving on, Doug tried to visualize a time line. "How long you figure it took the cabin to burn down? Forty-five minutes? An hour?"

"Maybe. There was zero humidity. I didn't pay that much attention to time, to tell the truth. Our concern was preventing a disaster on this whole mountain."

Doug and Ted strolled toward the pond's bank nearest the ridge road. "You're a forest scientist. What's *your* opinion? Will a road really damage that stream and pond the way she thinks?"

"Honestly?" Ted's brow arched. "I don't know for sure, but I suspect she's right."

Doug sighed. "I hope she'll sell that house to Miller if he still wants to buy it. When I finish remodeling, my place will be big enough for the two of us."

"Boy, I don't know. She loves that house."

At the pond's edge, Doug looked back at the ridge. "How far is it from here to Miller's timber?"

"The boundary's about a mile to the south."

"I don't remember seeing him here fighting the fire. Yet besides Alex and her house, he's the guy with the most to lose. Why didn't he show up? If I was in his shoes, I would." Until his conversation with Culpepper, Doug hadn't wondered about Miller's absence from the fire fighting. "Did anybody besides the sheriff ever talk to him?"

"I heard from him myself a couple of days later. Said he was up north looking at a logging job or he would have brought his equipment and helped us. He was real grateful for the job we did."

"I'll bet."

The next day at dusk, after a long day's drive through a variety of extreme and beautiful landscapes, Doug reached the town of Challis, located at the edge of the Challis National Forest. To the southeast, Borah Peak rose like a twelve-thousand-foot wall. He stopped for a sandwich before calling Cindy.

She told him to meet her behind the bleachers at the roping arena. Challis wasn't much larger than Callister. He had no trouble finding the arena. He killed his pickup lights as he turned behind the bleachers. The sky was clear and there was moonlight. Cindy's battered Blazer waited for him, parked out of the way under the bleachers just as she said it would be. The mere fact that she felt a need for such secrecy told him her information would be devastating to somebody. He left the Silverado and went to her rig. Apparently her interior lights didn't work because they didn't come on when he opened the door. The night air was cold and the minute he slid onto the seat and closed the door, the windows began to fog, leaving them sitting in an eerie blue-gray darkness.

"You hiding out?" he asked her.

"What do *you* think?"

"I'm glad you changed your mind about talking to me."

"What are you gonna do for me after I tell you what you want to know?"

"Everything in my power to help you."

"But you're not a cop anymore. And you never was an Idaho cop. Why should I believe you can do anything?"

He sensed her nervousness, could hear a tremble in her voice. It had been three years since he had questioned a witness or a suspect, but the routine came back to him as if he had done it yesterday. "Because I know somebody who can and if you didn't already believe that, you wouldn't have called me."

"There's no telling what Kenny might do to me if he finds out I talked to you."

"Let me make it easy. Just give me simple answers. Was Miller at the cabin with you and Charlie the night of the fire?"

Staring straight ahead, she nodded.

"The next question's obvious, kiddo. Did he do something to Charlie?"

She sniffed and ducked her head. "They had a fight."

"And Charlie lost?"

She nodded again and wiped her eyes, then jerked the latch on her door and scooted out. Doug left his seat, too, and rounded the front end of the Blazer. She was attempting to dig out a cigarette with shaking hands. He reached for the pack and bumped one out, then held the lighter for her.

"Kenny threw Charlie across the room. He hit his head on the woodstove. Kenny's real strong and Charlie wasn't a big guy. Charlie just sort of folded up on the floor."

Doug thought of the autopsy report and the official cause of death. In all likelihood, McGregor would have survived his head injury if someone had helped him escape the cabin before he burned to death. "What did you do to help him?"

She broke into sobs, her shoulders shaking. "Help him? He wasn't moving. And he was bleeding something awful. Kenny said he was dead . . . and I didn't have any clothes on."

She drew on her cigarette, then wiped her nose with the heel of her hand. "Then Kenny dumped lantern gas everywhere and lit a match. I tried to tell the dumb fucker he was gonna burn up all his trees, but he was blind drunk and pissed off."

End of story. A small part of Doug had always been amazed at how simple most murders were. People were killed by people they knew.

"Did Miller harm you?"

"I didn't give him the chance. I took off and hid in the trees. I seen him choke a dog once with his bare hands. I ain't forgot it."

Doug mumbled curses, his eyes narrowing as he tried to picture the man choking a dog. Miller was just plain mean and even more violent than Doug had thought. "Then what?"

She sniffed. "He staggered around outside a few minutes, then got in his truck and left. The next thing I knew, Alex showed up. I don't know what I woulda done if she hadn't come."

"You left out what Miller was so pissed off about."

She stared up at him. It was too dark to see her eyes, but she was stalling. She drew deeply on her cigarette. The tip burned bright orange in the darkness. "Charlie said Kenny stole some trees."

How the hell did somebody steal trees, Doug wondered. "Fill me in."

"Kenny logged some trees off Forest Service ground and some old people's from Pennsylvania. Charlie knew about it."

Doug went back to his conversation with Alex. *Charlie was in over his head with something . . . always out of money . . . gambled . . . restaurants in trouble.* "He wanted money from Miller to keep his mouth shut? How'd he know about the trees?"

"I don't know. I just know he had some pictures."

"Did he ever actually collect any money?"

She nodded. "Kenny paid him once. I don't know how much, but he was pissed off about it. Told Charlie he wouldn't ever do it again."

"Where's the pictures?"

"I don't know. Charlie said they were in California. That's part of why Kenny got so mad at the cabin. He told Charlie this was the last time, but he wanted the pictures first."

"So when Charlie pressured him for more money, Miller jumped him?"

"That ain't what they got in a fight about, but it's why Kenny set the cabin on fire."

"I'm listening."

"Me and Charlie was on the bed and Kenny was in the recliner, watching. I told you he liked watching." She turned her back and leaned her elbow on the Blazer's front fender. "Charlie couldn't, you know, do anything. He was too drunk. He said it was my fault his dick went limp. He started pushing me around. He even hit me. Kenny always took up for me when we was kids growing up. He dragged Charlie off me. That's when Kenny threw him across the room."

Doug marveled that Alex could be surrounded by so much corruption, yet stay apart from it. No wonder she had built high walls. "So there wasn't a real fight, then? Sounds like Charlie was defenseless."

"Even if he'd been sober, he couldn't have fought against Kenny. Nobody can. Kenny said he'd get rid of his problem with the goddamn trees once and for all. I didn't know what he meant at first. Then he started throwing the lantern gas around. That's when I told him he could lose all his trees next door. He didn't even hear me. I didn't like the look in his eye, so I ran outside."

A bone-deep weariness spread over Doug. Once he had thought all the evil in the world was concentrated in Los Angeles County. How could he have had such tunnel vision? He drew a hand down his face. "One more thing. Does Jim Higgins know all this?"

She nodded. "Him and Kenny are good friends. Hell, Jim's worked for Kenny ever since I can remember. He ain't really a sheriff. He's a truck mechanic."

Doug clenched his jaw. "Right."

"You wanna know something funny?" Cindy dropped her cigarette on the ground and ground it out with her shoe. "Me and Charlie didn't even intend to go to that goddamn cabin. He was in the Eights and Aces waiting for me to get off when Kenny came in, wasted on Wild Turkey. He's the one wanted to go to the cabin. I didn't want him with us 'cause I knew Charlie was going back to California and I prob'ly wouldn't see him for a long time. I was mad 'cause I thought Kenny just wanted to go off to the bushes somewhere. He's so afraid somebody'll find out about him. Maybe he wanted to talk to Charlie about the money and the pictures all along. Kenny always gets what he wants."

"Not this time, Cindy. Not this time."

"Am I gonna be okay?" she asked in a tiny voice. "You promised. I can't be in jail or anything. I gotta be able to take care of my kids. I mean I'm all they've got."

"I'm gonna help you." And Doug meant it. "Stay where you are until either I or a lawyer named Bob Culpepper contacts you."

After cautioning her again, Doug left Challis. He stopped in a little town at the junction with the interstate and spent the night, then headed on to Boise the next morning.

Culpepper beamed at the information Doug passed on to him, told him Jack Dunlap's office already had the state police in Region Three alerted. Alex would be back tomorrow. The lawyer and Doug agreed the news about her husband should come from Doug.

Doug rented a room and ordered a dozen roses.

The hour-and-a-half flight from LAX to Boise gave Alex an opportunity at last to do some serious thinking about the relationship she had allowed herself to stumble into with Doug. She had spent a whole day digging out additional stories of the shooting in which he had been wounded and three others killed. An entire newspaper page had been devoted to the funeral of John Bascomb's teenage son, during which, she remembered hearing, Doug had been in the hospital fighting for his life.

Until the shooting, Doug's police career had been exemplary, filled with awards. It would have survived the controversial shooting but for the affair with Bascomb's wife. News stories didn't reveal how long the cuckolded husband had known about the relationship, but the world knew the sordid details within a few days after the teenager's burial.

In a small L.A. newspaper, Judy had discovered another fact that had seen little publicity. Since the kid's death, Bascomb's wife had been treated in the ER for injuries from spousal abuse at least three times. What Alex had learned only supported what she already knew. Doug Hawkins was not the loose-cannon, woman-chasing lout she had first believed him to be. If anything, he took on too much responsibility for the shortcomings of others. He was good and strong, the kind the helpless looked to for support. The kind a woman would fall in love with.

The kind she had, perhaps, already fallen in love with.

Did she want to give their relationship a chance? Judy had told her she was crazy if she didn't jump into it with both feet. She must concur with her assistant's opinion because that's what she had done—jumped in with both feet and both hands. And try as she would, she couldn't be unhappy about it.

She enjoyed the way he fussed over her. So many years had passed since she had shared her days with someone who cared if she lost a sale or dented her car or broke a nail. Nor had she felt those same concerns for anyone else. The only living beings she had to worry about were cats. She had disciplined herself not to need the companionship of another human being, not to want it.

She crossed her arms and hugged herself as she realized, for the first time, really, that Doug Hawkins was her man. And he would be waiting for her at the airport. She could hardly wait to see his beautiful silver eyes, the smirk she had learned to enjoy the sight of. She wanted his brawny arms around her, holding her and protecting her. She wanted his husky, sexy voice whispering his lusty intentions in her ear. And she damn sure wanted him to follow up on those intentions.

Her plane touched down on schedule. He was waiting

with a brilliant grin and a huge bouquet of roses. He looked mouthwatering gorgeous, wearing a green pullover, jeans and rough-out boots. His hair showed a hint of curl and touched his collar. She forced herself not to race through the concourse into his arms. When they met, she melted into his embrace, wasn't even embarrassed when he kissed her for everyone to see.

Doug felt as if she had been gone a month instead of a week. He had been lonesome and horny and lost the whole time she was away. Having her in his arms again reinforced what he already knew—he didn't like her flitting in and out of his life like a hummingbird. "God, I've missed you," he told her.

He chose a highway rest stop just out of Callister to tell her the truth of her ex-husband's death. She cried and he closed her into his arms and rested his cheek on her hair. "I'm sorry," he whispered.

"Poor Charlie. He was such a victim. Not just of his own excesses as an adult, but of where he was born. Of course, he could have taken control of himself at any time, but he chose not to. Something was missing inside him."

"I lied to you when I told you I was going to scout out some hunting sites. I was afraid you wouldn't understand if I told you in a phone call I was going to see Cindy."

She pulled away and looked down on the small stream that ran at the bottom of the canyon. "I might not have understood. There's certainly been bad blood between Cindy and me. But you know what? She's a victim of the same elements Charlie was. Weakness and ignorance. I probably don't hate her as much as it appears I do."

Doug went to her and slid his arm around her waist, pulled her against his side. "Culpepper's a good friend. He's taking the whole mess to the attorney general. Including Jim Higgins's performance as sheriff. If it's any consolation, Charlie's murder won't go unpunished."

She nodded. "Bob's wanted to do that all along. I've kept him from it. It's just that I hated to see Charlie's weaknesses thrown out there for all the world to see unless there was a good reason. He depended on me to protect him. And I did for as long as I could."

Doubting if he could ever love her more than at this moment, Doug set her away and placed a reverent kiss on her lips. "Let's go home," he said.

She sniffed away tears and smiled. "Yes. Let's do."

# Chapter 30

Doug and Alex, lying spoonlike, came awake in the dusky blue of daylight. They had scarcely closed the front door yesterday afternoon before they fell into bed and made ravenous love. He had kissed her everywhere, taking her to shuddering heights and whimpering lows. She still felt his slick essence between her legs.

With a low growl, he brushed her shoulder with his lips, moved to her nape. Without opening her eyes, she squirmed her bottom into the curve of his hairy groin. His hand smoothed along the outside of her thigh, caught her behind the knee and eased it up toward her chest. She felt open and vulnerable until the thick head of him pushed into her. His hand cupped her breast and molded and kneaded. Her nipples grew rigid and achy and those little sounds she had now come to recognize came out of her throat. He began to move inside her in slow, tantalizing strokes and she moved, too, keeping his lazy rhythm. His hand moved down over her belly, his fingers found her slippery softness. She purred and pushed the needy little kernel at the top of her sex against his skilled fingers. As pressure built, she rode his thick length until indescribable pleasure washed through her and her deep muscles contracted around him. She heard his groan, felt his body grow taut for a few seconds as his hot semen filled her. On a sigh, she drifted back to sleep in his arms.

The distinct sound of a truck grinding in low gear woke her a second time. She grabbed a robe and dashed to the living room windows. A truck tractor pulling a low-boy trailer loaded with a CAT labored up the driveway. It was being led by Kenny's 4x4 and the bastard was behind the wheel, his arm hanging out the window, motioning the truck to follow him.

She turned to see Doug behind her, grim-faced. "I thought they were going to arrest him," she cried.

Doug's arms closed around her. "Shh. Any day now."

She hid her face against his chest, picturing the pond's pure, clear water clouded with silt and talc, dead and dying fish floating to its surface. She had never felt so helpless.

"Let's get a shower and get dressed," Doug said. "We'll go to my house. At least you won't have to watch."

She didn't argue. Sitting in her living room, watching her driveway and Old Ridge Road change before her eyes, was more than she wanted to bear. While she made arrangements for her phone calls to be referred to Doug's number, he packed up her computer and files. She threw some clothing, toiletries and cosmetics into a bag. They loaded it all into his pickup and her Jeep and together with Maizie and Robert Redford, left her house. On the way down the driveway, a dump truck loaded with gravel forced them to pull to the side and wait while it passed. She had an insane urge to leap out of the Jeep and throw rocks at the dump truck's cab.

The stay in Doug's house turned from a weekend into a week. A cold front moved in and brought rain. Winter's bite could be felt in the air. A detective from the state police called and came down from Lewiston. When she and Doug led him to her house and the cabin site, instead of her rock-strewn driveway, they discovered a smooth gravel surface. After she had told the detective all she knew about Charlie's death and shown him the site, she gathered more clothing and personal items and they returned to Doug's house.

With no firm timetable from the detective, she willed herself to establish a routine and wrote down a schedule: work out on Doug's NordicTrack early in the morning, then phone calls, faxes and E-mails until noon. Bookkeeping and collecting the receipts at Carlton's in the afternoon.

She forced herself to not look across the valley to her house, but sometimes, in weaker moments, she did. She could see no change in the landscape with her eyes, but she could feel it in her soul.

She felt tired and weepy and blamed it on the stress of worrying what Kenny was doing behind her house and what the police were doing in Meridian. Doug was attentive and patient with her outbursts of temper and tears. And he was loving and supportive in a way she had never known.

By Thursday, she had made a decision. It wasn't in the stars for her to live in Callister, Idaho. Besides being expensive, her ten-year residency had been filled with trouble, both for herself and for others. She would return to her business in Los Angeles and rethink her plans for her future. If Doug loved her as he said he did, he would accompany her.

She broached the subject over a dinner of delicious steelhead trout steaks he had barbecued on the grill.

"I can't go back," he said.

She presented her arguments, how he could do the same things in Los Angeles he was now doing here and probably be more successful, make more money. And they would travel back to Callister often.

"I can't do it, Alex. Not even for you. And I don't want to travel back and forth. Guess I'm a stick-in-the-mud. I like being rooted in one spot."

She heard the resolve in his voice, even saw it on his face, but wasn't she a negotiator by trade?

Friday stormed in with winds, rain and dropping temperatures. Excited TV meteorologists predicted a severe winter. Doug brought up skiing and making a trip to Sun

Valley. She maintained the thread of his returning with her to Southern California.

At midmorning on Friday, Ted roared into the driveway and came to an abrupt halt. Before either Doug or she could reach the front door, he was clambering across the deck. He swung through the doorway without knocking, breathless with excitement. "Jesus Christ, Doug, the state cops came in here and arrested Jim Higgins. Another bunch of 'em went out to Kenny Miller's shop with a warrant, but nobody knows where he is." Ted's gaze shot to her. "They're saying he killed Charlie, Alex."

She began to tremble all over, could feel herself breathing. Doug came to her side and put his arm around her shoulders. "You okay?"

She nodded.

"You hear anything about Cindy?" Doug asked Ted.

"Somebody said they picked her up over in Challis." Ted paced in front of the fireplace. "My God, I can't believe this. I didn't even know those guys were investigating that fire. Until this morning, nobody ever said a damn word to me." Then his expression changed to one of dawning and he leveled a squint-eyed look at Doug. "That day we went up to Granite Pond. You did this, didn't you?"

"Relax, Ted. Soon as Miller's in custody everything will settle down."

Alex's stomach began to roil. She backed away from the conversation and sank to the sofa. She didn't know what was wrong with her. She had never reacted this way to shocking news. Doug came to her side and took her hand, looked into her face. "It's gonna be okay now. The hard part's over."

Alex knew she wouldn't relax until she knew Miller was locked up. But would he ever be arrested? He had enough money to be anywhere he wanted to, including out of the state, out of the country. Doug's gaze swung to Ted. "There's a deputy here, right?"

"Yeah. Rooster Gilley. As a lawman, he's damn near as worthless as Jim was. But he's honest."

"That counts for something," Doug said.

After Ted went on his way, Doug left the room and returned with a 9 mm automatic and loaded it while he sat beside her on the sofa. He would defend her. She knew he would. If necessary, he would die trying. She started to weep inside. What would she do if something happened to him? She loved him.

"Where's that .357, sweetheart?"

"In my purse. Why?"

He looked at her across his shoulder and grinned. "You know, one of these days we're gonna have to get you a permit."

*Permit. Who cared?* "Are we—are we going to need guns?"

He sat back and took her into his arms. "It's just a precaution. Don't worry."

Days passed. Kenny's whereabouts remained unknown. The cops were turning over every rock. Jim was indicted on a laundry list of charges. Doug understood all of it, but she didn't. With Kenny a fugitive, Cindy was hidden away in a secret location.

And all the while the Miller Logging Company's logging in Swede Creek Basin continued.

The story made Boise TV. Reporters showed up and/or called for interviews, but both she and Doug said no. They came to Carlton's and tried to film and question her and Doug. He escorted them outside and sent them away.

The town hummed with so much gossip and speculation, the buildings seemed to lift off their foundations. Business in Carlton's doubled as the curiosity seekers came and were too embarrassed not to buy food or drink. Doug helped Estelle behind the bar.

He refused to allow Alex to go away from his house without him accompanying her. He had never said in words that he expected a confrontation with Kenny, but he didn't have to. Who knew what a maniac might do?

She worked at winding up the Salt Lake project, sometimes did the same chore twice to keep her hands and mind busy. In a conversation with a Utah highway engineer, paging back through her planner seeking a critical date, she came across a note she had made to pick up her good beige slacks from the cleaners. She had soiled them when her period had started in the middle of a traffic jam in Boise. It was six weeks ago.

She paged ahead from the date, trying to remember if she'd had a period since then. Well, she must have. It had just slipped her mind. Other than sometimes having cramps, she paid little attention to the schedule.

"Alex?" the engineer on the phone said. "You there?"

"Oh, James, I'm sorry. Someone just came into my office. I was distracted a minute. Listen, can I call you back tomorrow?"

"Sure. By tomorrow afternoon I'll have this problem solved."

They hung up and she went through her planner page by page. She simply hadn't had a period for a month and a half. Dear God. Could she be pregnant? Of course not. A very good gynecologist had told her years ago to forget ever having any more children. A brazen fact flew at her. Not since the very first time had she and Doug practiced birth control. She felt weak and began to tremble.

She glanced out the door of the small bedroom Doug had given her to use as her office, debating if she should tell him her worry. He was in his own office working on his computer. They had developed a pattern of leaving each other alone in the morning hours to pursue their respective projects.

Well, she wouldn't panic and no need to panic him. Missing a period probably had something to do with stress.

Or menopause. After all, she was almost thirty-seven. She had read that some women started the change early.

Still, she should check and alleviate the concern. Didn't she have enough to worry about without adding that? When she went to Carlton's to pick up the receipts she would go by the drugstore and buy one of those pregnancy test things advertised on TV. Her mind began sorting at how she would be able to buy it without Doug seeing her. She pulled off the deception by telling him she wanted to pick up perfume in the drugstore. He waited out front in the pickup, then they drove down the street to Carlton's.

They left the bar early. Back at the house, while Doug cooked dinner, she took the pregnancy test to the bathroom. When it turned out positive, she lapsed into stunned silence, but what she really wanted to do was curl up in the corner and howl.

Doug had cooked grilled chicken and steamed broccoli and made a green salad. How healthy could you get? She minced at the food and kept her news to herself until she thought through the ramifications.

Doug made conversation, but she was so preoccupied that for her part, she mostly grunted. There were at least a hundred reasons why she couldn't be pregnant.

"There's a good old movie on tonight," Doug said as they cleared the supper dishes from the table. "Glenn Ford and Rita Hayworth. *Gilda*. Wanna watch?"

"Uh, sure," she said.

"What's wrong? This thing with Kenny getting to you?"

Well, it was now or never. Being pregnant was a secret hard to maintain. "Oh, nothing much. Just a little thing like the rabbit dying."

"Rabbit? I thought we just had cats."

"You've never heard that tired old saw?"

Doug searched his mind a few seconds before the information sank in. His heart made a jump. He nearly dropped the stack of plates in his hands. "You're not saying—"

"You know damn well what I'm saying." She burst into tears.

He hated seeing her upset, but he couldn't stop the silly grin he felt spreading over his face. He set down the plates and took her into his arms. "Good Lord, Alex. Is it true? I can't believe it."

"I don't know. I passed the test. Or I failed the test. Or something."

He felt giddy and silly. There was a God after all. He pulled his handkerchief from his back pocket and dabbed at her tears. "And you've kept this a secret how long?"

She cried some more. A thousand images swirled through his head as his brain tried to wrap around the idea of fatherhood. He tried to visualize her pregnant, her belly swollen with his child. His chest felt so full, he thought he might cry, too. "One chance in fifteen thousand, huh? Guess my little soldiers are some of those determined ones."

"Don't make jokes. This isn't funny. Something will have to be done."

He didn't let himself think about what she might mean by that statement. He set her back and looked into her eyes. "Damn right. We'll get married. Live like normal people. Go to ball games and get a dog. The cats will just have to live with it."

She wailed against his shoulder. He patted her and held her, planning. He would build a cradle with his own hands. Go to Toys "R" Us the next time he was in Boise. He would teach his kid to play football so he could go to a top college on a scholarship just like his old man had done.

"You don't understand." She sniffed and wiped her nose again, her breath hitching. "I can't do this. I've already done it and I failed."

"Already done what?"

"I've—I've already had a child. I killed her."

# Chapter 31

"What?"

Doug had been almost afraid to ask the question, wasn't sure he wanted to hear the answer. The feeling crawling through him could only be described only as cold and black. Had any part of her life ever been normal and ordinary? She was sniffling now, struggling to halt tears. He put an arm around her shoulder and guided her to the dining table, pulled out a chair, eased her into it, all the while dreading to know what caused her such anguish.

She propped her elbows on the kitchen table, blew her nose and wiped her eyes. "They say pregnancy makes women over-emotional. It's hormone imbalance or something."

He didn't know much about pregnant women, but he didn't think hormone imbalance had anything to do with her emotional state. He leaned forward, took both her hands in his. "We'll both feel better if you tell me."

She shook her head. "It was so bad."

"Tell me," he urged softly.

She freed her hands and stood, went to the window, staring out, arms wrapped around herself. He stayed where he was, watching and waiting.

"Have you ever done something that cost you so much you couldn't recover?"

If she hadn't been so distraught and if the question hadn't been so ironic, Doug might have laughed. But *his* failures were a topic for another time. "What, Alex?"

She turned her perfect profile to him and looked at the floor. "Her name was Holly. . . . She was pretty and sweet and fun. She looked like Charlie. You probably never saw him, but he used to be a handsome man. . . . He—*we* loved her so much. And we killed her."

She turned back to the window and he saw an almost imperceptible shake in her shoulders. He left his chair with a sigh and went behind her, putting his hands on her arms. "Alex—"

"It was before we bought this house in Callister." She made a gesture toward Wolf Mountain.

She stared out the window, talking into the night in a soft monotone. "I dropped her off at a birthday party and went to the restaurant. Charlie had taken the lockbox key and I wanted something from it. When I got there, he was drunk. He wouldn't give me the key, insisted on going with me to the bank. We left together in my car and I stopped by and picked up Holly from her little friend's house."

A sense of foreboding began to build in Doug. He hated hearing what he knew was coming. "How old was she?"

"Ten. I tried not to fight with Charlie in her presence. It upset her. But even then, Charlie could be out of control when he was drinking. Anyway, our daughter climbed into the backseat, didn't buckle her seat belt. Charlie and I were so involved with ripping each other to shreds, we paid no attention."

She made a sound that resembled a laugh, but Doug heard the bitterness.

"It was pouring rain. I was speeding. I said some nasty things. You know me and my sharp tongue." Another round of tears and sniffles followed. "He blew up and yanked the steering wheel. The car went into a spin. . . . I lost control. We plunged over an embankment and rolled over, down the hill. She was thrown out and the car . . . passed over her."

Doug couldn't keep from sighing. He wrapped his arms around her and laid his cheek against her hair. "Alex—"

"Don't," she said, pulling away and leaning her backside against a sheet of plywood that substituted for a counter. "I don't want your pity."

He related to her feelings, thinking of his own pain, his own sorrows. Pity wasn't something he wanted either. "Not pity, sweetheart."

"Charlie didn't know what to do. We were torn between trying to make amends with each other on the one hand and dealing with grief on the other, plus I had a severe head injury. He felt so guilty. I did, too."

Doug's mind flew back to the night he had taken her home after Miller bloodied her nose and blacked her eye and he recalled tracing with his thumb the long scar hidden by her hair.

Her lips twisted into a bitter smile. "Holly and her dad were great pals," she went on, sorrow oozing like drops of blood. "She was very smart and mature for her age and they played this word game together and . . ." She turned to him then, lifted her arms and let them fall back to her sides. "There. That's my sad tale."

Her troubled eyes zeroed in on his. "You can see why it's impossible for me to have more children. I'm not entitled. I mean, I've proved I'm not—"

"It was an accident."

"Don't you think I've told myself the same thing over and over? It doesn't erase what happened. And it doesn't make me fit to be a wife and mother. I don't want to be, ever again."

"Let's go into the living room," he said, taking her elbow and urging her to the sofa carefully, as if she might bolt if he made the wrong move. They sat down, but she scooted away, all the way to the far end, her shoulders scrunched as she braced her elbows on her knees. "I'm only a few weeks, not too far along to have something done. It'll be easy in L.A. and—"

"Hey, are you kidding?" he said softly. "Forget that. We'll be good parents."

She looked across her shoulder at him. "Didn't you hear me? I don't want to be."

What he saw in her eyes was a need for reassurance and support. Without hesitation, he scooted down the sofa beside her. He leaned forward, he, too, bracing his elbows on his knees. "I've told you how I feel. I believe you feel the same. Isn't it logical we would have children?"

"I'm too old," she blurted, as if she were grabbing frantically for any excuse. "I'll soon be thirty-seven. Old women shouldn't have babies."

"Unh-unh. Won't fly. You're not old. Besides, nowadays women in their fifties are having babies."

"Well, that doesn't mean they should."

He drew her into his arms and leaned against the sofa back, holding her. "I don't believe you wouldn't want our kid. I can see how you'd be afraid, but I'm here. And I'll be here. I want us to get married."

"All we've done is insult each other and . . . and screw. We don't even know each other."

"Shh." He turned her face to his and laid a finger on her lips. "All we've done is make love, Alex. And we know enough. We know we have a connection that's rare. Why wouldn't we extend it by fostering a life?"

She huffed out a humorless laugh. "I was better prepared to be a mother when I was sixteen than I am now. I'm not sure how calculating the cap rate on an apartment complex qualifies you for changing diapers and burping babies."

"Chasing down sociopaths doesn't qualify you either, but I don't doubt for a minute I can do it. It's all about love and caring, Alex. I'll tell you something about me. My old man split when I was a baby. My mom died when I was eight. I don't even remember her. My older brother and sister-in-law gave me a roof to keep me out of foster homes, but that's about all they supplied.

"Back then, I thought a mom and dad were just about the luckiest things a kid could have. I always believed if I ever had a kid of my own, I'd know just what to do to make him feel loved and wanted because I knew plenty about how it felt not to be."

Her hand found his and her fingers interlocked with his. "I have no doubt you'd be a wonderful father. You don't think I'm too mean to be a mother?"

He smiled. "We have nothing to debate."

He had given up on fatherhood, couldn't believe it had been handed to him at this late moment in such an unexpected way. But then, much of life had come to him in extraordinary fashion. The only explanation he could think of was one he had come to terms with long ago—it was meant to be. "Hang with me on this. I'll never make you sorry."

He stroked her hair, bent his head and touched his lips to hers, his emotions hovering close to the surface. Her lips trembled beneath his and her palm came up to his jaw. He whispered her name and closed his arms around her, loving her and the idea of her so much his heart ached. "You don't even realize how good you are. You're the best woman I've ever known." The statement wasn't a lie or even an exaggeration. Indeed, he had never known any member of the opposite sex as strong and loyal and giving.

She smiled and lowered her head. "That's crazy."

"Don't ever think any part of this is crazy." He stood and pulled her to her feet. She didn't resist. He kissed her all the way up the hall to the bedroom, where he undressed her, savoring the soft beauty of her body. He even removed her watch and rings, wanting her clothed in no artificial trappings. He kissed the breasts that would nourish his child, made love to the belly where his seed had taken root, held his breath as he eased into the warm sanctum of incubating life. Heat. Desire. Need. And love and tenderness. Each was inseparable from the other. She came with clawing fingers and hitching breaths. He followed, his body jerking and shuddering. Afterward, he kissed her countless times, couldn't stop, couldn't leave her. They drifted to sleep still joined.

*   *   *

They awoke to a sunny day. The storm had moved out in the
night. Lying in the circle of Doug's strong arms, she still found
it hard to believe a lover could be as tender as he had been last
night. How could any woman not love him? She snuggled
closer.

Awake now, she found her mind going at once to the pregnancy. Doug seemed sincere in his happiness about it. If he had
shown the slightest qualm, she would have been forced to seri-
ously consider an abortion and she doubted she could have han-
dled it. But at the same time, facing motherhood again terrified
her.

She could remember no more than pieces of being pregnant
twenty years ago when she was but a kid herself, but she recalled one thing. Back then she had been fearless. Charged with
looking out for herself, her child and her husband, who had always behaved like a child, she had lived by instinct, doing what
needed doing, whatever the task might be. Life had battered her
mightily since then. Her instincts were no longer arrow-straight
and compass-true.

Her next thought was how long would she be able to work?
She couldn't abandon the Salt Lake project and the financial
boon she expected from it. The multimillion-dollar deal should
have closed back in August, but a protest from an environmental
group had put it off. Now two months past the original date set,
she knew too well that every day dragging past the closing put
the deal at greater risk of failure.

Beyond that, if it didn't wind up soon, she would be showing
up for meetings with a protruding belly. She tried to picture the
scene, but the image wouldn't jell.

Doug's arm was wrapped around her waist and she lifted his
hand, trying to ease from under it.

His hand tightened on her midsection. "Caught ya. Where
you sneaking off to?"

"The shower."

"Not without me." He threw back the covers, moved over

her, framed her face between his hands and kissed her thoroughly. "Morning," he said at the end of the lush kiss. "Last night was incredible. You're incredible. And beautiful. And I love you."

Oh, he was good for her.

Doug thought she seemed happy. He sure was. Perhaps confession *was* good for the soul. They shared breakfast cooking chores and after they ate, she said she wanted to go back to Wolf Mountain and bring the Acura to his house. He drove her up the driveway that, compared to its previous state, seemed like a superhighway.

"It's silly not to stay here," she said as they strolled across the deck. "We may as well be comfortable while you rebuild your house."

He turned the knob and pushed the door open. "You know, I thought we locked—"

"Oh my God!" Alex stood paralyzed.

Doug gaped at the sight before them. Soiled dishes and Styrofoam food cartons littered the living room tables. Trash and several items of clothing dotted the living room floor. A spoiled-food odor permeated the air. Oil paintings had been slashed, sculpture broken. Doug's adrenaline surged as he contemplated the possibility that the vandal was still in the house. "Wait here," he told Alex.

He walked toward the kitchen, his pulse thumping. Alex was right behind him. He should have known she wouldn't stay behind. As he made the right turn to cross the kitchen, headed for the bedroom, pain exploded in his left shoulder, tore through his arm and torso like a red-hot spike, taking him to his knees. At the same time, a hand grabbed Alex's wrist and dragged her into the kitchen.

She shrieked. "Kenny!" Doug recognized Alex's cast-iron fireplace poker in the logger's hand. From the floor, he dove into Miller's midsection as the poker swung again. The blow deflected off the granite cooking island with a loud *thunk*.

Doug's left arm hung useless at his side and he couldn't lift it.

He fended off the poker with his right forearm, looking for an opportunity to land a blow.

Alex flailed at their attacker with her fists and was suddenly free. She scuttled away. She could see Doug's bad arm was helpless as he tried, one-armed, to fight Kenny off. He couldn't defeat a monster like Kenny.

*Knives*! Knives were in the kitchen, but she couldn't reach them. She lunged for her purse, shoved her hand inside, wrapped it around the .357 and fired through the wall of the purse.

The sound of the shot indoors nearly split her eardrums. Kenny screamed and staggered back against the breakfast bar, a dark patch spreading on the side of his blue T-shirt. Doug's eyes darted her way. She struggled to her feet, shaking the purse away from the pistol.

Kenny's nose ran, tears streamed from his eyes. "I'm shot. The fuckin' bitch shot me. Get me some help."

Alex was frozen in place. "Sweetheart. You okay?" Doug crawled to her, took the gun and leveled it on the monster.

"I—I think so."

"You got your cell with you? Call the sheriff's office." Alex dug in her purse and pulled out the phone—thank God it was in one piece—and punched in 9-1-1. Doug climbed to his feet and stumbled to where Kenny lay on the floor groaning and swearing. He pulled up Miller's shirt and examined his side. "Flank shot," he said to the monster. "You'll live."

Doug hadn't yet met Rooster Gilley. After Miller had been hauled away in the ambulance, the skinny deputy sheriff introduced himself, then turned to Alex. "Those cops from Lewiston think Kenny must have been staying up here in your house for the whole time he's been missing. His foreman's been bringing him food. They arrested him, too."

Doug looked across Alex's living room and dining room at the mess Miller had made of the normally spotless house. "Looks like it," he said.

Gilley leveled a questioning look. "Doug, I think I'm supposed to get a statement?"

"Let it wait, Rooster," Alex said. "Can't you see he's hurt? We're going to the emergency room."

Doug didn't argue. The fingers of his left hand had gone numb.

Alex drove him to the Callister hospital, where Doug had his second encounter with Dr. Thornton. He had seen him the first time examining Charlie McGregor's corpse lying in the cabin's ashes.

"I don't think anything's broken," the doc said as he outfitted Doug with an arm sling, "but some of that metal in there might be badly bent." His round belly jiggled as he laughed at his own joke. "I'm going to refer you to an orthopod down in Boise all the same. Somebody did a helluva fine job on that arm and it ought to be looked at by a smarter man than me." Finished, he poked his glasses into his pocket and turned to leave. "I'll be right back with some pain meds."

"That sounds dangerous," Doug said to Alex after the doctor left the room. "I could be unconscious for days." He slouched on the examining table and let Alex soothe and pet him, enjoying every minute of her attention. With his good arm, he pulled her close and kissed her.

"Don't get any ideas about going downtown and talking to Rooster or those guys from Meridian," she said, fussing with his sling. "I'm taking you home and putting you to bed. I want the father of my child to get well and be in topnotch shape because I intend to be a cranky, demanding pregnant woman."

Doug grinned through the searing pain in his shoulder. "Oh, yeah? And what if I turn you over my knee?"

"Don't forget, I've got the pistol and I can hit where I aim."

"Sweetheart, we're gonna *have* to get you a permit if you're gonna carry that gun. I don't want my wife arrested and I don't want my son born in jail."

# *Epilogue*

Alexandra McGregor married Douglas Hawkins a few weeks later. His brother as well as Ted's mother showed up for the small ceremony. Ted stood beside Doug as best man and Alex's assistant, Judy, flew up from California.

Out of jail on bond, Cindy was already back to work at the Eights & Aces and engaged to Butch Wilson.

With the sheriff in jail, law enforcement temporarily rested on the shoulders of the deputy, Rooster Gilley.

Logging ceased in Soldier Meadows. Jailed, facing murder charges and monumental legal fees, Kenny Miller became almost docile. He eagerly sold Soldier Meadows back to Alex, including the logs already cut and decked for hauling.

After the purchase was final, Doug drove Alex around the five sections that were Soldier Meadows and Kenny's log landing. He stopped the Jeep on Old Ridge Road. They climbed out and looked down on Granite Pond. He pulled Alex in front of him, wrapped his arms around her thickening middle and rested his hands on her belly.

"I could fix this," she said. "I could sell all these cut logs and use the money to clean up the stream and pond. I might look into turning the whole glade into a park."

"But I thought you loved it."

"I do. But it's so beautiful it seems a shame not to share it. I don't have the same attachment to it now that I did. Before you, it was all I had to care about."

"Don't forget this," Doug said, his hands tightening on her stomach.

"No," she said, smiling. "I won't." Her hands covered his. "What would you think if I turned the house into a museum? It does have historical value. There's a good road now. I could charge admission and use the money to maintain the park."

"Ever the entrepreneur, aren't you? You mean you'd be satisfied to live in my house?"

"Well, not entirely. I think we should buy the rest of Stewart's place. Have some stock and a garden. Maybe even some chickens."

"We're gonna be farmers?"

"It's not out of the question that we would have more kids. They'll need horses to ride and chores to do."

"More kids, huh? I could handle that. It *was* fun making this one."

"I'd like to help Cindy's kids, too. Everybody in town thinks one of them is Charlie's and I wouldn't be surprised if it's true. Maybe I could set up a fund for their education. I believe in education, even though I have none."

Doug laughed and held her tighter. "You're a special woman, Alex. Do what you must."

And because she was Alex, she did.

*Crack!* A rifle shot pierced the morning stillness.

"Mamaaa!"

Isabelle Rondeau's heart streaked up her throat. The plastic bottle of dishwashing soap she had taken from the cupboard fell to the floor. She tore from the kitchen through the mudroom, through the screened-in porch, out the back door.

Her ten-year-old daughter, Ava, came running toward her in rubber boots that reached clear to her knees, splattering through grass left wet from last night's storm. "Mama! Mama! Something happened to Jack!"

Just outside the backyard fence, Isabelle caught Ava in her arms. Heart pounding, she dropped to her knees on the cold grass, grabbed the girl's narrow shoulders, and looked her up and down. She yanked open her puffy nylon coat and searched for injury, but saw nothing wrong.

"He went next door and—" The child began to wail.

"Ava, Ava, don't cry. You're all right." Isabelle rushed her hands over the girl's long russet braid. "Show me," she said in a calm voice that masked a sense of foreboding.

"Over there." The small voice hitched. A trembling little hand pointed toward the hillside some three hundred feet away, on the other side of two barbed wire fences.

Isabelle strained to see through the gray veil of morning fog and spotted a dim image of black and white on the ground. *Jack. Oh, God, no* . . . A sick feeling oozed through her stomach. She pulled her daughter's thin body close and enclosed her in an embrace. "Shh-shh. Mama's here."

Instinct urged her to sprint to their fallen dog's side, but the same instinct told her it was too late and Ava needed her presence more than the dog did.

Looking past her daughter's small shoulder, Isabelle panned the pasture that stretched between her house and the county road. Her two mares grazed down by the far fence. Her eyes traveled over to the side pasture that held the stallion Dancer. The horses appeared to be fine. One sliver of anxiety quelled.

She swung her gaze back to the black and white spot, then on up the <u>hill</u> to a massive log house that looked as if it had been hewn from the mountainside against which it stood. A lazy trail of smoke drifted from its rock chimney.

Tears welled in Isabelle's throat. To compound her anguish, the cold fog turned into a heavy mist and stabbed her face with prickles of chill. Her body began to quake from the cold.

With one last furtive glance at the black and white spot on the hillside, she put her arm around Ava and walked her toward the old house where they had taken up residence, the house of her own miserable childhood.

Ava tried to look back, but Isabelle held her shoulders firmly and steered her straight ahead. "But—but, Mama—"

"Shhh. Let's go inside."

She guided Ava through the porch to the square mudroom where heavy coats hung on iron hooks made of horseshoes attached to the plywood wall. A row of assorted boots lined up beneath them. Still shaking, Isabelle stopped and stripped off her daughter's muddy boots. "Honey, your socks are soaking."

"Is Jack gonna be okay, Mama?"

Swallowing around the lump in her throat, Isabelle removed her own boots, then led her weeping child into the living room. A low fire burned in the red brick fireplace.

The gloom of a cold and foggy day forced itself through a pair of two-over-two windows, but the fire and rustic furnishings made the room feel cozy. "We have to get you warm. I don't want you to get sick."

She knelt before her daughter, peeled off her wet coat and socks, and urged her to a seat on the sofa in front of the fireplace. "Your feet are ice cold," she said, rubbing the slender bare feet between her hands. Her own shearling-lined slippers sat on the hearth and she grabbed them up and slid them onto Ava's feet.

Ava sobbed. "He isn't going to be okay, is he?"

Hugging her daughter close, a dozen reassuring fibs ran through Isabelle's mind. They were useless. The ten-year-old was too wise to be fooled by an unrealistic tale, and the dog meant too much to raise false hope. "I don't think so, but I'll have to go see."

"Go now, Mama. Go now."

Isabelle's heart kept up a rapid tattoo as anger seethed inside her, but she held it in check and pushed back a tendril straying from the braid that hung down Ava's back. "I will in a minute, but we need to put a log on the fire. Want to help me?"

Ava's sobs abated to weeping and sniffling. She wiped her nose with the back of her hand. "No."

"Okay. You just get warm. It'll only take me a minute."

Shivering inside her damp clothing, Isabelle added another log from the rock woodbin beside the fireplace.

By the time the embers had been stoked to a roaring blaze, Ava had ceased crying and was staring into the orange flames. "I hate it here. I don't know why we had to come."

*Oh, Ava, please don't hate it.* Isabelle had been nervous enough about returning to Callister, Idaho, without her daughter hating it. God knew, she hadn't accumulated scrapbooks full of happy memories of her childhood here. But after all that happened in Texas, the allure of an unencumbered roof over her head and the opportunity to build a secure nest near her only family had beckoned like a comforting hand.

"This is where our family is, sweetie, and that's important." She removed Ava's wire-rimmed glasses and wiped them clean on the tail of her flannel shirt. "While you get warm, I'll go next door and see what happened."

"I want to go, too."

"No, sweetheart. You need to stay where it's dry and warm." She set the glasses back on Ava's nose. The lenses magnified her dark brown eyes to where they looked huge and owl-like. "You keep an eye on the fire."

Her daughter didn't respond, but she was calmer now. Being given a task, a responsibility, had always settled her. *Too old for her ten years.* The thought sent a stab of guilt all the way through Isabelle's heart.

On her way out the door, Isabelle yanked her down coat off a hook in the mudroom. Tears hovered near the surface. She stamped to her pickup, shoving her arms into the coat sleeves and zipping up as she went. The Sierra fired on demand and Isabelle charged down the long driveway, through potholes and puddles, sending muddy water flying. At the county road, she made a sharp right turn, drove a few hundred feet and made another, then sped up the smooth gravel road that went to the house of Art Karadimos.

On the left, just below the house, Jack lay uphill from a huddled band of grimy sheep, their fleece turned gray by the wet conditions. She halted the Sierra and sprang out, tucked through the strands of a barbed wire fence, and dashed to the four-year-old border collie that had been with them since puppyhood.

She dropped to her knees and ran her hand over his hair, now wet and dark stained. She had no trouble spotting where a bullet had pierced his chest. Art had always been a crack shot. A sob burst out. "Dammit, Jack. Why didn't you stay home?"

She wiped her eyes on her sleeve, trying to think. Jack couldn't be left here in the sodden pasture, but how could she take him home, knowing Ava would see him shot and bloody? But what else could be done? Without a doubt, even now, the ten-year-old was watching out the window.

On a hard swallow, she lifted the dog's limp body and carried it to the Sierra's bed. "Friggin' sheep," she mumbled, slamming the tailgate shut. She climbed behind the wheel and plowed up the road to the hillside log house.

The owner was standing there grizzled and withered on his front deck, his face a scowl behind a drooping mustache. His shoulder leaned against a thick log porch support.

She lurched to a stop, leaped out and stomped to the edge of the deck. "That's my daughter's dog you shot!"

"I warned you yesterday." He threw a fist in the air. "I won't have him running my sheep."

"You didn't have to shoot him. You could have called me."

He huffed, then turned his back, walked into the house and slammed the door.

"You're a mean bastard, Art Karadimos," she shouted at his front door. "You always have been. You were mean to my mom and dad. You were mean to me and my brother."

Silence. She picked up a baseball-sized rock and hurled it with all her strength against the side of the house. It clunked against the thick log wall and bounced off. "I'm back, damn you! I gonna live here and there's nothing you can do about it! I'm gonna call the sheriff! You can't just shoot somebody's dog!"

Stamping back to the Sierra, digging in her coat pocket for her cell phone, she came up empty-handed. The phone was lying on the kitchen counter back at the house. "Dammit!"

She roared back down the long driveway. At the sagging lodgepole entrance to her own place, she braked hard and collected herself. She was all Ava had to look up to. A daughter shouldn't see her mother fall apart.

"Get a grip, Isabelle," she muttered and eased up the driveway.


Sheriff John Thomas Bradshaw, Jr., listened to the breathless female voice on the phone.

". . . shot . . . my little girl's dog. . . . He . . ."

"Where are you, ma'am, and who shot him?"

"I'm at . . . home. . . . in my barn. My neighbor . . ."

John groaned mentally. In the six months he had been sheriff of Callister County, Idaho, he hadn't been called on to investigate much and he couldn't recall from his twelve weeks of cop school if dog shooting incidents had been addressed. "Tell me who you are and where you live, ma'am."

When he heard her name, his mental groan grew louder. Izzy Rondeau. He remembered her from high school. Pretty, sweet-natured, sort of quiet. Had a long mop of naturally curly red hair that flew wild and free as a windstorm. Frizzy Izzy, they had labeled her in school.

She was calling from her folks' house, so the neighbor would be Art Karadimos, a gnarly old geezer who raised sheep and damn sure had it in him to shoot her dog. Or even her, under the right circumstances. He was one of John's dad's best friends.

"Just stay where you are. I'll be out there." John disconnected and grabbed his jacket and battered Stetson off the top of the filing cabinet behind his desk.

He clumped up the steep stairs leading out of the courthouse basement that housed the sheriff's office and jail. Outside, he drew into his lungs a big helping of chilly air, thick with moisture. Nothing like spring in the mountains.

He scooted behind the wheel of the sheriff department's Blazer, looking around as he plugged the key into the ignition. Through the gray mist, he could see the entire town in silhouette. With few cars parked along the one main street, things looked quiet this morning. He fired the engine and nosed east.

The Karadimos and Rondeau places were about fifteen miles out of town. Because they were the only two dwellings at the end of Stony Creek Road, Callister County's four-man maintenance crew kept the gravel passage in only fair shape. The Blazer furrowed through mud ruts and rattled over wet potholes, making poor time and giving John's mind an opportunity to dwell on Izzy.

They had been in 4-H together, both had raised steers. A

couple of years older than he, she'd had a woman's body when a lot of the girls his age looked more like boys than girls. He spent his whole sophomore year at Callister High School sporting a hard-on, watching her heart-shaped butt twitch up and down the hallways in tight Wranglers. And dreading the day she would graduate and take that vision away from him.

He invited her to a rodeo once to watch him rope, but his being a high school rodeo calf roping champion at the national level hadn't impressed her. She'd had eyes only for Billy, who wasn't a champion at anything.

John reached the weathered Rondeau gate that could use some shoring up, slowed just past the cattle guard and looked at two horses grazing on his right. Their images were dim in the fog, but they looked like mares. Izzy had fooled with horses when they were teenagers, probably would have competed in rodeo if she'd had some support from somebody.

A white frame house of no particular style hunkered at the end of a half a mile of driveway. Its most obvious distinctive features were a long porch across the front and wood siding badly in need of paint. A barn, in need of more than paint, and a couple of outbuildings with attached corrals loomed to the left and slightly back from the house. John ground his way uphill toward the complex.

He pulled to a stop in the tire tracks worn into the grass in front of the house. A woman zipped up in a bright blue parka stood at the front gate waiting for him. Izzy. John recognized her, even with a hood covering her hair. One arm was wrapped around a little kid who seemed to be all coat and boots.

John swung out of the Blazer and walked over. Unable to tell if she recognized him, he lifted his hat, offered his hand and introduced himself.

"Oh, yeah," she said, shaking hands and looking up at him with eyes dark as coffee. John had always wondered what deep secrets those eyes hid. "I recall, sort of. You were in Paul's class in school."

Paul Rondeau. Izzy's bad-ass little brother. He had been

in trouble from the first grade forward and not much in that regard had changed. He had already tested John's authority once by arguing when John confiscated his truck keys and kept him from driving drunk. "That's right. I was."

"This is my daughter, Ava."

The kid frowned up at him from behind glasses sheened with moisture. She had dark brown eyes, freckles and rosy cheeks like her mother. And red, swollen eyes.

"Ava." He touched his hat to her, but she didn't move a muscle or change her sour expression.

"I didn't know you were the sheriff," Izzy said. "Last I heard, you were rodeoing."

John chuckled. "I quit. Slim pickings if you don't hit the good money." What he didn't say was when he had reached the brink of the good money, his life had caved in and he had lost his concentration. "I'm filling out Jim Higgins's term. You probably heard, he went to jail. The commissioners appointed me. Let's see, you left town, what, around fifteen or sixteen years ago? With Billy Bledsoe, as I remember."

"Seventeen," she said curtly.

John waited for more, but all that came was an awkward pause. "Okay," he said, finally, "where's your dog?"

She tilted her head toward a fairly new, mud-spattered GMC truck parked beside the barn.

"Let's have a look."

"Go in the house, Ava," she told the kid.

A defiant little chin thrust forward.

He dug a stick of chewing gum from his shirt pocket. "Tell you what, Ava—"

"You can't bribe me with gum," the little girl said, not changing her expression or removing her hands from her pockets.

"Ava, go," Izzy ordered, her tone firmer. The kid stomped into the house and slammed the front door.

John followed Izzy toward the pickup, glancing back at the door to see if the glass pane fell out. "How old is she?"

"Ten. Please try to overlook her rudeness. She's headstrong. And mature for her age. . . . She's upset."

"Yeah, I guess she would be." John wondered if his ten-year-old son knew what a bribe was.

At the pickup, Izzy opened the tailgate where a pretty, but very dead, little border collie lay on the truck bed. He had probably been shot with a .22, the varmint gun of choice. The sight hurt John's heart. He loved animals and he especially loved working dogs. Anger leaped into him. "What happened?"

"I don't know. I was in the house."

A little flutter danced through John's stomach. Art was a grouchy old codger, but surely he had more sense than to fire a gun onto Izzy's property. "Where was he when he got shot?"

She didn't answer right away, but pushed her hands into her coat pockets and stared at the ground. "Over there on the hillside, just below Art's house."

John threw a glance at the grazing herd of maybe a hundred sheep. *Uh-oh.* It didn't take a genius to see what happened. "Tell you what. I'll go up and have a talk with him. See if we can get to the bottom of this."

"What good's that going to do? I want the son of a bitch arrested."

So much for the quiet, sweet natured girl from high school. "Ma'am, er, Izzy—"

Those warm brown eyes gave him a glare cold enough to freeze ice cubes. "No one's called me Izzy in years. The name I use is Isabelle."

John hesitated a few seconds, unable to interpret the vibes coming off her in waves. One of the many things he remembered about her as a kid was she had been a puzzle. It appeared that much hadn't changed. He ducked her piercing gaze and shook his head. "Look, just hang on here till I get back, okay?"